MW01229169

THE FEAST OF
THE VAMPYRE

A Story in the On the Trail of the Vampyre Universe

KEN JOHNSON

Printed Worldwide
First Printing 2024
First Edition 2024

10 9 8 7 6 5 4 3 2 1

ISBN: 979-8-9892390-4-7 (eBook)
ISBN: 979-8-9892390-5-4 (Paperback)
ISBN: 979-8-9892390-6-1 (Hardcover)

10 9 8 7 6 5 4 3 2 1

Cover design by Vikki at https://www.fiverr.com/s/yGyAwq

THE FEAST OF
THE VAMPYRE

To my wife, Suzie

Who is no fan of Horror and will never read this book

Yet without whose patience and support it wouldn't exist.

I love you, Honey

ACKNOWLEDGMENTS

First and foremost, I'd like to thank all the fans of the On the Trail of the Vampyre series, both the listeners on the YouTube channel narrated by Viidith22 and the readers of the stories since they first went to print in October 2023. Your kind praise, support, and requests for continued stories have motivated me to write this current monstrosity, and I sincerely hope it does not disappoint. Thank you all from the bottom of my heart.

Because of their keen interest in my work, which means a lot to me, I'd like to give a special shout-out to my two biggest fans, Jerry Miller and Jordan Andrew Harrison. As a horror writer, what would I do without my own versions of Annie Wilkes? No, I'm just kidding, guys. You are truly the BEST!

Of course, I owe a big thanks to Viidith 22 for his captivating narration of my stories on YouTube. His riveting storytelling really made the OTTOV series come to life and helped create a fan base long before I decided to go to print. He's going to shit when he sees this 105,000-word story, but I'm sure he will tackle it with his usual passion for excellence.

Lastly, a very special thanks to a very special friend, Craig Smith, an unabashedly old-school patriot who still flies Old Glory with pride. An outdoorsman with a love of nature, Craig has a keen interest in zoology, specifically marine biology, entomology, ornithology, mammalogy, and herpetology (have I left anything out?).

It was his biology lesson of the more esoteric, and shall I say, quite bizarre, aspect of the male bat's sexual organ that inspired me to throw that little factoid into this story, albeit on a much, well, LARGER scale befitting the King of the Mortis Vamyres. I dare say Bram Stoker would never have come up with this one!

PREFACE

Welcome back, vampiric readers. So good to see you again. This delectable tale, which I have titled *The Feast of the Vampyre*, is the eighth installment in the On the Trail of the Vampyre (OTTOTV) series. If you haven't done so, please make sure you read up through *On the Trail of the Vampyre, Diary Entry #5*, before beginning this story. *The Feast of the Vampyre* is a prequel within the OTTOTV "universe" and takes place more than 45 years before Jack Walker faces the group of fanatical vampyre familiars led by the enigmatic Professor Victor Hellriegel and his esoteric cult, The Stygian Seekers of the Ethereal Light. Set in German-occupied Poland in the steamy summer of 1943, the story will fill in the blanks left by Diary Entry #5 and explain how Victor's father, SS-Haupsturmführer Ernst Hellriegel, already with a dark soul and blood on his hands, falls under the spell of one of the most evil and sadistic Mortis Vampyre of all time, known as Wojciech. You will learn the origins of how Wojciech came to be and follow his predatory trail of seduction and murder across Europe through the centuries.

Just as with my earlier prequel, *The Vampyre Tapes*, this is a "multi-period" story using a "dual-timeline narrative." In other words, it is a story that shifts between contemporary and historical subplots. *The Feast of the Vampyre* is a story that begins with a letter written in the late 1980s, but the real tale is told through the 1943 journal entries of a premier homicide investigator with the German criminal police…on special assignment to Nazi-occupied Poland. An assignment that would change his life forever.

However, unlike *The Vampyre Tapes*, which was for the most part 100 percent fiction, this story is a true piece of "historical fiction." It contains real facts, and real names, dates, places, and events.

Why is this story set in WWII Poland, you may ask? Sure, the prequel to the Wojciech saga could be set in any location and any era. But I had a particular reason for choosing the Polish city of Kraków and the year 1943. Since I was very young, I was always a student of history, with a particularly keen interest in Germany's "Third Reich" period and the resulting Holocaust—the Nazi's concerted effort to exterminate European Jewry. As a history buff, I had the unique opportunity of being assigned to Germany for a total of nine years during my time in the U.S. Army, and five of those years were in Munich (München), the birthplace of the Nazi Party, which the Nazis called *Hauptstadt der Bewegung*, or "City of the Movement." Not far from Munich is Dachau, the Nazi's first concentration camp set up in 1933. I remember at the time being awed by the size of that camp, but I soon learned that as time went by, the Nazis increased dramatically the size and scope of the camps, particularly those outside of Germany. Over the next couple of years, I took it upon myself to visit several other concentration camps— Buchenwald and Flossenbürg, both in Germany, and Mauthausen in Austria. Then, it was time to visit the mother of them all, the extermination center at Auschwitz-Birkenau near Kraków, Poland. I'll never forget until the day I die my visit to Auschwitz. Two U.S. Army buddies and I decided to drive from Munich. It was 1990, and with the fall of the Iron Curtain and the end of the Cold War just the year before, it was still a relatively new experience to be able to drive into the former Communist Bloc. But I remember being treated like kings by the hotel staff when we stayed overnight in Kraków. Tourists from the West were still a novel thing, and our Deutsch Marks went quite far in exchange with the Polish Zloty. In the morning, we set off for Auschwitz. It was a bitterly cold winter day, and the barely trafficked, two-lane road we were traversing had only recently been cleared of snow and was thus still treacherous. We drove carefully, but we hit an icy patch near a crest in the road, and our car lost traction. We fishtailed all the way back down the slope, narrowly missing any trees along the way and, fortunately, any other cars as well. Miraculously, we came to a stop with no damage or injuries. Shaken but with resolve, we drove on and finally reached the camp shortly afterward. What we found surprised us. Auschwitz had been severely neglected under the Communist regime of 1945-1989 (many people don't realize anti-Semitism didn't end in Poland after WWII...in fact, there was an intensification of Polish antisemitism in 1945-48, which some have argued was worse than prior to 1939; hundreds of Jews were killed in anti-Jewish violence). The camp was nothing like you would find today. It was not yet a well-trafficked tourist site (I remember seeing only one other car, it too with German plates). There was no welcome center, no guided tours, brochures, or maps. The Birkenau camp, which sprawls more than 400 acres, was wide open, and once we entered through the infamous main rail gate, we were free to roam wherever we chose. None of the 30 or so brick prisoner barracks or the 20 remaining wooden structures (the "horse stable barracks") were cordoned off or protected against vandalism or souvenir taking. I'll never forget roaming through the barracks that housed the female prisoners...the glass in the windows had long been broken out, graffiti was on the walls, and bricks and debris littered the floors...they were basically in the same state as they were in 1945. The winter wind whistled in through the broken panes, reinforcing the already ghostly and eerie atmosphere of the place. The bitter cold only helped to complete the mood of suffering. I could easily visualize the freezing masses of men, women, and children as they huddled in misery along the rail line as they waited to be sorted for the gas chambers. Eventually, we came across the ruins of the four large buildings that had housed the gas chambers and crematorium, blown up by the SS as they abandoned the camp. Little is left of the huge structures that existed both above and underground that made up the machinery of death. Which has made it easier for the Holocaust deniers to proclaim,

"There wasn't really a gas chamber down there." For me, the visit I made to Auschwitz-Birkenau that day so many years ago made a lasting impression. As such, I wanted to weave it into this tale. When the protagonist in the story, German police inspector Otto Geisler, visits Birkenau and sees firsthand what is truly going on there, he, too, leaves the camp shaken but with his eyes now open to the truth.

By making this story a work of historical fiction, I know I'm taking a bit of a chance. I fully realize that some people would rather stick needles in their eyes than read history. Many find the subject boring as hell and still have bad memories of sitting through a monotonous high school history class. This is a vampyre story, yes, and it has all the action, suspense, and steamy eroticism you've come to expect from me, but it is also a dark tale of real-life death and suffering. The story covers a bleak time in our world's history when man's cruelty to man was most evident. It is my wish that you, the reader, will appreciate the history addressed in this book, and if you know little to nothing about the Holocaust, that it may prove informative. As the philosopher George Santayana wrote in 1905, "Those who cannot remember the past are condemned to repeat it." Unfortunately, in today's world, I often see this warning go unheeded. While working on this book, I learned that writing historical fiction is a lot harder and takes longer than straight fiction. Much research was undertaken to make sure that any historical references in this story—names, dates, places, and events—are as accurate as possible. I also endeavored to immediately translate in the narrative most of the German or Polish words when they were first used so their English equivalent would be immediately clear. To further aid the reader, I've included a quick reference key to the SS and military ranks used in the story.

I'm also breaking new ground in another way with this novel. Yes, novel! If you were paying attention, you'd notice that up to this point, I only used the term "story." Unlike my earlier works, this book is a true novel, with a word count of around 105,000 words. All my earlier books were technically "novellas," as, for the most part, they were under the threshold of 40,000 words. So, in a way, one can say this is my "Magnum Opus," or greatest work thus far. It involved much time and dedication, and I feel proud of the end product. It is indeed lengthy, but I hope that the story will be gripping and captivate you right up to the very last page.

Oh, and one final tidbit for the history buffs out there or any cinematic enthusiasts. You may see within this story some inspiration taken from the 1967 WWII mystery film, *The Night of the Generals*, starring Peter O'Toole, Omar Sharif, Donald Pleasence, and Charles Gray. In the film, O'Toole plays German Army General Tanz, a psychopathic serial killer, a sadist with a proclivity for slicing up prostitutes. After the murder of a prostitute, who was also a German agent, in German-occupied Warsaw in 1942, Major Grau of the Abwehr (German military intelligence), played by Omar Sharif, starts an investigation. After Tanz kills another prostitute in German-occupied Paris in 1944, then Lieutenant Colonel Grau resumes his investigation and concludes that Tanz is the killer. Grau confronts Tanz, who has transferred to the Waffen-SS, but unfortunately, it's the same day, 20 July 1944, that German army officers attempted to assassinate Adolf Hitler, and Tanz uses this as a pretext to label Grau a traitor and shoots him. Fast forward to 1965, and Tanz gets out of prison after serving 20 years as a war criminal. He kills yet another prostitute in Hamburg, but this time the murder draws the attention of Inspector Morand of Interpol, played by Philippe Noiret. Morand worked with Grau in 1944 and became certain the killer of the prostitutes in Warsaw and Paris was at it again. Morand finds a witness to the 1944 killing, Tanz's driver, Army Lance Corporal Hartmann, played by Tom Courtenay. For some reason, Tanz had let Hartmann live if he agreed to go forever into hiding. At a reunion dinner for Tanz's former panzer division, Morand confronts Tanz. When he produces Hartmann as his witness, and Hartmann says "You should have killed me, General," the stunned Tanz knew the jig was up…he asks for a pistol and goes into a vacant room to shoot himself. This is one of my favorite cinematic historical dramas, having first watched it upon its original release (yes, even at the age of seven I was a history nerd as well as a horror buff). If one has seen this movie, one can spot a couple of parallels to my story. First, one of the murders in the film takes place in German-occupied Poland, specifically Warsaw, in 1942. In my tale, all the murders take place not too far away, in the Polish city of Kraków, in 1943. Then of course, there is the similarity between Lieutenant Colonel Grau and the protagonist in my story, SS-Standartenführer (Colonel) Otto Geisler. Both characters are the same—they are both investigators, obsessed with a strange craving for absolute justice, where one murder is just as horrendous as the murder of hundreds. In the movie, Grau is seeking justice for the simple prostitute; in this story, Otto seeks the same for the murdered women of Kraków. All around them, a world war rages, and people are dying by the millions, but they are obsessed with finding their murderer and getting justice for the victim.

Which brings me to my final thought. This is a dark tale. It is a story of a sadistic, evil vampyre, and it is a story of a sadistic, evil regime made up of normal men. Men who could gas and burn thousands of people a day, then go home for dinner with their family, listen to Wagner and Beethoven, and read bedtime stories to their children. Is Wojciech right when he tells Inspector Geissler, "Who is the real monster?" Is Wojciech really any worse than the evil that man has seen fit to do to his fellow man? Wojciech is irredeemably a monster, yes, but is he any worse than a human monster? I'll let you be the judge.

All right, enough of the philosophical bullshit. Let's get to it. So come now, dear reader, pull up a chair and turn off the lights; it's time to go back to 1943…and get back on the trail of the vampyre!

Ken Johnson Northern Virginia October 2024

KEY TO GERMAN RANKS USED IN OTTO'S JOURNAL

Ranks of the Shutzstaffel (SS)

Reichsführer-SS	Leader of the SS
SS-Obergruppenführer	Lieutenant General
SS-Gruppenführer	Major General
SS-Oberführer	Senior Colonel
SS-Standartenführer	Colonel
SS-Obersturmbannführer	Lieutenant Colonel
SS-Sturmbannführer	Major
SS-Hauptsturmführer	Captain
SS-UntersturmführerSecond	Lieutenant

Ranks of the Wehrmacht (German Armed Forces)

Oberst	Colonel
Hauptmann	Captain
Feldwebel	Sergeant First Class
Obergefreiter	Senior Corporal

"Hell is empty, and all the devils are here."

- William Shakespeare

"Whoever fights monsters should see to it that in the process he does not become a monster."

- Friedrich Nietzsche

"Those families that lose a loved one to the scourge of the Vampyre should have no illusions of the dark transformation that will follow. That person's soul is lost forever, replaced by the black heart of evil. Whether a woman of great virtue or a man of pious devotion, they will be corrupted both in the flesh and the spirit upon the bite of the vampyre. Alas, even a god-fearing man of pure mind and spirit, a man of the highest morality with love and dedication to family, will succumb to the Devil's hand. He will become a beast, only seeking to fulfill the most decadent and wanton desires. Woe to a loved one who does not heed this and falls prey to the vampyre's seduction. Then they, too, will become one of the damned."

- An excerpt from *Liber daemonum et inmortuorum,* the fabled book on demonology and the history of Homo Nosferatu Vampiris, commissioned in the sixteenth century by the emperor of the Holy Roman Empire.

PART ONE

The following letter was received by the Committee for the Scientific Investigation of Claims of the Paranormal on 23 July 1989:

Dear Sirs,

My name is Kevin Geisler. I am 43 years old and currently live in [REDACTED], Michigan. My father, Otto Geisler, passed away just a few months ago, in March of 1989. Otto had made it to the ripe old age of 83, no small feat for a man in the higher-risk profession of law enforcement, who lived in Nazi Germany during the tumultuous twelve years of its oppressive dictatorship, and who endured the overall death and destruction of the Second World War. He had seen a lot, witnessed a lot, and done a lot, my father. After immigrating to the United States after the war, he met my mother in Detroit, and I was born in 1947. Otto eventually found work in the field he loved so well—homicide investigations. Employed by the Michigan State Police, he rose through the ranks to become their top homicide investigator and profiler, receiving many awards and decorations along the way. Despite a turbulent life, he managed to die peacefully in his home of the past 39 years, a seemingly content and happy man, having lived a full life and realizing the American dream.

I could enthrall you with countless adventures and anecdotes of his time as a police investigator, but that is not my purpose here. By sending you this letter, I am hoping to solicit your comments and opinions that may allow me to reach some kind of understanding, maybe a rationalization, of the strange entries I have found within an old journal or diary that belonged to my father. I had only recently discovered it upon going through his personal effects, all left to me in his will. My mother died several years ago due to cancer, and I have no siblings. As such, Otto was my only family. While he had left several boxes of other journals detailing the many criminal cases he handled when he was the premier German criminal police inspector from the late 1920s to the end of the Second World War in May 1945, this particular journal was treated much differently. I found it separately, kept in a metal lockbox. I never did find the key and eventually had to break the box open. Inside, I found three things: the journal, handwritten in German, a catholic crucifix, and an antique knife with a pearl grip and what looks to be a Latin inscription etched on the blade. The journal contains daily entries written during what was described as a special assignment to German-occupied Poland during the summer of 1943. In all my years growing up, my father never mentioned this assignment or what had supposedly taken place there. As far as I knew, he had never left Germany at all during the war. And then there is the narrative itself—it is so fantastic, almost too unbelievable to take as fact. If it had been written by someone other than my father, I wouldn't take it seriously. It sounds like the missive of a madman, but I assure you, my father was anything but. He was the most scientific, reasoned, and rational man I ever knew.

I am hoping that through the Committee's prior research on this particular subject matter, you may have case histories of the period that can substantiate or verify the historical references in my father's account, specifically the events that he describes taking place in the Polish city of Kraków from July to August 1943.

I believe that the Committee is the best entity to look into my father's story since your charter promotes scientific inquiry, critical investigation, and the use of reason in examining these types of strange and extraordinary accounts. My father, too, as an investigator, held the same philosophical position of scientific skepticism.

I also know that the Committee will conduct this inquiry discretely. I loathe that my father's journal entries, specifically the more fantastic and lurid aspects of his tale, become privy to the fringe or less savory adherents of the occult, demonology, and vampirism that may use the journal for their own purposes.

I have never read much about the paranormal or the supernatural, nor am I a believer in such things as vampires, werewolves, ghosts, spirits, or evil demons. I profess to know very little of these esoteric subjects. However, upon doing some recent reading, I have learned that in Eastern Europe, where my father's account took place, the folklore and belief in nosferatu— the vampyre—is at its strongest. Maybe what my father experienced in his account was true, or maybe it was a delusion shaped by his environment and the strong beliefs of the superstitious locals. You be the judge.

First, above all else, the Committee needs to understand the type of man my father was. He was born Otto Hans Geisler in Landsburg am Lech, a small town southwest of Munich, on the Ides of March 1906. He had a good childhood; his father, Heinrich, was a highly successful attorney and later a judge within the German state of Bavaria. Otto was too young to have participated in the Great War, and his father had been too old, so the family remained fairly unaffected by its horrors. As such, the surprise of Germany's surrender in 1918 was a shock to Otto's family, as it was for most Germans. The German Empire and the Kaiser were no more, and in its place was now the strange experiment in parliamentary democracy called the Weimar Republic. And with it came the economic chaos of hyperinflation, which peaked at over 200 billion percent – billion with a "b" – in 1923. Times were difficult, even with his father's judicial career, but nevertheless, Otto was ultimately accepted into the Ludwig Maximilian University, or University of Munich, in 1924. Over the next four years, Otto became a voracious student, concentrating his studies in the fields of criminology, behavioral sociology, and psychology. His father wanted him to pursue a law degree, to become an attorney, or even to be a judge like himself, but Otto was adamant – he wanted to join the police. It turned out my father had a keen interest in abhorrent behavior and criminal psychology. After Otto graduated in 1928 with full academic honors, he was accepted into the Kriminalpolizei, the Criminal Police, or KRIPO for short. The KRIPO was distinguished from its counterpart, the Schutspolizei, the uniformed municipal police, by its plain-cloths detectives. Basically, the KRIPO's mission was similar to that of detectives in police departments around the world – they investigated the more serious crimes of murder, rape, and arson. Soon after coming on board, Otto had the fortunate good luck of catching the eye of Ernst Gennat, then the director of the Berlin criminal police. Gennat was one of the most gifted and successful criminologists in Germany and is credited with creating the first dedicated homicide division within the Berlin police. Under Gennat's tutelage, my father soon distinguished himself with his ability to "read" crime scenes and analyze the available evidence to a highly successful and actionable degree. They didn't have the term "criminal profiling" back then, but the ideas were nothing new, even going back as far as the late 19th century, when investigators began to use psychology to understand and attempt to apprehend infamous killers such as Jack the Ripper. In that case, London physicians George Phillips and Thomas Bond used autopsy results and crime scene evidence in the fall of 1888 to make informed predictions about the Ripper's personality, behavioral characteristics, and lifestyle. Father Otto had been heavily influenced by this era of "Positivist Criminology," which believed that biological, psychological, and sociological factors determined criminal behavior. Rejecting the earlier

"Classical Criminology" school of thought, Positivism marked a shift towards more scientific and empirical approaches to the study of crime. Otto studied the works of Positivist scholars like the Italian criminologists Cesare Lombroso and Enrico Ferri, who emphasized social and economic factors as contributors to criminal behavior that are outside the control of the offender.

My father took these philosophies and developed his own unique tools for new and innovative analysis of crime scene evidence—the examination of the perpetrator's methodology, his criminal signatures, and his forensic connections to other crimes. As a result, Otto would build an accurate profile of the criminal by ensuring a thorough examination of a crime scene to identify notable psychological traits of the perpetrator, such as psychopathologies, behavioral patterns, or demographic variations.

By the late 1920s, the Weimar Republic had entered its "Golden Age," a time when the German Reich enjoyed greater stability, economic security, and improved living standards. As the Republic flourished, so too did my father's police career. One of his earliest murder cases was the infamous "Vampire of Dusseldorf," a sexual sadist who terrorized that German city for most of 1929. Due to the sheer savagery of the murders, the diverse backgrounds of the victims, and the differing methods by which they had been killed, initially with scissors, then by knife, and finally by hammer, the police and press theorized they were the work of more than one perpetrator. My father disagreed and provided a psychological profile of a middle-aged male with a history of an abusive childhood and cruelty to animals, with a likely criminal record possibly going back decades and including other self-gratifying crimes such as arson. Eventually, a man named Peter Kürten was arrested, and authorities were amazed at the accuracy of Otto's assessment. As a child, Kürten was forced to watch his parents have sex, and as a teen, he resorted to bestiality with the sheep, pigs, and goats in the local stables, obtaining his greatest sense of elation if he stabbed the animals just prior to achieving orgasm. The first murder Kürten definitely committed occurred in 1913. During the course of a burglary, he encountered a nine-year-old girl asleep in her bed. He strangled the child, then slashed her twice across the throat with a pocket knife, ejaculating as he heard the blood dripping from her wounds onto the floor. Over the following years, Kürten was arrested and went to prison multiple times for burglaries and arson. In 1929, Kürten's fantasies reached the pinnacle of their depravity as he began his spree of terror in Dusseldorf. Kürten would spontaneously ejaculate as he knifed his victims. In one case, he returned to the scene of the crime with a bottle of kerosene and, setting the young child's body alight, achieved orgasm at the sight of the flames. Kürten was ultimately arrested in 1930 and convicted of nine murders, although he admitted to 68 crimes, including 31 attempted murders. My father was present as Kürten was escorted to the waiting guillotine on the second of July 1931. With his belly full from his last meal of schnitzel, Kürten excitedly asked the executioner, "Tell me, after my head is chopped off, will I still be able to hear, at least for a moment, the sound of my own blood gushing from the stump of my neck? That would be the pleasure to end all pleasures." After the execution, my father published a detailed study of the Kürten case. It was the first analysis ever done of a psychosexual killer and influenced European law enforcement's understanding of serial murder, sexual violence, and sadism. In his case study, Otto was also one of the early users of the term "serial killer." This term is commonly attributed to FBI Special Agent Robert Ressler, who used the term "serial homicide" in a 1974 lecture in the United Kingdom. However, the term "serial killer" was actually coined in the 1930s by Otto's boss and mentor, Ernst Gennat. In German, the word Gennat began using was "serienmörder," which can be translated to "series-murderer."

My father's ability to render these types of exacting psychological profiles led to an increasing number of arrests, and as a result, almost every murder case to cross his desk had a higher-than-normal closure rate. As you would imagine, this enamored Otto with his superiors within the police, as well as municipal and political leaders in charge of public safety. In 1931, Otto was awarded the highest police medal for exemplary service, personally bestowed upon him by the Weimar President, Paul von Hindenburg. By 1932, Otto's reputation for cracking unsolvable criminal cases was such that he was invited to both London and Paris to teach his profiling techniques. He had been invited to lecture in the United States as well, but before he could do so, everything changed. Along came Adolf Hitler.

I need a moment here for a quick history of the evolution of the Nazi police state. Please bear with me. To explain what happened to Otto's KRIPO once the Nazis took over, I need to introduce several more acronyms. Trust me, when it comes to organizational structure, no one does bureaucracy like the Germans. One could say that bureaucracy is Germany's pride and joy. Although the term originally comes from the French, and the actual concept dreamt up by the Egyptians some 5,000 years ago, it is the Germans who have refined it into a system that regulates every last detail of every single area of life.

When the Nazis came to national power in 1933, Germany, as a federal state, had many local and centralized police agencies, which often were uncoordinated and had overlapping jurisdictions. Heinrich Himmler, chief of the Schutzstaffel, or SS, sought to fully absorb all the police and security apparatus into the structure of the SS. To this end, in 1934, Himmler first took over the Prussian Secret State Police, the Geheime Staatspolizei or Gestapo. By June 1936, all police forces throughout Germany were united, following Hitler's appointment of Himmler as "Chef der Deutschen Polizei," the Chief of German Police. Himmler immediately reorganized the police, with the state agencies statutorily divided into two groups: the Ordnungspolizei, the Order Police or ORPO, consisting of both the national uniformed police and the municipal police, and the Sicherheitspolizei, the Security Police, or SIPO. The SIPO consisted of two complementary, plainclothes investigative police forces—Otto's KRIPO, and the more infamous Gestapo.

While the KRIPO initially kept a level of independence because its structure had been longer established, many within the SIPO were encouraged to become members of the SS. As a minimum, as an apparatus of the state, members were expected to be members of the Nazi Party. This was anathema to my father, who hated the Nazis. Throughout the 1930s, he found it abhorrent that the police were politicized and weaponized against the German people. He detested the fact he himself had become a cog in Hitler's Police State, where the police were all-knowing and all-reaching, permeating into the lives of every German. This police state reached its zenith in September 1939, with the beginning of the Second World War, when Himmler created the Reichssicherheitshauptamt, the Reich Security Main Office, or RSHA, as the overarching command organization for the various state investigation and security agencies. The new organization encompassed the intelligence service, security services, secret state, and criminal police. The SIPO was officially abolished, and its departments were folded into the RSHA. Father's KRIPO became Department 5 of the RSHA. The official mission of Department 5 was to standardize criminological methods and equipment, apply scientific research and experience in the investigation and prevention of crime, conduct criminological training, provide data for policy decisions and legislation, nationalize police surveillance, maintain a national criminal register, and investigate severe crimes.

Unfortunately, the KRIPO had an even darker mission. As the detective force of Germany, they were responsible for investigating "normal" crimes such as theft and murder. But during the nazi regime, they became a key enforcer of policies based on Nazi ideology. As part of the nation's security police, the KRIPO worked closely with the Gestapo, the regime's repressive political police force. Together, they conducted the widespread arrest of Jews, political opponents, professional criminals, male homosexuals, Jehovah's Witnesses, Gypsies, and the people whom the Nazi regime categorized as asocials—vagrants and beggars, alcoholics, drug addicts, prostitutes, lesbians, pacifists and the disabled and mentally ill. The Nazi state gave the KRIPO the power to eradicate their racial, social, and criminal enemies by preventively and indefinitely detaining them in concentration camps. After 1938, these concentration camp inmates were detained under either KRIPO preventative detention or Gestapo protective custody, neither process subject to judicial review. Between 1933 and 1945, the KRIPO sent more than 70,000 people to concentration camps. At least half of these prisoners died as a result of Nazi brutality and neglect.

When World War Two began, the KRIPO's mission turned the most sinister. The KRIPO was one of the sources of manpower used to fill the ranks of the Einsatzgruppen, SS mobile killing units sent to occupied territories in the East – namely, Poland and Russia. Several senior KRIPO commanders, among them my father's boss, SS-Gruppenführer Arthur Nebe, were assigned as Einsatzgruppen commanders. In the occupied East, their units perpetrated atrocities, including mass murder of Jews, communists, prisoners of war, and hostages, and played a key role in the Holocaust. By 1942, when the war provided the Nazis the machinery and the seclusion necessary to execute their Final Solution to the Jewish Question, the KRIPO was instrumental in the round-ups of Jews, Roma, and other undesirables for their deportations to the extermination camps.

Now, you may rightfully ask, was my father one of these men? One of the KRIPO officers with blood on his hands? I can assure you he was not. After the war began, and as the distinction between "ordinary" crimes and political crimes blurred so that there was no longer a clear distinction between the criminal and political police, Otto had grown to hate the very organization to which he belonged. But for him, even with war raging all around him, the core mission of the criminal police remained: track down murderers and get justice for victims and their families. That may sound like a dichotomy; with the war causing murder on a mass scale, what is the point of solving the murder of one? I think in my father's mind if he could solve the murder of, say, a housewife, a shopkeeper, or a young child, it was one soul avenged. Father was a moral man, maybe one of the few in the Nazi police apparatus, and this surely would have been his downfall, but fortunately, Himmler recognized Otto's superior detective skills, and throughout the war, he was allowed to continue to do what he did best – solve civil murder cases.

I remember sitting on my father's lap as a child, spell-bound, as he told me about one of the more infamous murder cases of the Nazi era. The case of the notorious "S-Bahn Serial Killer." Even the nickname made me shiver. For those of you who are non-Germans, "S-Bahn" stands for the "Stadtschnellbahn" or city rapid railway. Basically, it is the municipal rail system of most German cities. It mostly runs above ground, but in the inner cities, it may also run underground, sharing space with the "U-Bahn" or underground mass transit system.

Over two years, beginning in August 1939, women were assaulted, raped, and murdered along the S-Bahn line in the Friedrichsfelde district of Berlin. The perpetrator targeted women whose husbands were serving abroad in the German military. He would choke, threaten with a knife, or bludgeon these solitary and vulnerable women, but in the beginning, murder was not part of his modus operandi. Later, the man's violence escalated, and he began to attempt to murder his targets. Three women were attacked and stabbed but survived. In the hopes of making sure future victims were dead, he began throwing the bodies off the moving train, but in some instances, several victims were found along the tracks still alive.

By October 1940, he had begun to attack the women by either strangling, stabbing, or crushing their skulls with a thick piece of telephone cable or iron bar. It wasn't long before railroad workers began to discover the bodies of his victims littered alongside the rail tracks. One such victim was a twenty-six-year-old nurse named Elfriede Franke. Spotting Franke in the second-class train compartment at the Karlshorst station, the killer wasted no time—or words—and, removing the iron rod from his jacket, slammed it hard into Franke's head, forcing pieces of her skull into her brain. She immediately fell down onto the floor of the carriage. Satisfied that the young nurse was indeed dead, he opened the door of the carriage, allowing the cold air of the winter night to rush into the compartment. Then, dragging Franke by her feet, he threw her body into the darkness. Just thirty minutes later, his sexual perversion still not satiated, the killer spotted another victim on the platform of Karlshorst station. He knocked out a nineteen-year-old named Irmgard Freese whom he had spotted walking alone. After crushing her skull with three blows, the killer ripped off her clothing and raped her.

On the very day that these two women were murdered, the police operation to catch the S-Bahn murderer was taken over by the Serious Crime Unit of Berlin's Kriminalpolizei. My father was called in. He immediately ordered the interview of the survivors of the assaults. Each of them described their assailant as wearing the black uniform of a railroad worker. There were eight thousand railroad workers and very little else to go on, but one thing Otto noticed was that on several victims, the train ticket was missing, indicating that the killer may have been a ticket inspector. Using a psychological profile developed on the murderer, Otto's interviews resulted in several possible suspects. One of the names mentioned was Paul Ogorzow. As it turned out, Ogorzow had been the exact opposite of what the police had been looking for…he was a family man, a loyal Nazi, a veteran of the Sturmabteilung or SA, and was spoken highly of by his peers and superiors within the Deutsche Reichsbahn. Otto's KRIPO superiors did not want to believe that the infamous killer could be a Party member and a member of the SA, no less. But Otto was insistent that his profile added up. After obtaining Ogorzow's uniforms, Otto personally inspected them. He discovered blood on Ogorzow's jacket and trousers, with a large amount found in and around the crotch area of the trousers. My father arrested Ogorzow on 12 July 1941. He was interrogated and, after being put face-to-face with one of the surviving victims, confessed to the crimes but blamed his actions on alcoholism and a Jewish doctor he claimed had incorrectly treated him for gonorrhea. Ogorzow pleaded guilty to eight murders, six attempted murders, and thirty-one cases of assault, including rapes. Despite his Nazi credentials, he was sentenced to death on 24 July 1941 and was executed by guillotine two days later at Plötzensee Prison. As was usually the case with such executions, a charge for the wear and tear of the guillotine blade was sent to the prisoner's relatives…in this case, Mrs. Gertrude Ogorzow.

As a result of his cracking the S-Bahn killer case, Himmler promoted my father to SS-Standartenführer, or Colonel, and awarded him the War Merit Cross without Swords, and, much to Otto's chagrin, the Nazi Golden Party Badge with the initials "A.H." on the rear, personally approved by the Führer himself. After that, my father's reputation and loyalty were assured within the Nazi Party, and he was nearly untouchable within the KRIPO. Nevertheless, he had to keep his criticism of the regime to himself while carefully maintaining his allies and keeping his enemies under scrutiny.

It was in the summer of 1943 when my father was summarily called to Himmler's office in Berlin for a meeting. He had met with Himmler many times before, but this time, the urgency of the meeting was unusual. Otto was understandably nervous, not knowing the nature of the visit. When he walked into the room, he immediately recognized Hans Frank, who, since October 1939, had served as the head of the General Government, the territory of German-occupied Poland. From that moment, my father's life changed forever.

My father's journal will now take up the rest of the story. You will find it enclosed with this letter. The initial entries are consistent with his nature— short, business-like, and direct to the point. As events unfold, the entries become more emotional, and he takes great care to document his conversations in greater detail. The end of the journal is, well, truly terrifying…as well as heartbreaking. If what he described did happen, then there is no wonder why my father kept the journal locked up for forty-five years, firmly out of the light of the day.

Sincerely yours, Kevin Geissler

PART TWO

(Translated from the original German; some German and Polish words are kept for realism and clarity)

10 July 1943 –

At ten this morning, I received a telephone call from Reichsführer-SS Himmler's adjutant and told to report to his office at Prinz-Albrecht Strasse no later than one in the afternoon. When I asked the adjutant the subject of the meeting, he seemed curt and said he had just been told to make sure I would be there in short order. I had been to Himmler's office many times over the years, but this time, I admit I had a knot in my stomach due to being so abruptly summoned and no reason given. When I arrived, there was none of the usual waiting, and I was ushered in immediately. While I had anticipated some form of urgent meeting with other KRIPO or RSHA officers, I was quite surprised to see that the only other person in the room was Hans Frank, the General Governor in charge of the German occupation of Poland. I knew he didn't make it back to Berlin all that often. Frank looked glummer than his usual dour self. I soon learned why. Apparently, the authorities are experiencing a situation in the area surrounding Kraków, the seat of the General Government in Poland. An unsolved number of murders over the past several months. Horrific murders almost exclusively of young women.

Throats tore out, almost animalistic, which led to exsanguination. Autopsies indicated they were raped and bitten around the genitals. Most were posed provocatively. I was shocked when Frank told me that the numbers were nearly 27 dead. Why hadn't I heard about this before? I asked. Frank indicated that in the beginning, most of the murdered women were Poles. At first, a few prostitutes. Then, some women from the Jewish ghetto. Frank really didn't care if the Poles killed themselves. It was of no concern. After all, the territory was slated to become ethnically German "living space" by deporting and exterminating the non-German population or relegating it to the status of slave laborers. The Blue Police initially had the case, of course. The Blue Police were the Polish police auxiliary allowed to work under the authority of our KRIPO. But they were inept, and no progress was made, and the murders continued. But now, according to Frank, the situation has become "unacceptable." How so, I asked the General Governor. Because, he replied, recently, the murders began extending to German nationals. Thirteen German women in total had been killed, he said. Five of them were ethnic Germans married to Polish husbands. Four were with the German Army—two nurses, one signals specialist, and one administrative secretary. The others had been members of the Nazi Party. The first was a young female typist assigned to the Reich Ministry of Armaments. Then, two days ago, a young girl on Frank's own administrative staff was attacked in her flat in Kraków. She had been raped, sodomized, and left strung up like a deer carcass. The last straw came last night when two women of the SS-Helferinnen Korps, or female SS auxiliary, were found butchered. The shocking aspect of these murders was that they didn't take place out in the Polish neighborhood but rather within the confines of the local concentration camp, where they were serving as Aufsehrinnen or "overseers" in the female section of the camp. Which camp? I asked Frank. A facility called Auschwitz, he replied. The SS had complete control within the camp, and the possibility of a prisoner being the killer had been discounted. Most significantly, the wounds inflicted on the bodies matched the previous killings in Kraków. As such, it was unfathomable how the killer could have entered the camp and killed the women. The murders now had the full attention of the SS. "Otto," Himmler instructed me, "you are to go to Poland immediately. The chief of the KRIPO in Kraków will be expecting you. He has been ordered to provide you with all the resources you need to conduct your investigation. You have complete authority. You will answer directly to General Governor Frank and myself. Is that understood?" I acknowledged my instructions and began to stand up. "One more thing," Himmler said, looking over at Frank, who suddenly looked even more uncomfortable. "The bodies of the earliest victims disappeared from the city morgue," Himmler continued. "The bodies of German nationals and members of the Party…a totally unacceptable affair. I regret their theft may hamper your investigation, Otto." Then Himmler turned to me, his eyes cold. "But trust me, the Poles will pay dearly." And with that and a hearty "Heil Hitler," I excused myself and made immediate plans for a flight out of Berlin.

11 July 1943 –

I flew out of Rangsdorf at 0655 hours on a Fieseler Fi 156 Storch. The weather was good, and since the pilot flew low to avoid being sighted by any Allied aircraft, I had a good view of the countryside as we crossed into Poland. Just under two hours later, I arrived at a Luftwaffe airfield outside Kraków. I was picked up and taken to Wawel Castle, the seat of the Reich's General Government. There, I was greeted by SS-Obergruppenführer Friedrich-Wilhelm Krüger. As the Höherer SS-und Polizeiführer-Ost, or Higher SS and Police Leader (HSSPF) in the General Government, he has command of all police and security forces in German-occupied Poland. He is not a pleasant man; he has a reputation for cruel efficiency as he implements terror in the occupied area on a large scale. Krüger uses public executions by shooting or hanging to intimidate the population, and for every German killed by the Polish Home Army or the resistance, ten random Polish citizens are shot in retaliation. As if the mass murder of the Polish intelligentsia and the cultural genocide of Poland's property and history wasn't enough, I heard an even worse rumor— that Krüger was behind the systematic kidnapping of thousands of Polish children from their families for Germanization, forced labor, and, in some cases, medical experimentation. Of course, he's not alone in carrying out these terrible programs. Krüger introduced me to his deputy, SS-Oberführer Julian Scherner, the SS and Police Chief for Kraków. As the city's police chief, Scherner rules Kraków with an iron hand. Under Frank's and Himmler's directives, his main remit has been the deportation of the city's Jewish population. Last year, in May 1942, Scherner led *Aktion Krakau*, using his police battalions to encircle the Kraków ghetto, where the city's Jews had been relocated since 1941. Over the succeeding year, the Jews were "resettled" and sent off to concentration camps. Scherner is, if anything, highly efficient. Both he and Krüger were cordial, but with Scherner in particular, I could tell he wasn't pleased to have an outsider flown in from Berlin to take charge of a police investigation in his city. I think things sat better with both of them after I promised to keep them informed on the investigation's progress, despite the fact I was instructed to report directly to Frank and Himmler. A small concession to make sure I wouldn't have to be looking over my shoulder.

After our brief discussion, Scherner took me downstairs, within the bowels of Wawel Castle, to a secluded wing that had been set up with office space. My new staff waited for us, all of them hand-picked to work the case with me. I was pleased to learn that my deputy and chief investigator will be SS-Obersturmbannführer Manfred von Albrecht. Manfred is long in the tooth, a seasoned KRIPO investigator even before the Nazis came to power. About the same age, he and I go way back, first meeting during the Peter Kürten case. With his close-cropped salt and pepper hair and patrician good looks, Manfred looks every bit the part of the royalty he descends from.

However, he is an unpretentious, modest man of extraordinary focus and dedication. Like me, he might be considered "old school," where solving the case is more important than Party politics. I know I can trust him explicitly. I was equally pleased to see SS-Sturmbannführer Felix Schellenberg, who will be my senior detective. Felix is a protégé of Manfred's, having worked under his tutelage on several assignments. Tall, blond with classic Germanic good looks, Felix is several years younger than Manfred and I, but he has become a good, solid investigator. I worked with him on a murder case last year in Munich, and I found him to be highly observant and intuitive, with a keen ability to analyze cases objectively and avoid assumptions. I know I can depend on him. However, I was not so pleased to learn that SS-Haupsturmführer Ernst Hellriegel was assigned to the team. Ernst is a competent investigator, but he's also an ardent Nazi, and as such, I detest the man. He has blood on his hands, having volunteered to serve early in the war with an Einsatzgruppe during the invasion of Poland and once again with Einsatzgruppe C during the invasion of Russia. I heard that he participated in the Babi Yar massacre of September 1941, during which some 34,000 Jews were stripped naked, led to ravines, and machine-gunned. Overall, a rather detestable man. I'll have to keep a close eye on him. There are also two females on the team. My heart skipped a beat when I saw that one of them was Dr. Anna Müller, a civilian pathologist and forensics specialist from Stuttgart. We have met several times before at various professional seminars, and I've greatly enjoyed reading her papers on wound and blood splatter analysis. Anna is younger than I, in her early 30s, and exceedingly attractive. But I've always felt that it was her gregarious personality and quick wit that was the most pleasing. My last encounter with Anna was during a crime conference in Berlin about six months ago when we had gone out for drinks together one evening. I remember having a fabulous time, the both of us laughing and just letting our hair down for a change. I felt there was good chemistry between us, but alas, the next day, the conference was over, and she went back to Stuttgart and myself to Berlin. The demands of the job were back, and life moved on. But now, here she is. The other woman on the team is Fräulein Elsie Best, who was sent over from the Kraków SS secretarial pool and will serve as our files manager and typist. She is young, about 21 years old, but comes across as very professional and capable.

While speaking with everyone, I learned that Manfred, Felix, and Anna had also just arrived in Kraków, having flown in from Germany yesterday. Ernst Hellriegel is the only investigator who was already here; he had been assigned to the local KRIPO staff for the past several months. By early afternoon, I was shown my office, and Felix had already placed the case files on my desk. Before reading the files, however, I wanted to see the bodies of the latest murder victims. At least the ones that hadn't been stolen. Felix made the arrangements and then drove Anna and me to the city morgue, located not far from Wawel Castle. When we arrived, we were met by a fellow German named Dr. Max Weber. He was the coroner for the city of Stuttgart but had been flown in two days ago to replace the previous coroner and staff, who had been Poles. They had been taken out and summarily shot after the theft of the bodies, which Weber explained included the corpses of the four females assigned to the Wehrmacht and the one young typist from the Reich Ministry of Armaments. "Do you suspect the Poles?" I asked. Weber shook his head. "Not unless they steal their people as well. The earliest murder victims, all Polish, had been sent over to a designated non-Aryan mortuary…and I heard they disappeared a day or two after being brought in." I pondered this for a moment. "So how did the thieves break into this place?" I asked, "wasn't there some kind of security?" Weber shrugged. "Before he was shot, the Kraków coroner claimed the morgue was locked up tight. The locks on the doors were never broken into. He said the bodies just disappeared. As if they got up and walked away." During our conversation, I learned Weber has over thirty years of experience and has several advanced degrees in medicine and pathology. Anna and I are very impressed with his credentials, and I think we can definitely count on his opinions as we go along.

Together, the three of us spent the next hour examining the wounds on the two SS-Helferinnen, and those suffered by Frank's secretary. I learned that the secretary's name was Johanna Liebl, and she had worked on Frank's staff since he became the Governor-General of Poland in October 1939. The two SS women were Magdalene Haas and Irma Koch. Haas had been serving as an Oberaufsehrin, or Senior Overseer at the Auschwitz women's camp, while Koch was a Blockführerin, or Block Leader. All three women were young, between 22 and 25 years of age. We all agreed that we are dealing with a sadistic killer who makes Peter Kürten look like a novice. It appears the killer somehow subdues or overpowers his female victims. None of the victims had defensive wounds, which indicate they had not put up any kind of struggle. Some kind of anesthesia could be involved, but Weber found no evidence of this. All the women were sexually assaulted and in the most brutal fashion. Ravaged, really. By something abnormally large. They had been bitten, the bites confined mostly to the genital, stomach, buttocks, and breast areas. After analysis, the bite marks were thoroughly baffling. They were of an unrecognizable nature; the size, shape, and bite pattern were all off. The killer's mouth would have to be almost twice as large as that of a normal man, and the depth of the punctures far exceeded normal teeth. It was postulated that perhaps the killer was wearing some kind of oral contrivance. The cause of death was exsanguination, due to a bite to the neck, penetrating the artery. Under such circumstances, the body completely loses its ability to pump blood after losing about 50 percent of blood volume. The heart stops pumping, and without the pressure, much of the blood stays and pools within the body. Yet, all our murder victims were found virtually bone dry. To add more mystery, very little blood was found under or around the victims, or anywhere around the crime scene for that matter. It was as if the blood had been purposely drained from the bodies. Weber found no evidence of any needle marks from a blood extraction apparatus. And in the case of the two female SS guards, there was virtually no time for such a transfusion to take place. Apparently, they were found less than 30 minutes from last being seen. Anna put forth the possibility that the killer had drank the blood, but even she had to acknowledge it would have been impossible to drink 5 liters of blood in that amount of time and so cleanly. I've encountered this extreme hematophagy before, but not to the degree of removing an entire body's worth of blood. Such a killer risks hemochromatosis, a condition of excess iron in the body that can lead to organ damage. What happened to the victim's blood is a mystery. But I have a feeling it is a key component in the killer's psychology. Anna took vaginal smears from victims, as well as samples from their bite marks and throat wounds, to examine later, and hopefully, we'll get a blood type of the killer.

At the end of the day, an officer from Scherner's staff took me to the flat where I'd be staying. It's in a building formerly used as housing by members of the Polish government but has now taken over for the use of General Government and Nazi Party officials. It's adjacent to the main market square in the Old Town of Kraków, now renamed, of course, Adolf-Hitler Platz. It's an easy 15-minute walk to Wawel Castle, so this will be most convenient. I've been told that the square is the largest medieval plaza in Europe, covering an astounding 40,000 square meters. From the balcony of the fourth-story flat, I can see the beautiful architecture of St. Mary's Basilica, with its unique two differently-sized towers, as well as the 70-meter tower of the old Town Hall. In the center of the square is what they call the "Cloth Hall," dating from the thirteenth century, which is packed with market stands and shops. Even under German occupation, the hall seems to still be a hub of activity and commerce. From what I've seen, Kraków remains a beautiful old city. It has fared far better than Warsaw, which has had much of its historical architecture razed.

12 July 1943 –

I spent most of the day reading through the case files. Apart from the sheer violence and brutality of the sexual assaults and the culminating bloodletting, there is yet another aspect of the murders that seems to set these cases apart from the norm. Specifically, the changing venues of each murder. Most killers have their favorite hunting grounds, a neighborhood, or an area they are familiar with and feel safe in. Yet, these murders have taken place in a wide and diverse areas. The early killings of street prostitutes took place in the city's red-light district...the ancient profession still flourishing under the German occupation. Then, there was a shift towards attacks on young women living in the squalid tenements of the Polish ghetto. These areas were in central Kraków and involved mostly Polish nationals. After a fashion, the killer shifted again, making several attacks within the military districts, notably involving the two German Army nurses that were raped and killed within the barracks of a military hospital. The typist for the Reich Ministry of Armaments lived in an upscale flat not far from Wawel Castle. Poles had long been evicted, and only members of the Nazi party were allowed in the building. She was found sexually brutalized in her fourth-floor flat, with the door to the balcony found open. Later, Frank's secretary was murdered in yet another part of Kraków, in a large residence that had once been a Polish villa but had since been confiscated by the General Government. Her murder had been exceptionally brutal...after being sexually assaulted and sodomized, and one of her breasts nearly bit off, she had been hung upside down from a huge crystal chandelier in the home's main foyer. As with many of the other murders, police found a window had been left wide open. The area in which she lived had been assessed as safe and secure, where other party apparatchiks had been domiciled. Lastly, the two SS women were killed within the confines of the concentration camp where they worked. This location is the most intriguing. How did the killer get in and out of a secure facility run by the SS? Could the killer be an SS officer? Tomorrow, I intend to go and visit this Auschwitz camp and have a look for myself.

13 July 1943 –

This morning, I left with Felix, Ernst, and Anna to go to the camp, about an hour and a half drive from Wawel Castle. A two-car security detail accompanied us. Felix briefed me during the drive that Auschwitz was actually a complex of over 40 camps in occupied Poland. The main camp, or Auschwitz I, is located in Oświęcim, about 65 kilometers from Kraków. Just three kilometers from there is a second, much larger camp in Brzezinka called Auschwitz II-Birkenau. A further seven kilometers to the East is Auschwitz III-Monowitz, a labor camp for the chemical conglomerate IG Farben. In the outlying areas are dozens of subcamps.

We were going to the Birkenau camp, which I was surprised to learn was 150 hectares in size or about 371 acres. It currently holds an astonishing 90,000 prisoners. Most of those were Jews, but there were also Poles, Gypsies, Jehovah's Witnesses, Homosexuals, Communists, and other "undesirables." I was shocked at the numbers and asked why so many were being centralized in a camp so far East, in occupied Poland. Felix just gave me a sad smile and shook his head, a gesture that indicated I should already know the reasons why. Ernst Hellriegel, ever the staunch Nazi, spoke up and said, "They are all enemies of the state, Standartenführer. At least they are now all out of Germany." I looked at the contemptible little shit, wanting to chastise his lack of humanity, but I held my tongue. It was a confrontation best saved for another time.

When we arrived at Birkenau we drove through an imposing brick gatehouse that ushered in a three-track railroad spur. As we drove past, I could see a train that had pulled up next to a long ramp that extended into the camp. The rail cars were all open and appeared to be offloading a new delivery of incoming prisoners. It was a terrible sight; thousands of people were pouring out of the packed cars and being ushered out to the ramp. At first glance, it looked to be pure chaos, with the guards shouting directions and dogs barking and snapping at the prisoners. But then I could see there was an orderly process being carried out, with all the people being divided into two columns. One column looked to be men and older boys, and the women and children of both sexes in the other. I spotted a couple of SS officers mingling in the crowd, quite obviously medical personnel, as they were wearing white medical coats, one with a stethoscope around his neck and holding a clipboard. They looked to be making selections amongst the newly arrived children, for God only knows what. In a moment, we had driven past, and I was left with a fleeting sight of the children, desperately clinging to their mothers, crying, with absolute terror plastered on their young, innocent faces. Until the day I die, that image will forever be burned into my consciousness, a single snapshot of man's complete inhumanity to man.

It took another minute or two driving through the camp to reach the headquarters complex. Even though I was briefed on the camp's size, I wasn't prepared for what I saw. I had been to Dachau, the first concentration camp established by the Nazis outside of Munich after coming to power in 1933. It was several years ago, before the war. I needed to interview one of the inmates, who was an eyewitness to the murder of a young couple I was investigating. The month before, the hapless fellow had been labeled a communist, arrested, and sent to Dachau. At the time, I had thought that the Dachau camp was impossibly large, but I realized it was truly minuscule compared to the sprawling monstrosity I was now traversing. We drove past row after row of horse-stable-like barracks; they seemed to go on forever. At last, we reached a car park adjacent to the camp's administration building. As we got out of our vehicles, we were met by the Auschwitz commandant, SS- Obersturmbannführer Rudolf Höss. I immediately took a dislike to the man. I already knew from his file that in his SS career, he had always served with the SS-Totenkopfverbände, or "death's head units" that ran the concentration camps. He joined the SS in 1934 and was immediately assigned to Dachau. In 1938, he moved on to Sachsenhausen concentration camp, where he honed his brutal skills. There, he led a firing squad that, on Himmler's orders, killed August Dickmann, a Jehovah's Witness, who was the first conscientious objector to be executed after the start of the war. Höss fired the finishing shot from his pistol. Himmler was so impressed with Höss that he dispatched him to evaluate the feasibility of establishing a concentration camp in western Poland, and Höss' favorable report led to the creation of the Auschwitz camps and his appointment as commandant in May 1940. In my view, Höss is just a thug, a high-paid jailer who has been given a full remit to mistreat, beat, torture, or murder any prisoner assigned to him. He has no police or investigative background and can't be compared to the many professional detectives and investigators in the KRIPO. I fear that someday, however, we will all be viewed as one monolithic SS, forever associated with the death's head units of the camps.

When he greeted me, Höss appeared nervous. He no doubt was under a lot of pressure to explain how two of his female SS guards had been sexually assaulted and murdered in what was supposed to be a secure concentration camp. He pointed to an area just outside the perimeter of Birkenau. He explained that the garrison consisted of nearly 3,000 total SS, and of those, 50 were female. When off duty, they lived and slept in the SS barracks that were located just outside the perimeter. Thus, the two murdered SS women would have normally been in their barracks rooms outside the camp, but on the night in question, they had pulled guard duty within the women's section of the camp. Along with a large entourage of SS functionaries, we then walked with Höss as he escorted us towards the women's camp, which, in reality, was its own subcamp within the larger confines of Birkenau. And as such, it was far inside the main perimeter. With the omnipresent guard towers and roving guards, it would have been impossible for an outsider to have infiltrated so far inside. As we walked together, Höss seemed almost proud of what he had accomplished during his time as camp commandant. He boasted how Birkenau was built by 10,000 Soviet prisoners of war supplied by the German army. Construction of the camp began in the autumn of 1941, and by the following spring, only a few hundred of the original 10,000 prisoners were still alive. Höss seemed to smile when he added that the prisoners assigned to build the camp survived on an average of two weeks. I wasn't surprised. Everyone knew Soviet military prisoners of war were treated harshly. However, they were the lucky ones. Soviet Jews, political commissars, and all communists were systematically targeted for execution. As we arrived at the women's camp, Höss informed us that over ten thousand women were held there and lived in barracks that consisted of sixty-two bays, each with three "roosts." A roost was originally supposed to hold three prisoners, but this had been increased to four. To sleep, sit, and keep belongings, each prisoner had their own space that amounted to the surface dimensions of a large coffin.

We finally reached the murder site itself. It was between two of the prisoner barracks that ran parallel to each other, with about a 10-meter strip of ground between them. We could quickly determine that the area was in a blind spot—out of sight of the closest guard tower. Anna was the one to ask the obvious question—surely, some of the prisoners in the adjacent barracks had heard the cries or screams of the women during the killings. Höss simply nodded to his adjutant, who then disappeared into one of the barracks. Soon after, he was back with three women. They wore prisoner's white pajamas with vertical blue stripes. The poor women looked pitiful; they were so emaciated their bodies looked almost skeletal. They were shaking in fright, no doubt scared beyond belief being in the presence of Herr Commandant. "I'll tell you upfront," Höss told us, "These Jewesses talk utter nonsense. What they have to say is ridiculous. It has no value to your investigation." I turned to the women. They were obviously terrified even to speak. "Herr Commandant," I ordered, "I want a private space where these women can speak freely. Please set up a room where my staff can do a proper interview." There was no way I was going to interrogate the women with their SS guards standing right over their shoulders. Höss looked displeased but ordered his staff to set it up. While this was being done, we spent the next hour examining the killing site. Höss confirmed that when they found the bodies, there was virtually no blood to be found on the ground, although the ground between the buildings was disturbed with indentations that seemed to show the initial struggle had taken place there. There was only a trace amount of blood on the side of one of the wooden barracks where one of the bodies had been positioned. I say positioned because when the SS found the bodies, their uniforms had been all but ripped off, and they were nude. After having been sexually assaulted, ravaged, and bitten, one woman had been placed with her back up against the side of the barracks wall. The other woman had been placed on top of her, but in reverse, with the first woman's arms up and holding the second so that they appeared to be conducting some perverted lesbian act. Unfortunately, with all the commotion and confusion when they were initially discovered and with no one having investigative expertise, no photographs had been taken of the scene before the women had been pulled apart. Thus, all we are left with are the descriptions from the SS guards that had discovered them. But it seemed enough—the MO clearly fits that of the earlier murders. The killer seems to have a penchant for sexually defiling his female victims, followed by further debauchery and humiliation of the corpses. Despite the absence of the bodies, we tried to proceed with a standard crime scene analysis. Felix took photographs of the scene, first by working outwards with perspective shots, taken at every angle, and gradually moving inwards for the close-up, detailed photos. Manfred took measurements to capture the topographical dimensions of the entire area. I took sketches per my habit, making annotations in the margins based on my first-hand eyewitness evaluation. Working around all of us, Anna methodically took samples of the blood from the side of the barracks, as well as some of the grass and dirt where the scuffles had taken place. From time to time, as we did this, I could see curious prisoners looking out from the barracks windows. I felt pity for them as I could clearly see the abject misery painted across their faces. I would leave this horrendous place at the end of the day, I thought to myself, as would Höss, returning to his villa outside the camp, where his wife and five children would await him, ready for a family dinner. But those poor wretches of Birkenau will likely never see the outside world ever again.

Once we were done at the crime scene, we returned to the administration building, where we proceeded to interview the eyewitnesses to the murders that Höss had provided. Two of the women spoke German, and one required the assistance of a translator. We took their sworn statements. I could see why Höss was skeptical of their value. Still, it was hard to see any reason why they would make up such a fantastic story. Especially one they know the SS will not accept. Höss would like to interrogate them with more aggressive techniques to get the "full truth," but I bade him not to do so. I have a feeling they have related to us truthfully what they witnessed despite it seeming utterly fantastic. I'm going to write down here for the diary a partial summary of two of the women's lengthier statements:

Partial statement from Prisoner 22454 (Polish Jew): "I woke up from a fitful sleep, cold and shivering. Someone had stolen my blanket a few days before, and sleep was hard to come by. I could see the moonlight coming through the windows and knew it was in the middle of the night. The crowded bay was filled with the usual sounds of whimpers, moans, and incessant coughing. But I began to hear something that sounded like it came from right on the other side of the wooden wall of the barracks. Some kind of slapping sound. I had never heard something like that before, so I got up. At first, I thought a guard was slapping an inmate, but it was too rhythmic. I had to walk down a few bunks to be able to look out a window. From an angle, I could then see what was making the sound. It was a man fucking a woman guard. I could tell it was a guard because although her skirt was missing, she still wore the blouse of her SS tunic. I could see the death head's patch clearly on the collar. I couldn't see her face clearly because of the angle and the blood, but I realized she looked a lot like one of the guards we've nicknamed 'Mara.' (Note: I later learned that in Slavic mythology, *Mara* is a malicious spirit who torments people in their sleep…her name is associated with nightmares and fear, as she feeds on the despair and anguish of her victims.) The man was rutting like an animal, pounding into her violently. He looked to be in his 40s or 50s, with long dark hair combed back and tied behind in a ponytail. There was a bit of grey along the man's temples. He wasn't wearing a military uniform, German or otherwise. He was wearing nice clothes, a dress shirt and tie…I guess you could say a man's suit. I hadn't seen a man dressed like that since before the war. I could see a gold chain that was dangling down from around his neck. As I watched, he occasionally bent his head down and tore out pieces of Mara's neck with his teeth. I could see his bloodied mouth. Yet all this time she was being bit, Mara had her arms around the man, holding him tight, her legs spread wide and wrapped around the man's back, as she bucked her hips up to meet his thrusts. There was no doubt she was welcoming the sex. Enjoying it even. At one point, the man reached down and ripped off Mara's tunic top, throwing it aside so that he had better access to her breasts. I watched in horror as he bent down and chewed on her breasts with his wide maw. A minute later, as the man came to orgasm, he threw his head back and opened his mouth, moaning in pleasure. It was then I could see he wasn't human. He couldn't be. His mouth was full of jagged teeth, dripping with Helga's blood. I could see his eyes were red as they glowed in the moonlight. I fought the urge to scream, and I had the feeling the man would look up at me at any second. The thought of that chilled me to the bone. I ducked away from the window and went back to my bunk. For several minutes thereafter, I could hear sounds of movement outside the barracks wall, but I did not dare go back to take a look. I lay huddled in fright until about a half hour later when I heard shouting from the other guards."

Partial statement from Prisoner 9945 (Romani): "I had gotten up to go to the bathroom. I went into the latrine to relieve myself. The shit and waste were up near the top of the toilet holes, and the barracks stank more than usual. As I was making my way back to the bunk, I heard a strange sound coming from just outside the wall. Some kind of slurping sound. I took a look through the closest window, and I could see a man I'd never seen before. I've been here a long time, and I know he wasn't SS or anyone who worked in the camp. He was well dressed and in a nice suit as if he were just coming back from a dinner party. He was on his knees, his face bent down over a nude woman. I could see his mouth was on the woman's neck, not in a kiss, but latched on wide and hard. With each slurp, I could see his Adam's apple bobbing. Once in a while, he would burp, his mouth losing its grip ever so slightly, and blood would pour out of what I could see was a wound in the woman's neck. He was drinking her blood. I glanced over the ground next to her, and that's when I saw what looked like an SS tunic. I knew then she was one of the guards. When I looked further down the row between the barracks, I saw another nude woman. She was lying still. I looked back at the man. I'd say he was in his 50s. He was tall, with long, greying hair, combed back along a thin scalp. From what I could see of his face, his flesh was thin and taut. It was like looking at a skull. I suddenly remembered the stories my grandmother used to tell me back home in Romania. The stories of the *strigoi*, the vampyre, the undead. As if reading my mind, the creature looked up, and I swear he looked right at me. His eyes were glowing red and malevolently. His face was smeared with blood. He smiled, but it was more like when a dog bares his teeth…a warning to stay away. I backed away from the window and ran back to my bunk. I kept expecting the monster to come for me next. Maybe he still will. Or worse yet, those two guards. They will soon also turn to *Strigoi*.

That's why I came forward. The SS beat me because they think I'm lying, but I know what I saw."

After the interviews with the women, I made sure to see Höss again. I told him the three women were material witnesses to the murder and, as such, needed to be protected. I ordered him to ensure their safety and well-being, and when or if I needed them, they had better be well-fed and in good health. I could see he wasn't at all happy with that. To him, Jews and Gypsies are "Untermensch," sub-human. But he knows I am reporting directly back to Himmler, so he dare not disagree. As we left Höss' office, Felix came up alongside me. "Nosferatu? Really, boss? Who's going to believe any of this nonsense? They must be playing us," he said. I shook my head. "For what reason?" I replied. "You saw those women. They're scared out of their minds. They face the wrath of the SS for sticking to those stories. But I think they're even more scared of the man they saw. Of course, he's not a vampyre. But fear does some strange things to people's perception. And if they are already predisposed to believing in the vampirism folklore and legends of their homeland, they may, well, read more into what they actually saw. But at the least, I think we now have a working description of the killer."

Minutes later, we were packed up and ready to head back to Kraków. It was then I noticed a plume of smoke coming from a building with a large chimney. The plume was massive; the smoke came roiling out of the chimney, thick and black, stretching far into the sky. "What's that building?" I asked Höss's adjutant, a young SS captain, who had escorted us back to our waiting vehicles. "That's Krematorium II, Standartenführer" he said, "and the building next to it is Krematorium III." I knew that the SS used crematoria ovens to burn the corpses of inmates who died from neglect and disease. But these two crematoriums were truly massive affairs. How many people were dying here, I wondered to myself. "How many crematoria, or ovens, are there?" I asked curiously. "Well," the captain replied, Krematorium I is over at the main Auschwitz camp. It's very small. It has just three double-muffle ovens, so a total of six ovens. It can only burn 340 bodies a day. Here at Birkenau, we have a state-of-the-art system courtesy of Topf and Sons. Krematorium II and III, which you see here, each have five three-muffle ovens, for a total of 15 individual ovens. Both Krematoriums are capable of burning 1,440 corpses every 24 hours. And over there," he paused as he pointed across to the other side of the camp, "we have two more, Krematoriums IV and V, that can each burn 768 of the dead in 24 hours." My head was reeling. According to the captain, the Birkenau camp has the capacity to burn over 4,440 corpses a day! But surely, I thought, that many people can't be dying here daily, no matter the starvation and ill-treatment. It was only then I noticed the line of people near Krematorium II. They were walking down steps and disappearing from view. Not into the building, but somewhere underground. I didn't see any exit. "Gas chambers," Anna whispered in my ear. I looked at Felix, and the look on his face told me all I needed to know. I found out later from both Felix and Anna that the rumors had been circulating for months, that the SS had moved on from the Einsatzgruppen, with their less efficient methods of shooting or gassing by mobile gas vans, to the much more effective gassing in a large fixed facility that can kill vast numbers and, with adjoining crematoria, efficiently burn the bodies. The SS even found a gassing technique that worked far more quickly than their previous use of carbon monoxide from exhaust fumes. They are using something called Zyklon B, a cyanide-based pesticide. And where better to do this than at secret locations in the occupied East, far away from the German public? I had been too busy, too focused on my work, to have fully understood what monstrous plans the Nazis had set in motion. Only Ernst Hellriegel seemed nonplussed. He stood there, eyes wide with obvious admiration. "Such a highly efficient operation," he praised the SS captain, "a perfect killing machine." I felt like pulling out my Walther and shooting the pig right there on the spot. There's no humanity, no empathy in the man. I knew then I was looking at a psychopath, a sociopath, at the very least. As we drove through the gates of Birkenau to head back to Kraków, I could still see the plume of black smoke billowing out of the chimneys of the krematorium. What I first took for snowflakes began to flutter down lazily on the breeze. Wispy white flakes, some of them sticking to the car's windshield. Then I realized, with growing horror, that it was no midsummer snowstorm. It was human ash, the incinerated remains of the people I saw disappearing underground. They had been selected simply for who they were and then had walked down those steps and into oblivion. At some point, I felt Anna take my hand. As I looked silently into her eyes, I could tell she sensed my sorrow and my revulsion. With a nod and a little squeeze of the hand, she told me she felt the same way, too.

(Addendum Entry) It's just after 4 a.m., 14 July. I got to bed late last night, and after witnessing the horrors of the Auschwitz camp, I found sleep to be impossible. But if things can get worse, they just have. I received a phone call from Manfred. He informed me there had been another break-in at the morgue. The bodies of the two murdered SS women and Han Frank's secretary are gone. Worse yet, Dr. Weber, the coroner, is also missing. I'm going over immediately.

14 July 1943 –

The team and I spent the morning over at the morgue. The bodies of the murder victims have been taken. There's no doubt their theft was the goal of the break-in because there were three other bodies that were left behind. One was a young Wehrmacht soldier who died in a traffic accident three days ago. The second was an employee of the Deutsche Reichspost, the German national post office which has taken over the Polish postal system, who had suffered a fatal heart attack the day previous. The third was a woman, a secretary with a German construction firm, who died from an accidental fall down a flight of stairs. What we can't understand is that, after the first break-in of the morgue, Dr. Weber had changed all the locks to the doors and had upgraded all security protocols. Yet, as before, the body snatchers were able to get in and out without any lock being picked or any door being breached. Two nightguards were on duty, but they saw and heard nothing out of the ordinary. The most troubling aspect is that the likable Dr. Max Weber has also disappeared. He was last seen by one of his departing assistants around 11 p.m. and by one of the nightguards in the examining room around midnight. He was reportedly working late to get another autopsy completed. His last words to the guard were that he hoped to be done within the hour. When the guard came back during his rounds 30 minutes later, the doctor had vanished. He immediately noticed the doors to three of the mortuary cooling units were hanging open, and the spaces within were empty. There are already rumors starting that Weber may have been part of the body snatching, but I don't think so. I think there's something else going on here. We've put out a bulletin with Weber's description to the police and security services, as well as to the local Wehrmacht commands. If he's still alive, I desperately need to speak with him. Needless to say, Himmler and Frank were furious. Especially Himmler, who now sees the situation as a direct attack on the SS. I think he sees it as some plot by the Polish resistance.

15 July 1943 –

No updates regarding Weber. Himmler has now ordered a full squad of SS men to guard the morgue. He is determined that there shall be no further body thefts. He is also flying in another coroner from Munich. A doctor Ziegler. I'll be picking him up at the airfield tomorrow afternoon. Despite the distractions, today I completed a basic framework of my psychological profile of the killer that I will be presenting to Himmler and Frank. Up to this point, I've been careful not to provide either of them with too many operational details of the case, particularly the more lurid details and description of the killer as recounted by the three Birkenau prisoners. I don't see any benefit in doing so at present, and I certainly don't want to start some kind of crazy rumors about a vampyre walking the streets of Kraków. While the animalistic neck wounds on the victims and their unexplainable blood loss still mystify me, I know the killer is a mortal man. A psychopathic and sadistic killer, but nevertheless mortal. The following is the psychological profile I've completed thus far:

KRIPO Case Nr. 43-0715

Assessment: The Kraków killer is a male, likely around thirty to forty years old, and a native of Kraków or the surrounding area. He appears to know his killing fields very well and is comfortable with his surroundings. He likely came from a dysfunctional background involving sexual or physical abuse, drugs, or alcoholism. He likely has disorganized thinking, manic depression, and a feeling of resentment towards society brought on by his own failings, sexual frustrations, a history of abuse or neglect at home, and an inability to be social or socially accepted. People who knew him as a child or adolescent probably witnessed behaviors such as daydreaming, compulsive masturbation, and isolation. He likely had a wild imagination that would often drag him into a fantasy world. A crucial factor in his development as a serial rapist is the role of fantasy. The action of penetration brings on a sense of triumph and conquest. In his case, he never had the opportunity to learn intimacy due to childhood restraints, and he substitutes intimacy with control, which is obtained by inflicting bodily harm on the victim. Each victim has meaning to the killer, and the intimacy of the murderous act is part of a close bond between himself and the victim formed in the killer's fantasy and delusions. The killer was probably "highly sexed" in childhood and may have been known to look into bathrooms through keyholes on females undressing or initiating sexual games— sometimes amounting to rape—with girls at school. The killer sees himself as dominant, controlling, and powerful. Fire is power, and power and control that puts the victim at his mercy are very appealing to him. As such, he probably has a history of fire-starting and arson. He holds the power of life and death, and in his own eyes, he perceives himself as God. In his fantasies and his enactment of the murder, he becomes God. By raping and biting his victims, he is desecrating and defiling their bodies, and by removing or drinking their blood, he is taking their life force and absorbing it into his own. As such, he enjoys having the ability to strike terror into people's hearts, controlling the lives of thousands of city residents who are held in his grip of terror. He is a sociopath and lacks a conscience, feels no remorse, and cares exclusively for his own pleasures. As the killer's pleasures increase, so will his escalation of violence. The number of attacks will likely increase, as will the ferocity of the killings as he seeks to gain more and more pleasure. The positive for law enforcement is that as the killer becomes less organized and more frenzied in his attacks, he will likewise take more risks, becoming over-confident and sloppy.

Recommendations: This investigative team recommends immediately that 1) There should be a city-wide mandate that all unaccompanied women now be escorted, particularly during hours of darkness. As with the Paul Ogorzow case, female detectives can be deployed in the killer's known operating areas as bait. However, appropriate surveillance and backup are essential due to the viciousness of the killer's attacks; 2) Kraków police files, including pre-war records, be reviewed for arrests or convictions for the following crimes: Arson, Rape, Sodomy, Voyeurism, cross-referenced for any multiple hits, then rank ordered by number of linkages.

16 July 1943 –

Anna came to my office this morning as I was discussing the psychological profile with Felix. She had the results of her examination of the samples taken from the murdered SS women and Frank's secretary. This case is getting all the stranger. Even as I write this, I still find her results inexplicable. If I hadn't known Anna's expertise in the forensics area, I would think she was either incompetent or insane. "I found the attacker's saliva in all of the bites," Anna led off. "As you know, saliva contains around 99 percent water, but also white blood cells and epithelial cells. I isolated those, and they are consistent with necrosis. As you know, necrosis is the death of cells in organs or tissue. Most people would probably equate it to gangrene. Necrosis in the mouth could indicate several things, one of them being osteonecrosis of the jaw, a disorder that occurs when cells in the jaw bone die. Could also be from a seriously neglected periodontal disease or some other disease or injury to the body." I was mulling over this information and what it could possibly mean when I noticed Anna had gone quiet. I looked at her. She was fidgeting with her notes and looked decidedly uncomfortable as if she was trying to form the right words for what came next. "All right," I told her. "You've got something else. Let's hear it." Anna cleared her throat, then dropped her bombshell. Her analysis of the semen found in the victims was even more unbelievable. According to the test results, vaginal and rectal swabs were positive for male semen in all three women. However, the age and condition of the semen samples were not consistent with a recent sexual assault. The semen was not fresh. Not by a long shot. According to Anna, the sperm cells contained in the semen were in the first stage of human decomposition called "autolysis," or self-digestion, which begins immediately after death. As soon as blood circulation and respiration stop, the body has no way of getting oxygen or removing wastes. Excess carbon dioxide causes an acidic environment, causing membranes in the cells to rupture. The membranes release enzymes that begin eating the cells from the inside out. Anna's summary of what this meant still resonates in my mind and continues to bring chills to my spine: "Because autolysis is the first stage of decomposition and takes place immediately after death, usually at about four minutes or so," she said, "it is as if the depositor of the semen in the women was someone who had just died. This confirms it…the killer is a corpse." Felix and I stared at Anna for several moments, waiting for the punchline to the joke. Or the "I gotcha." However, she just continued to stare at us with her detached clinical persona. I finally realized that she was dead serious. Pardon the pun. "That's insane," I told her simply. "It's scientifically impossible. The murderer can't be a dead man." Anna gave me a shrug. "It's science that proves that he is. I've run the tests three times. The results are the same," she told me. I sensed that there was someone else in the room, and I turned around. It was Hellriegel. The little weasel had been spying on us and had heard everything. "The old Gypsy at the camp was right," he mused. "The killer is a Nosferatu, a vampyre." I scoffed at his words. "He's just a man, Ernst. And he's going to be brought to justice the same as any murderer." Anna grabbed my arm. "There's one more thing, Otto." For the first time, her clinical expression changed to one of apprehension. She was clearly rattled. "I found a glycoprotein in the salvia. It seems to act as a natural anticoagulant, which allows blood to flow more readily. There's only one animal I've ever heard of that has this type of protein in their salvia." "Which one?" I asked, almost not wanting to know the answer. She glanced nervously over to Hellriegel. "Vampire bats," she said.

Frankly, after that revelation, it was almost a relief to leave the office in the late afternoon to pick up the new coroner, Dr. Hans Ziegler. His flight from Munich landed on time. I found out that he was fairly young, in his 30s, tall, with an infectious smile. I took a liking to him immediately. Not just because he is a fellow Bavarian, but I can tell he has a solid scientific and medical mind. He asked a thousand questions about the case on the drive back to Wawel Castle. He was so excited and had such an exuberant attitude that I only then realized that the poor chap was told nothing by the SS about what had happened to his predecessor. If he knew about Dr. Weber disappearing from work in the middle of the night, along with a roomful of corpses, I don't think he would have been so excited about coming. When we got back to Wawel, I took him aside and briefed him on everything. Even Anna's findings about the killer being a corpse as outrageous and unbelievable as it is. I'm not the type to let someone stay in blessed ignorance, especially when their life could be at risk. After I filled him in on the history, some of Ziegler's boyish exuberance dissipated, but he maintained his professional demeanor. He thanked me for my candor and honesty and vowed to do his best to support the investigation. I thanked him in turn, telling him that's all I could ask.

17 July 1943 –

My God! There was another murder last night. And it was particularly gruesome. And damn it, it's going to have political repercussions, which I fear will bring even more unwanted pressure on the team to get results and quickly. The victim was a cinematographer assigned to Josef Goebbels' Propaganda Ministry. She had been in Kraków for the past several weeks, working on a propaganda film on the success of the Germanization of Poland. Her name was Gertrude Brunner. Apparently, she was a young protégé of Leni Riefenstahl, Hitler's favorite propaganda film producer, and the director of the "Triumph of the Will," a well-known documentary of the 1934 Nuremberg party rally. I saw a publicity photo of Brunner and could see she was strikingly beautiful. Tall, blonde, slim, and physically fit, with all the right Ayrian features. But dear God, she's certainly not beautiful anymore. The killer was particularly brutal this time. As I had predicted, he is becoming more frenzied, escalating his violence.

Brunner was found in the bedroom of her fourth-story flat overlooking the Vistula River, located in the Kazimierz district of Kraków, just south of Wawel Castle. Ironically, Kazimierz was the former Jewish quarter of Kraków before all the Jews were deported south of the river to the Podgórze district where the Nazis had set up the Jewish ghetto in 1941. Podgórze was chosen as the site of the ghetto instead of Kazimierz because Hans Frank believed Kazimierz was more significant to the history of Kraków. And, of course, south of the river would be more out of sight, out of mind. When the Jews of Kazimierz were ordered to relocate to the ghetto, they were allowed to bring just 25 kilograms of their belongings. The rest of their possessions were taken by the Treuhandstelle, the German Trust Office. The Jews of the Podgórze ghetto are gone now, too. Just a few months ago, in March 1943, the final liquidation of the ghetto was carried out under the command of SS-Untersturmführer Amon Göth, a rather detestable creature who runs the nearby Kraków-Płaszów concentration camp. I haven't had the pleasure of meeting the man, but I don't doubt, with the blood on his hands, he is of the same murderous ilk as the Auschwitz commandant Rudolf Höss.

Brunner was discovered when one of the members of her film team became worried when she didn't show up for the morning's film shoot and convinced the building's manager to open up her flat to check on her. They discovered a sight that would undoubtedly haunt them for the rest of their lives. Even in the midst of brutal war, there are some images too nightmarish to process. I arrived less than an hour after getting the call with Manfred and Felix in tow. When we entered the hallway outside Brunner's flat, we found an ashen-faced young police officer standing shakily, his eyes downcast, still breathing hard. I noticed that there were flecks of vomit on the front of his otherwise impeccable uniform. I knew then whatever was inside was horrendous. As soon as we entered, the smell of blood and death hit us like a tsunami. It quite literally smelled like a charnel house. I steeled myself and entered Brunner's bedroom. We found her spread eagle on the bed, on her back. She was nude. Her breasts had been bitten off, and bite marks had reduced her stomach, genital area, and inner thighs to a bloody mess. She had been sexually assaulted and sodomized by something extremely large, certainly not by normal sex, but something that ravaged her, causing severe tearing and hematoma. Brunner's body looked to have been drained of blood per the usual MO, but this time, all the pre-mortem wounds had left a considerable amount of blood all over the bedroom.

Manfred was the one who saw it first. It's inexplicable, and I'd probably have a hard time believing it if I hadn't seen it with my own eyes. There were bloody handprints on the walls and the floor, but some on the ceiling, too. Together with partial footprints. It looked like the killer had somehow been crawling along the ceiling. Scuttling around like a spider. I know how it sounds. Totally insane, I know. But why would the killer take the time to fabricate such an intricate ruse? For what purpose? And how in dear heaven was it done? It seems that with every new murder, we end up with more unanswered questions. This whole case is turning out to be an enigma wrapped inside a riddle.

We spent the next several hours in the flat, making sketches, taking photographs, and interviewing the building's other residents. Anna arrived and collected samples for forensic testing. Speaking of which, I have not dared divulged to either Himmler or Frank the results of Anna's forensic testing indicating necrosis and autolysis in the killer's semen and saliva. They would think her a charlatan or an incompetent at the very least, if not totally mad. I do not want to lose her if they recall her back to Berlin. I still don't know if I accept her findings, but I have confidence in her professional acumen.

18 July 1943 –

This morning I attended Brunner's autopsy. Since his arrival, Dr. Ziegler had time to review the autopsy notes from all the previous victims, so he was well versed with the MO of the killer. As we suspected, Brunner's body had been completely drained of blood. She had lost a lot of blood pre-mortem due to the numerous bites she had sustained and the huge chunks of flesh that had been torn out around the most sensitive parts of her body. The killing wound was, without a doubt, the bite to the neck, penetrating the jugular vein. An arterial bite into the carotid artery would have ended her life quicker as it carries oxygenated blood to the brain, vice the jugular, which carries deoxygenated blood back to the heart, but nevertheless, it was fatal.

Brunner had been raped and sodomized by something large and phallic-shaped, but nothing was found near her body that could have been used for that purpose. Some kind of artificial device had obviously been used, but semen was also found inside her body. Copious amounts to be exact. Much more than could be possible from a normal male. Zeigler felt that maybe three or more men were involved because of the amount collected. Samples were taken to hand over to Anna for further analysis. Zeigler also collected samples from the bite marks and skin found underneath Brunner's fingernails, which quite possibly may be the killer's. There was also a ragged piece of black fabric found near Brunner's hand. It may be a piece of clothing torn off the killer. Anna is going to work around the clock to test the samples, and I should know more in 48 hours.

A very interesting development happened after I had retired back to my flat for the night. I opened a bottle of Schnapps and sat down to go through some of the case files, taking notes for an update I must give soon to Himmler and Frank. Later, after several shots of the brandy, I sat there, lost in my own thoughts, rehashing the details of the case as we knew them. We have a man, a voracious killer of women, who rapes and defiled his victims. A man who is sexually insatiable. A man who bites his victims in the neck, killing them, and then somehow drains them completely of their blood. A man who somehow managed to get in and out of one of our most secure concentration camps. A man that eyewitnesses have described as virtually a demon or a vampyre. A man that leaves bite marks larger and deeper than those of a human. A man that crawls on ceilings. A man that scientific analysis says is a corpse. I chuckled to myself. I couldn't wait to brief Himmler on those latest conclusions. I'd be brought back to Berlin and locked up in a mental asylum. Or worse.

My reverie was broken by a sudden knock on the door. It was quite late, nearly midnight. If it was someone from my team they would have called ahead. I took out my Walther PPK and clicked the safety off. Although my flat wasn't far from Wavel Castle, still in the secure zone of Kraków, and had excellent security since it was reserved for General Government and Nazi Party officials, I wasn't taking any chances. There was a war going on, after all. I cautiously opened the door and looked back and forth. The hallway turned out to be empty. No one was there. But they had left something. A package lay next to the door. I picked it up and took it inside. After re-entering the flat and locking the door, I took a look out my fourth-story window. I didn't see any waiting cars or anyone lingering along the street outside. I went over and sat back down at the table.

The package was a large, thick envelope tied together with twine. It looked like some kind of a dossier or file. I carefully untied the twine and opened it. The package consisted of a large rolled-up document resembling a scroll, accompanied by two bound manuscripts or journals. There was also a short letter, hand-written in German. "It's important you read this," the letter read. "I know you will find it, well, informative. I'll contact you again when I can. Be very careful, Inspector. The thing you seek is very cunning, and he knows you are on his trail." It was signed at the bottom with just the letters "S. K." Very interesting, I thought. Looks like I might have received an anonymous tip on my case. But what did he mean, "the thing" that I sought, not "the man?"

I brushed that thought aside as I first took out the rolled document. I unrolled it, spreading it across the length of the table. I could see it was a detailed drawing of a family tree. I looked at the top and determined it showed the lineage of a family with the name of Batowski. Polish, I realized. The tree began with a Batowski born in 1375, and indicated a marriage in 1394, resulting in five children. The tree continued to branch out from there, showing the marriages and children born through the years. Then, near the bottom, I noticed one name in particular had been circled. The name was Wojciech Batowski, born in 1562 from the union of Stanislav Batowski and Karolina Lewandaska. Stanislav and Karolina had one other son, Henryk, who in turn showed a marriage and two offspring. Wojciech, however, looked to be the end of his own line, with a marriage indicated but no children. I noted that all the names on the tree had dates of birth, marriage, and dates of death annotated, but Wojciech Batowski had a question mark next to a cross, the European symbol to denote death. Apparently, no date of his death was known or recorded.

After rolling the family tree back up, I took out the document that looked like a manuscript of sorts. It consisted of approximately 50-75 typed pages, many of which had inked annotations at the margins. The last several pages were also handwritten. It looked like a research paper that the author had continuously updated with new information. I returned to the first page and started to read.

From my fair grasp of Polish, I could see immediately the paper was a biographical sketch of the same individual circled on the family tree: Wojciech Batowski. As stated, born in 1562 in Kraków. Just a few years before the 1569 Union of Lublin, which created the Polish-Lithuanian Commonwealth—a single state formalizing a real union between the monarchies of Poland and Lithuania and creating one of the largest and most populous countries in Europe. Young Wojciech was born into nobility, the Batowski name having a long lineage as part of the Crown of the Kingdom of Poland. The record showed that Wojciech went to the top schools of the day, receiving an enlightened education. By all accounts, he was interested in science, and in particular, astronomy—the study of planets. By age 20, he grew tired of academia and yearned for action and adventure. With his noble connections, he obtained a commission as an officer in the famed Polish Hussars, the elite of the Polish cavalry, alternatively known as the winged hussars because of the large wings worn on their armor, which were intended to demoralize the enemy during the charge. The Hussars were a formidable force; they would charge enemy soldiers, impaling them on deadly, intricately designed lances and making entire units flee from the battlefield. As part of the military, Wojciech finally found the niche he was suited for. During the battle of Byczyna in 1588, he fought with distinction alongside the Polish military commander and Great Crown Hetman, Jan Zamoyski, leading to an overwhelming victory for the Swedish-born king-elect Sigismund III Vasa, over the army of his rival to the Polish throne, Maximillian III, Archduke of Austria.

Then, in 1591, when he was 29, the dashing young officer met a woman and fell madly in love. Her name was Nataszja. She was the daughter of a Colonel in Wojciech's regiment. At 25, she was simply stunning; no one could deny her features were carved by angels. Slim, blonde, with child-like eyes and full lips perpetually curved into a warm smile, she was seductively alluring yet at the same time genuine and compassionate. Her vulnerable quality masked a strength that only Wojciech could seemingly see. He was totally captivated by her charms, and after a brief courtship, they were married in May 1592.

In 1598, upon the death of his father, Wojciech inherited the royal title of Count, and became a loyal consort of the Polish-Lithuanian King, Sigismund III Vasa, who ruled the Commonwealth from 1587 to 1632. During the battle of Kokenhausen in 1601, Wojciech was reportedly fearless in the face of the enemy, earning great respect from his men by leading several charges even after being wounded, setting an example for all to see. The battle was later notable as one of the greatest victories of the Polish Hussars, who defeated their numerically superior Swedish adversaries. In 1605, Wojciech, now a Colonel in the Hussars, fought in the Battle of Kircholm, another battle of the ten-year Polish-Swedish War. The battle was decided in 20 minutes by the devastating charge of Wojciech's Winged Hussars. The battle ended in the decisive victory of the

Polish-Lithuanian forces and is remembered as one of the greatest triumphs of Commonwealth cavalry.

Even as his country perpetually called for him, Wojciech never failed to find time for his beloved Nataszja. By all accounts, he doted on her, lavishing her with his love and affection. His brother, Henryk, once wrote: "My brother has shown himself to be the consummate warrior—decisive, cruel and efficient when dispatching the enemy—yet when in the presence of his beautiful Nataszja his manner becomes as gentle as those of a lamb, his voice soft and caring. He becomes a man possessed by the greatest of love." It was one of the sadistic ironies of life that Nataszja never bore Wojciech any children of his own. By 1608, they had tried for 16 years, but Nataszja could never get pregnant. If Wojciech was disappointed, he never showed it. His love for Nataszja seemed to overcome this loss. They had each other, and they were happy. And Nataszja, for her part, never stopped loving her man in uniform.

Then, in the winter of 1609, tragedy struck. The symptoms were mild at first; Nataszja began experiencing fatigue and some lack of appetite. A few weeks later, she developed lower back pain and began losing weight. When she was hit with belly pain, Wojciech became alarmed and called in the best doctors his resources could buy. However, nothing they could do helped, and soon Nataszja was bedridden with a fever. Her skin turned yellow with jaundice, her urine became dark, and she vomited up any food they tried to feed her. It was "the wolf," doctors informed Wojciech. What doctors in the 1600s called cancer, because of its nature as an aggressive and destructive disease. Nataszja was dying, and there was nothing Wojciech could do to save his one and only love. By spring, she was dead. Wojciech was inconsolable over the loss of his beloved wife. As Henryk wrote in a letter to a close friend: "My brother is like a sailing ship cast adrift on a windless sea…he knows nothing of where he is headed. He is despondent and has no sense of purpose. I worry for him." Wojciech had Nataszja buried in the family plot just beyond the walls of his castle, and was seen making daily pilgrimages to the gravesite, standing alone, speaking words that only the spirits could hear.

Meanwhile, the Machiavellian intrigue amongst the Polish monarchy marched on, and with his power and authority secure, Polish King Sigismund III initiated a policy of expansionism and invaded Russia in 1609 when that country was plagued by a civil war known as the Time of Troubles. In 1610, Count Batowski , Colonel of the Winged Hussars and a favorite of the King, was called to the royal palace in Kraków and asked once again to go to war. "He took the commission eagerly," Henryk again wrote. "Nothing is left for him in Poland anymore, except for sadness and regrets. I fear that only on the battlefield will he find solace…as it is a place where men such as he, full of bitterness and anger towards our Lord God, are eager participants in that of man's inhumanity."

On July 4, 1610, at the height of his fame and glory, Wojciech led his unit once again during what was to be known as the Battle of Klushino. The Polish-Lithuanian forces, numbering about 6,800 men, of which 5,500, or about 80 percent, were Wojciech's Winged Hussars, faced off against a numerically superior force of about 30,000 Russians, augmented by nearly 5,000 Flemish, French, Irish, German Spanish, English and Scottish soldiers; mercenaries fighting for the Russia's ally, Sweden. The battle began around 4 a.m., taking place on a flat agricultural field, crossed by a high village picket fence, reinforced by improvised fieldworks, which allowed the Hussars to charge only through narrow gaps in the line. The first part of the battle consisted of Wojciech's Hussars repeatedly charging the fortified Russian positions, attempting to break them. The Polish-Lithuanian forces continued to make ferocious attacks, some accounts indicating the Hussars charged eight or ten times. Unfortunately, their attacks on the Russian infantry, hidden behind fences, and using firearms, were not successful. Further, the Polish riders had lost most of their long lances in the initial assaults, limiting the shock of their charge. A fight with swords and sabers occurred. During one of these charges, Count Batowski, Colonel of the Winged Hussars, was hit by a volley of Russian matchlock fire and was felled off his mount. The battlefield was chaotic and smoke-filled, but there were three eyewitnesses from fellow Hussars who saw Colonel Batowski after he was shot. All three accounts were never reconciled with what took place in the weeks to follow.

One of the Hussars, under fire himself and attempting to withdraw, recounted that he looked down from his horse briefly and saw his Colonel, shot and bleeding from the chest, lying on his back, staring up into the pre-dawn sky. "He was still alive," the man said later, "I could see his lips moving, as if in prayer." A second Hussar, also falling back and returning to the Polish line, claimed that he saw a man dressed in a black hooded cloak, kneeling beside the Colonel and leaning down over his face as if speaking to him. "The hooded man came out of nowhere," the Hussar later stated, "He was wearing a dark cowl, like those worn by monks. He wasn't a soldier, nor was he a mercenary. I figured him for a marauder, pillaging the dead on the battlefield. I would have stopped him, but then my mount was shot and I fell to the ground. I blacked out for a moment. When I came to, I was being carried back to our lines. I lost sight of the Colonel again." The third account is the most bizarre. Another Hussar, himself wounded and lying on the ground, swore that he saw a figure in a black cowl moving amongst the dead and fallen. A man, but yet not a man, the soldier insisted. "I saw what looked like a man moving from body to body. But he wasn't walking…he was keeping low to the ground…scuttling to and fro. He looked like a black spider as he moved along. He would pause and peer down at each body as if looking to see if they were alive or dead. My blood ran cold at the thought of him coming my way. I knew if he did, it would be the death of me. For an instant, he turned his head towards me. I caught a brief glimpse of his eyes, which seemed to glow red, despite no light shining into them. But he turned and scuttled off in the other direction, towards the forest. It was becoming light with the dawn, and I thanked our God in heaven."

Wojciech's body lay on the field through most of the day as the battle continued. Eventually, after a failed Russian counterattack, the left flank of the Russian forces was broken, and the Russian center disintegrated. Overall, the battle lasted about five hours, resulting in Russian losses of about 5,500 men and Polish losses of just 400, 100 of them being Hussars, including Wojciech. The battle is remembered as one of the greatest triumphs of the Polish-Lithuanian cavalry, and the victory enabled the Poles to take and occupy Moscow for the next two years. With little time to spare as the Poles pursued the retreating Russian army, the Polish dead, including Wojciech, were given hasty battlefield burials. As Count Batowski, Colonel of the Winged Hussars, was lowered into the ground, he was encircled by his grieving cavalrymen, paying their final respects to their fallen leader. As the Polish army chaplain gave a final prayer, Wojciech was covered with dirt, bloodied by the hundreds of men who had also fallen upon the same battlefield.

And there the story would have ended concerning Count Batowski; just a sad footnote in the otherwise glorious history of the Polish Winged Hussars. But, what followed became a true mystery, an inexplicable event that, at the time, drew wonderment by some, and doubt and fear by others. A little over two weeks after the Battle of Klushino, friends of Count Batowski were astonished to see him return home one night, arriving on a carriage from the East, totally unscathed, clearly alive and healthy. As he walked into his castle-like estate on the outskirts of Kraków, his staff and servants, having been told of the death of their employer, were in complete shock and disbelief. One young servant girl reportedly fainted straight away after seeing the Count. Over the coming days, Wojciech never gave a full accounting of what had happened, even to his brother Henryk, only saying he hadn't actually been shot but had blacked out after being felled from his horse. He claimed to have awoken on the battlefield the next day, the area by then left deserted by the advancing armies. Still disorientated, and not knowing where his army had gone, he slowly made his way back west to Poland. Naturally, the Hussars gave a hero's welcome to their leader, but privately, many officers and cavalrymen present at the burial KNEW the body they put into the ground was Wojciech's. After all, the corpse wore the Colonel's uniform, replete with all his medals and decorations. It was HIM, they whispered, shot in the chest by an arquebus, but no one dared voice what everyone was thinking…that the Count had somehow returned from the dead. After that, he was nicknamed "Wojciech the Fortunate" by his troops. But the glory and accolades did not last for long. Within a week of his return, Wojciech had resigned his commission and left the military. He had not left his castle since returning home, even to meet his benefactor, Sigismund III, the King of the Polish-Lithuanian Commonwealth. He became a recluse, never meeting anyone during the day. He only held court, hosted dinners, and visited with friends during the evening hours. Many of his servant staff left during this time, now afraid of the idiosyncrasies and strangeness of their employer, although a loyal cadre remained, enough to keep the household running. Over time, the Count's circle of friends diminished, and there became fewer and fewer visits to the castle. Information is scarce as to the Count's later years, as he became more and more reclusive, seen by few people except for his brother Henryk. The last meeting between the two brothers took place in early 1624, and it did not seem to go well. In a letter to a close friend, Henryk had written: "In a way, I feel that my brother did indeed die on that accursed battleground in Russia so many years ago. Whilst his body still appears young and vibrant, like that of a man in his 40s, his soul seems to be gone. There is a dark presence within him; I feel no love or affection coming from him…our discussions are always curt and perfunctory. Since his return, I have never met with him during the light of day. I will no longer take Darek and Albina to the castle to see their uncle."

Later that year, some fourteen years after his wounding at the Battle of Klushino, Count Wojciech Batowski disappeared one night at the recorded age of 62. His personal effects were all left behind, including his clothing. It was as if he just walked out the door with what he had on his back. A search was conducted, but it was perfunctory as, over the years, the castle had garnered a reputation that kept many of the superstitious locals uncooperative. With no body found, no death was ever reported, and the Count was never seen again. The castle and grounds were left vacant, abandoned by Wojciech's brother, who wanted nothing to do with it. It was left to decay and rot over the centuries, and now, in 1943, little was left except its brick foundations and scattered remnants of the walls.

After finishing the biography, I set it aside. What a tragic, sad story, I thought. For this Wojciech fellow to have left the military at the height of his career, throwing away all the honors and accolades, even from the King, and sequester himself inside the walls of his home for the remainder of his life, becoming a recluse even from family…it indicates some serious psychological disorders with the man. The mental anguish he suffered from the loss of his beloved wife Nataszja was certainly one tipping point, and then God only knows what subsequent mental breakdown he may have had as a result of being nearly killed in battle. One thing we Germans learned during the Great War is that the horrors men see in battle sometimes come back to haunt them, and some are never the same again.

I then pulled out the third and last document. I immediately froze, the hair standing up on my neck as I read the heading. At first, I wasn't sure if I had translated the Polish correctly. The heading read: "The Vampyre Batowski: Historical Activity and Victims." What the hell, I thought. I took an involuntary look around the room, almost thinking it was some kind of prank. Could Hellriegel be behind this? He's already come to the crazy conclusion our killer is Nosferatu, a vampyre. But what about the results of Anna's forensic testing? Namely, the killer's cells were in autolysis, the first stage of human decomposition that begins immediately after death. Which would make him a walking corpse. And the fact that his salvia also contained dead cells and a natural anticoagulant similar to that in the vampire bat. How can that be explained? I haven't been able to refute her findings. It's science, after all. And I've always seen myself as a rational man, a man of details, facts, and evidence. So, what to make of this? I had no choice but to continue to read.

It wasn't until 3 a.m. when I finished. I sat back in my chair, stunned. Could it all be true, I thought? The document, which I'll refer to as the "Vampyre Chronicle," had contained hundreds of entries noting dates and locations of disappearances and killings attributed to the supposed vampyre Batowski, most of them involving girls and young women, spanning over the past 300 years. Several of the entries documented sightings of the Count after he disappeared in 1624, confirmed sightings by people who knew him, who swore he hadn't aged a day since they last saw him. There were far too many entries to write down here in the journal. But a few stood out:

The first entry was dated 1626. The Polish village of Wadowice, 50 kilometers southwest of Kraków. The population was terrorized over an eighteen-month period, during which time thirteen young girls disappeared. Several more killings took place in the years after, in villages further away, expanding like a concentric ring.

In 1632, in the Moravian village of Ostrava, then occupied by Danish forces after the Thirty Years War, six young women disappeared. One woman came back months later, her husband claiming she was tapping on the window in the middle of the night to be let in. He would have done so, too, but was stopped by his brother, who was staying the night. The brother, who had spent time in the Old Country of Romania, held up a crucifix, and the woman screamed and disappeared into thin air.

In 1639, in the city of Vienna, at that time the de facto capital of the Holy Roman Empire under Hapsburg rule, Count Batowski's younger brother, Henryk, who had last seen Wojciech shortly before he disappeared from Kraków fifteen years previous, was in Vienna visiting a friend. He swore later to family and friends that he had seen Wojciech standing on a moonlit street, and he didn't look a day older than fifty, even though he would have been 77 years old. Henryk would shudder when recounting how his brother had looked right at him, his eyes aglow with a reddish malice, smiling maliciously before disappearing into thin air. Later, when Henryk would describe Wojciech's mouth of wicked-looking teeth, he would break down in tears, shake uncontrollably, and repeat the words, "Wurdulak…Wurdulak…Wurdulak."

The occurrences of missing and murdered women continued southwards over the decades. In 1652, the city of Graz, at that time under the Hapsburg Monarchy, experienced a wave of missing girls, none of them to be seen again. In 1660, Ljubljana, a Slovenian city then under the control of the Hapsburg Monarchy, experienced the horrendous murder and mutilation of seven young women, one of them the mayor's sixteen-year-old daughter. A man by the name of Frankowski, who was a young officer at the Battle of Klushino fifty years earlier, now aged 73, was visiting Ljubljana at the time. Frankowski swore he saw his old commander, Colonel Wojciech Batowski, while standing outside the inn where he was staying. Batowksi drove by in a carriage, and sitting next to him was a young woman. Frankowski recognized his former Colonel easily because Batowski, who would by then be 98 years old, looked exactly the same as that day on the battlefield so many decades before…a man in his late 40s. But what really unnerved Frankowski was when the carriage passed him, the man turned his head and looked him in the eyes, smiled, and brought his right hand up, fingers straight, touching his forehead. A military salute for a fellow soldier.

In the years to follow, the killings continued to move southwards, from Central to Southern Europe, then down into the Balkans. From 1683 to 1685, in the sleepy village of Banja Luka, then under Ottoman rule, over a terrible two-year period, the town's population of young women was nearly decimated by a rash of killings and body snatching. Sixteen young women were found murdered and sexually assaulted, with their bodies later disappearing from their graves. Seven other girls disappeared completely and were never seen again.

The killings reached their furthest location to the south during 1724-26. In that three-year period, in the Croatian city of Split, at that time ruled by the Venetian Republic, over a dozen young women were found raped and murdered. Their bodies later disappeared. This time, a local man was accused of the crimes and sentenced to death. He professed his innocence until he was publically executed in the city square. Despite the execution, three more women were attacked. The city was in total panic, but mercifully, the killings eventually ceased. The real killer was never caught.

During the rest of the millennium, the killings began to move northwards. A girl here, several girls there, all the villages up the eastern coast of the Adriatic experienced terror as their young women disappeared or were found in horrendous states. In 1740, the city of Trieste, a city under the Hapsburg monarchy, experienced a rash of disappearances of young women. After the seventh woman disappeared, three priests from the Catholic Church arrived from Rome, who seemed to be conducting their own investigation. Several residents spotted the priests around the local cemeteries at night. After two weeks in Trieste, they too disappeared, never to be seen again. Over the next several decades, killings and disappearances continued all along the northern shore of the Adriatic. The list of villages experiencing terror and sadness went on and on. In the year 1796, as the 18th century began drawing to a close, the City of Venice, then under the control of the Venetian Republic, was the scene of the next carnage. Over a six-month period, seven young women disappeared. Three men also disappeared, all husbands of the missing women. In two cases, not just the husband disappeared, but the entire family. Seven children in all went missing, ranging from one year old to nearly twelve. The disappearances only ended when Napoleon Bonaparte conquered Venice in May 1797 during the War of the First Coalition.

In the nineteenth century, the killing spree slowly progressed westwards through Europe. In 1806, fifteen young women were raped and murdered in the city of Genoa, a year after Napoleon annexed it as he proclaimed himself the King of Italy. The killings were followed by a rash of grave robberies, with the murder victims dug up from their graves and disappearing. Residents recounted a mysterious stranger who arrived in town, a self-professed vampyre slayer, a young man, maybe in his 30s, who was from the old country in Eastern Europe. The man was seen carrying a bright silver dagger with an ivory handle. He asked about a man named "Wojciech." A week after he arrived in town, he was found with his throat cut, hanging upside down, tied to a Cross of Saint Peter, an inverted cross seen as an anti-Christian or Satanic symbol.

There continued to be sporadic cases of unexplained murders or disappearances of young women along the coastline of the Ligurian Sea over the next several decades. The next large rash of sadistic murders took place in the Piedmont city of Turin, 200 kilometers inland from the coast, in 1862. Turin had recently become the capital of the newly-proclaimed United Kingdom of Italy. Over a six-month period, four entire families were found murdered. The women and young girls fared the worst; they had been sexually ravaged, and most had bite marks all over their bodies. The cases gained the attention and curiosity of the local Italian medical community when it was revealed that all the victims had been found completely drained of blood. Investigators soon became frustrated as they became deluged by scientists and medical experts coming from all over

Europe. Even priests from Rome showed up and began asking questions. The public spectacle then became a three-ring circus when the local cemetery was vandalized, and the bodies of the murder victims disappeared. Talk of vampirism ensued, and soon Turin was inundated by so-called vampirologists and investigators of the occult. The final straw was when the cemetery became the focal point for various satanic cults that held nightly rituals there in honor of the undead. The police tried to disperse them but to no avail. Over the next two weeks, six cultists and one occult investigator disappeared during these nightly vigils, gone without a trace and never seen again. After this, even the most ardent devil worshipers would no longer step foot into the cemetery, fearful of whatever roamed amongst the headstones in the darkness of the night.

Over the next twenty years, sporadic yet unexplained disappearances took place all along the coastline of the Ligurian Sea. In 1883, the French city of Nice was in the midst of its pro-Italian movement, despite the repression carried out since the French annexation in 1860 under the Treaty of Turin, namely, the French government's policy of Francization of Italian society, language, and culture. During that sweltering summer, the bodies of several young Italian women were found defiled and murdered. Public anger and suspicion naturally turned towards the French, that was, until the 17-year-old daughter of the French military garrison commander, Général Francois Daladier, was also found murdered. As the months progressed, there was an equal number of victims from both sides. What couldn't be explained was who was removing their bodies from the city's cemeteries. Once again, mysterious priests from Rome arrived to lend "assistance" to the police investigation. Then, in the fall, word filtered back to Nice that the daughter of Général Daladier had disappeared from her family's gravesite in Paris. Daladier, still in Nice, committed suicide with his service revolver. Two days later, his wife swallowed poison. The rash of killings stopped as quickly as they started.

In 1924, the French city of Marseille experienced a bizarre occurrence. In May of that year, within a span of three days, five young girls were raped and murdered. Late one night, there was a shootout and commotion at the city's morgue, where the bodies of the girls had been kept. Police reports later described two young women who had entered the morgue and tried to desecrate the bodies of the murder victims by cutting off their heads. They were caught in the act, and after a police shootout, they somehow escaped. By chance, a policeman at the scene who got a good look at the women recalled engaging them in conversation at a bar two nights before. As best as he could remember, one of the girls was named Bethany. Her friend introduced herself as Althea.

In 1936, the killings resumed in Seville, a city in southern Spain, then under the control of Francisco Franco's Nationalist forces. With the Spanish Civil War raging all around them, the discovery of seven young women found raped and butchered over a ten-month period was simply attributed to sectarian violence between the Republicans and Nationalists. Amidst the ongoing war, even the priests stayed away. It was the perfect killing ground.

In early 1939, just before the war, there was a bizarre news story that came out of St. Gallen, a city in eastern Switzerland, not far from the principality of Liechtenstein. The young daughter of one of the town's businessmen was found missing one morning, her bed having never been slept in, and the window wide open. On the nightstand was the 17-year-old girl's diary. In it, she wrote of sneaking out at night for several weeks to meet a young, handsome man; the girl was smitten and felt she might be in love. A school friend's name was mentioned in the diary as also sneaking out to meet with the young man; the trio would meet in the nearby woods and have sex. Investigators spoke with the girl, and she said they first met the man one night while they were hanging out and smoking in the woods. Although they "weren't that type of girl," she described how they ended up having sex with the young man. It was so intense, so overpowering, the girl claimed, that they couldn't stop themselves from coming back for more. Then, the night previous, the man tapped on her bedroom window and asked her to come out. But her parents were still up, and when her father walked into the room, the man disappeared. That no doubt saved her life. The girl described the man as being in his early 20s with long black hair, muscular and well-built, and so cute he was "to die for." When asked the man's name, she remembered it right away. Because it was so cute, she said. It was "Wojo."

From 1939 to 1940, in the area around the Austrian city of Linze, nine young women were killed or went missing in a year. Most of these women, in their late teens, were members of the National Socialist Woman's League. The numbers of the missing increased as the nearby Mauthausen concentration camp went into full swing. In 1942, an uncle of one of the murdered girls, who lived in Berlin, swore he saw his niece along the Kurfürstendamm one evening. There was no chance of mistaken identity because he even spoke with her. She told him he was her favorite uncle and that he shouldn't worry about her as she was very happy now. She said she might come to see the uncle and his family sometime if he invited her. He, of course, replied yes, she was welcome anytime. Upon hearing his brother's account, the girl's distraught father had her grave opened back up in Linze. It was empty.

I put the vampiric chronology down and realized there was a pattern. If true, the vampyre Wojciech had migrated over the past 300 years all through Europe. Settling into one community for a year or two where he did his killing. From Kraków he traveled south into the Balkans, then back up to the north of Italy, and then all the way over to the bottom of Spain, then back up through France, Switzerland, and Austria to…yes, of course, back to Poland. Back to Kraków, his birthplace, and where it all started. But why the migration? What drew him to those places? I think I know why. Many of those places were going through tumultuous times, either plague, war, or some social upheaval. It is easier to kill when killing is already going on all around you or when the populace is otherwise distracted.

It's nearly dawn now. When I get to the office, I'm going to show everything to Manfred and Felix…and Anna too. I need to get their opinions on this. I can't bring myself to believe any of it; my whole life's work has been rooted in science, logic, and reason. Yet, I have a gnawing feeling that this case may be turning out to be something far, far larger than we can imagine. Larger than any of us. If everything I read in the documents is true, we're just another event in a timeless ritual, and we are way out of our depths.

19 July 1943 –

It was a very busy day today. I no sooner walked in the door than Manfred told me that Governor General Frank wanted to see us. He wanted an update on the case, particularly about Brunner. He was undoubtedly getting heat from the Propaganda Ministry and that clubbed-footed Goebbels. I spent the next three hours with Frank, time I could have spent addressing the case, but there was no choice. Manfred briefed Frank on the overall status of the investigation, and Felix covered all the investigative interviews. I let Dr. Ziegler discuss Brunner's autopsy, keeping to the basics. Finally, I briefed the criminal profile I had developed on the perpetrator thus far. I explained that we felt we were getting close, that the killer was becoming more frenzied and erratic, and this would mean he would make mistakes. Frank seemed placated but wanted to know how the bodies from the morgue had disappeared and what the status of Dr. Hans Weber was. I could offer no rational explanation as to how the bodies disappeared, but fortunately, Frank was quick to jump to the insinuation that Weber must have been involved and had been the one to take the bodies out of the morgue. He almost seemed to want to pin the murders on Weber as well until I reminded him that the murders had started before Weber had been flown in from Stuttgart. With no options of my own to explain the body thefts, I went ahead and let Frank believe Weber was behind them. At that point, I didn't think it would matter. I have a gut feeling that Weber won't be seen again.

As we left Frank's office, Felix joked, "Well, that went well. At least we're not in front of a firing squad." I had to laugh with him. "We probably would be," I replied, "if we had let Anna brief her forensic findings. Imagine telling Frank his administrative assistant was raped by a dead man. It will be interesting to see what Anna gets off the Brunner samples. Hopefully, proof that the killer is as alive as you and I." As we continued back down to our basement offices, I turned to Felix and told him, "I want you guys to grab Anna, then come see me in my office. I was given something last night that I need to share with you. You may not believe it, but we need to go over it." Felix looked at me curiously. "Got it, boss. What about Hellriegel? Should I get him too?" I stopped for a moment to consider. I was loathe to bring that sadistic son of a bitch into our discussion, but he was a member of the team. And a fellow officer. I had to bring him into it, but I dreaded what conclusions the man might draw from the curious history of Count Batowski. Despite my reservations, I gave the nod to Felix.

Thirty minutes later, I had the whole team assembled in my office. Manfred, Felix, Ernst, Anna, Elsie, and Dr. Ziegler. At first, I had planned to exclude Elsie, my secretary and admin assistant, as I felt she was too young and she was not an investigator. Moreover, I didn't want any note-taking or a record kept of the meeting that could leak out. Felix assured me that Elsie was mature beyond her 22 years and was highly dependable, loyal to the team, and would keep anything discussed to herself. I relented, and a bit later, when we were all assembled, I explained how the package was delivered to my door by the mysterious "S. K." I unrolled the Batowski family tree, then recapped to the group what I had learned from the biography of Wojciech Batowski's life. I hesitated before I brought out the Vampyre Chronicle. I knew from that point on that the document would change how we looked at this investigation forever. If we even took it seriously. Since it was in Polish, and I was the one who had the best literacy, I read it out loud. When I was done, there was silence in the room. Manfred spoke up first. As the oldest investigator, I wasn't surprised when he scoffed at even the possibility a vampyre was the killer. "Horse shit," he exclaimed loudly, "someone's trying to play us." I could see Felix and Anna as they exchanged glances. I knew they were the ones who were privy to Anna's lab results. Ernst Hellriegel's reaction was the most bizarre; he just smiled and said, "He's back. He's back home. Back home to his city. Full circle." For once, I wasn't sure if Hellriegel was full of bullshit. We spent the next hour going over the evidence we had. Manfred sat stoically as Anna summarized her forensic findings. Findings that pointed to a perpetrator who was supernatural…and the perfect definition of a vampyre. Felix recapped the eyewitness accounts of the Auschwitz inmates, describing a non-human fiend that raped and fed on blood. Hellriegel recounted the unexplained thefts of corpses from the morgue and the disappearance of Dr. Weber. Disappearing bodies of victims, just as recounted in the Vampyre Chronicle. Bodies that maybe don't stay dead. Bodies that maybe come back. Weber's replacement, Dr. Ziegler, discussed the strange wounds inflicted on the bodies, bite marks too large and no match to a human being, the bites to the necks, and the unexplained blood loss. In the end, I think everyone in the room came to the conclusion that we were facing something we had never encountered before. Manfred conceded the forensic and eye-witness evidence was compelling, but he stopped short of actually saying the words that we were all thinking…that our perp was a vampyre. How would we even begin to fight something like that? We all agreed that the mysterious "S. K." held the key. Whoever he was, he must have been investigating Wojciech for years. Maybe even tracking him across

Europe. Was he, well, a vampyre slayer? I almost laughed just thinking of it. But the team agreed that if I could meet with him, we would probably get some answers to our questions. And right now, all we had were questions. But we don't know who S. K. is or where he is. All I can do is wait until he contacts me again. After we adjourned, Anna came up to me. She was concerned about the warning in S.K.'s letter—That Batowski knows we are investigating him. And that maybe he knows that we are starting to figure out who and what he is. She is obviously worried for me. I squeezed her arm and told her I'd be fine. That I was a big boy, and if all else failed, I had my Walther PPK. She looked dubious, but then she did something that I didn't see coming. She bent forward and planted a kiss on my cheek. "Just be careful," she said softly, the concern showing in her eyes, and left. My emotions are now in turmoil. I admit Anna has had my eye for years. She's smart, the best in her field, but she's not pretentious. I've always felt comfortable talking with her, and she makes me laugh. Something I rarely do these days. I feel like, well, we have a special connection. I had never suspected that she may feel the same about me.

I was just about to leave for the day when Hellriegel came to see me. I suspected trouble the minute he walked into my office. The little shit was smiling like a cat that just swallowed the canary. Without fanfare, he told me he had an approach we should consider to catch the vampyre Wojciech. So quick for him to believe the supernatural angle, I thought. However, I was curious about what he had in mind, so I asked him to explain. Hellriegel told me what we should do is gather a dozen Jewesses from Auschwitz and use them as an offering to Wojciech. He admitted he had done a lot of research into the occult and claimed to know the incantations that he believed would summon the vampyre. Wojciech would come for the Jewesses, to drink their blood provided as an offering. I was stunned. "You mean you want to use Jewish prisoners as bait?" I spat. "Are you mad?" It would be necessary, Hellriegel told me. To draw the vampyre in. Once he makes an appearance, we could speak with him. I couldn't believe what he was saying. "Speak with him?" I asked, incredulously. "If this Wojciech does exist, and I'm not convinced of that, what would we speak to him about? The son of a bitch needs to be arrested and put away forever. Or better yet, executed." Hellriegel shook his head adamantly. "No," he replied excitedly, "Don't you see? There is so much we can learn from this vampyre. Thousands of years of knowledge. Everything we want to know about vampirism. About immortality. And we are the chosen ones…you, me, the others. All of us have the chance of a lifetime. To reach out, to make contact." "You're insane!" I exclaimed in utter disgust. Hellriegel just continued to smirk his twisted smile. Then, what he said next chilled my blood. "I don't think so, Obergruppenführer. You'll see. You'll all understand…very soon." Then he saluted and walked out of the room. I swear I've had enough of him. He's clearly becoming unhinged. If I could, I would relieve him of his duties immediately. But I can't. We're already under a microscope, and I don't want Himmler to think we don't have a cohesive team. And bring my leadership into question. I must speak to both Manfred and Felix. Together, we will need to keep a very close eye on Hellriegel from this point on.

20 July 1943 –

I arrived at Wawel Castle a bit late today. Along the way, I stopped at a Polish coffee house, where they brewed it the old-fashioned way in a brass Turkish coffee pot called a *cezve*. The coffee was thick, rich, and delicious. It was just the pickup I needed. When I walked into the office, Anna was already there waiting for me. "I have the forensic results from Brunner," she announced without fanfare. The grim look on her face told me everything I needed to know, but I asked her to get Manfred, Felix, and Dr. Ziegler together so she could brief us all at once. A half-hour later, we had everyone assembled. "First, here are the results on the semen samples," Anna began. "As you already know, Dr. Ziegler found, well, an astonishing amount of semen found in Brunner's body. First, you have to understand that the average volume of a male's ejaculate is about 3.4 milliliters, although some studies show amounts as high as 5.0 milliliters. Basically, the volume of a teaspoon." Anna paused for several moments, and I could see she was struggling to keep herself composed. When she resumed, her voice was shaking, and I could see her hands trembling as she held the file. "In Brunner's body, Dr. Ziegler recovered at least 23 milliliters of semen. That's enough for five, maybe even seven men." We all sat there for a moment, stunned. "Was she a victim of gang rape, then?" asked Manfred. Anna shook her head. "No. Not unless all five men were corpses. As with all the other previously collected samples, the cells contained in Brunner's semen were in autolysis, the first stage of human decomposition." The room was quiet. "And it's impossible to get a blood type. There's nothing there. If other men were involved, ordinary men, I should be able to get some blood typing. There's none. And there's another weird thing with the semen." The room remained quiet, waiting for Anna to continue. "Healthy semen has between 15 million to over 200 million sperm per milliliter of semen. Yet, there was almost no sperm in the semen found in Brunner. The sperm that was isolated was just a mass of decomposing cells. Sperm is really an independent, single-celled organism, basically a living cell, like a living amoeba. There was virtually nothing alive in my sample. Bottom line, the huge amount of semen is from one man...and he's not alive." Felix let out a nervous laugh. "Well, one thing we have to give to him, he's one virile son of a bitch." I had to smile despite Anna shooting Felix a look of disapproval. "What about the saliva samples?" I asked. "Same as last time," Anna replied. "The killer's saliva in all of the bites wounds were consistent with necrosis...the cells were all dead or in the process of dying." I nodded. "And the samples collected from under Brunner's fingernails?" Anna looked at her notes. She had regained some of her composure and was back in clinical mode. "This is where it gets really interesting. It was skin all right. And it was also consistent with necrosis." Manfred slapped his hand on the table. "Good for Brunner. She managed to get a piece of the bastard." Anna nodded. "It would appear so," she said. "You said it was interesting," I asked, "why is that?" Anna smiled. "It was what was also under the nails. Not just skin. I found salt." We all exchanged glances. Felix asked first. "You mean, like table salt?" Anna shook her head. "No, not processed table salt. These particles were various shades of grey, resembling unpolished granite rather than the white crystalline substance you are thinking of. It's rock salt. Salt particles from a natural brine. And…" Anna's voice trailed off as she pulled out an evidence bag. It contained the piece of cloth we found in Brunner's flat, not far from her hand. "This piece of cloth has exactly the same salt particles. I think it's definitely a piece of clothing worn by the killer, and Brunner managed to tear it off during her struggle." I looked at Anna admiringly. What a piece of forensic detective work. "Anna…" I began, feeling the excitement building. I knew we had something big here. "Where do you think that kind of salt came from? It's not like we have an ocean around here." Anna nodded. "I don't know," she said, "but I'll start looking into it." I smiled. "That's the best lead we got so far. Great work, Anna."

21 July 1943 –

The good news: no murders last night. The bad news: Ernest Hellriegel didn't report to work today. We've begun a search. A lot going on. I need some sleep. I'll have to catch up tomorrow.

22 July 1943 –

The last 24 hours were a blur. To recap, SS-Haupsturmführer Ernst Hellriegel went missing yesterday. When he didn't report to work, Felix and I went over to his flat. It was located down the block from mine in a building reserved for junior military officers. We didn't have any problem getting in; the door was left unlocked. We were shocked by what we found.

The flat was a mess, littered with discarded and dirty clothes, unwashed dishes, and trash that hadn't been taken out in days. But all that paled in comparison with what we found on the floor of the main room. A large pentagram ringed with a circle had been drawn in chalk. Not a normal pentagram; the cross had been inverted. It was a sigil used by practitioners of the occult or those performing a satanic ritual. There were single Hebrew letters at the five points of the pentagram spelling out "Leviathan," the ancient serpent from the biblical *Chaoskampf.* In the center of the pentagram was Baphomet, or the Sabbatic Goat. Around the top of the pentagram was the Hebrew name "Samael," an archangel in Talmudic lore, a figure who is an adversary, seducer, and destroyer. Along the bottom was the name "Liltih," a female figure in Mesopotamian and Judaic mythology, said to be the first wife of Adam and supposedly the primordial she-demon. Candles sat around the outside circle at the points of the pentagram. They had long ago died out, burnt down to nothing. Scattered around the floor were books and manuscripts, many of them ancient codex volumes that looked to have covers made out of leather or some kind of skin. They were all in various languages—Aramaic, old forms of English, German, French, Latin, and even a couple in Arabic. From what I could decipher, the tomes were a mix of black magic, spells, and incantations. Closest to the pentagram was a book in Latin titled *Liber incantationum, exorcismorum et fascinationum variorum,* or "A book of Incantations, exorcisms, and various fascinations." I had heard of it…a fifteenth-century goetic grimoire manuscript concerned with demonology and necromancy. What the hell is it doing here? I had asked myself…isn't this book in a museum? Nearby, I spotted a tattered manuscript handwritten in Mittlehochdeutsch, or "Middle High German," which would date it generally between 1050 and 1350. There are nuances in the older language that differ from modern High German, but I could translate the title to read *Necromantic Spells: How to Manipulate the Energies of Life and Death.* Next to it was a dogeared book in French, published in Paris in 1912, titled *Le manuel du nécromancien,* or

"The Necromancer Handbook." Overall, it was an impressive collection of occult books. It looked like Ernst Hellriegel had been a busy boy. A very busy boy.

In Hellriegel's bedroom, we found another drawing, this one on the wall. It again depicted Baphomet, the goat's head that has a long history with occultism and devil worship. This depiction had exceptionally long horns and a grinning mouth that appeared to be dripping blood. On the unmade and rumpled bed, lying open and upside down was a book in Polish. Compared to the ancient tomes scattered in the other room, it was a relatively new book, a little over a decade old, printed by a Warsaw publishing house in 1932. The title was *The Vampyre in Eastern Europe: Legend vs. Reality.* The author's name caught my eye. Stanislaw Kaminski. Could this be the same "S.K." who paid a visit to my flat the other night? It seemed too much to be a coincidence. "Jesus, boss," Felix whispered, "what the fuck is Hellriegel up to? This place looks like some kind of satanic shrine. It's giving me the willies." I couldn't disagree with him. The place was a monument to Ernst Hellriegel's insanity. "On the outside, Hellriegel is the perfect SS man," I told Felix. "He is dedicated to the Führer and the Party. A poster child of the blond Ayrian, the German Übermensch. An adherent of Lebensraum, the German expansionism for 'living space.' And, to this end, the regime's policies for the systematic elimination of those inferior—the Jews, Slavs, Gypsies, the feeble, the infirmed, and the mentally ill. And, of course, one might as well throw in the undesirables, the homosexuals, communists, and the dissident clergy. But Hellriegel has qualities that put even the thugs in the SS to shame. You should have seen his eyes light up when he saw the gas chambers and crematoria at Auschwitz, Felix. He sees nothing wrong with the regime's policy of mass murder. Hell, he enjoys it. That's why he volunteered twice for the Einsatzgruppen. It's a disgrace that he is a KRIPO detective. He should just transfer to be one of the Death's Head guards at the camps. There, he would be in his element. But now, it looks like the man has immersed himself fully into the occult…black magic, devil worship, God only knows what. I don't know when or where Hellriegel obtained all those books in the other room, but they're evil books, Felix. Books on raising the dead. I don't know what's up his sleeve, but most frightening of all, Hellriegel has already accepted the existence of the vampyre…this Wojciech. He actually admires him. Admires him as a perfect killing machine. He told me he wants to make contact with Wojciech, to speak with him. I think that's what he was trying to do here: invoke some incantation to summon what he thinks is a vampyre. But I don't think he had any success because he mentioned something about needing blood to use as an offering. He had the idea of using blood from the female Jewish prisoners for the ritual." Felix looked at me, astonished. "That's right," I summarized, "Ernst Hellriegel is totally insane. And I fear he's out there right now, trying to obtain blood for his little ritual. We may end up with another murder on our hands. But this time, not from our killer. This time, it may be from one of our own."

Before we left the flat, I instructed Felix to put a 24-hour guard in place in case Hellriegel returned to the Pentagram to initiate his ritual. I also ordered that all the books be bagged and brought back to our office for further study. The one book I took with me was Stanislaw Kaminski's *The Vampyre in Eastern Europe*. I had a feeling it was going to make the most interesting reading.

We spent the rest of the afternoon putting out arrest warrants for SS-Haupsturmführer Ernst Hellriegel. We placed all Wehrmacht and SS checkpoints on alert. The strange thing is that no military checkpoints ringing the city of Kraków reported anyone with Hellriegel's identification leaving the city in the past 48 hours. Either he slipped through using an alias, or he never left.

Near the end of the day, I knew I couldn't delay any longer to inform the Reichsführer and SS chief Krüger of the disappearance of one of their SS officers. I went to Governor-General Frank's office to place the call to

Berlin so that he would be part of the conversation. The call went better than I had expected. I told Himmler the truth, with slight variations. I reported that Hellriegel had suffered a mental breakdown or psychotic break, probably from the stress of working the case and witnessing the depravity of the crime scenes. I told the truth about finding the pentagram and evidence of him performing satanic rituals. I even told the truth that Hellriegel believed the killer was some sort of vampyre, and that I think he disappeared because he was out looking for it. As I predicted, that did the trick. Himmler immediately agreed that Hellriegel must have lost his mind. That he was a stain upon the professionalism of the SS. The last thing Himmler wanted was a rogue officer on the loose who could bring embarrassment to the SS or, worse yet, the Führer. And Krüger was mortified that Hellriegel had been on his staff for months, and he had never seen such a thing coming. Both men agreed that we needed to find Hellriegel as soon as possible. I now have carte blanche to track him down and arrest him.

All that was yesterday. Today, we've extended the search throughout the entire borders of Poland, but no indication of Hellriegel's movements has been forthcoming. I have a strange feeling that he hasn't gone far. Kraków is the supposed vampyre Wojciech's killing grounds, so Hellriegel must believe he will find him here.

The good news is there haven't been any new murders since Brunner, so that is a positive thing. This afternoon, Anna announced she had some updates for us on the piece of material found near Brunner's body. When we all convened in the conference room, I could tell whatever she had must be good. She was wearing a wide, Cheshire Cat grin. "So, I checked out the type of salt I found on the evidence. It didn't take long to figure it out. If we were locals, we'd already know. Here's the thing. Kraków is famous for its salt mines! They've been obtaining salt from the underground brine for centuries. The salt from the Brunner crime scene is consistent with what comes from the brine lakes in the local salt mines. And there are two mines not far from here. The Wieliczka mine is 14 kilometers southeast from here, just 30 minutes away. The other is the Bochnia mine, 30 min east of Wieliczka." I stared at Anna in awe. Before I could think, I blurted out, "Anna, I could kiss you!" Manfred, Felix, and Dr. Ziegler burst out laughing, and Anna, cheeks turning red, said, "Well, Otto, this is probably not the place and time." Then, after a pause, she continued, "And there's something else." Her tone had changed serious, and gone was the display of joviality she had a moment before. Everyone leaned in closer. "Regarding that strip of material," she continued, "it's made of wool. From the density of the weave, fiber content, and the dye used, it's not a piece of modern clothing. If I had to guess, I'd say it's at least three hundred years old." The room once again fell into a dead silence. Anna summarized what it all meant. "The killer is a corpse, and the clothing he wears indicates he is centuries old."

23 July 1943 –

I can't believe what has happened. Gertrude Brunner's body has gone missing! But not from the morgue this time. As if disappearing from the morgue was bad enough, this is much, much worse. Brunner was due to be flown back to Berlin today for an elaborate funeral, fit for a dedicated National Socialist, arranged by none other than Josef Goebbels and his Propaganda Ministry. Dr. Ziegler had prepped the body for shipment, and she had been placed in the best ornate six-sided wooden coffin we could find in Kraków. A little after 6 p.m., SS guards took the coffin out to a waiting hearse. I was not present, and neither had I planned to go to the airfield to see the body off. From the reports we received, the hearse and several escort vehicles arrived at the Luftwaffe airfield without incident, and in short order, the coffin was loaded onto a waiting Junkers Ju-52. The aircraft had been prepped to be able to receive the coffin, with seating available for several dignitaries returning to Berlin. The flight manifest indicated that in addition to the two pilots and one Luftwaffe flight crewman, there were six members of the Reich Propaganda Ministry and two political leaders of the General Government on board. The flight took off at 8:51 p.m. The evening flight was deliberate, in the belief the lone plane would be less detectable than during the day. The weather was clear, and those watching its departure said the plane took off normally. Yet, with the flight less than a half hour out, something happened. Luftwaffe military flight controllers received a frantic message from the pilot, saying that there was a disturbance on board. There were screams, and within a minute, all transmission was lost. The next report was of a plane crashing into a field between the Polish cities of Katowice and Opole. It didn't exactly crash and looked like the pilot had tried to make a controlled landing. The landing was rough, but while it had lost a wing and landing gear as it hit the ground, it miraculously hadn't exploded or caught on fire. Within minutes, local authorities had reached the wreckage. What they found defied any clear explanation.

From the preliminary reports I have received, the cabin of the aircraft was intact, and interior damage was minimal. The seats were intact, but very few of the passengers were sitting in them. They were not strapped in, as one would expect during an emergency landing. They were all found out of their seats, dispersed all around the cabin. They were all dead. But not from trauma that could have been caused by the controlled crash landing. The "injuries" were far too severe. Blood was sprayed everywhere. One statement reported the whole cabin looked painted red, there was that much blood. It was fairly easy to figure out where it had all come from. The throats of nearly all the passengers had been cut. Or torn open. In addition, one woman was missing her eyes. One man's face was completely missing. One of the Propaganda Ministry officials had what looked like a camera shoved so hard down her throat that it could barely be seen. The two pilots were the only ones still in their seats. Regardless of what took place in the main cabin, they had remained in control long enough to land the plane. But whatever killed the passengers got them too; their throats were torn out just like the others. One responder said the pilot's eyes had nearly popped out of his skull, and his mouth was wide open in a silent scream. What had been so horrendous, so terrible, to cause such a fright? There was one clue. Bullet holes were found in the cabin. One of the political officers had pulled his service pistol and had been trying to shoot something. But what?

But then came the most incredible revelation. In the rear of the aircraft, Gertrude Brunner's coffin was found. It was still strapped down and secured for flight. That had fortunately prevented it from being tossed around the cabin during the turbulence of the crash. If so, it certainly would have caused a lot of damage and possibly would have killed someone. But in this case, that didn't matter…everyone had been killed anyway. But the thing is, the coffin had been opened. The lid sat upright, revealing an empty satin interior. The shroud she was wrapped in left discarded like an unwanted skin. One report said the first man to enter the plane was a local farmer who owned the field where it had landed. Along with his son, they were inside the plane within a minute or two. When he saw the empty coffin, he grasped his son, and together, they ran screaming from the wreckage as if the Devil himself were in pursuit. I couldn't blame them. Not at all. The coffin was empty, and Gertrude Brunner, the National Socialist martyr, was gone. Ironically, the plane was full of corpses, but the one corpse that mattered had been taken. Snatched. Or had she?

By midnight, the wreckage was being picked over by a near army of SS and military investigators. A nationwide search is now underway for Brunner's missing corpse. Needless to say, Goebbels is furious. Thankfully, no blame has come my way. The flight, the security, and the passenger list had all been arranged and approved between Hans Frank and the Propaganda Ministry. From a brief conversation I had with Frank, the powers to be are already concluding that the downing of the plane was an act of sabotage, even though no evidence of an explosive was found. Frank is pushing hard that the Poles are somehow involved, even though there is no evidence to support that theory either. After all, everyone on the plane were dedicated National Socialists. But Frank felt it was possible that a Polish saboteur could have been a stowaway, waiting for the right time to reveal himself to take over the plane. His motive was to steal Brunner's body and thus embarrass the Reich. He may have even been wounded by the brave political leader who had managed to fire off a few shots, but in the end, he had managed to take Brunner's body off the plane and into the nearby woods. I thought the theory was complete bullshit, of course, but to speak anything contrary would be foolhardy and unproductive. All I know is that I have my own investigation to run, and I feel like I'm getting close.

It was well into the early hours of the 24th when I finally had time to assemble the team—Manfred, Felix, Anna, and Elsie, in our basement office. Hans Ziegler joined us too. I broke out a bottle of Polish Slivovitz I had recently purchased. It's a rather pungent liquor made from fermented plums, mostly a mainstay of the Slavic countries of central and eastern Europe. It's definitely an acquired taste. "Fuck," sputtered Manfred after downing a shot. "This stuff will burn the hair off of one's chest! Don't we have any good German Schnapps?" I smiled at my old friend. "Sorry, this is the best I could do under the circumstances." Anna gave me a coy smile as she raised a glass to her lips. "Well, I don't have any hair on my chest, and I like it just fine, Otto." Felix gave me a knowing wink, and I could feel my cheeks redden in embarrassment.

Manfred was the first to get down to business. "OK, I know what you're going to say, Otto. Gertrude Brunner got up out of her coffin after the flight took off and slaughtered the passengers, leaving the pilots to manage to crash land the plane before they, too, were attacked and killed. At some point during the melee, one of the political leaders pulls his pistol and tries to shoot her. He's killed along with the rest, and then when the plane comes to rest in the field, Brunner walks off into the night." He paused, then looked us all in the eyes before concluding. "Brunner is now a vampyre, just like all the others who disappeared from the morgue. Does that about sum things up?" Felix, ever the pragmatist, responded with a mischievous smile, "Ja, that's about it. No wonder you are the Chief Investigator, Obersturmbannführer." With Manfred giving his young protégé a steely look, I interrupted. "I truly don't know, Manfred. But we have to be honest with ourselves. Wouldn't a saboteur have just blown up the plane? Or if one was on board, wouldn't they just shoot the passengers? Since when do saboteurs go around biting out people's throats? How could such a person have overpowered all those people? Whatever happened was so fast the pilots barely had time to get the plane on the ground. And why steal the body? Why not just desecrate it, or throw a hand grenade to destroy it? Why take the body into the woods? They surely know they can't get very far lugging a body. Nobody was waiting for them with a car; the landing site was completely arbitrary. Those are the facts. I know the alternative seems insane, but it all adds up. Brunner is not the first of the killer's victims to seemingly get up and disappear. Only this one didn't just walk out of the morgue; she dropped in by Air Special Delivery." When I was finished, no one spoke. In the quiet room, we all grappled with our inner thoughts…and our darkest fears. Young Elsie looked the most scared, and I couldn't blame her. When she joined our investigations team, she had no idea the nightmare things were about to become. Her training as a secretary in no way could have prepared her for being thrown down such a terrifying rabbit hole of the supernatural. Hell, even my most seasoned investigators are unnerved. Strangely, Anna seems to be handling it the best. Vampyres…demons…succubi, all elements seemingly outside the realm of the physical and natural world. Yet, Anna is approaching it all clinically and still through a scientific lens. I'm proud of the strength she's showing, and it's helping me greatly to maintain my own inner composure.

24 July 1943 –

It was around 3 a.m. before we all left the office last night. Due to the lateness, Felix volunteered to see Elise back to her flat, which was further away than the rest of ours. As for me, I slept fitfully. Anxiety coiled in my stomach like an angry snake, and I couldn't shake a sense of impending dread. At one point, I succeeded in nodding off, but it wasn't for long, having been jolted awake by a god-awful dream. In it, Brunner was out there in the night, walking amongst the weathered pines of what looked like a thickly wooded forest. Moonlight drifted down through the tree's canopy, illuminating her pale naked body. All the terrible wounds inflicted by her murderer had healed, and her lithe body once again appeared beautiful…attractive…seductive even. Even in the dream, I felt aroused as I watched the firmness of her buttocks as she walked, her melon-sized breasts full and upright, the nipples long and erect in the cold…a cold she could not feel, not now, not forever. Then, I watched as she came to a clearing and gazed out towards the open field before her. There was a small farmhouse and, next to it, a barn. I could see the shimmering glow of lantern light coming from inside the home…or perhaps it was from the fireplace, its smoky plume rising from above the chimney. Then, with horror, I could see the Brunner-thing smile, lips extending nearly ear-to-ear, the mouth becoming unhinged to show rows of monstrous teeth straight out of hell itself. As saliva dripped from her mouth, her eyes took on a look of anticipation…excitement…and a terrible thirst that could not be denied. Brunner started forward, taking her first step towards a new life, an existence that would never end, the perpetual state of the undead.

After that terrible nightmare, I couldn't return to sleep, my imagination spinning whole tapestries of the torments the occupants of that small farmhouse must have received at the hands of the hellish fiend once named Brunner. I left early for Wawel Castle, the short walk in the dark only increasing my sense of dread and foreboding. It didn't help that the clouds had rolled in, bringing a summer drizzle that further served to add to the bleakness of the morning. Because of the early hour, my office was still empty, and I took advantage of the solitude to re-read the case file and, in particular, the background info on Brunner. I kept wondering if there was some reason she was chosen by the killer other than being a young female. But with the wide disparity amongst all the victim types and no common denominator, I just couldn't determine any linkage or reasoning behind her killing. All the murders seemed to be random, just targets of opportunity, necessary to satiate the killer's immediate bloodlust. No different than the tiger in the wild…our killer was just an animal driven by its basic and overarching instinct.

As I had foreseen, it didn't take long for the leadership to start looking for a scapegoat for what is now officially labeled as "sabotage" of Brunner's plane. Initially, poor Dr. Ziegler's name came up, and there were questions about whether he had replaced Brunner's corpse with some kind of assassin. Fortunately for Hans, his two morgue assistants, as well as three SS guards, witnessed Brunner's body in the coffin as he closed the lid just a few minutes before 6 p.m. She was there, that is indisputable. The coffin was then never out of sight before the SS honor guards wheeled the coffin out only minutes later. It was all complete nonsense, of course. The next person to come under the microscope was the young Luftwaffe flight NCO on the plane. His name is Josef Dieter, and he holds the rank of Feldwebel. His job as the flight sergeant was to assist the pilots, ready the cabin, ensure the passengers were seated and secured, secure the doors, and ensure the overall safety of the passengers during the flight. There was some thought he might have tampered with the coffin in some way, but once again, there were witnesses from the ground crew that he had help tying down and securing the coffin in the rear of the aircraft with the assistance of the SS escort, and after that, the two political leaders were seen taking seats next to the coffin where it would have been in their view at all times. At any rate, Dieter had an impeccable service record, having served in air operations in both the

French and Russian campaigns. So, who was left? No one was willing to accuse the two political leaders, both representing the various districts in Kraków where Brunner's team was doing their filming. They sponsored her visit and took care of all the logistics for the film shoot. They had been escorting the body back as a show of respect and sympathy for the family and probably to assuage a bit of guilt that she had been murdered in a city that was declared subjugated and fully under German control.

With all that said, Reichsführer-SS Himmler, no doubt influenced by Frank, now believes the murders on the plane and the snatching of Brunner's corpse had to be an inside job, a move by the Polish resistance to embarrass the Reich. At first, he wanted reprisals, and although it was outside my scope as a murder investigator, I convinced him that would be counterproductive, that the SS should put its resources into finding the perpetrators and, by extension, Brunner's body. It helped a great deal that there is no love lost between Himmler and Goebbels. It's no secret that Himmler, filled with the elitist missionary zeal of the SS, has nothing but contempt for a man who is notorious for his extramarital affairs and infidelity. Goebbels, in turn, believes himself an intellectual, feeling more at ease in the company of literary and movie people while looking down on the crude philistines of Munich, the leading group within the Nazi Party...and of course, Himmler is a Bavarian, born in Munich. As such, Himmler is not going to bend over backward to placate Goebbels, no matter how furious Goebbels may be over the body snatching of his precious propaganda princess.

By late afternoon, I finally had time to sit down with Manfred and Felix to begin making arrangements to pay a visit to the salt mines. While I was tied up with the Brunner matter, they had made inquiries, and they informed me that since the occupation, both mines had halted their salt production. Now, the mines are in the process of being converted to underground facilities for German wartime manufacturing to improve the supply to the Wehrmacht of necessary supplies of weapons and ammunition. The underground industrial sites will be run by Albert Speer's Reich Ministry of Armaments and War Production, augmented with engineers from Organization Todt. It is planned that they will bring in several thousand Jews from the forced labor camps in Plaszow and Mielic to work in these underground armament factories. My God, is there ever an end to the inhumanity of the SS? We are not just exterminating the Jews; we are using them for slave labor, literally the same thing, working them until they die of disease or starvation. I do not doubt that if we lose this war...which since Stalingrad, I believe is a near certainty...we Germans are going to be judged harshly by the victors, and deservedly so. As a country, we will have to forever live with the shame of what has been taking place here in the occupied territories. And I will have to live with the personal shame of being even the smallest cog in this apparatus of misery and death.

"This doesn't sound like much of a lair for a centuries-old vampyre," I sighed, looking at Manfred and Felix, "not if there is a presence of hundreds of German soldiers within the mine." Manfred nodded, and said, "That's true, but the Wieliczka mine is vast. It reaches a depth of 327 meters or 1,073 feet. To put that into perspective, it is deeper than the height of the Eiffel Tower by approximately 10 feet. It consists of nine levels with horizontal passages and chambers extending over 287 kilometers or 178 miles. There is an underground lake, and several large chambers, four of them actually, that are chapels of worship dug into the salt rock by the miners. I was told that several sections in the lower levels have been left derelict and abandoned due to flooding. There are areas where someone could hide or avoid detection if they wanted to." I digested the information Manfred provided, and, after further discussion, it was decided we have no choice but to go take a look. The brine salt is our only lead linked to the killer. We decided to set out for the Wieliczka mine first thing tomorrow morning.

I've had a chance to read portions of *The Vampyre in Eastern Europe: Legend vs. Reality*, the book we found in Hellriegel's flat. It has proved to be very, very informative. From the book's preface, I learned that Stanislav Kaminski was a highly respected and esteemed professor at the University of Warsaw. At the time of the book's publication in 1932, Kaminski had been with the university for eleven years, where he taught history. He was born in Warsaw in 1885. At that time, Poland was not yet a sovereign state, having been divided since 1795 by the great powers of Prussia, Austria-Hungary, and Russia. Kaminski did his undergraduate studies at the University of Warsaw, graduating in 1907 with a degree in history. His graduate studies were interrupted by the Great War that broke out in 1914. Kaminski evaded conscription into the Russian army, which had control of Warsaw at that time. Like many other young men, he believed that Poland's best chance for independence lay in a victory of the Central Powers over Russia, followed by the defeat of the Central Powers by France and Britain. In August 1915, the German army finally entered Warsaw, and Kaminski immediately enlisted, swearing loyalty to the Kaiser. By March 1918, the Treaty of Brest-Litovsk ensured the end of Russia's rule in Poland, and soon after, upon Germany's defeat and the end of the war in November of that year, Poland became an independent country. Kaminski returned from the war and returned to graduate school, concentrating on historical archeology. In 1921, at the age of 36, he was given a professorship at his old alma mater, the University of Warsaw. There, he taught history, with one of his favorite classes being Eastern European legends and folklore. From 1929 to 1931, Kaminski took several sabbaticals from teaching. He traveled all over Europe, conducting research and interviews for his long-planned dissertation on the legends of Nosferatu – the Vampyre. In 1932, he published his work as *The Vampyre in Eastern Europe: Legend vs. Reality*. I found the book itself fascinating. It goes way beyond simply summarizing the generic legends of vampyres in Eastern Europe; it's a well-documented account of specific vampyre cases and sightings, all backed by meticulous research of municipal, clerical, medical, and familial records dating back hundreds of years, much of it further augmented by comprehensive oral histories from those still alive and available to give it.

There were several names of purported vampyres mentioned in the book, but two stood out. The first, of course, was the Pole Wojciech Batowski. The longest chapter in the book was dedicated to him, titled "The REAL Vampyre Count," an obvious reference to the fact he was a real Count of the Crown of the Kingdom of Poland, as opposed to the fictitious Count portrayed in Bram Stoker's 1897 book, Dracula. Most of the information in Kaminski's book was the same that I had received in the mysterious package from "S.K." except that, being published in 1932, it had not included the latest string of murders attributed to Wojciech, up to and including those in Linze between 1939 and 1940. It was obvious from the book that pursuing the bloodthirsty and enigmatic Count Batowski was a years-long obsession for Kaminski. A passage in the book made this conclusion inescapable: "The fiend that was once Wojciech Batowski, the esteemed Count of the Polish Crown, and the beloved Colonel of the Polish winged hussars, today exists purely a beast, ravenous for blood and the thrill of debauchery and limitless sadism. His soul has been lost forever, replaced by the black heart of pure evil. For over three centuries, he has terrorized humankind, feasting upon the innocent, the pure, and the chaste. He will keep killing and fulfilling his decadent and wanton desires until he is hunted down and destroyed. Even the undead, the vampyre, can be killed, but only by following the ancient rituals of the Church, and backed by God's righteous might. The challenge for the vampyre slayer is finding the creature in its lair, at a time when it is vulnerable. This is my goal—to find Wojciech and forever eradicate the evil he brings to this world. As long as I live and breathe, I will track him down and have him face God's justice."

Another name mentioned in the book, contained in a lengthy chapter titled "The Queen of the Undead," is a female vampyre called "Alexandria."

I found this chapter particularly interesting because whereas Wojciech's modus operandi is the defiling and murder of young girls and women, this Alexandria seduces and feasts upon predominantly young men. In a chapter titled "The Linkage between Vampirism and Demonology," Kaminski goes into great detail about how the lines between these dual beliefs have been blurred over time. The vampyre and the succubus/incubus are, Kaminski argued, often one and the same. Both the vampyre and the succubus are parasitic in nature. They are creatures of the night, both seducing their victims and having sexual intercourse. The vampyre needs its victim's blood, whereas the succubus, according to religious tradition, needs semen to survive. The vampyre "drains" its victims of blood, the demon of their sexual energy, virility, and manhood. In Kaminski's theory, Wojciech is not only a vampyre, he is an incubus—albeit one that revels in sexual sadism and torture. The vampyre known as Alexandria is Wojciech's counterpart— a vampiric succubus. According to legend, she is almost as old as time, with one account saying she was born in Roman Egypt, in the ancient city of Alexandria, hence her name. Just as with Wojciech, Kaminski documented many of Alexandria's attacks throughout the centuries, as she migrated from North Africa and up through Europe, seducing and enslaving young men for her sadistic pleasure. In September 1890, two vampyre slayers commissioned by an esoteric arm of the Vatican were on her trail when she is believed to have snatched Louis Le Prince, the French inventor of an early motion-picture camera, possibly the first person to shoot a moving picture sequence using a single-lens camera, off a train traveling to Paris. His body was never recovered. I was astonished to see her name further linked to the infamous Hinterdkaifek murders that took place in 1922 not far from where I grew up in Munich. The killings took place six years before I joined the Kriminalpolizei, but in the early 1930s, while attending a crime conference in Augsburg, I met one of the original investigators who had worked the case back then. He recounted that during one night, six inhabitants of the small Bavarian farmstead were killed, all struck dead by a mattock. The strangest thing to investigators was that the murderer stayed amongst the corpses for three days, making themselves at home, with no sense of urgency to depart. Kaminski's book claims that, once again, the Vatican records confirmed that two vampyre slayers were hot on Alexandria's trail, but arrived at Hinterkaifek too late, and just narrowly missed her. This revelation intrigues me. Who were these slayers? Has the Catholic Church been hunting the vampyre while keeping their existence a secret from humanity? Are there other organized groups out there with the sole purpose of hunting the vampyres down? Is that what happened to Kaminski? Is he now also a vampyre slayer? Either way, I have a feeling that he's out there, still tracking the whereabouts of the vampyre he calls Wojciech. I believe now that Stanislav Kaminski and "S.K." are the same man, and that he sent me that packet of information to help steer our investigation in the right direction.

According to Kaminski's book, these vampyre slayers protect themselves with blessed crucifixes and holy water. The sign of the cross will ward off the vampyre, and the water will burn them severely. And if the vampyre pays a visit to one's home, it must never be invited in. I've instructed Felix to procure crucifixes so we will be protected when we visit the mines. It will be hard to get them blessed in German-occupied Kraków, but there are still Catholic priests in hiding. We'll find them. We are the SS, after all. The only thing I don't know is how we can kill the vampyre if we find him. In his book, Kaminski mentions a special blessed and holy knife that must be used to decapitate the vampyre, and an incantation that must be uttered to destroy the creature's spirit. But I have no idea where such a knife can be found.

The mysterious "S.K." wrote, "I'll contact you again when I can." If that was Stanislaw Kaminski, I hope that he does and soon. But I have no idea how he can still be in Poland, let alone be alive. Thanks to the Nazis, and in particular my KRIPO, teachers and professors such as him were rounded up right after the war began, and most have been killed or sent to the camps. The first killings of Polish intelligentsia took place soon after the German invasion, lasting from autumn 1939 until spring 1940. It was called *Operation Intelligenzaktion*. As a result of this operation 100,000 Polish people were killed, among them 61,000 Polish nobles, teachers, entrepreneurs, social workers, priests, judges, and political activists who were on the Reich's "enemies list." The mass murder of Polish intellectuals and the elites of Polish society continued with a second phase called *AB-Aktion*, resulting in the arrests of more than 30,000 Polish citizens. About 7,000 of them, including teachers and professors, were subsequently massacred secretly at various locations, including at the infamous Palmiry forest. If Kaminski is here in Kraków, he must be living under a different identity and nationality or, perhaps, he's a member of the Polish resistance.

25 July 1943 –

We left for the Wieliczka mine right after dawn. I decided to use the ruse that we had a credible lead on the whereabouts of SS-Haupsturmführer Ernst Hellriegel. I figured it would be far more accepting than announcing we were on the trail of a vampyre thousands of years old and suspected of committing the Kraków murders. In addition to Manfred and Felix, we had a platoon of Waffen-SS at our disposal. I couldn't risk telling them the real reasons for the search and prayed desperately that I was not putting any of their lives at risk. Anna wanted to come, of course, but I would hear nothing of it. Before we left Wavel Castle, we did a double check of what we were going to take. "Here are six vials of blessed holy water," Felix announced. "Two for each of us. Blessed and sanctified. It wasn't easy. We SS have been very efficient. Poland was a predominantly Roman Catholic country before the war. Not anymore. Thousands of churches and monasteries have been systematically closed, seized, or destroyed, and most of the priests have either been killed or sent to labor camps. However, there is a clandestine underground seminary here in Kraków that the church still manages to run, set up by the Archbishop of Kraków, Cardinal Adam Stefan Sapieha. We had help getting the water blessed through one of the Cardinal's students, a young Pole named Karol Wojtyła. Imagine the look on the young man's face when a German came asking for help, and holy water no less. I think he could tell from my face that I was into something serious, and needed the protection. He also provided me these blessed crucifixes." Felix then handed out a crucifix to Manfred and me. They looked old and weathered and were the Catholic types that depicted Jesus nailed to the cross. "I hope the stuff is really blessed," opined Manfred, "it would be a great way to eliminate some Germans if they just gave us tap water." I had to smile at my old friend. "Ah, so you really do believe in vampyres now, Manfred? We are indeed making progress."

Our convoy arrived at Wieliczka in good time. We were greeted by the Wehrmacht commander in charge, a young-looking Oberst named Heinz Brandt. My first thought was that he was young for a full Colonel, and I wondered why he wasn't assigned elsewhere to combat duty. Then I noticed the gold wound badge he wore on his tunic, followed by the empty left sleeve which was pinned to the side. Wounded in action, he was no longer suitable for the front lines and was given the assignment to oversee the construction of the armaments facility in the mine. After the perfunctory "Heil Hitler!" he was all business. "I got word you're here to look for your missing SS-Haupsturmführer," he said, and I couldn't help but notice how he had stressed the "your." No doubt the Army was enjoying the fact that the SS also had men that went AWOL—Absent Without Leave. "I can assure you he's not here," Brandt continued. "We've checked every inch, and there is nowhere he could be hiding. Far too many people are working down there not to have run into him. And even if he was there, how could he survive? Our field kitchen is here, above ground, and no rations have gone missing. Anyway, he could never come up or go down on the surface shaft lifts without being seen. I think you're wasting your time." I was

THE FEAST OF THE VAMPYRE

already prepared with my canned response. "I understand, Oberst," I said, "He may not be here now, but we have intelligence indicating he was here for at least a time. So, we need to look for anything he may have left behind or any clues that could lead us to where he is now. A slim chance, I know, but I have to report back to Reichführer-SS Himmler at the end of the day with any progress. You know how it is." At the mention of Himmler's name, the Oberst's demeanor suddenly changed, as I knew it would. "Of course, Standartenführer, I am here at your disposal. My men will render all the support you need. Come, let's go in. I have the maps of the mines ready for you."

Felix had given us a heads up on the enormity of the mines, and how intensive the search would be, but I don't think I fully comprehended the daunting task before us until I studied the diagrams and maps of the mine. Our search would have to cover nine levels underground, consisting of 245 kilometers of galleries and corridors, 2,500 chambers, and 180 shafts connecting caverns across all nine levels. I also learned that there were 26 different surface shafts that provided access and ventilation. If the vampyre was down there, he probably used one of these vertical shafts for ingress/egress from the mine. He wouldn't be riding one of the lifts like Brandt was expecting Hellriegal would have to do. After some discussion, it was agreed that Manfred would take one of the Waffen-SS squads and do a sweep of levels one through three, Felix levels four through six, and I would take the deepest levels at seven to nine. Radios wouldn't work down there, but I learned there are phones at various stations on each level, connected by landline, so it would be possible to check in or call any of us if assistance is needed. With that, we set forth, departing downwards in the lifts. The lifts were small and could only hold a few men at a time, so it took some time to get all of the twenty-member teams down to their assigned levels in the most expeditious manner. As I boarded my lift to head down, I couldn't help but notice Oberst Brandt eying the satchel I was carrying. No doubt he was wondering what I had in it. I smiled inwardly. My, wouldn't he be surprised to discover it contained holy water and crucifixes? I mused. After the doors shut, it wasn't long before I had my team down on the seventh level. Once again, I wasn't prepared for the reality I found myself in. One of the pleasant surprises was that the level was brightly lit. Strings of electrical lighting snaked along the corridors, many of which were shored up with timbers painted white by the miners of long ago, serving to reflect the light further and resulting in well-lit walkways as we progressed. We made good time in the corridors, but the many chambers were a different matter. Many of them were huge and served as chapels for the miners. I learned the Baroque St. Anthony Chapel is the oldest preserved underground chapel in the mine, created between 1690 and 1710. In addition to its altars and many detailed bas-reliefs, the chapel is also home to several freestanding statues carved from salt blocks, including those of the Virgin Mary and St. Anthony of Padua, the patron saint of ore minors. The largest chapel is that of the patron saint of salt miners, St. Kinga. Work began on the chapel in 1896 and continued up until the war. It is completely carved from salt, from floor to ceiling, including the altar and other decorations, the most remarkable being the large chandeliers made from salt crystals that were adapted for electricity.

By mid-day, all the teams had finished one level and had moved down to the next. Rather than going back up to the surface for the noon meal, Oberst Brandt had arranged for rations to be brought down to us. We took 30 minutes for lunch and a rest break, and during that time I checked in with both Manfred and Felix. They all reported no significant findings. And so it went. Corridor by corridor, chamber by chamber, a very painstaking process. Most were easy to search, but there were a few chambers that had been left derelict or blocked off, with no lighting, perhaps because the salt was limited in the rock there. These deserted chambers naturally drew most of my attention, as they would have served as the more likely place for the vampyre to be hiding. As we began searching the lowest level, we encountered even more of these unfinished or unwanted chambers and corridors. We then had to resort to old mining lanterns that Brandt had provided. It was painstaking and slow. Worse, none of us realized how cold it was going to be down that far in the mine, and even our jackets weren't keeping us warm enough. Then, around 2000 hours, I realized it would be sunset in just less than an hour. If Wojciech was there, he'd be awakening and we would have lost our element of surprise. Our time was fleeting if we were going to catch him when he was most vulnerable. At one point, I spoke with Manfred on the landline. Both he and Felix had finished with their levels. I instructed him to take the men and inspect all the ventilation shafts that led to the surface, and to leave one man guarding the surface vent until relieved. I knew Manfred understood the purpose of the order, but I figured Brandt would think it crazy to guard a shaft that a man couldn't climb up or fit through. Not a man, I thought wryly, just a murderous, sadistic, evil son of a bitch.

My team finished the search at 2150 hours and we returned to the surface. I don't think I was ever so happy to feel the omnipresent warmth of the Polish July night. I ignored Oberst Brandt's smug "I told you so" look as the doors to the lift opened and I walked back out to the mine's entrance. "I trust you are satisfied, Standartenführer," Brandt said, with a well-pleased tone, "please tell Reichsführer Himmler that the Wehrmacht is always willing to assist the SS in their hour of need. Is there anything else I can do for you?" I ignored the insult and sent out an order recalling all the men. It was then that I glanced up on the mountainside overlooking the mine, and saw one of the SS men beginning to walk back down. Apparently, he was one of the men guarding the ventilation shafts. What caught my attention was the one-story building up on the ridge, just behind the man. It looked derelict and abandoned, one or two of its windows now broken out and the wooden roof beginning to cave in. "What's that building?" I asked Brandt. "Just an old logistics control station I think," he replied hesitantly. "It's not used and was left abandoned years ago." Yes, and right next to a surface shaft too, I thought to myself. "Manfred, Felix, come with me," I barked. We used our torches to light the way as we climbed up the steep mountainside. When we reached the building, I could see the nearby shaft. It was large, with a hinged grate cover. Hell, I thought, it was actually large enough for a man to fit through, let alone some spectral creature. "Let's go," I ordered, already feeling something akin to anxiety mixed with excitement in the pit of my stomach. Like some big revelation was coming, something that wouldn't be good but at the same time something that would be a vindication. Without another thought, I kicked in the old wooden door of the building. It fell off its rusted hinges more than it opened, but nevertheless, in seconds we were in. As we cast our torches around the room, it was a bit like stepping back in time. It was littered with old debris from times long gone…clearly, there had been no effort to have cleaned things out. There was a rotting wooden desk against the wall, on top of which was one of those old candlestick telephones from around the turn of the century, still sitting there like it was ready to receive some ghostly call from the distant past. Another desk lay on its side on the floor, its contents disgorged all over the floor like a meal gone bad. In one of the corners was an old wire-frame bed, missing its mattress and now looking skeletal with its rusted springs. Probably a flop bed for the night shift, I thought. Next to it, a file cabinet had its drawers hanging open like hungry mouths, showing deteriorating files black with mold and mildew. Log books, forms, and other old mining records lay scattered all over the floor. Many were damp and deteriorating due to leakage from several small holes in the collapsing ceiling. In addition, several panes of window glass were broken and missing, further ensuring the room was now at the mercy of the outside elements. I spotted an old corkboard on the wall; pinned to it were several schematics of what looked like some kind of pumping system. Next to it on the wall was a calendar, opened perpetually to the month of April in the year 1928. Brandt had been right…the place was abandoned years ago. On the far side of the room, we reached a wall with another door. Judging from the exterior size of the building, I knew this was an interior wall and there was another room on the other side, about the same size as the one we just walked through. I opened the door and led the way inside. I noticed immediately that this room had so far fared better than the first. The ceiling was still pretty much intact and there was no leakage from above. In addition, this room had no windows. It didn't need any because it hadn't served as office space. Instead, the room was a mechanical room, containing control panels of now useless buttons and lights, and long-dead dials and gauges. Three massive pipes, each with diameters larger than myself, fed into the ground like huge octopus tentacles. I guess that it was once a pumping station used to bring the salt brine to the surface, but judging from its age and size was probably made obsolete by the late 1920's and was replaced by a larger and more efficient pumping system. I didn't have much time to dwell on that theory, because when I walked over to the other side of the piping I knew immediately that we had found it. The lair of the vampyre Wojciech. There was no doubt. Because the mattress to the old bed in the other room wasn't missing, it was there. On the floor. It was filthy and reeked of mold and old mattress stuffing. There was no reason for it to have found its way into the pump room, hidden behind the pipes. Of course, nothing is impossible, and perhaps it was thrown there during the facility's shutdown. But what clinched it was what was lying all around the mattress. It was enough to remove any doubts at all. Felix let out a loud whistle. "Christ, boss, that fucker has been real busy." "My God, added Manfred, "it's a sick trophy room. He's no different than any other common serial murderer we've encountered." I nodded. I cursed out loud, totally frustrated. "He was here, just today. While we were down in the mines. We had the right idea but not the right place. At sunset, he rose and knew we were here, and got the hell out. He'll never be back. We lost the one good chance we had." We all stood silent for a while, the air heavy with the sense of defeat. At last, I turned to both men. "I want this entire area photographed. And detailed diagrams made. And then everything must be bagged and tagged. Even the fucking mattress. Maybe it most of all."

Manfred and Felix clicked to attention with a loud "Jawohl!" I took one last look at the detritus that had been collected, stacked neatly in piles against the wall. Ah, the stories they will tell, I thought. There were countless women's panties, brassieres, and stockings. In one corner was a stack of wigs. In another was a pile of jewelry—rings, necklaces, and pendants. Sitting on top was a *Goldenes Parteiabzeichen* or NSDAP Golden Party Badge. I didn't have to look at the serial number on the rear to know who had been the owner. The only victim that had one was Gertrude Brunner, Joseph Goebbels' propaganda princess. And who was now out there, somewhere. Maybe still in the woods she disappeared into, or…maybe she's already back in Berlin, where her loved ones are…maybe asking to be invited in, ready to give them a special embrace. I shuddered at this thought and turned to leave.

When we all returned to Wawel Castle, Anna and Elsie were waiting for us, anxious to learn our results. I called Hans Ziegler and asked him to come over from the morgue, and then I filled them all in. When I was done, I could tell Anna felt vindicated that her forensic analysis and findings about the brine salt had led us to the vampyre's lair. She immediately requested that the mattress and the clothing be dropped off at the lab, where she would get busy with their testing. Although slim, there may be clues to be found to help us decide where else he may be holding up. We debated for a few minutes on how we were going to explain to the higher-ups what we found. The mattress was one thing, but Brandt and his men clearly observed us as we walked out with bags containing the other evidence we had recovered. No one knew the bags contained the personal effects of the Kraków murder victims. It probably wouldn't go over well to brief Reichsführer Himmler that they were all sexual trophies kept by some predatory vampyre. Then Felix spoke up. "Boss, everyone knows we were there looking for Hellriegel, a rogue SS officer who has gone AWOL. All we have to do is leak what we had discovered in his flat…the goat, the pentagram, and all the books on the occult and demonology. He is deranged, and most likely dangerous. And clearly, he is the Kraków murderer." We were all silent for a moment. Hellriegel was a despicable human being, and he may indeed be mentally dangerous, but to pin on him all the Kraków murders? That was a step too far. If he was later caught, he'd be branded a serial murderer and executed. I couldn't have that on my conscience. But then, Anna broke the silence. "Yes, Felix is right," she said. I was stunned and stared at her in disbelief. How could Anna, of all people, be willing to frame a man for murders he didn't commit? "Otto, you're too focused on catching the bad guy to realize that it's you who is on very thin ice," she said bluntly. "You're the chief inspector in charge of the Third Reich's premier murder investigations team, sent to Kraków at the personal behest of the Reichsführer-SS. But it's a team that will never "solve" the case, will never make an arrest, and never bring a killer to justice. Because you have no one human that you can place into handcuffs…no normal man that you can parade into headquarters in triumph. You need someone you can bring to justice for the crimes." Anna took a pause and then looked at all of us. "Hellriegel is not a good man. He salivated over how efficient the krematorium were at Auschwitz. He suggested to Otto that Jewish girls be killed to offer a blood sacrifice to the vampyre. He's a worshipper of demonology and the occult. He's clearly a dangerous man, and for all we know, he may already be a murderer. And, unlike the rest of us, he was here in Kraków since the beginning of the murders. Add it all up, and one could argue Hellriegel had the means, motive, and opportunity to kill all those women. So I ask you if this team has to produce a killer, who is better than him?" Anna had laid it out so succinctly, so clearly. God help me, it makes sense. Even if I succeed in tracking the vampyre Wojciech down and somehow killing him, I still need to be able to close the case. And right now, I don't even know how such a being can be killed. I had just given Anna a nod, to show her I understood, when Elise spoke up. Young Elsie, who had never before had much to say during our previous team discussions, this time asked one simple, yet brutally direct question: "But what happens if you arrest Hellriegel and the murders continue?" God help me, I don't have an answer.

26 July 1943 –

I should have been dead tired after the long day trekking through the mine, but last night I just couldn't sleep. I was incensed that we had narrowly missed the vampyre Wojciech, but at the same time, exhilarated for we had found his lair and taken away his sanctuary. More than anything, I had a profound sense of satisfaction that we had recovered the sick bastard's trophies. He had spent a lot of time and effort collecting the personal effects of his victims, and I figured seizing them was a tremendous blow to him. But what kept me awake was the team's discussion back at Wawel. Anna was right. My head is on the chopping block to catch a murderer, and I will never be able to produce one. Pinning the murders on Hellriegel could be easily done, but of course, from a moral perspective, could I do something like that? And Elsie was right. Even if I did cast the blame on Hellriegel, what would happen if Wojciech isn't caught or stopped, and the murders continue? I'd pay a political price in embarrassment even more than if didn't catch the killer in the first place. I am in a damnable position.

I stayed up late and continued reading more of Stanislaw Kaminksi's *The Vampyre in Eastern Europe: Legend vs. Reality.* Eventually, I put it down and went to bed. Sleep evaded me as I kept tossing and turning, my thoughts continuously returning to the case. I kept seeing the terrible images of the hideous wounds inflicted on the bodies of the murder victims. I visualized the vampyre gleefully copulating with the SS guards at Auschwitz, his head thrown back, mouth open, and red eyes rolled back in ecstasy. Anna's forensic reports that conclude the killer is a walking corpse flashed like neon lights. Cardinal numbers reflecting the growing number of disappearing bodies danced behind my closed eyelids like spinning tops.

I could see horrific images of Ernst Hellriegel, crazily chanting around the goat head pentagram and candles in his flat. The mysterious S.K.'s biography of the enigmatic Count Batowski continued to replay over and over. And finally, I could even smell the dilapidated and filthy mattress we found at the mine, on which the vampyre had made himself at home while hiding from the sun's rays, the thing stained with semen and blood of his victims. All of these images spun around in my head like a whirlpool of unwanted despair. It didn't help that the temperature of the July night was a sweltering 30 degrees. My flat kept the heat inside despite opening up the windows. I almost wished I was back down in the coolness of the mines. Around three in the morning, I felt compelled to get out of bed and try to get some fresh air. I went out onto my balcony and looked down upon the newly named Adolf Hitler Platz. All part of the Germanization of Polish street names. The plaza, bustling with activity in the day, was quiet in the dead of night. I rested my arms on the railing and looked below. The moon was full, its silvery glow highlighting the darkened shops and restaurants circling the square. At least there was a bit of a breeze blowing in over the nearby Vistula River. Then I saw something in the corner of my eye. A slight movement near the fountain in the center of the plaza. I stared at the fountain for several moments, seeing nothing out of the ordinary. Then, I saw a man step out from behind it, illuminated in the moonlight.

Despite the sweltering heat, my blood froze in my veins. The man was tall and gaunt, his face skeletal, wrapped with skin the color of a porcelain death mask. His dark hair, accented by streaks of grey along the temples, was pulled back along his skull and tied into a knot behind his head. He was dressed impeccably, in a suit complete with a dapper pocket square. One of the details of the male wardrobe that contributes to defining the style of a true gentleman. It was Wojciech. Fear choked me as I watched his pupils appear to devour the whites of his eyes, glowing a predatory red like those of a hungry fox appraising a packed henhouse. He just stood there for several minutes, glaring up at me. I could feel malevolence and hatred radiating from the hideous luminescence of his corpse-like expression. I should have moved inside, but my bones had turned to Jelly, and I found myself continuing to stand there, our eyes locked. Part of me wanted to stand up to him, to show him I understood what he was, and that I wasn't intimidated. In reality, I could feel nothing but blind terror, and I have no pride in admitting that. I prayed that it was only a dream and that I was safely back in bed. Any illusions that were the case were dashed when the monster smiled. The change from an intimidating and threatening scowl to an amiable, almost friendly smile, was so sudden and such a bizarre contrast that it made the breath catch in my throat. But this was no friend of mine. As I watched, transfixed, the vampyre's smile became abnormally wide, a repulsive rictus that I will never forget until the end of my days. As his malignant lips drew apart, he revealed a mouth full of jagged, pointed teeth dripping with saliva that glistened in the moonlight. A frightening sight in itself, but noncomparable to the horrific visage of two incredibly long, curved incisors that began sliding outwards from man's maxilla as I watched, half mad in terror. The fangs of a malignant viper. It was an image straight out of hell. I wanted to scream, but fear had choked me, and blind terror had stolen any words I sought to utter. Bile raged into my throat as the vampyre took several steps forward, clearly deciding to come for me. I felt my heart pound as fear stabbed into my chest like a thousand sharp knives. But then, he stopped and raised his arms and covered his eyes. After a moment, he moved them down to cover his ears. A few seconds later, he covered his horrible mouth. I realized what he was doing. It was a monstrous parody of the three Japanese wise monkeys, Mizaru, Kikazaru, and Iwazaru. See no evil, hear no evil, speak no evil. It was a message...a warning. The bastard was telling me to lay off the investigation, to stop meddling in his affairs. The fiend gave me one last monstrous smile, and then, as quickly as he appeared, he vanished. It happened so fast my eyes could barely register what had become of him. I think the man changed into something, something that flew, but fast, too fast for a bat or anything in this world. He was there one second; the next, I caught a glimpse of a dark shape shoot across the plaza and off into the darkness of the nightscape. It was enough to propel me back to my senses, and I quickly retreated into the flat. I locked the door. I am not ashamed to say I did not sleep the remainder of the night, and I was never so grateful to see the sunrise in the morning. As I write this now, in the comfort of the daylight and the sounds of humanity in the bustling plaza below, it would be almost too easy to dismiss the whole thing and conclude that I simply imagined it. Perhaps I was dreaming after all. Or was it some kind of hallucination? Have I been working this case too hard? No, I'm sure of what I saw. The visage of the fiend's horrible maw was burned into my consciousness. It was him. Count Wojciech Batowski. He came to warn me. But I won't be intimidated. But how to catch him? I am off to Wawel Castle now; I will continue the day's entry later.

Continuation entry: As soon as I got to my office, I assembled the team and filled all of them in—Manfred, Felix, Anna, and Elsie, about what I had seen last night. Specifically, Wojciech's warning. No one doubted what I described, although Manfred, ever the skeptic, went through the motions and asked if I might have been dreaming, but I don't think he even believed that himself. It was now official; none of us could deny what we were facing. As a man of science, I never would have believed in the existence of the Nosferatu—the Vampyre. Nor Anna. All the evidence is now conclusive. The eyewitness testimony, the forensic evidence, the strange occurrences of disappearing corpses, Kaminski's historical records, and, with last night's encounter, the appearance of the vampyre himself, attempting to warn me off. Anna is now very concerned for my safety. I insisted I would be fine staying in my flat alone tonight, but Anna would hear none of it. She will be staying with me, a prospect that would have thrilled me under other circumstances, but now I must accept with great reluctance. At least if she's with me, I'll know she's safe as well. Frankly, I'm concerned for everyone on the team. I've instructed them to take one of the blessed crucifixes to their flats at night, as well as a vial of holy water, and to keep them close at hand. I don't like being on the defensive, but until I can get a lead on where to find Wojciech, it's the best we can do.

27 July 1943 –

Last evening, Anna and I felt the need to get out of my flat for some fresh air. We decided to go out for a drink at a local bierstube that was about a 5-minute walk down the street. I had stopped in there several times and had come to learn that it was a favorite watering hole for many officials of the General Government, as it was well-secured and safe for the German occupying forces. When we went inside, I could see it was fairly crowded; the tables were full of boisterous drinkers, swinging their glasses of beer back and forth as they merrily sang traditional beer songs. The place looked a lot like any beer hall back in my native Bavaria, and I felt right at home. Anna and I found a secluded area in the back that had a few empty tables. We asked the barmaid for a local beer, curious to try a Polish brew. She returned with glasses filled with Grodziskie, a famous brand still allowed to be brewed under the occupation. I took a long pull. It was a smokey Pilsner, flavorful and hoppy. Anna liked it too. We sat there for a while, recapping the case and trying to decide what our next steps were going to be. Perhaps fifteen minutes later, I sensed the presence of someone standing next to us. I looked up as a man pulled out a chair and took a seat across the table. He was tall, older, perhaps in his 60's. He was probably at one time a handsome man, with high cheekbones, patrician looks, and bright blue eyes. But now, with a face drawn and haggard, he looked like a man worn out. His blue eyes were tired and hollow, and his skin was overly pale and sallow. This was the face of a man who has been to places no one ever wants to be, and has seen things no one ever wants to see, I thought. Nevertheless, the man gave me a slight smile. "Herr Inspector," he said, in nearly perfect German, "my name is Stanislaw Kaminski."

Anna and I immediately exchanged glances. "You're 'S.K.,'" I said simply. "The one and the same," Kaminski replied. "Please forgive the subterfuge, Inspector. But as a Pole, vampyres are not the only thing I have to fear these days I'm afraid. I wanted you to have the information, but I was hesitant to give you my name. Not until I could check a few things out." I nodded. "Let me guess, I said, "You wanted to know whether or not I'm a dedicated National Socialist, an adherent of the Party's policies of genocide, extermination, and large-scale ethnic cleansing of the Slavs and Jews of Eastern Europe." Kaminski chuckled, but his eyes never wavered from mine. "Well, you ARE an officer in the SS, after all," he said, "and a rather senior one at that. You have the trust and respect of Heinrich Himmler himself. You are here in Kraków at his direction, and you are answerable only to him and Governor-General Hans Frank. The same Frank, I might add, who is in charge of reducing the numbers of Polish people through mass murder, ethnic cleansing, enslavement, and extermination through labor. The same Frank that just four months ago liquidated the Kraków Jewish ghetto, first by summarily shooting 2,000 Jews, then transferring another 2,000, those that could work, to the Plasnów forced labor camp, run by SS-Untersturmführer Amon Göth. The rest of the Jews, approximately 3,000, were sent to the Auschwitz-Birkenau killing center to be gassed. Your SS has a lot of blood on its hands, Inspector." Continuing to lock eyes with Kaminski, I replied, "I regret sincerely that all that is true," I replied. "I see you've done your homework. But I have to assume that since you are sitting here in front of me, at the risk of being arrested, your research on me also provided information that makes you comfortable to do so." Kaminski leaned in closer and lowered his voice even further. "I know you're no Nazi, Inspector." He turned his eyes to Anna. "And neither are you, Dr. Müller. You both joined the Party out of reluctance, to do otherwise would have been professional suicide. And you had no choice in joining the SS when the KRIPO came under its control once the Nazis came to power. Unlike your peers, you are not ideologically motivated. You have a complete disdain for the Nazi police state and its persecution of political and religious dissent. Your only motivation, your raison d'être, is solving murders, seeking the truth, and obtaining justice for the victims. You are here in Kraków with no other agenda except to catch a killer. The killer of women, be they German, Polish, or even a Jew. Because for you, Inspector, justice is indeed blind. That's a rare trait in today's world. That's why I'm here, inspector. Because I know you are a good man with exceptional moral character. And I trust you. But with this case, your investigatory zeal is not going to be good enough. You are not pursuing a normal man, you see. Your usual psychological analysis will not work. Yes, Count Wojciech Batowski was a man once, even a man of virtue and honor, but over three centuries ago his soul was lost forever. He is what my Slavic people call an *upiór*…a vampyre. He was bitten in Klushino, you see. As he lay, vulnerable on the battlefield. It was not uncommon for the vampyre to find easy prey this way during the many battles in Europe. Wars make the perfect feeding ground. With the bite of the vampyre, the Count became corrupted in both the flesh and the spirit. Now, he thinks more like a beast than a man, seeking only to fulfill his most decadent and wanton desires. But what makes him truly dangerous and a very formidable foe is that, in addition to his evil cunning, he retains the intelligence of a man. He can perceive, reason, comprehend, plan, and remember. You have never faced such an adversary before, Inspector. This is why I reached out to you by sending Batowksi's biographical information and the historical record of his crimes so that you would know what you were dealing with. It is also why I was desperate to see you tonight." I gave a glance over to Anna. She was staring at Kaminski intently. "To give me more information?" I asked hopefully, but somehow sensing there was more to it. Kaminski shook his head. He smiled, but it looked like the smile you would get from your local undertaker. "To warn you," he replied.

As Kaminski paused, I caught the eye of the barmaid and ordered another round of beers. I figured whatever Kaminski was going to tell me warranted something stronger, so I ordered a round of shots of Slivovitz. Anyone who has drank it knows it tastes like shit and goes down like firewater, but it seemed appropriate at the moment. When the barmaid departed, I said, "Alright, before you give me the warning, I want to ask you something. I've read your book, *The Vampyre in Eastern Europe: Legend vs. Reality*. I know you've been researching Wojciech Batowski for probably close to two decades. Not just him, but others of his type…the *upiór*. I don't think you left academia and your position with the University of Warsaw just because of the war. You're a vampyre slayer, aren't you? You're out there…looking for him, right?" Kaminski nodded and spread his hands on the table. "Yes. It wasn't a path I thought I would have ever ended up choosing. But fate can thrust upon us some cruel choices, Inspector. So, you read my book. Well, there's one detail I left out in the preface. I just couldn't write about it. It was still too raw, and talking about it in the book would have been like pulling a scab off an old wound. You see, I had been married. Her name was Alicja. We met soon after I returned from the Great War, and I began teaching at the university. She was much younger than me, almost by ten years. She was one of my students, and I was smitten with her from the beginning. And her with me. But I was a professor, and we maintained a professional relationship until she finished her degree. We courted for another year as our love grew even more intense. We got married in the spring of 1922, taking our vows in the All Saints Church, the largest church in Warsaw. For the next several years we were so happy. But it was the spring of 1928 when I got down on my knees and thanked the Lord for the blessing he had brought us. Alicja was pregnant. We had tried for so long, and then…it happened. We were both ecstatic, and all was perfect with the world. But then…" Kaminski trailed off, remaining silent for a long moment. He wiped a visible tear from his eye before he continued. "Alicja disappeared in August 1928. She took a trip with some of her girlfriends to visit Bordeaux, the well-known wine district of France. We both had an interest in wines, and I thought it was a nice chance for her to go on a group tour. According to her friends, she stepped out of the chateau where they were staying just after dinner for a short walk. She never came back. A local resident later recalled seeing her speaking to a man. An older man with long hair tied behind his head. My father and I traveled to France and looked for months, but we had no leads, and within a year, the Gendarmerie gave up the case. Then, in 1929, I was approached by a group that, for the first time, had some concrete information on what had happened to her. This group is…well, unique, and they have knowledge of the Vampyre going back almost to the beginning of recorded history. They told me the name of my wife's killer…that it was shockingly one of my own countrymen, a Pole who lived centuries ago by the name of Wojciech Batowski. They asked me to join their group because of my…commitment to see justice for Alicja. And they needed more of our kind. I didn't need any prodding. Since then, I've been working with them, not just to track down Wojciech, but many, many others."

"So you're not alone in this," I stated. "Who is this group? How could they have records of the vampyre going back centuries? And what do you mean, they need people of our kind?" I asked. Kaminski looked around the room and leaned in closer before answering. "This will be a bit difficult to accept, Inspector. And a bit fantastic, but trust me, it is true. We all think of the vampyre as an evil, monolithic entity. That they look upon man simply as cattle, needing our blood to stay alive, yes? Well, that's only half right. In reality, there are two bloodlines of the vampyre, two clans. The original bloodline is called the Vampyre Magnus. They still have to drink blood to survive, as any animal must kill to eat their prey, but they learned to satisfy this need without feeding on humans and have dedicated themselves to living amongst us in peace and harmony. In fact, Inspector, it was not far from your city of birth in Germany, where the Magnus codified this pledge millennia ago. Led by their most charismatic and influential elder, known simply as "Der Eisern," or "The Iron One," the Magnus clan held a conclave in Steppach, near present-day Augsburg. It was there that the clan made the declaration that they would live amongst the humans in peace and would never again feast upon human blood to survive. And they do live amongst us, Inspector. They hide their true identities well and camouflage their lifestyles so they are never seen in public during the day. However, through their intermediaries, many are successful and influential people who contribute to our society. Doctors, lawyers, engineers, artists, architects, the list can go on and on."

I had listened to Kaminski intently. His story was so outrageous, so fantastic, that I studied him closely for signs of insanity, paranoid schizophrenia, or at the least, a delusional disorder. But yet, he seemed rational, cogent and reasoned. "So I take it the other clan is not so benevolent," I said, prompting him to continue. "The other clan is called the Mortis," he explained. "Its name says it all since the Mortis remains a primal clan, animalistic, sadistic, and reveling in death. Whereas the Magnus is highly organized, with an agreed-upon hierarchy led by their council of elders, the Mortis tend to be fragmented, with no central leadership. Unlike the Magnus, most Mortis live outside the comforts of human existence, in a primitive manner, as hunter-predators. Their lairs are usually in abandoned, desolate locations, away from human activity, and which afford them protection from the sun's rays and seclusion from their enemies while they are most vulnerable. They are, for the most part, solitary hunters, although in recent years, we have found some Mortis enclaves with several other vampyres, possibly indicating a shift towards better cohesion and communication. Not a good development, I might add. But the most horrific aspect of the Mortis is that they are evil, the true vampyres of our nightmares and ancient legends. They retain none of the human qualities of the Magnus…they are incapable of warmth, empathy, and love. Quite the opposite…they have a wicked proclivity for sexual sadism and seduction. The female Mortis are succubus-like vampyres that use decadent and animalistic sex to hypnotize, seduce, and feed upon their victims, men and women alike. Their male counterparts are likewise sadistic killers, often raping and maiming as they go along. Some, like Wojciech, simply like to deflower young women, whereas others have been known for their pedophilia and proclivity for young boys and men. All of them are unholy creatures and damned in the eyes of God.

"Total opposites," I mused, "I can't imagine the two clans get along very well." Kaminski shook his head and let out a chuckle. "They are, and excuse the pun, mortal enemies. The Magnus not only pledged to never feed on the human race but to assimilate and live amongst us in peace. As you can imagine, this is made difficult when the Mortis goes on killing sprees, drawing attention to the vampyre of both clans. In truth, it's the Mortis that has served as the basis for the evil and seductive vampyres we have come to know in legends and folklore. And in modern times, in literature and the cinema. For centuries, the Magnus have fought to keep the Mortis in check, not only to ensure their own survival as they live among humans but also for humanity itself. The Magnus are our protectors, our first line of defense against the evil of the Mortis Vampyre. It's a constant fight that has gone on for centuries, with the Magnus selecting some of their very best to track down and eliminate their Mortis adversaries."

Kaminski picked up his shot glass and downed the last of his Slivovitz. I signaled to the barmaid to bring another round. "I have worked with a few of these Magnus vampyre slayers. I spoke of them in my book, although I described them as vampyre slayers from the Vatican. This is based somewhat on truth, as an esoteric wing of the Catholic Church did indeed hunt vampyres down for centuries on their own accord. Anyway, it is my Magnus benefactors who have trained me and given me the knowledge and tools to go after the Mortis." The barmaid arrived with the drinks, and Kaminski swirled his shot glass for a moment before continuing, raising his eyes to lock onto mine. "But you see, Inspector, the Magnus have their limitations. They cannot move around in the day. They cannot come across the Mortis asleep in their lair when they are most vulnerable because they, too, must rest during the day. No, they need someone who can move around freely in the daylight and, oftentimes, someone who can interact with others as only humans can do. This is why, centuries ago, the Magnus started enlisting the aid of humans to also serve as vampyre slayers. There have been only a handful of us, perhaps one or two each generation, as the selection criteria are tight; only those with the inherent goodness of soul, purity of character, and strength of resolve are chosen." Kaminski gave a wry chuckle and said, "I guess I made the cut," then downed his shot of Slivovitz.

We were all quiet at the table for a moment until Anna broke the silence. "So, Stanislaw, you said you were here with a warning for Otto. What is it?" Kaminski sighed, then said, "Just the inevitable, I'm afraid. Since your visit to the mines and finding his lair, Wojciech knows you are on to him. He's probably not happy, and he might try to come for you or…" Kaminski's eyes glanced over to Anna…"Or the ones you care about. And the other members of your team." I burst out in a laugh, although admittingly, it was devoid of any humor. "I think you're a bit late with the warning, Kaminski," I said dryly. "Wojciech already paid me a visit. Last night. He was standing out in the square outside my flat, looking up towards my balcony. Just flashed me a wide smile…not one I will soon forget." Kaminski didn't seem overly surprised, just nodded. "So, you've seen him yourself," he stated flatly. "You know he's real." I downed the rest of my Slivovitz. "It was adding up even before. Anna's forensic evidence, the Auschwitz eyewitness accounts, the crime scenes, the disappearing bodies, the history on Wojciech you provided, and then what we found in the salt mine. Having the bastard make an appearance just made it official. I know he's real, and I now have a face to the name. And I know he must be dealt with before he can continue to be the scourge he is, wantonly killing and feeding on the helpless." Kaminski leaned forward. He almost looked younger, more virile, and invigorated. He had a purpose now. "Have no fears, inspector. I will teach you what you need to do to protect yourselves.

And the tools to kill Wojciech, if you can find him when he's vulnerable. We're in this together now. And frankly, if there ever was a time we could get Wojciech, it is now. At least as long as he stays here in Kraków. Which I think he will, at least for a while yet. I feel there is something that brought him back here, to his birthplace, although I'm not sure what it is yet. But we're getting close. Very close." I looked at Kaminski and nodded. I had made my decision. I looked at Anna, and she nodded in return. I turned to Kaminski and held out my hand. "Well, here's to combining forces. The German police and the Polish vampyre slayer. An unlikely union, but if we can kill that bastard Wojciech and get justice for his victims, then I'm all in."

Later, Kaminski said he wanted to head back to my flat, where he could hand over another package he had prepared for us. A package of vampyre-fighting tools. We started to get up from the table, but then Kaminski paused. "Oh, you have a man, an SS-Haupsturmführer Ernst Hellriegel," he stated. I looked at him with surprise. "Yes," I replied, "he's been missing for a week now." Kaminski scowled, his lips turning downwards in disgust. "Yes. I hate to have to tell you this, Inspector, but Hellriegel is a lost man. He has made contact with the Count, and has completed the blood oath, swearing his loyalty, and now has become what we call a familiar, a willing supplicant to the vampyre." Anna gasped, and I heard her ask, "But why? Why would he voluntarily go to Wojciech? He's an SS officer! How could he fall so easily under Wojciech's spell?" Kaminski's eyes momentarily looked down at the table, his expression saddened, resembling a father who was steeling himself to explain the blunt facts of life to a naïve child. "The vampyre can easily spot those of us who are spiritually vulnerable. Those with weak moral character, lacking God's virtues of loving-kindness, compassion, sympathy, and equanimity. Your man already had a black heart, incapable of empathy and love." I thought of Hellriegel, and how he looked at the krematorium at Auschwitz with both awe and admiration. "You got that fucking right," I spat. "He's an evil son of a bitch. And I suppose evil attracts evil. He must have stood out to Wojciech like a shining beacon." Kaminski nodded in agreement. "As a familiar, Hellriegel will serve his master with unswerving loyalty, perhaps with even the promise to be made into a vampyre himself someday. He'll be just as dangerous as the vampyre, and he can walk amongst us in the daylight, so be very, very careful." Oh, don't worry, I thought to myself, if Hellriegel comes for me, I'll be ready for him. And then I'll put him down like the rabid dog he is.

"I have a question, Stanislaw," said Anna. "Does the Magnus Vampyre clan also have familiars?" Kaminski chuckled and replied, "Now, that's a good question, young lady. They do, indeed. Unlike the Mortis, the Magnus only recruits the most virtuous men and women of pure hearts. They are often placed in positions that can provide help or support to the Magnus, as obviously, they can get things done in the day while working amongst their human counterparts. As an example..." Kaminski paused and pointed towards a large table across the room. In the center, there was a sign that read "Stammtisch," German for "regular's table." Seated around the table was a group of men hoisting their beers in reverie as they engaged in gregarious conversation. "See the man wearing the Bavarian-style jacket? He's Karl, the owner of this beer hall. After the Germans confiscated this place from the previous Polish owners, Karl was allowed to buy it and reopen it for the German occupation forces. In his position, Karl has gotten to know just about everyone; he's a virtual "who's who" of what's happening in this city. He knows a certain Wehrmacht general who comes here some nights with his mistress. He knows the member of Frank's staff who comes here to have a drink with his homosexual lover. He knows the SS officer who is running an illegal cigarette enterprise. And, Inspector, he knew you liked to come in for a beer from time to time. The man heading the investigation into the Kraków murders. He's the one who told me you had come in tonight. Because you see, Anna, Karl is a Magnus familiar. He is very well-placed and very useful. From the outside, he's a German profiteer of the war, but in reality, he's one of us. Through his contacts, I was given a new set of passports and identification. I now go by the name of Josef Fischer, just another German profiteer in Kraków. I'm even a member of the Nazi Party." With that revelation, Anna and I looked at each other in amazement. The Magnus maintained a stable of familiars serving as support agents that probably put the best ring of clandestine SS informants to shame. It was all incredible.

Five minutes after returning to my flat, there was a knock on the door. Kaminski AKA Fischer had told us that a colleague would be delivering a package per his request. After opening the door, Kaminski took the item and thanked the man. He then brought it over to a large table that I had cleaned off to make room. It was some kind of cloth satchel, rolled up and secured with two cloth ties. After untying it, Kaminski proceeded to unroll it, spreading it across the table. At first, due to the glint of the metal, I thought it contained medical or operating devices. Then, I could tell this was not the case. Instead of a satchel for a doctor, it was something more appropriate for a member of the clergy. The inside pockets were filled with various accouterments of the church, namely, several crucifixes and vials of water. "These are blessed crucifixes," Kaminski explained, pulling out one of the crosses. "Not just any crucifix will do. It must be sanctified by a priest, reserving it for God's sacred and holy purpose—a powerful symbol of redemption, sacrifice, and victory over sin and death that will protect us from the evil of the vampyre. If you hold these at arm's length, you can keep the monster at bay. Hit them with it, and you will burn them severely with the power of the Lord." Kaminski then removed one of several small bottles from the satchel. "And these are vials of blessed holy water. It too will repel the vampyre and cause them great pain when touching their skin." He then took out something from the remaining pocket. Unlike the other items, this one didn't look like it had any place in a priest's bag of holy implements. It was a wicked-looking knife, its blade about seven or eight inches long. One edge looked razor-sharp, curling up to a very nasty pointed tip, ideal for fine slicing. The other edge was serrated, suitable for cutting through tough materials. The blade was bright and highly polished and etched with the inscription *Deus lux mea est.* Kaminski held the knife up into the light. I could see the handle was made of an extraordinarily beautiful white ivory. "The knife blade is pure silver, and the inscription is Latin for 'God is my Light.' This knife is more than 500 years old, originally used by an esoteric wing of the Catholic Church dedicated to hunting down and killing vampyres. Legend has it that twenty-five were made for the church's vampyre slayers, all blessed personally by the Pope. Many have been lost to time and generations, but the Vampyre Magnus has recovered several of them, and they are now used by us. I have my own, and this is for you. This…" Kaminski raised the knife higher to emphasize his next point. "This is the only way you can kill the Mortis Vampyre. Crucifixes and holy water will hurt and damage them. But only the sacred knife can extinguish their evil forever. But pay attention, this is very, very important. There is a sacred ritual that must be adhered to. The knife is blessed, but to unleash its full righteous might, you must dip or wash the blade in fresh holy water. A thrust to the creature's heart will severely wound it, and it may appear to be dead. But unless you take the final step, the vampyre can rejuvenate. To kill it, to deliver the coup de grâce, you must decapitate the vampyre. You will find the serrated edge of the knife particularly useful for this. Cutting through the tendons and bones of the neck is harder than one may think. Before you begin, again wash the blade in holy water. Then, as you remove the head, incite the holy words *Adjure te, spiritus nequissime, per Deum omnipotentem,* Latin for 'I adjure thee, most evil spirit, by Almighty God.' Say it correctly, and say it with true conviction. Only then, with the head removed, will the vampyre be truly dead."

I put the knife back in the cloth pouch and rolled it up. "I'm curious," I said. "You spoke about the Magnus Vampyre slayers, who for centuries have tracked down their Mortis counterparts. And that they took you under their wing and trained you as a slayer as well. How did they find you? Do you still know them? Are they here in Kraków?" Kaminski pulled out a chair from the table and took a seat. "Hmmm…" he said, and for a long moment he went quiet. His face took on a wistful, almost dreamy expression, like he was in another place, another time. Just when I began to think he wasn't going to answer the questions, he spoke. "It was the spring of 1929 when I was in the depths of my despair over not finding my missing Alicja. I had given up all hope and was beginning to spiral down the bottomless pit of self-destruction. I had begun drinking heavily, and this had affected my teaching, my position at the university, and my standing with friends. I was even contemplating suicide. The week before, I had illegally purchased a Nagant M1895 revolver of old Imperial Russian manufacture from a rather unscrupulous dealer I managed to find in one of the more notorious crime quarters in Warsaw. I was caressing the pistol in my pocket, my fingers oily from running them around the warm, naked steel, as I sat at a table outside a tavern in Warsaw's Castle Square. It was early evening, and there were still quite a bit of people bustling through the square. I didn't immediately take notice when someone stopped and stood next to the table, looking down upon me. When I sensed their presence, I looked up. And when I did, my first thought was that I was looking into the face of an angel. It wasn't just because the young woman was stunning, because she was. She was very young, maybe around twenty, with beautiful blond hair fashioned with very long ringlet curls, made popular by silent screen actresses like Lillian Gish and Mary Pickford. She had gorgeous sapphire blue eyes, which almost seemed to shine in the lamplight. She wore a coordinating set of knee-length checkered wool tweed knickers with a vest jacket worn over a brown shirt. Below her high socks, she wore a clean pair of oxford shoes. I was a bit surprised at her attire since, in those days, it was still rather taboo for a woman to be wearing pants, although women's knickers fell into a gray area and began to be accepted as sportswear. With her clothing exuding a sense of freedom and rebellion, I could tell she was a woman who didn't live by social norms or what others thought. But what really captivated me, what I couldn't believe I was actually seeing, was the soft glow, or halo, that was around her head. Like a crown of light. She radiated a sense of calm, tranquility, and serenity. When she smiled, I felt awash with a sense of well-being and peace that melted my feelings of despair, loneliness, and regret. 'You don't need that gun, Stanislaw,' she said gently, sitting down across from me. 'That is what he wants, don't you see? The man you seek thrives on human fear and sadness. Don't give him the satisfaction. Instead, hunt him down like the dog he is. Only when he is destroyed will you have true justice for your beloved Alicja. And for the tens of thousands of his other victims.' I sat stunned, not knowing how she knew about the gun and not caring. I only cared about what else she had said. 'How? How do I find him?' I asked. She reached over then, taking my hands into hers. And when she did, the last vestiges of my sadness and despair completely evaporated, replaced with new feelings hard to describe…a mix of confidence, excitement, and a sense of anticipation. 'You are a good man, Stanislaw Kaminski,' the young girl said, 'of pure heart and soul. Come with me, and I will teach you everything you need to know, and then you will know your true destiny.' I didn't even have to think. Without hesitation, I squeezed her hands, signaling agreement, and that was the beginning of everything."

Over the next hour, Kaminski told the rest of his story. Anna and I listened with rapt fascination. In the following days after meeting the girl, Kaminski learned that her name was Bethany, and although she looked like a young flapper, she was actually three hundred years old. She was from the benevolent Magnus clan and was herself a vampyre slayer, entrusted more than a century earlier by her clan's elders to track down and kill the Mortis. Kaminski discovered Bethany was one of her clan's most powerful and successful slayers, having killed thousands of Mortis over the many years of her remit. Because of her feared reputation, the Mortis took to calling her *Rhamnousia*, the name for the Greek goddess of divine retribution and justice. More commonly known as *Nemesis*, she is the goddess who enacts retribution against those who succumb to hubris or arrogance before the

Gods. *Nemesis* has a rough translation of "to give what is due," and she is usually depicted as having angel-like wings and holding a sword, but in some images, she can be seen holding a balance and scales, maintaining the balance, and making malefactors face the music. Kaminski was taken under Bethany's tutelage, and over several months, she taught him the history of their craft and all the ancient rituals he would need to become a slayer himself. Over time, he was introduced to several of Bethany's Magnus colleagues as they traveled throughout Europe. One of these was another young woman who called herself Althea. Kaminski determined that Bethany and Althea were close friends and had worked together over the past one hundred years in an attempt to track down one of the very worst of the Mortis Vampyre. Her name was Alexandria, the "Queen of the Vampyres" that Kaminski had later written about in his book. From Bethany and Althea, Kaminski learned that Alexandria was considered the top priority for the Magnus slayers. She was, in effect, the Mortis "Public Enemy Number One." This was predicated on Alexandria's propensity for sheer death and destruction wherever she went. She didn't just feed on her victims by taking their blood; she would harvest their sexual energy first, using her sexual hypnotism to seduce and defile them through animalistic and decadent sex. No human was safe, male or female, from her sexual appetites. Her debauchery knew no limit. But what made her most dangerous was that, whereas most Mortis were solitary creatures, hunting from their secluded lairs, Alexandria would create nests composed of her sexual slaves, those she turned, or even as a worse fate, those she did not, human familiars who existed only for her endless bidding. Kaminski told us that Bethany and Althea had tracked Alexandria from the Middle East and all through Europe, and although they had been very successful in killing many of her minions, Alexandria had somehow evaded them at every turn. Kaminski realized that Alexandria had become Bethany's obsession and that she had committed herself to spend centuries, or as long as necessary, to find and destroy the creature now calling herself "Queen" of the Mortis Vampyres.

But the reason Bethany had come to Warsaw in the spring of 1929, Kaminski explained, was not because of Alexandria. The Magnus had, for hundreds of years, also been on the trail of another ancient Mortis vampyre. A fiend that defiled and fed upon young girls and women. A Polish man who once went by the name of Count Wojciech Batowski. The same monster that had snatched his beloved Alicja. The Magnus had known of Stanislaw's loss suffered at Wojciech's hands and his never-ending grief. "They said they needed my help," Stanislaw smiled, "but in reality, they saved me and gave me purpose once again. They believed in me, and I vowed never to disappoint them. And that's how it all started," Kaminski concluded. "I started taking sabbaticals from teaching whenever new leads came up concerning Wojciech's whereabouts. I tracked him from southern France and on into Spain. In 1936, I just missed him in Seville. The Spanish Civil War was raging, and I almost got killed myself when I got caught in a gun battle between Republican and Nationalist forces. The next time he came up on my scope was in 1939, with the missing girl in Switzerland. It appeared that Wojciech was moving East. This was confirmed when the nine girls went missing in Austria. I began to have a theory. I wasn't sure, but I had a gut feeling he was coming home to Poland, possibly to Kraków, his birthplace. When the rash of murders began in the city two months ago, I knew he was here. I still don't know why, but it doesn't matter. I'm going to end it. End it here, in the city where it all began." I looked at Kaminski. The man had lived through hell and had both the love of his life and future child taken away from him. The years of hunting the Mortis had taken a toll on him, and he was prematurely aged. Yet, I could see the fire in his eyes, his determination to avenge his wife's death blazing there like an eternal flame. The man would never give up, I realized. Not until he killed Wojciech, or Wojciech killed him.

28 July 1943 –

This morning, Anna and I walked together from my flat to Wawel Castle. We are in full swing of the summer now; the air is thick and muggy as if waiting for a breath. The air dripped with something else, too. I could feel it…and I think Anna could too—a feeling of omnipresent dread that is hanging over the city. I couldn't shake the feeling that things were going to get worse before they got better. A whole lot worse. It didn't take long for my suspicions to be confirmed. When we arrived at Wawel Castle, it was a madhouse. The first thing we heard when walking into the office was a man crying hysterically. Anna and I ran into the conference room to find Felix trying to console a man sitting at the table, his head down into his folded arms, alternatively sobbing and talking gibberish. We joined Felix in trying to get the poor man to calm down. The KRIPO uniformed police who had brought the man in stood over in the corner. According to them, they had found the man roaming the streets, totally hysterical, babbling about his girlfriend coming back from the dead. The man was so distraught that Anna ended up giving him a sedative. It took about 30 more minutes to get the man to a rational state where we could interview him. When we did, he recounted the most horrific story. His name is Hans Dietrich. He is a Hauptmann in the German Army, assigned to the Kraków's military district. He had been dating Han Frank's secretary, Johanna Liebl, for about a year before her murder. Their relationship had become quite serious, and just before her death, they had decided to become engaged. The KRIPO had interviewed Dietrich after Liebl's murder, but he was out on maneuvers during the timeframe in question and was cleared of any suspicion. Dietrich was left to mourn his loss, which was further exacerbated when he learned his fiancée's corpse was stolen from the morgue on July 14th. All this was too much for Dietrich, and he had recently requested reassignment out of Kraków, even if it meant deploying to the Eastern front. Dietrich said he didn't much care; the pain was too great, and he no longer had much to live for.

Then, late last night, he claimed he had just left a bierstube frequented by Wehrmacht officers not far from the garrison when someone called out to him. It was late, and the small cobblestone alley he had turned into, a shortcut back to the base, had no other pedestrian traffic. So Dietrich was quite surprised when someone called out his name. A familiar voice, female. The alley was not well-lit, either, and the only light shining out to the street came from a few windows along the pathway. Dietrich struggled to see through the darkness but couldn't see anyone. Then, he heard a soft voice say "Ich bin hier, mein tapferer Ritter." *I am here, my brave knight.* He froze then. The only one who ever called him "her knight" was Johanna Liebl. It was a nickname she had given him in jest, making fun of his strict military bearing. Dietrich never liked it, but over time it stuck. Now, he knew for sure he didn't like it. He didn't like it at all. As he watched, a beautiful woman stepped out of the gloom. As gorgeous and radiant as he remembered her. Slim, petite, with voluminous brunette hair fashioned in classic curls. Her dark eyes looked different, though; they seemed to sparkle with a reddish glow. "Johanna?" Dietrich had sputtered, still not comprehending the apparition before him. The woman smiled and took several steps forward. No, not walking, Dietrich realized. As he watched, not truly comprehending, she drifted above the cobblestones towards him, her feet never touching the ground. He started to take a step back but found he couldn't. It was her crimson eyes. They had become circular whirlpools, spinning, twirling…pulling Dietrich in. He suddenly noticed her mouth was larger than he remembered; the lips he had loved to kiss now stretched nearly from cheek to cheek. "Ich habe dich vermisst, Dietrich," she said. *I've missed you, Dietrich.* It sounded guttural, less distinct. Because now her mouth was full of teeth, rows of sharp little knives, accented by two large incisors that glistened with saliva. At last, Dietrich tried to scream, but he could not; his body was paralyzed, held in a vise-like grip of some unseen power. "Halt mich fest, meine Liebe," *Hold me tight, my love*, the Johanna-thing cooed as she placed her arms behind Dietrich's neck, pulling him into her embrace. What happened next was difficult for Dietrich to recount. Not because he couldn't remember but because of the shame he felt when recalling the memory. It took some time for us to get the full story. In a nutshell, Dietrich claims he no longer felt fear when Johanna pulled him into her embrace. Instead, when he felt her ample breasts crush against his chest, he became sexually aroused. When she raked her fingers through his hair, he wanted, no, needed her. He felt himself moaning when he felt her tongue move up and down his face, tasting him, and he nearly climaxed. When Johanna reached down and felt his hardness, she whispered, "Ja, Ja, sehr gut." *Yes, yes, very good*. Then, without warning, her mouth clamped down over Dietrich's lips in a monstrous kiss. As Johanna thrust her tongue into his mouth, he experienced wave after wave of erotic pleasure, which he likened to an extreme sexual orgasm. He stood there, his body racked with spasms, for how long he couldn't recall. Eventually, he could feel her hot breath on his neck. " Jetzt wirst du für immer bei mir sein, meine Liebe," she purred. *Now you will be with me forever, my love.*

Suddenly, Dietrich's ecstasy was broken by a nearby shout. Two other men had entered the alley and had stumbled upon them. They were Wehrmacht soldiers who had just left the bierstube, and they were drunk. Having set eyes upon the beautiful woman before them, they began to stagger towards her. The thing that had once been Johanna whipped her head about in a snarl. The men, in their drunken state, didn't at first notice the woman's anglerfish mouth. By the time the ghastly image registered with them, it was too late. The vampyre was on them in a heartbeat, biting and slashing at the men's throats. Dietrich stumbled backward, his mind beginning to clear once he was out of Johanna's embrace. He watched in horror as the woman he once loved now sat astride one of the men and greedily drank the spray of blood spurting out of his carotid artery. The blood spray had saturated her hair, which now hung down grotesquely over her face, making her look like some monstrous Gorgon of ancient mythology. Dietrich screamed, his mind no longer capable of processing the carnage taking place before him. His last coherent memory before he ran from the passageway was the image of Johanna turning her head to look at him, smiling, as her teeth clenched a dripping piece of flesh.

KRIPO officers reported that within the hour, they had searched the alley where Hauptmann Dietrich had claimed to have the encounter with his dead fiancée. They found no bodies, but there was indeed huge amounts of blood, pooling between the cobblestones and sprayed against the walls of nearby buildings. We subsequently sent out an urgent message to all Wehrmacht commands to do a head count of all assigned personnel. Just before noon, we received word that two soldiers had not reported back to their unit, the 501st Signal Battalion, after their evening pass expired. Their names are Feldwebel Günther Tanz and Obergefreiter Klaus Bauer. We've placed an alert out with all authorities to look for them. Frankly, I doubt they will ever be found. Not alive, anyway. There's no doubt what got them. Unfortunately, by the end of the day, the military claimed criminal jurisdiction and placed Hauptmann Dietrich under arrest on suspicion of murder. No one believes his story that Johanna Liebl, a woman who was murdered and then her corpse stolen from the city morgue, would suddenly show up alive and well, or, as the Hauptmann described her, some kind of vampyre. I would have liked to have kept Dietrich in SS custody, but I had no official reason to do so. Dietrich was taken to Kraków's Capital Defense Garrison, which houses the city's military forces, numbering some 30,000 strong, pending a court-martial on the murder charges.

By early afternoon, as the dust was settling a bit on the Dietrich arrest, Anna and I finally had a chance to assemble Manfred, Felix, Elsie, as well as Dr. Ziegler, to fill them in regarding Stanislaw Kaminski's unorthodox appearance to us in the bierstube last evening, incognito as a German citizen named Josef Fischer. I recapped how Kaminski had become a vampyre slayer with the death of his wife, and his revelations about the two clans of the vampyre—the Magnus and the Mortis. Further, how they use their stable of human familiars to aid them during the day. Lastly, I unwrapped the satchel containing the silver knife and repeated Kaminski's instructions on how to decapitate and kill the creatures. As one could expect, we were hit with dozens of questions, and Anna and I did our best to answer them. Thank God Anna had been present during the meeting with Kaminski. Unlike my nocturnal encounter with the vampyre Wojciech outside my flat, this time I wasn't alone, and Anna backed me up one hundred percent and could fill all the gaps in our discussion with Kaminski. After three hours, even Manfred, once the most ardent skeptic, was fully convinced of Kaminski's story. And now, thanks to Kaminski, we have the knowledge and the tools to defend ourselves…and to kill Wojciech if we can track him down. With Kaminski passing us the intelligence and any potential leads developed from the Magnus familiars, we have a real chance of tracking the son of a bitch down. In the meantime, it was agreed that none of the women on the team should be alone at night. Anna would continue to sleep over at my place, and Elsie would be staying with Felix. They were both quick to agree and the fleeting smile I saw them exchange only confirmed my suspicions that something is going on between the two. Well, all the better, I think.

Late afternoon was no less busy than the morning. I spent about an hour with Hans Frank. He's in a foul mood, and I guess I can't really blame him. First and foremost, Kraków still has a mass murderer of women on the loose. On top of that, we now have an apparent murder of two army men, by one of their own. And of course, our rogue SS man, Ernst Hellriegel, is still unaccounted for. Frank is also still smarting over the hijacking of the plane that was carrying the corpse of Gertrude Brunner, Goebbels' propaganda princess, which has caused him considerable embarrassment. Frank is still inclined to cast most blame upon the Polish resistance, but with the pressure he's under, he's looking for answers. He asked where I was on the murder investigation. I only could tell him that we had a clear understanding of the killer's methodology and a working understanding of his motivation. As such, the profile we had developed on the man was our best lead to find him at present, and this had been disseminated to every police and security agency in the city. We have also deployed a virtual army of undercover officers at strategic locations where women may be most vulnerable. Frank seemed satisfied with that and dismissed me in due course. Only I know that we are spinning our wheels, and wasting resources in a wild goose chase that will never net the perpetrator. The vampyre Wojciech will never be caught by traditional means, but only by close collaboration with Stanislaw Kaminski and the Magnus.

29 July 1943 –

Last evening Kaminski came to my flat. We had agreed to meet nightly and compare notes to see if either party has developed any leads worth pursuing. Anna and I had just finished dinner, and I offered Kaminski a plate. He accepted, and we sat down at the dining table. Before I even got the words out of my mouth to tell him about Hauptmann Dietrich, he said he had already heard Dietrich's claims of seeing his dead lover. I was surprised at this since that information had not been released to the public. As far as anyone in the public knew, Dietrich had been arrested for the possible murder of the two Army men. When asked, Kaminski just chuckled and said he "had sources." I suspect a Magnus familiar is on Frank's staff or in the Wehrmacht command. Or, perhaps even in the KRIPO. It doesn't much matter I suppose. One way or the other, Kaminski is going to know everything we know.

Kaminski told us he wanted to discuss what we could expect when hunting the vampyre. "To separate fact from fiction," he chuckled. As he explained it, not everyone killed by a vampyre returns as one. If they are merely killed at the hands of the vampyre, they remain dead. But once bitten, the creature's saliva invades the host's body, changing it cell by cell, and once the victim dies, either through immediate exsanguination or later death, that person will become one of the undead, typically rising from the grave no later than the next nightfall. Or, getting up and walking out of a morgue. Kaminski told us that if Dietrich's account was correct, the two Army men would no doubt turn. He said Dietrich's escape was a miracle, but he would be surprised if Johanna Liebl didn't come after him again. Vampyres, he said, especially soon after turning, frequently retain vestiges of their human existence. They are drawn to those they loved or knew, and to places they had lived, or enjoyed, while they were alive. Therefore, it was not uncommon for them to return home, asking for permission to come inside. And, at least for a while, they may set up their daytime lair close to the locations they frequented often while still alive. This can sometimes help the Slayers to locate the more recently turned victims of the vampyre. Kaminski then said something that made my blood turn cold. "What we are witnessing is what I call the 'contagion effect.' As a vampyre like Wojciech settles in a particular area, in this case, the city of Kraków, he will turn others. Of course, first, he has his way with them in the self-gratifying and sadistic manner you have seen. But they will turn. And this becomes a ripple effect of sorts and grows by exponential progression. One vampyre makes another, then two, and then those two make four, then eight, then sixteen, and so forth." This is why, Kaminski said, the slayers are so important. This contagion must never get out of hand. The faster it can be controlled, the better. While the ultimate goal is to take out the prime carrier, in this case, Wojciech, the underlings must also be destroyed before they can multiply. "Think of a set of concentric rings that will radiate out of Kraków, extending across Europe, Russia, or Africa," Kaminski said. That thought makes me sick, and truly afraid for mankind. No wonder the Magnus is so adamant about hunting down and destroying the Mortis. They are truly the first line of defense for the preservation of the human race. And human slayers like Stanislaw devote their lives to protecting all of us. Such an awesome responsibility, and a terrible burden. Unfortunately, if my math is correct, the number of Mortis in Kraków is growing rapidly, with at least four of Wojciech's victims unaccounted for. Not even counting the initial victims that disappeared from the morgue when it was under Polish control, there are the two Auschwitz guards, Magdalene Hass and Irma Koch, Frank's secretary Johanna Liebl, and the propaganda princess Gertrude Brunner. And now, I'm afraid, two more can be tallied as well—the two missing Wehrmacht soldiers, Feldwebel Günther Tanz and Obergefreiter Klaus Bauer. The contagion is spreading.

30 July 1943 –

I received reports that Dietrich had been screaming from his cell that he was innocent. And that he is afraid his former fiancée will come for him. Everyone thinks they are just the ravings of a madman. A madman and a killer. I feel terribly for the man because no one will ever believe him. Kaminski's warning that Johanna Liebl may come back for him bothers me a great deal. I wish I could move him to a holding facility under the control of the SS, where I could better protect him. The last thing we want is for yet another person to be turned and added to Wojciech's growing army of the undead. But Dietrich's in a military stockade, under the control of the Wehrmacht. I can't so much as get a crucifix to him for protection. He has many guards watching his cell, so I can only pray that they will serve as some kind of deterrence against any visit by his former lover.

31 July 1943 –

Anna and I are both lucky to be alive. If it wasn't for Stanislaw we'd be dead for sure. Or worse. All this time I had been fearing an attack by Wojciech, but what happened last night was completely unexpected. And I blame myself for leaving us so vulnerable. I should have been better prepared. It had been close, very close. The day itself had been uneventful;

there had been no new murders and no sightings of Hellriegel. I needed to complete an update I must give Reichsführer Himmler, so Anna and I left Wawel Castle a bit later than usual. It didn't take long to walk the few blocks back to my flat. Anna cooked us some dinner, which was actually my favorite—Bavarian schnitzel with spaetzle. It was around 10 p.m. when, at my suggestion, we took the plates and moved out on the balcony. The inside of the flat was insufferable, hot, and stuffy with the summer heat, so I figured we would sit outside and enjoy the slight coolness offered by the night's breeze. As Anna and I sat and ate, our conversation eventually drifted to better times. Aided by a bottle of wine I had opened, Anna and I were soon managing to laugh and, just for a while, escape the dark reality we had found ourselves in since arriving to Kraków. I could never tire of Anna's blue eyes as they twinkled in the moonlight, or when she would throw her head back, her laugh a sweet melody of song. Nor when she would continuously brush back wayward strands of her chestnut brown hair being blown by the evening's breeze. I watched all of this in the rapturous manner of a satiated addict. At some point, Anna and locked eyes with each other, both of us suddenly growing silent. The look in her eyes told me she felt the same, but then she reinforced it with words. "I'm so glad we met again, Otto. Here, in Kraków. Despite everything. Years ago…when we last met…I should have said something then. You add something so special to my life. You make me laugh, and you make me happy. A new experience for this boring scientist, I'm afraid." I smiled at her revelation and then replied. "Oh, you're far from boring, Anna. On the contrary, you are the only brightness I've ever had in my life. A life dedicated to the job, a job surrounded by death. You make me feel alive, Anna. I…I don't think I could part with you again." Before we both knew it, we both leaned over towards each other, and we kissed. Our first, and it was everything I had always thought it would be. My heart hummed like a high-voltage wire, and at that moment, I knew I was in love with her.

"Oh, how sweet," came a raspy voice from the other side of the balcony. Anna and I twirled around, surprised, the looks on our faces probably almost comical, like those of two adolescents caught in the act of their first illicit kiss. Our movements caused the bottle of wine to topple, and then shatter upon the concrete floor. "Oh, my, what a waste of good alcohol," came the voice again. My eyes could barely register its source, my brain unable to process who I was seeing. What I was seeing. It was Anna who said it first. "Max? Dr. Weber?" The thing sitting in the corner chair sat relaxed, arms on the rests, with legs crossed. Looking just like another house guest, enjoying the evening out on my balcony. Except for his clothes. He was still wearing his doctor's scrubs from the morgue, but his once immaculately clean and sanitized appearance was gone, his clothing now stained, dirty, and torn in several places. His well-groomed hair was in disarray, and his fingernails were cracked and caked with dirt. The tight skin of his face was the color of bleached parchment, and his bulging eyes looked like two grotesque orbs straining to break free of their skeletal cage. He smelled of rot and decay, and it was everything I could do to not vomit up Anna's dinner. Max's eyes shined silver in the moonlight. "I know, I know," he said. "My sudden appearance must be a bit shocking, and I apologize for just, well, dropping in." He gave another throaty chuckle, seemingly amused at his attempted witticism. Dread gnawed at my insides as I frantically thought about what I needed to do to rid us of the monster before us. "I didn't invite you," was all I could manage to say. Weber smiled, his lips stretching far wider than any human had a right to do. "Oh, I see you've been speaking to our good friend Stanislaw Kaminski. Sorry Otto, if you had remained inside, I would have needed your invitation. But out here..." he waved his hand across the balcony. "Out here, I don't. We vampyre can't enter the confines of one's home, or domicile without an invitation. The walls become physical barriers through which we cannot pass. It's all bullshit, I know. And I don't even pretend to understand it myself. Something about a man's home is his sacred castle. Anyway, do you see any walls out here?" Weber said, chuckling. Anna, ever the pragmatic scientist, went right to the main question. "Max, what happened to you...the night you left the Morgue?" The eyes of the thing that was once Dr. Weber sparkled, now taking on a reddish glow as he leaned forward, uncrossing his legs. "I was working late, intent on finishing the last autopsy. I didn't hear the doors open to the refrigerated units. The first thing I knew was when one of the SS women jumped me from behind. I felt pain when she bit into my throat, but it didn't last long. I blacked out, and when I awoke, I was lying in an alley not far from the morgue. I didn't know how I got there, I was already changed, I could tell that. I could see my surroundings through a new prism, in which everything was brighter, more colorful, and, I don't know, more vibrant. And my sense of hearing, taste, and smell was a thousand times more sensitive than before. As I sat up, I could even hear the heartbeat of a rat that was next to me. Just like your heartbeat right now, Doctor. It's beating like a drum." Anna gasped as I looked her way. Her face had turned ashen, and she had placed her hand up over her heart. Weber smiled broadly, knowing he had scared her, the sadistic son of a bitch. But then he continued. "It was still dark, but I could sense the dawn coming. My skin was already getting prickly. Then I felt hands on me...pulling me. It was my new benefactors. They took me into their lair, where I was welcomed. I became one with the Mortis. And I felt at home."

Anna wouldn't let it go. I could see a tear slide down her cheek. "But Max, you have a wife, and a son, back in Stuttgart. You can't let them go. You have to fight to stay with them. With us." Weber waved his hand dismissively. "They are gone to me, now," he said. "You could say that was the night I was reborn, Doctor. Born into a better existence. Before that, I was just like you. Living a meaningless life, going through the petty daily motions that humans do, all the while just destined for the grave and oblivion. You seek financial security, success in your careers, thrilling travel, and a comfortable home with a healthy family. And most laughable, you're taught to devote your short lives striving for intangibles such as love, compassion, respect, kindness, generosity, and all the other useless human traits. How much time you waste, Doctor! The time during which you could REALLY live, satisfying your basic emotions. Your basic cravings. To do what you want...pursuing all your sensual pleasures and sadistic fantasies. Fucking, torturing, killing...having the power and the choice to do what you want. Think of it, Doctor, fulfilling all your hedonistic desires without any judgment...or limitations."

"Max, no, it's not you," Anna cried, "you were a good man, I could tell! Please, no, this can't be happening!" The monster that used to be Dr. Max Weber threw his head back and laughed. A long, malevolent laugh that was devoid of any human warmth or humor. It sounded like it was coming from the depths of Hell itself. I knew then that Anna and I weren't going to get off that balcony alive. Not unless I could do something. I had only one thing that could maybe buy us a few seconds. But Dr. Weber was already taking the initiative. "Oh, Anna," he purred as he slowly got up out of the chair. "Don't think I never noticed that fine body you tried to hide under all your lab clothing. So slim, with perky, firm breasts. A body meant for sensual pleasures. Especially now. As a doctor, surely you are aware that at 33 years of age, you are now reaching your sexual peak. In fact, studies I have read indicated that if you measure the frequency of orgasms, women are orgasming the most often in their early 30s. You are at the apex of your sexuality, Anna. Yet you consistently deny yourself, always act so prim and proper, supposedly dedicating your life only to science. But look at you tonight, in that fine dress, a little shorter at the hem, and even showing a bit of your cleavage. You wanted Otto to fuck you, right? I could even smell it on you when I arrived. Your anticipation and desire. Your wetness."

"That's enough!" I yelled, jumping up. "Leave here! Leave here, now!" But Max just smiled even more broadly, his mouth taking on the aspect of a fanged and sphincter-like maw. My innards lurched as two long incisors slid down from his upper jaw. Curved and very sharp. Bubbles of saliva pooled around his lips in anticipatory hunger. His eyes began glowing a bright red. "I don't think so, Otto. The Master wanted me to come here tonight. To finish you. You're a thorn in his side, you see. You and that prick Kaminski. I'm not to turn you, just kill you. But sweet Anna…" Weber turned to her, wearing a lecherous leer. "…I have plans for you. I'm going to show you what a real man can do. Just a warning, it will be a bit painful at first, but you'll get used to it. You might even beg for more!" Max threw his head back and let loose a sadistic cacophony of evil laughter. I had had enough. A minute earlier, I remembered what Stanislaw had placed in my suit coat pocket the last time we met, telling me to keep it close in the event I needed it, and I thanked almighty God that he had done so. I took out the blessed crucifix and slapped the Max-thing on the right cheek, hard. It was a good smack, hard and straight on. Max howled and reeled backward, clutching at his face. I could see the skin sizzling, darkening in the shape of the cross. Even being outside, I could smell the burning flesh as the smoke caught the night's breeze. I grabbed Anna's arm, trying to pull her inside the flat. But she was still sitting, and it took too many precious seconds before she could push the chair back and get on her feet. By the time she did, I felt a hand tear at my shoulder, long claws digging through my clothes and into my skin. I barely could register that it was Max, because he was transforming into something even more monstrous, more hideous. He shed his clothes as his body became more bulbous, growing a thick black fur as I watched. His arms became impossibly long, and a fleshy membrane of skin expanded from his chest, attaching to his arms and forming spines that soon clearly became translucent, bat-like wings. I watched in horror as Max's nose split into a fleshy, pointed protuberance, becoming snout-like, and his ears elongated to long, banana-like ears, filling with the same black hair as his torso. His eyes became wider in their sockets, giving him a dog-like appearance. He had become, in all appearance, a large black bat.

I let out a scream as Max's claws dug deeper into my flesh. Before I knew it, he had picked me up like I was a rag doll and threw me across the table. I landed on the other side of the balcony, slamming into the side of the railing. I was lucky; a little higher, and I might have sailed over the top, falling four stories down to the plaza below. As I sat, stunned, I watched through blurred eyes as the Max-Bat-Thing advanced on Anna. It had just reached her, its claws reaching out, and with open wings ready to envelop her into a cocoon of death, when I saw a man step out onto the balcony. With a practiced snap of his wrist, he cast out a stream of liquid from an open vial in his hand. The spray hit Max across his wings, and they immediately began to smoke and sizzle. I realized it was holy water. Max back peddled, screeching as the trail of smoke followed him. Before he could recover, the man took out a long knife and thrust it right into Max's side. He took it out and thrust it back in again, this time twisting it back and forth. The vampyre gave out an unholy shriek and then collapsed to his knees. As I got back up on my feet, Max toppled over, and I could see a horrendous black ichor pouring out of the wound on his side. It pooled on the floor of the balcony, rancid and foul-smelling. "Stanislaw," I managed to croak out. I watched as he took out another vial of holy water and poured it over the blade of the knife. In the moonlight, I could easily see the inscription etched into the blade: *Deus lux mea est.* He kneeled down and began sawing off Max's head. I looked over to Anna, who was now sitting on the floor, her back against the railing on the far side of the balcony. She looked uninjured, thank God. I could see she was watching with clinical interest as Stanislaw performed his gruesome task. As a forensic scientist, she knew as much as I did about the difficult and bloody task that Stanislaw was undertaking. The human head, because it sits on top of the spinal column, requires less musculature at the back of the neck. There is so little muscle in our necks that you can quite easily feel the main blood vessels, the lymph nodes, and the vertebrae through the skin. In short, it is much easier to decapitate a human than a deer, a lion, or any of the other animals that are more usually associated with hunting trophies. But nevertheless, this is not to say beheading is easy. Human necks may be, compared to other mammals, quite flimsy, but separating heads from bodies is still hard to do. Even when the executioner or assassin is experienced, it can take many blows to cut off a person's head. Thomas Arthur, comte de Lally, the famous French general, was executed in 1766, before the French Revolution and the invention of the guillotine. When he knelt, still and blindfolded, the executioner's axe failed to sever his head. He toppled forward and had to be repositioned, and even then, it took four or five blows to decapitate him. Then there was Mary, Queen of Scots, who famously needed three strikes to sever her head in 1587. The first hit the back of her head, while the second left a small sinew which had to be sawn through with the axe blade. Even when the victim is already dead, severing the head can be difficult. When Oliver Cromwell's three-year-old corpse was decapitated during his posthumous execution at Tyburn, it took the axe man eight blows to cut through the layers of cerecloth that wrapped his body and finish the job. The terrible truth is, that the swift decapitation of a living person requires a powerful, accurate action, and a sharp, heavy blade. Watching Stanislaw do his business reinforced that beheading is an extremely bloody business, both brutal and effective. When he was nearly done, having sawed through skin, muscle, sinew, and spinal bone, I could hear Stanislaw recite the scared words *Adjure te, spiritus nequissime, per Deum omnipotentem.* He then placed the disembodied head on top of the vampyre's deflated chest. Max's eyes looked like two grotesque orbs straining to break free of their skeletal cage, and his mouth was frozen in a rictus scream. His blood, black and foul-smelling, pooled all around the body. A beheading is a vicious and defiant act of savagery, and I supposed that was what made it a fitting end to the evil scourge that is the Mortis Vampyre.

As it turned out, Stanislaw had stopped by to pass on a lead he had on Ernst Hellriegel. When I failed to answer the door, he "let himself in." As I have now come to learn, Stan is a man of many talents. When he heard the commotion on the balcony, he immediately came out and saw the attack on Anna. "A textbook dispatch," he told us later. "That's how it's done." And I am forever grateful. Not for saving my own life, but for saving Anna's. I owe Stan a debt that can never be adequately repaid.

Continuation Entry: Now, on to the events of today. On the way to Wawel Castle, Anna and I grabbed a copy of the *Krakauer Zeitung*, a German-controlled newspaper published by the General Government for public consumption. The arrest of Hauptmann Dietrich is now front-page news. His picture was prominently displayed, along with those of the soldiers Bauer and Tanz. Upon reading the article, it appears the newspaper is already shaping the story that Dietrich viciously killed the two men during some kind of drunken altercation. A nice, clean narrative that excludes any of Dietrich's rantings about his fiancée coming back from the dead. The story also conveniently glosses over the fact that Dietrich had no blood at all on him when he was found, nor does it address the issue of what Dietrich did with the bodies and how he could have even picked two large men and moved them on his own. Both men outweighed Dietrich by about 23 kilos. It's obvious that Hans Frank is going to let Dietrich take the rap. At least one murder case was solved, all tied up with a nice neat bow.

After arriving at the Castle, I immediately assembled the rest of the investigatory team and briefed them on last night's attack. That the vampyre hadn't been Wojciech but our missing former colleague, Dr. Max Weber. And that he was nothing like the gregarious and friendly coroner he was before, that he had become a vile, sadistic monster who surely would have raped Anna and killed me if Stanislaw Kaminski hadn't intervened. I described how Stanislaw had used the spray of holy water to burn and disorientate Weber, followed by a thrust of the silver knife to incapacitate him, and finally, the final coup de grâce with the decapitation. Afterward, Stan had taken the body, saying he would have it cremated so that no trace remains. We thought that best, rather than reporting the once-missing doctor had been found with his head cut off. Kraków already had too many gristly murders in the news, and there was no sense in seeing Hans Frank go on another tirade. I told the team this was a cautionary tale, and we all needed to double down on our safety measures. Everyone needed to keep a vial of holy water with them at all times, as well as a blessed crucifix, to protect themselves if attacked. When I was finished, everyone was silent for a time. They realized that things had gone way past just receiving a warning to lay off. We now were all potential targets for assassination. Either at night, in the gristly embrace of a vampyre, or by day, at the mortal hands of some Mortis familiar. Felix, ever the stalwart soul, broke the silence by saying, "Uh, I think I need to pay another visit to the underground church. We're going to need a shitload more holy water."

At least I had a bit of potentially good news to pass on. I told the team that Kaminski has a lead on Hellriegel's whereabouts. The lead was passed to Stan from a Magnus familiar who believes that he spotted Hellriegel in the small village of Dobczyce, about 30 kilometers southeast of Kraków. Earlier, Stan had passed out a photograph of Hellriegel to all his operatives. It was Hellriegel's official SS file photo, which I had provided him. The man just happened to have one in his pocket to make a comparison when he saw Hellriegel come into the small bierstube he was in to have a drink. It was just by chance that the operative, who lived in Kraków, had stopped by the small village to see a friend. He reported that the man, believed to be Hellriegel, wasn't in uniform but wore a dark jacket over a shabby-looking pair of khaki trousers. He was quite a bit thinner than in the photo, but the resemblance was still unmistakable. The familiar made note of Hellriegel's eyes, however. "They looked sunken," he recounted later, "with puffy skin and black rings underneath. Like a man who hasn't slept in days. Or a man haunted by things he shouldn't have seen." After he had finished his drink, Hellriegel left the establishment without speaking with anyone. The informant couldn't leave his friend to follow Hellriegel, but he watched as he cut across the road on foot and disappeared into the woods. For me, what proved to be the conclusive piece of evidence that the man seen in Dobczyce was indeed Hellriegel was the drink he was seen to have ordered. A shot of Jägermeister, a dark German liqueur, which I had seen him drink on several occasions. The narcissistic bastard would always boast that, as a KRIPO murder investigator, he was indeed a Jägermeister—a "master hunter." With the sighting confirmed, I put out an alert to the local SS and security forces around Dobczyce to be on the lookout for Ernst Hellriegel, and to arrest him on sight.

1 August 1943 –

Last night was quiet and uneventful, thank God. Anna and I stayed in the flat after dark, and we made sure to affix a crucifix on the outside door of the balcony. Manfred, Felix, Elsie and Hans did the same at their respective flats. Stanislaw had told me he wouldn't make our nightly meeting, so Anna and I spent the evening playing Schafkopf, a card game very popular back home in my native Bavaria. Bavarians consider it their "national" card game, although of course, with the rise of the Nazis we lost the "Frei Stadt Bayern" status we had enjoyed since 1918. We needed four people to play, and fortunately, we found two neighbors in the building who knew the game well. Both were from Bavaria. There was Oskar from Fürth, a civil engineer brought in by the General Government to reconstruct Kraków in the spirit of other great cities of the Third Reich. Kraków was chosen by Hitler as the capital of the General Government, and Poland's spiritual heart will eventually be rebuilt to become a racially pure metropolis, a flagship German city in the East— the *uralte deutsche Stadt Krakau,* or "ancient German city." There was only one inconvenient problem, though. Up until the occupation, Kraków had been a major Jewish cultural and religious center, so before the city could be Germanised, the Jews needed to be removed, along with the Poles. Now that the Kraków ghetto has been all but cleared out with the mass deportations to the camps and the Jewish population of the city cleansed, engineers and city planners like Oskar are now free to design and establish pure German neighborhoods. The fourth player was Helga from Bayreuth, who is a bookkeeper with the Reich Ministry of Economics. She no doubt was sent to Kraków to work in collaboration with the SS Main Economic and Administrative Office, which had the mission of exploiting slave labor for armaments manufacture and construction projects. In the past few weeks, I've learned that all in all, there are around 457 camp complexes in German-occupied Poland. The major concentration and slave labor camps consist of dozens of subsidiary camps scattered over a broad area. Millions of camp inmates are used virtually for free by dozens of major German corporations like Krupp, IG Farben, Bosch, Diamler-Benz, Volkswagen, Messerschmitt, and Siemens. It's big business, and as with any successful business, meticulous and detailed bookkeeping is essential. I suppose it would be easy for me to judge both Oskar and Helga, each having a role in the destruction and exploitation of the Polish people. But then I have to remind myself that they are just low-level functionaries in the overall Nazi machine. They are decent people with pleasant personalities and loving families—Oskar has a wife and two children back in Germany. They're not monsters like Hellriegel. But yet I wonder…someday we Germans are going to be held to account for the horrendous things we've done not only to Poland but in all the occupied lands. Will we be able to defend our actions by explaining we were just cogs in the system, that we were, well, just following orders? Is someone like Helga, a bookkeeper of blood money, any less complicit in the exploitation and suffering of the Poles than the SS guards of the camps? Time will tell. And I have a feeling Germany's reckoning is not that far into the future.

Today was the first of August, and I owed an update to Reichsführer-SS Himmler on the Kraków murder case. Initially, he wanted me to fly back to Berlin for a formal presentation, but I convinced him that doing so would take too much time away from working the case. Himmler acquiesced, and I was able to brief him by telephone from Han Frank's office. Kraków Police chief Scherner also sat in. We put the call through at 0900 hours. Himmler seemed irritable and preoccupied. He pointedly remarked that today marked exactly twenty days since I arrived in Kraków, and yet I had made little progress in identifying and arresting the killer. His impatience to have the killer caught and the case closed was clearly evident. I had prepared a briefing that I hoped would indicate some progress and have a positive spin to it. Of course, it was total bullshit. Only my team knew that we were not pursuing a mortal man. I needed a story for Himmler that would buy us more time in the hopes of tracking the vampyre Wojciech down. Himmler wanted a sign of progress, so I was going to give it to him. I reminded the Reichsführer that we had developed a solid psychological profile of the killer and that it had been instrumental in focusing police attention on the critical areas of the city where he would most likely frequent as he searched for potential victims. That hopefully put us one step ahead of the killer. In addition, we have increased our numbers of undercover KRIPO officers, both male and female, throughout the city, looking for any indicators of the behavior associated with the killer. We also have recruited an entire stable of informants amongst the German population in Kraków to report any suspicious behavior seen among their friends, neighbors, and co-workers. Finally, and perhaps more importantly, I noted that there had been no further killings since Gertrude Brunner's murder on 17 July, some 14 days or two weeks previous. This was a welcome development and may indicate the killer had himself been killed. If he was Polish (Himmler will never consider that the killer could be one of the German occupiers), there is the possibility he had been rounded up and either executed or sent to one of the labor camps. Of course, the lack of murders could also mean the killer had just moved on to some other killing ground in Poland or elsewhere. The bottom line was that either way, with the absence of any more murders, we had no further evidence that could provide leads and move us forward in the case. I knew Himmler wasn't happy with that lack of closure, but what I told him seemed to placate him for the time being. "Very good, Otto. It's a good sign the attacks on German personnel have seemed to have stopped. Let's hope the murderous bastard finds himself in one of the camps, where he will be dealt with accordingly."

Himmler's next question was addressed to Frank. "Hans," he asked, "where are we with the Brunner thing? The woods were thoroughly searched around the crash site. So, what happened to her body? If it was the Polish resistance, then why didn't they take credit? Is there any update?" Frank replied that, under his direction, the General Government had rounded up and interrogated hundreds of suspected resistance figures, seeking verification that there had indeed been a Polish plot to bring down the plane. He spoke coldly and dispassionately about the various torture methods used to elicit their confessions. But in the end, the interrogations hadn't produced anything definitive. Under Frank's orders, all of them, including around 30 women, were taken out and summarily shot. The fat bastard is one cold son of a bitch. But I can't help but share the guilt. Only I know what truly became of Brunner, and I know all the Poles Frank had executed had no blood on their hands. It's on mine.

Then Himmler threw a curveball. "I heard there is an army Hauptmann arrested there in Kraków who killed two other soldiers. He is claiming he saw his old fiancée, Johanna Liebl. Isn't that your secretary that was killed, Hans? Whose body was supposedly stolen from the morgue?" Frank shot me a surprised glance, then cleared his throat. It was clear he never told Himmler anything more than what had been printed in the *Krakauer Zeitung*. "The ramblings of a madman, Heinrich," Frank replied. "It's clear that Hauptmann Dietrich had some kind of mental breakdown. He claimed his dead fiancée came to him in the same alley where he killed his fellow soldiers. Liebl had already been dead 18 days by then. And nearly two weeks after her body was stolen. The man is off his rocker, and right now, he is being kept in a padded cell before his courts-martial." I could hear Himmler as he let out a grunt, having made his point but having no reason to pursue the matter further.

"Alright," Himmler continued, "so tell me where we are at with SS-Haupsturmführer Ernst Hellriegel. Hans, what steps has the General Government taken to track him down?" Frank shot me another glance, but this time he smiled. He was going to throw that hot potato back into my court and let Himmler know Hellriegel's disappearance was an SS issue. After all, Frank worked for Hitler and was not answerable to Himmler. In the early days, before becoming the Governor-General of Poland, Hans Frank had been Hitler's personal legal advisor, and later, after the Nazis came to power in January 1933, he served as the lawyer for the Party. "I believe Standartenführer Geisler has an update for you, Heinrich," Frank smoothly replied. I nodded at Frank; I had foreseen this question and was ready. "Based upon an informant's tip, we had reason to believe Haupsturmführer Hellriegel had been holding up somewhere around the Wieliczka salt mine, just outside of Kraków. We meticulously searched the entire mine, all nine levels, taking most of the day. In the end, we found where he had been staying, in an abandoned pumping shack on the mountainside just above the mine. We think we had just missed him. But then yesterday, another tip came in from someone who spotted Hellriegel in the small village of Dobczyce, about 30 kilometers southeast of here. All resources have been dispatched to the area. Our instructions are to arrest him on sight, and if he resists, to shoot to kill." Himmler grunted again, then replied, "Well done, Otto. This Hellriegel is a complete disgrace to the SS. And in particular to the professionalism of the KRIPO. I know you must be taking that very personally. I have complete confidence that you are doing all you can to find him. Please notify me immediately when you have." With that, we exchanged our Heil Hitlers, and Frank hung up the phone. As I turned to leave, Frank cleared his throat and asked, "Otto, I heard your team took out bags of evidence from the shack where Hellriegel was hiding out. You didn't mention that to the Reichsführer. What was in them?" I had also prepared for this question. I was not willing to frame the murders on Hellriegel just yet. "Some of Hellriegel's clothing and personal effects. We're hoping Anna can get some clues off of them to indicate where else he has been, just in case the Dobczyce tip doesn't pan out." Frank seemed satisfied with that, and I promised to update him as soon as I obtained anything significant.

Later in the afternoon, Anna got with me to let me know the results of her forensic tests of the mattress we found at the salt mine. "It was saturated with dried semen," she reported, "and a lot of it. And all the sperm cells were in autolysis, the same as the other samples." As I stared at Anna, I knew I had to ask the question that I probably didn't want the answer to. "Why so much semen on the mattress? Didn't he just use it to flop down on, uh, while sleeping during the day? Anna shook her head sadly. "Otto, I found trace amounts of other fluids, too. Female vagina fluids. And blood. Real human blood. Was hard to see since the mattress was so filthy. But there's a mixture of all of it—Wojciech's semen, women's vaginal fluids, and blood." I felt bile rise in my throat as I considered the next question. "You said women...plural." Anna nodded sadly. "Yes, Otto. Women. It's hard to tell, but from blood typing, it looks like there are at least six. He was bringing women back to his lair to, well..." Anna's voice faltered, and she was unable to finish. I felt the realization rock me like a middle-weight's left hook. "To continue feasting upon his female victims," I concluded. "An unholy meal of rape and depraved sexual sadism, of deliciously ravaged flesh and exquisite pain and delight. But just as the cat eventually tires of playing with the mouse, the vampyre eventually moves in for the real prize. The feast is concluded with the eternal wine of human blood, the Vampyre sexually climaxing as the hot spurts of the coppery elixir fill his mouth and throat. No, that lair we discovered wasn't just a sanctuary from the sun's rays, it was also a pleasure chamber for his unholy fantasies. My God, the torments those women would have received are unimaginable." Without another word, Anna fell into my arms, and I embraced her tightly. It was such a terrible realization. We had always assumed only the rapes and murders we had investigated were the extent of the vampyre's carnage. But clearly, there are many more women we haven't identified. Women who suffered in ways that no one should have to do, dying most horrendously. But the worst thing of all…those women are still out there, looking forward to their own feast of the damned.

2 August 1943 –

This turned out to be a day like no other. Just when I think I've seen enough death and denigration. A day when bad news comes in and just keeps rolling in all day. It all started when I was contacted by the overnight KRIPO duty officer. I received the phone call a little after 4:30 a.m. He reported what appeared to be a double homicide. A young German couple named Klaus and Irma Fischer. The husband's body had been found in their flat next to Jagiellonian University in the Old Town District, not far from my place on Adolf Hitler Platz. The wife appeared to have been murdered in the bedroom. I was told the couple worked for the Reich Ministry of Science, Education and National Culture, apparently as some form of caretaker of the university, which has, along with the rest of Poland's higher and secondary education, been closed since the war began in 1939. I later learned that close to 200 of the university's professors had been arrested by SS Chief Krüger under *Sonderaktion Krakau*, and deported on cattle trains to the camps. All part of the elimination of the Polish intelligentsia as Kraków is re-shaped as the new German city of the East. I immediately called Manfred and told him to get with Felix and meet me at the crime scene. Before leaving, I asked Anna to call Stanislaw and have him meet me there as well. He had previously provided us with a contact number in the event we needed to link up outside of our nightly meetings. I had a feeling this double homicide was not going to be just a normal murder. After telling Anna I would meet her later at the office, I set off on the 15-minute walk to the Fischer residence. By then, it was a little after 5 a.m. and sunrise. It was early, but the August day was already beginning to get hot. Nevertheless, the morning walk through the Old Town area was pleasant, and the rising sun was a welcome respite from the darkness of the night. Soon, I arrived at the block of flats where the Fischers lived. I was taken aback to see Stanislaw was already standing outside. "It's apparently a double homicide," I told him. "Husband and wife. Don't know if it's the Mortis, but the odds are pretty good." Stanislaw nodded. "Glad you called. I was in the area anyway." I wasn't surprised at that. The man's like a ghost—everywhere and anywhere. The building was nondescript and consisted of three stories, with around thirty tenants. We walked the stairs to the third floor, to flat #34, and met the Ordnungspolizei officers who had reported to the call and secured the crime scene. After introducing Stanislaw as a colleague, I asked the officers to give me a quick run-down. They related that one of the tenants in the building had contacted the police after smelling something coming from the Fischer's flat. They went in and found the husband in the living room, dead. He had been dead for several days, they concluded. It appeared the wife had been murdered in the bedroom, but they couldn't find her body. I told the officers to stay and guard the front door. They nodded, faces ashen, clearly not relishing the thought of having to go back inside. I couldn't blame them, as even from the closed doorway, I could smell the odor of death. For the uninitiated, nothing smells as foul as a decomposing body. During the human decomposition process, dozens of different types of gases are released. During my career, most people have associated the stench to be akin to rotting fish, feces, mothballs, rotten eggs, rotten cabbage, and garlic. After one of the officers opened the door and I proceeded across the threshold, I nearly gagged from the horrific smell and was forced to pull out a handkerchief to cover my mouth and nose. To my amazement, Stanislaw looked unfazed by the foulness of the air. He was like an old soldier who had encountered death so many times on the battlefield he had become hardened to its stark reality. We proceeded down a narrow hallway that had a bathroom off to the right. It was then that I first heard the insidious buzzing of something coming from the far end of the hall. The sound got louder as I drew closer until it sounded like I was about to enter a hive of a thousand angry bees. When we stepped into the main room, which was a living room with an adjoining kitchen, we stopped cold. Sitting in a chair was a man, who I assumed was Klaus Fischer. But I wasn't sure. Nobody was going to be sure until an autopsy was performed. Because it was impossible to make his face out. It was covered with a black mask of pulsating blow flies, busily at work impregnating the skin with their horrific eggs, many of them already hatching and releasing a nightmare of white maggots that were coursing through the man's flesh. I watched in horror as maggots were winding their way out of the man's eyes, nose, and mouth, so many of them that they were dropping onto his chest and lap, where they would find new flesh upon which to burrow. Hundreds of the white worms had also dropped to the floor and almost seemed to be slithering their way towards us. I took an involuntary step backward in revulsion. This had been no recent murder; the man was clearly in the bloat stage of decomposition. His belly and extremities were swollen nearly twice their normal size with fluid and gasses, a new bacterial community now growing inside of him. "The open window," Stanislaw pointed out, "the summer heat and humidity from outside has sped up the decomposition process. And allowed the flies to make quick work of him. But look at his neck, and his blood-soaked shirt." I nodded. "Looks like a good chunk of his throat was ripped out. Bled out so quickly he didn't even get up out of the chair. Poor bastard." Just then, I heard additional voices enter the flat. Manfred and Felix. "Holy Fuck," muttered Manfred through his handkerchief as he entered the room, staring at the bloated, fly-infested body. "This might make me lose the wonderful schnitzel dinner my Fräulein friend made for me last night." Felix's eyes sparkled, and I could almost see him smiling behind his own handkerchief when he laughed, "You can stand to lose a few pounds, Herr Obersturmbannführer. We just passed the bathroom in case you need it." Manfred glared back at the younger officer. Technically, Felix was insubordinate to his superior, but the mutual respect and admiration between both men were too strong for Manfred to hold him to account. Manfred ignored the quip and turned to me. "So, where's the wife?" he asked. I pointed to the bedroom door. "We were told she was probably murdered in the bedroom, but there wasn't a body. Let's go take a look." We all exchanged glances and steeled ourselves for what we would likely see. If the husband were bad, the scene of the wife's killing would probably be much, much worse. For some unknown reason, the killer had left the door to the bedroom closed. Mercifully, the frenzied feeding of the flies would be confined to the ill-fated husband. I opened the door, and we stepped inside. I immediately noted that the room was in complete shambles. A table had been overturned, its contents ejected throughout the room. A lamp was smashed, and broken shards littered the floor. Picture frames had been torn off the wall and were smashed to pieces. The bed had been nearly overturned, and twisted sheets hung to the floor. Whoever had torn the room apart had been in a complete frenzy. There were splatters of blood on the mattress, no doubt from the wife. "So where's the body?" asked Felix. "She's gone," announced Stanislaw grimly. "We're too late. She turned and became one of the undead days ago." Manfred pointed to the mattress. "Not much blood, but the mattress is damp. Some spots are downright soaked." Before I could warn him, Manfred reached down and touched the ruined mattress and then brought his fingers to his nose and sniffed. "Christ almighty!" he exclaimed in revulsion, "Is this shit what I think it is?" "Yes," replied Stanislaw. "The vampyre is insatiable...and virile." Manfred broke away to go wash his hands in the bathroom sink. "That'll teach the old fart to touch evidence without gloves," Felix snickered. I shot him a disapproving glance, then turned to Stanislaw. "Judging from the husband's condition, I'm guessing all this happened two or three days ago. Maybe right after you killed Max Weber." The inference hung in the air for a few moments. I didn't mean for it to sound as accusatory as it did, and I regretted my words as soon as they left my mouth. But Stanislaw merely nodded in agreement. "Yes, it could be retaliation. The vampyre does not like losing one of their own. But it could also be a signal, another warning to leave things alone. To leave HIM alone. He clearly wants to demonstrate he can strike anyone, anywhere. So, he goes out and selects this random couple. He had no interest in the husband and killed him right away. The husband wasn't bitten, or he would have turned. Then, he takes the wife and ravages her in the bedroom. Now, she's standing by Wojciech's side, one of his growing minions. Klaus and Irma Fischer were innocents. Their only mistake was inviting the stranger into their flat. But to have done this because of Weber...well, perhaps. But it's a war, Otto. We can't protect all the innocents. And we can't let something like this deter us from going after the source of the evil...the source of all the pain, anguish, and destruction. Nothing, and I mean nothing, will ever stop me from my goal of eradicating that pestilence from the face of the earth. I will destroy Wojciech, or die trying." And as I looked into Stanislaw's steely eyes, I believed his every word.

A little after 7:30 a.m. I had just gotten off the phone with Hans Ziegler to let him know he could expect a body to arrive at the morgue that was in severe decomposition. We were just getting ready to head to Wawel Castle when I received word that there had been another double homicide in another flat, this one east of Old Town, in the Grzegórzki district of Kraków. I knew then we were in for a long day. Manfred, Felix, Stanislaw, and I drove over together. When we arrived, we were greeted at the street entrance by the Ordnungspolizei who had secured the site, as well as the neighbor who had made the call to the police. An Ordnungspolizei officer by the name of Schultz briefed us that the victims were a married couple, Gerhard and Frieda Kessler. In their late 20's, both were employees of the Reichsbank, and worked at one of the branches not far from their flat. The neighbor told us he had called the police after seeing a man leave the Kessler's third-floor flat. He had thought this very odd since the Kesslers never had visitors and certainly never in the middle of the night. He lived right across the hall and so had gotten a pretty good look at the guy through the peephole. The stranger had initially caught the neighbor's attention by the way he had been dressed. "The man was very dapper," the neighbor told us. "He was wearing an impeccable suit, very stylish, complete with a flashy pocket square. He wore a gold chain around his neck with some medallion. There was some image on it, I don't know…kind of like a scythe. You know, like the farmers use to cut down wheat. He came out the door and began to walk down the hallway but then stopped. He turned around and looked back. Not at the Kessler's place but at mine! I swear to God, it seemed like he knew I was on the other side of the door. I was never so scared in my life. He didn't look right. He was gaunt, with sunken eyes that looked red. You know, like one of those albino people. His face was so very pale, and even from the peephole, I could see the dark veins underneath the skin. I was petrified he was going to walk back towards my door. But he simply turned back around and walked away. And he was whistling. It was enough to chill my blood. My eyes were fixated on him until he left my view. I then looked back to the Kessler's front door. The man hadn't even closed it. And that's when I saw it. There was blood smeared on the doorknob. I hadn't looked at the stranger's hands, but it had to have come from him. I wanted to go check on the Kesslers, but I was terrified the man might still be there, lurking just down the hallway, waiting for me to come out. That's when I immediately called the police." Schultz concluded by telling us his team had answered the call and, after going inside, found the couple. "It's a horrendous sight, Inspector," Schultze said, his face grim. "Just be prepared. The condition of the woman is…well, you'll see for yourself. The killer is Goddamn psycho for sure." I couldn't help but think that if a seasoned police officer working amid the death and suffering that we have witnessed in this cursed war is rattled by what he saw up in that flat, then it must truly be a terrible sight. I nodded to him in acknowledgment and then turned to go upstairs.

As the neighbor had described, there was blood on the door handle to the Kessler's flat. The inside handle also. Upon entering, there was a small vestibule with a coat rack. A small stand had been overturned, and a lamp was on the floor. Everything else looked normal as we entered the Kessler's family room. Schultze had already told us that both bodies were in the bedroom, but we examined all the rooms we walked past, looking for anything out of the ordinary. But everything else looked in its place. The bedroom was at the far end of the flat. The door was open, but the room was dark. I went in first and turned on the light switch. There was an audible gasp from all the men as we stepped inside. In a way, maybe I would have welcomed a bloated and deteriorating corpse like Klaus Fischer's over what I saw in that bedroom. If I thought that Gertrude Brunner had died most horribly, raped and sodomized, the fate of Frieda Kessler was far, far worse. Similar to Brunner, Kessler was lying on her back, in bed, completely nude. Her long blonde hair cascaded around her face, still beautiful and unmarred, unlike the rest of her body. As with Brunner, her breasts had been bitten off, leaving a chest that resembled raw hamburger. But here, the similarities ended. Frieda Kessler had rope tied around her ankles, pulling both of her legs back up and over her head towards the headboard, where the rope was tied off. The effect was a lurid, sadomasochistic manifestation of the "missionary" sexual position. Her vagina, under normal circumstances, would have been predominantly displayed, ready for her erstwhile husband's penetration. Only now, it was a ruined mess. The woman's entire pubic area was one bloody maw. And that wasn't the worst of it. Her entire abdomen was ripped open as well. Not cut neatly from the outside, but judging from the flaps of skin and muscle that were flayed backward, now laying against the skin of what was left of her stomach, it looked like something massive had penetrated her from below and exited her abdomen. Like a harpoon, I thought crazily. Only much wider.

Something massive and with tremendous force behind it. She was basically eviscerated with the force of the penetration. She should have bled out very quickly, but although the bed was bloody, there was not nearly as much as it should have been with that kind of massive wound. Judging from her chalk-white complexion and the lack of lividity in her lower extremities, she didn't have any blood left in her body. No, despite the massive damage to her lower abdomen, the cause of death looked to be the bite that could be seen on her neck. There were two large jagged puncture marks, surrounded by several needle-like holes, all ringed by a still bright red welt. "The bite of a vampyre is lamprey-like," Stanislaw said as if reading my mind. "The creature latches on with rows of small, hooked teeth. The two curved incisors slash through the throat and penetrate the jugular vein. The lips clamp down to perform a tight seal, hence the red ring surrounding the bite. The vampyre's saliva contains a clot-dissolving substance that keeps the victim's blood flowing, allowing it to feed more efficiently. With a perfect seal maintained, the vampyre maintains a controlled, suctioned drain of the victim's blood, wasting precious little of it. The human body contains about four pints of blood, and the vampyre can drain this amount within just a few minutes." "Jesus," muttered Felix, "it looks like her stomach exploded. What the hell did he use?" Stanislaw shook his head sadly. "Batowski didn't use anything external, Sturmbannführer. He was in his true form when he did this. Do not think of the anatomy of a human male. The vampyre, in its true, bat-like form, has a much different physiology. This allows him to not just rape a woman, but to literally disembowel her. This is why the vampyre is a true demon; it derives its sexual pleasure from the pain and torment it inflicts. This poor woman went through hell before Wojciech satiated himself. The bite to her neck brought a welcomed death." I had no doubt Stanislaw was right. As I examined the bed, I noted the whitish stains, now dried and flaky, that populated nearly every inch of the sheets. The bite would have been a merciful end to the sadism inflicted on the poor woman.

"The husband's been bitten also," Felix stated as he kneeled over the man's corpse that lay on the floor next to the bed. "Same bite marks. And he's been sodomized as well. Poor bastard." I walked over and took a look. Gerhard Kessler was probably once a handsome man—tall, slim, with dark hair and chiseled features. Now, his face was a ruined mess. His nose was smashed, most of his teeth were missing, and one ear had been bitten off. He was still wearing what looked like a pajama top, but the bottom was missing. He was naked below the waist, and what looked like a broken end to one of the nightstands had been thrust into his anus. "Look at his hands," I pointed out. "A lot of abrasion to the knuckles. He put up a good fight. Judging from the pajamas and the wreckage in the other room, my guess is that both Kesslers were in bed for the night when Wojciech knocked on the front door. Gerhard goes to answer the door, and somehow, Wojciech gets invited in. There's a slight struggle, and Gerhard gets dragged back to the bedroom. He continues to fight, but he's no match for the vampyre. Gerhard is killed in front of his wife, and when he's done, Wojciech turns to Frieda." My eyes were drawn away from the hapless husband when I heard Manfred speak. "Gentlemen, it appears our over-sexed friend left us a message." I turned around, and Manfred was pointing to the wall behind us. When we walked into the room, we were so focused on the death scene in front of us that we missed it. The bedroom wall was a light sky blue, probably chosen for its benign and calming color. It was now marred with large, rust-brown letters that had been written with Frieda Kessler's own blood. Just two words: "BACK OFF." "You were right, Stanislaw," I told the old man. "Wojciech is warning us to stay out of his way. To stop investigating him...stop trying to find him. I have a feeling that this may be the first time anyone other than you and the Magnus vampyre slayers has been after him so relentlessly. Now he has us, KRIPO detectives, just petty humans, on his trail as well. We're on the trail of the vampyre, and he doesn't like it. Not at all." Stanislaw turned, and I could see his thin face was masked with a fierce resolve. "Good," he said, looking at all of us, "the centuries have made him overconfident. If his confidence is now rattled, he may slip up or make some mistake. Sayeth the Lord, 'I will punish the world for its evil, and the wicked for their iniquity; I will put an end to the pomp of the arrogant, and lay low the pompous pride of the ruthless.'"

After we checked the rest of the flat, Stanislaw took me aside. "Otto, we will need to take care of the bodies after you get them to the morgue. Tonight. As soon as the sun sets, they will awaken as one of the undead. They've both been bitten, and this is a certainty. And this time, we don't want them to escape. There has already been too much growth in the infection. Your coroner, Dr. Ziegler, is privy, yes?" I nodded. I had never thought of it in biological terms, but the vampiric curse was indeed an infection. Left unchecked, it would keep growing. Too many of Wojciech's victims had already been allowed to rise and walk off and out into the night. It was agreed we would meet at the morgue just before sunset. We would then deal with Klaus and Irma Fischer. They deserved the blessings of eternal sleep after enduring the horrific and painful deaths that ended their lives.

When we got back to Wawel, it was already mid-afternoon. We were all starving, having missed lunch, so Elsie went out to bring back some sandwiches from a local café. I filled Anna in on both sets of murders and what we had found. Her face was grim as I described the nature of Frieda Kessler's wounds. "We're going to need forensic testing of both bodies and the mattress, too," I told her. "Although I have no doubt what you're going to find. The same results as before. But maybe there is a clue in there somewhere. We need another break. Something to point us in the right direction. And you need to do the bodies ASAP. Stanislaw is going to meet us in the morgue before sunset. This time, we're not going to let Wojciech add to his stable of followers."

I spent the rest of the afternoon preparing some notes on the murders. I knew that at some point, I needed to brief Frank, but I couldn't afford to go see him and get tied up for the rest of the day. Around 7:30 p.m., I left for the city morgue. It was a short walk from Wawel Castle, and I had plenty of time before sunset, which was forecasted for 8:20 p.m. When I got there, Hans Ziegler was just wrapping up the autopsies of the Kesslers. Anna was there too, both of them in scrubs and masks. When she saw me, Anna smiled as she took off her mask. She no doubt was tired, but she still managed to look radiant. I watched as Hans draped sheets over both bodies, and I noted he had already stitched up the "Y" incision on their chests. After he and Anna had washed up and taken off their gowns, Hans took us to another room that served as his office. "I took full blood and fluid samples from both victims," Anna started. "Also, we found samples of male pubic hair on the woman. Skin scrapings recovered some foreign material from the husband's knuckles and from underneath the wife's fingernails. I'll get everything tested as soon as possible." Hans took a seat, looking glad to be off his feet, before he started summarizing the autopsies. "The husband was nearly beaten to death; all his injuries were pre-mortem. The leg from the nightstand was shoved into his anus with so much force that it completely destroyed the rectum, tore through the large intestine, lacerated the small intestine, and penetrated through the bladder, mesentery, stomach, and up to the liver. From these wounds, he would have eventually bled out, but it would have been slow, and you would have found tremendous amounts of blood at the scene. But before that happened, the killer inflicted the throat wound and began feeding on the blood. I would guess the vampyre's feeding takes place exclusively premortem. Ironically, a living heart greatly facilitates the feeding process. As long as the heart continues to pump, the stream of blood will remain high. Gradually, as the heart's beating slows, so does the blood pressure, and the volume of blood decreases accordingly. In the end, the vampyre is more sucking the blood out than he is drinking." My stomach lurched at the thought of the violence and amount of damage inflicted on Gerhard Kessler. He had fought valiantly to protect his wife but had suffered dearly for it. "As far as Frieda Kessler," Hans resumed, looking down at his notes, "She…she…" He abruptly stopped as his voice cracked. I watched as Anna reached out and gently squeezed his arm. I suddenly realized that all I really knew about Hans was that he was from Munich. Was he married? Did he have children? I felt ashamed I didn't even know. Hans smiled at Anna, nodded, and took a deep breath. "Rope burns around the ankles indicate she struggled a lot as she was tied up and subsequently raped. It would have been a terrible body position that made her completely vulnerable to the attack. She was completely helpless as he ravaged her. The question is—how did he inflict so much damage? A normal male penis could not have done this. Whatever it was, it was abnormally large, impossibly long. There was nothing left discarded in the room to have done that kind of damage. And nothing inanimate would explain the inhuman amounts of the killer's ejaculate. I have a theory, though…" Dr. Ziegler was abruptly cut off when another voice finished the sentence for him. "The vampyre has a baculum." We turned around, and Stanislaw had entered the room, followed by Manfred and Felix. "Yes," said Hans, looking surprised that his hypothesis was confirmed. Stanislaw came up to Hans and said, "You are correct, Herr Doctor. The male vampyre has a baculum, a penis consisting of bone, a feature confined to placental mammals, some as large as the gorilla or as small as a cat or dog. And of course, the bat. Another indicator that the vampyre is no longer a man, since the baculum is absent in human males, having disappeared through the process of evolution and our species' mating strategies, primarily monogamy. Did you know that the baculum of walruses is considered the longest at about 2 feet? Yet this doesn't even come close to the monstrous tool that raped Frau Kessler. Additionally, the baculum allows copulation to last for hours since it's bone and doesn't depend on blood engorgement as with the human penis. This makes for a horrific combination, a fate beyond comprehension for the vampyre's unfortunate female victims." The room was quiet as this revelation hung in the air. "The vampyre had his way with her," Hans summarized, "but he didn't go so far as to kill her. Not at first. Because again, he needed the living heart to continue pumping blood. So, at some point, he bites her and begins feeding. As the enzymes in his saliva start to clot the wound, he goes back to the rape, climaxes, and then returns to drink some more. God only knows how long the cycle continued. Eventually, she died from exsanguination and heart failure."

A couple of minutes later, Hans wrapped up the remainder of his autopsy findings. I had just thanked him for getting both autopsies completed so quickly when we heard what sounded like a cart being moved across the floor in the examination room, its wheels slightly squeaking as they turned. We all looked over to the door, but it was Stanislaw who had immediately recognized the significance of the sound. Within seconds, I saw him pull out a crucifix from the leather satchel he habitually had slung over his shoulder. Shit, I thought, as I looked down at my watch. It was 6:26 p.m., six minutes past sundown. Caught up in our conversation, we had completely forgotten the time. Stanislaw valiantly led the way into the adjacent room, the rest of us following behind almost like a pack of frightened school children afraid they were about to see the Boogyman. What I saw next was hard for my eyes to comprehend, even though we had expected it. Gerhard Kessler was sitting fully upright, on the edge of the autopsy table. The wheeled cart with the autopsy tools had been pushed aside. It was surreal to see the man sitting erect, with the "Y" incision on his chest, the ugly black stitches pulling the flaps of his skin tightly together. An impossibility…in the world of the ignorant. Kessler twisted his head back and forth, cracking his neck like a man who just woke up from a restful nap. "Hmmm…" he said, his eyes still closed as he stretched, "my ass feels like someone drove a truck up it. That was a hell of a ride." His eyes suddenly snapped open, his eyes glowing a predatory red. "God, I'm thirsty," he hissed, as his eyes quickly focused on Anna. Almost in a blink of an eye, he flew off the table towards us. Stanislaw was ready and, raising the crucifix, slapped it hard against the creature's cheek. I heard a sound like a sparked electrical circuit, and Kessler reeled backward, howling and clutching at his face. I could see smoke coming from between his fingers, and the smell of burning flesh filled the room. In those precious seconds, Stanislaw had taken out his silver dagger and quickly uncapped a vial of holy water. By the time he had dowsed the knife in the blessed liquid, Kessler had begun to advance on us once again. But he was so overtaken by pain and rage that he failed to understand the danger awaiting him. Stanislaw dodged the vampyre's flailing arms as smoothly as a seasoned boxer, coming up alongside him and thrusting the dagger directly into the creature's chest, just under the left armpit. A quick stab, in and out, so quickly I barely saw it. As Kessler whirled around, Stanislaw stuck him once more with the blade, this time on the right side. It was like watching a matador sparing with a bull, effortlessly jabbing the creature with banderillas. Kessler fell to the floor, viscous blood pouring from the wounds. Looking up into Stanislaw's face, he tried to speak but black ichor filled his mouth. Through the gurgling, he spat "Go to Hell, Slayer…and fuck your mother…you can kill me but you'll never kill the Master…you best sleep with one eye open old man…" Stanislaw, not one for a long dialogue, doused the blade with fresh holy water and thrust it down into Kessler's chest. The rotting, noxious fluid erupted out of the vampyre's mouth, nose, and even his eyes as the dagger tore through the monster's heart. The thing that was once Gerhard Kessler, a devoted son, brother, and loving husband, gave out one last garbled scream and then fell silent.

My brain had no sooner processed what I described above when I sensed movement behind us. I twirled around to see Frieda Kessler was now standing on the far side of the room, her glassy eyes taking in the corpse of her (finally) dead husband. The sheet that had covered her had fallen away to expose her naked body. But in death, Frieda's horrific injuries seemed to have healed themselves, and she bore no marks or scars to mar her shapely form. Her long legs were slim and muscular, leading up to a triangle muff of inviting hair. Her stomach was now flat and toned, in the middle of which was a belly button that suddenly screamed out in erotic intensity.

Her breasts were bulbous, full, and perky, the wide pink areolas surrounded her nipples which were enticingly long and erect. Frieda's face was as beautiful as the most alluring siren of Greek mythology; her blood-red lips, full and seductive, sat beneath a sculptured Greek nose. Her long blonde hair fell down over her bare shoulders, her porcelain skin clean and gorgeous. She was a goddess, with a body that no man could resist. Her eyes, once emerald green, had become spinning red orbs, a vortex that was drawing me in, sapping my free will. Frieda outstretched out her arms, invitingly. With her eyes drilling into mine, I had an uncontrollable urge to walk into them, letting them envelop me, pressing my body against hers, feeling her hotness as she ground her pubis against my growing hardness, tasting her full lips, her tongue thrusting against mine, the growing need building within me, wanting to fuck her, violate her, tie her ankles and pull her legs back, ready to impale her with my cock, hard and throbbing. I…I was lost, totally lost at that point. As I write this, I still burn with shame at those filthy and decadent thoughts. I learned later that all of us were affected the same way. Not just the men, but even Anna. She admitted she felt these impulses, ones that were not natural to her, of lying with Frieda, kissing her, tasting her, touching each other. Stanislaw had told us several accounts of the vampyre's succubus-like powers of sexual hypnosis and seduction, but my God, no human could prepare for such an onslaught upon their free will. I shudder to think of what would have happened if Stanislaw hadn't the strength to intervene. His slap sounded like a thunderclap in the room, and it stung as much as it was loud. It was hard enough to have left a handprint on my face, which, I admit, I'm content to wear as a badge of shame, rather than have faced the alternative. But it served its purpose. The pain immediately brought me back to reality, severing the telepathic ties with the vampyre. "Otto! Snap out of it!" Stanislaw barked. "Help me hold her down!"

The undead creature that once went by the name of Frieda Kessler hissed as Stanislaw advanced upon her, holding the crucifix out in his outstretched hand. As she backpedaled towards the wall, she shed the illusion of an alluring, seductive woman, the sham facade crumbling as she sneered, her mouth now a horrific assemblage of dagger-like teeth. "Back, shaman! Back charlatan!" she snarled in a guttural voice, no longer human. It reminded me of black water, sluicing through gutters choked with decaying leaves and clumps of garbage. I remembered my own crucifix and pulled it from my pocket. The vampyre hissed, her eyes wide and darting back and forth, her body beginning to twitch like an addict in desperate need of a fix. Within moments, Felix was standing by my side, now the three of us corralling the monster into a corner. "You will all die!" the thing screeched, back against the wall. "Cock suckers, sons of whores! You will all soon enjoy the sweet kiss of the Master!" "Shut your filthy mouth, unholy one!" Stanislaw shouted as he slammed his crucifix hard against her forehead. The vampyre fell to the floor and let loose with a high-pitched scream, an unholy cacophony that seemed to penetrate down to my very soul. The skin of the creature's forehead burst into flames, as well as her surrounding hair, the stench of which began permeating the room as smoke rose from the sizzling wound. I followed Stanislaw's lead by pressing my crucifix down upon her chest. There was another eruption of screams as Frieda's once-enticing breasts collapsed into each other, now becoming a mass of sizzling flesh, darkened in the shape of the cross. "Hold her arms and shoulders down!" Stanislaw commanded both Felix and I. "But be careful, don't get bitten!' Sound advice, I noted, as Frieda began snapping her jaws like a Bavarian nutcracker, her head turned from side to side, trying to take a bite out of either one of us. The vampyre's strength was inhuman, and it took everything for Felix and me to keep her restrained on the floor. "Hurry, Stanislaw," I urged, as he once again took out the sacred dagger to ready it with the holy water. But then, just as he had the vial in his hands, the vampyre's bucking torso knocked it out of his hands. "Damn it," Stanislaw exclaimed, as the vial went rolling across the room. The Frieda-thing started giggling then, like a little schoolgirl. "What's the matter, shaman? Lose your water? Piss your pants? Yes, like the little boy you once were, diddled by your step-father, his thick cock up your tight little ass, you liking it, bucking like a horse, so full of come…" Stanislaw smacked the vampyre once again with the crucifix, this time directly into the thing's face. "Be silent! You are of your father the Devil, and he is the father of lies! God will judge you harshly for your blasphemous words!" The vampyre's visage became unrecognizable as its eyes, nose, and mouth became sizzling masses of burning flesh. The final personification of the once beautiful Frieda Kessler was lost to eternity, and in its place was a ruined mass of scarred and smoking flesh. A moment later, Anna kneeled beside Stanislaw, and I was never so relieved to see a vial of holy water in her hands. No words were necessary between them as she uncapped the vial and he held out the dagger. No sooner had she doused the silver blade with the sacred liquid, Stanislaw plunged it directly into the vampyre's heart. This time, mercifully, there was no banshee-like scream, just merely a sharp intake of breath, followed by the sickening sounds of spurting blood, the noxious black ichor pumping out of the creature's mouth in time with its dying heart. "My God, is it over?" I heard Hans ask anxiously from over my shoulder. "No, not yet," Stanislaw answered, and I knew what had to happen next. Anna knew too, and she held out the vial of holy water. Stanislaw nodded, and, with one quick pull, removed the dagger from the vampyre's chest. It came out with a nauseating sucking sound. Anna poured a healthy amount of water over the blade, washing away some of the dripping black ichor from the blade. Without another word, Stanislaw moved to the top of the head, where he could get the best leverage, and then began the process of decapitation. All of us—Manfred, Felix, Anna, Hans, and myself—solemnly watched as the ritual played out, our mutual silence a form of homage to the memory of Frieda Kessler. At last, the gruesome deed was done. Stanislaw rolled off, panting from the exertion. After a few moments, he held out the bloodied knife towards me. I looked at it, dumbly. I wasn't sure what he wanted me to do with it. Then he said, "Gerhard Kessler needs to be finished off. And soon, before he reconstitutes. I don't know about you guys, but I'm exhausted." I glanced over across the room, where the husband's body still lay. Then I understood. "I can do it, boss," Felix offered. "No, it's okay," I replied. "Something tells me I'm going to need the practice."

I can't say it was easy, or pleasant, but several minutes later I placed Gerhard's decapitated head upon his chest. My forearms were covered with the thick, blackish vampyre blood. "Well done," admired Stanislaw, as I handed the knife back to him. "Well, opined Felix, "That was fun. I guess next time we'll be ready when those fuckers wake up. You most definitely want to take care of them before they can get up on their feet." Stanislaw chucked. "My fault, Sturmbannführer. I got sidetracked. But lesson learned, yes?" Indeed it was. But there was still one more task that needed to be done. We collected both bodies, and their heads, and put them on gurneys. We pushed them out into a corridor, and Hans led the way to the rear of the mortuary, and out to an enclosed garage that held two hearses. We loaded up both bodies in one of the vehicles. The final task couldn't take place at the morgue. Decapitation would be hard to explain to any of the Kessler family or next of kin, so there was only one answer. The remains would have to be disposed of. And the easiest means was cremation. But unfortunately, the city morgue didn't have a crematory, so the remains would have to be taken to the closest civilian crematorium near the outskirts Kraków. We decided to use the ruse of some contagious infection noted in the bodies, and they had to be destroyed immediately to stop the spread. Ironically, it wasn't far from the truth. For once, we'd been able to stop the spread of the vampirc infection before it could literally rise up and spread from the morgue. Manfred and Felix accompanied Dr. Ziegler, to provide police top cover if necessary. I didn't think it would be a problem. If Auschwitz-Birkenau could cremate over 4,000 corpses a day, then what's two more?

Anna had been uncharacteristically quiet after we had left the morgue. On the way back to my flat we made a brief stop at a small bistro in the Old Town to get something for dinner. We ate mostly in silence, Anna still seemingly lost in some contemplation unknown to me. I didn't push her to talk. I think we were both still shaken by the vampiric resurrection of Gerhard and Frieda Kessler and their transformations from a loving couple to a fiendish duo straight out of Hell. I suppose after the encounter with Max Weber we should have been hardened, better prepared for the extraordinary evil of the Mortis and the level of their malignant hatred towards we mortals. The sheer malice we encountered in the morgue, the vampyre's decadent, seductive powers…it was still unsettling. But despite all that, the most terrifying thing was how difficult it was to kill them. One mistake, one hesitation, and the vampyre could have easily had the upper hand. And they did not die easily. Nor was it pretty. Although I suppose if it was the other way around, our deaths would have been infinitely worse.

Anna and I had gone to our separate rooms for the night, both of us seemingly needing time alone to reflect on our inner thoughts. I found sleep eluding me, and I laid there for a while, hoping Anna would be all right. Outwardly, she put on a good front, strong, confident, and capable, but I still worried about her. That's when I heard the door to her room open. I figured she was heading to the kitchen for some water, or perhaps to the toilet. But then I heard her soft footsteps heading down the hall. Towards my room. I remained silent as I heard the door open. I watched as Anna padded across the floor towards me, wearing only her nightgown. She came to the edge of the bed and stood there for a moment. "I know you're awake too," she whispered. She reached up, pushed away the thin straps from her shoulders, and let her gown drop to the floor, exposing her naked body. I could see her full, round breasts in the moonlight casting brightly from the window. With the sweltering summer heat, I had no use for covers, so there was little between Anna and me as she climbed onto the bed and straddled me. "I don't want to be alone tonight, Otto," she said. "Yes," was all I could manage to say, my manhood already reacting to the weight of her body sitting upon it. I could feel her heat, hot and demanding, through my nightclothes. She bent down, and her lips found mine. She pressed softly at first, testing me, then harder as I responded, eagerly. How many years had I fantasized about this very moment, but never having the courage to pursue it? We soon were kissing hungrily, our tongues intermingling and prodding like coiled snakes. The world seemed dreamlike as she pulled back, the moonlight illuminating her face in a silvery glow. Without speaking, Anna started to undo the buttons of my nightshirt. I watched in silent expectation as she made her way downward. With each button, I could feel her fingers brushing against my skin, and she smiled softly when she was nearly finished. I moaned as she lowered her head and kissed my chest, licked my nipples, and slowly ran her tongue up to my neck. It was enough to drive me crazy. Her hands slid through my hair and I could feel our heated bodies pressed together, skin to skin. At last, when I could almost stand it no longer, she pulled my bottoms down and used her hand to slip me inside her. She gasped as I entered, and I moaned in pleasure as I felt her hot wetness firmly embrace me. Once she had me deep inside, she began a slow rotation of her hips. My erection grew larger and harder. Her vagina seemed to draw me in, and at the same time to press me out. I felt I was about to burst wide open. It was the strangest sensation, something that went beyond simple sexual pleasure. It felt as if something inside her, something special inside her, was slowly working its way through my organ into me. I had never felt as one with anyone else as I did at that moment. Anna let out a moan as I reached up and cupped her breasts, feeling the hardness of her nipples. She began moving up and down, excruciatingly slow at first, then faster and faster. Anna slapped hard against me, again and again, bringing me to the edge. Just when she knew I couldn't wait any further, her fingers dug into my shoulders and I felt her body shudder in climax. As she let out a scream, I thrust up my hips, exploding into her, a release unlike any that I felt before. Anna collapsed upon my chest, breathless, her skin slick with perspiration. I held her tight, feeling her heart beat wildly against my own. "My God, Otto," she panted, "that was…incredible." I kissed the bridge of her nose. "Indeed it was," I replied with a chuckle. "But I don't think I can take much of the credit; you did most of the work." Anna looked up into my eyes. The moonlight from the window gave her blue eyes a silvery reflection, and when she spoke next, I could swear I saw them sparkle. "I couldn't be alone tonight, Otto. To endure yet one more restless night sleeping apart from you. After today…with what happened with the Kessler's…it scared me. Really scared me. How love can exist one moment, yet die the next. How easily love can be taken away, stolen by a thief in the night, and replaced with eternal, never-ending hate. I want to have love, to embrace it, to cherish it, and never let it go. We may have the rest of our lives together, Otto, or we may have just tomorrow, that's up to God, but I won't waste one more night without telling you…showing you, how much I love you." A tear had slid down her cheek, shimmering like a line of silver mercury in the moonlight. I took my thumb and wiped it away. "Thank God for aggressive women," I replied, smiling. I flipped Anna over on her back. "No more wasted time," I said, looking down into her eyes. "Let's make the most of it, shall we?"

3 August 1943 –

When dawn came this morning, and I looked over to Anna sleeping by my side, I felt like I had been reborn; that it was the first day of a new life. I raised myself up, leaning on an elbow, and gazed down upon her face, and I knew I loved her with all my heart. I stared at her for I don't know how long, listening to the rhythm of her breathing, all the while drinking in her innocence, her beauty. When she finally stirred and looked up, she smiled. "Morning," she said, simply. "Morning," I replied. Few words were necessary. We made love yet again, an act as old as humankind, an affirmation of our undying passion. A baptism of our new life together.

We arrived at Wawel Castle a bit late to find Manfred and Felix already at their desks. As Anna scurried off to her lab, looking rather sheepish in front of the two men, Felix leaned back in his chair and flashed a knowing smile. "Hmmm…Dr. Müller seems to have a special glow this morning, sir," he opined. Manfred shot Felix his customary glare at the younger officer's forwardness, but this time didn't reprimand him. Instead, he turned back to me and smiled as well. "In this rare case, I have to agree with the Sturmbannführer. Otto, you do seem to have a bit of a pep in your step. Everything went well last night?" At that point, I noticed that even young Elsie had turned around from her typewriter, and was giving me her full attention. For some reason, I felt embarrassed to admit to anything in front of the young woman. I must have sounded foolish as I stammered out my response. I knew it was lame as soon as the words came out. "Anna…well…she was pretty shaken up after what happened yesterday at the morgue…she needed some comfort…err, I mean someone to talk to, uh, to give her support…" I trailed off. The grins on both men's faces had only become wider. At that point, I decided to quit while I was ahead, and proceeded to my office. At least the team can still manage a bit of levity despite everything that's happened. And I'm grateful for that.

This welcomed light mood did not last, however. The morning that had started so promising, seeming to herald in a day like none other, filled with renewed hope and glorious expectations, was changed a little after 9 a.m. when we received word that Hauptmann Dietrich had escaped from his cell at the army stockade. His absence was only discovered when the morning roll was conducted at 6 a.m. His bunk appeared to have been slept in, but he was gone without a trace. Three main points immediately drew the attention of the investigators. First, the door to the cell was still locked and secured. Second, the inmate's boots were still under his bunk. When he escaped, he would have done so wearing only his socks. Third, a small amount of blood was found on his pillow, which was assumed to have come from a nosebleed. Other than that, the cell was as it should be. It was still locked and secure. No window could have provided egress. If that wasn't strange enough, the guards claimed to have last seen him during their 3 a.m. rounds. Per the scheduled hourly rounds, they should have seen him again at 4 a.m. or at least 5 a.m. Yet, the guards claim they don't recall doing their last two rounds, that it seemed it wasn't long after the 3 a.m. round that it was time to do the 6 a.m. wake-up call. Either the guards were lying and were complicit, or time had somehow been frozen for them for two hours. The story the Army came up with was that the guards must have been drugged sometime after 3 a.m., although they can't explain how all three guards on shift could have been drugged at the same time. An investigation has been launched, and the commander of the Feldgendarmerie, the military police unit in charge of the stockade, is being questioned.

"God damn it!" I exclaimed as I crumpled the Army's radiogram and threw it on the floor in disgust. We all sat around the team's conference table, everyone's faces now glum with the realization that the vampyre had struck again. Anna put her hand on my arm in a comforting gesture and said, "It wasn't your fault, Otto. There was nothing you could have done." I looked at her and shook my head. "Yes, there was. I should have taken over jurisdiction from the military. I could have claimed Dietrich was a person of interest in our own murder case. The army wouldn't have challenged the SS on that. Then we could have put up some crosses outside Dietrich's cell, given him a crucifix and a vial of holy water. We could have at least given him a fighting chance. Now, he's likely just one more vampyre that has to be tracked down and destroyed. And we don't even know where the fuck to start."

"We do have something, though, boss," Felix broke in. "A courier just dropped off a note from Stanislaw. He has another tip on Hellriegel's location. This time, he was spotted in Raciechowice, a small village 35 kilometers southeast of Kraków, just eight kilometers from Dobczyce. Kaminski thinks Hellriegel is hanging around that area for a reason. Here's the note." Felix handed me the letter, and after reading it, I repeated it for everyone's benefit: "Otto, another one of our sources spotted Hellriegel as he drove away from a farm tractor repair business just outside the town of Raciechowice, not far from Dobczyce. He drove off in a dilapidated 1930s-era Ursus lorry, heading East down the MSR (Main Supply Route). The business owner said the man paid for five cans of kerosene after showing all the proper documentation, including a current General Government ration card. I'm convinced that Hellriegel is doing something at the behest of his master, Wojciech, and that the area is the key. There is something special about that area south of Kraków. I am researching the historical records once again to determine if there is any reason they may have an interest in this area. Meanwhile, I suggest the men you are sending to the area have instructions not to arrest Hellriegel on sight, but to try to follow him to where, perhaps, we can find Wojciech's lair. Regards, Stanislaw." I folded the note and turned to Felix. "Felix…," I began. "Already have drafted the order, sir," he interjected. "Effective immediately, all KRIPO and Ordnungspolizei will not detain the suspect once he is identified but will conduct a discrete surveillance, vehicular or foot, to monitor his movements, determine his activities, and identify any contacts or associates." I smiled. Felix was all over it. "Good man," I replied. "We are also distributing photos of Hauptmann Dietrich, Obergefreiter Bauer, and Feldwebel Tanz," Manfred added. "Dietrich is obvious—he is now considered an escaped fugitive. Bauer and Tanz may be vampyres by now, but the Army and the public still view them as missing persons. Presumed dead, but with no bodies recovered, we can still get away with having everyone keep their eyes out for them. The same goes for Irma Fischer. Officially, she is only missing after her husband was murdered and his body left in the flat. If any of these people are spotted, we may at least figure out in what part of the city to start looking for their lairs. Unfortunately, we can't have the men look for Johanna Liebl or Gertrude Brunner, as well as the two SS women, Magdalene Haas and Irma Koch…the word would get out that we are looking for dead people." I had to chuckle at Manfried's sarcastic summation. "Probably wouldn't go over very well, Manfred," I agreed. "Okay, that's about all we can do at the present. We have a lot of irons in the fire, and I hope something pays off soon. Meanwhile, everyone, keep your vigilance up. Limit your outside activities at night, keep the crucifixes up in your flats, and keep the holy water close at hand."

4 August 1943 –

Anna and I made love again last night. I'd swear it was even sweeter, more intense, than the first time. I find it ironic that I found her, that I found love, at the very time we both find ourselves in this living nightmare. A time when death and unspeakable pain and suffering are all around us. This damnable war is causing misery for tens of millions of people, but someday it will be over, as all wars eventually draw to their inevitable conclusion. But the scourge of the other evil we're facing, that of the vampyre, will continue century after century. That evil is perpetual, never-ending, and is all around us. Isn't it ironic that the vampyre has become the stuff of legends, relegated to myth and fantasy? Even though most sociologists agree that all legends have their basis in fact. The tales of vampyres have existed for millennia—ancient cultures such as the Mesopotamians, Hebrews, ancient Greeks, and Romans all had legends of such demonic entities and blood-drinking spirits. Here in Europe, vampyre lore has been exceptionally prevalent. There is the Russian *wurdulak*, the Polish *upiór*, the Romanian *moroi* and *strigoi*, the *mullo* of the Gypsies, the Albanian *shtriga* and *dhampir*, the Greek *vrykolakas*, the *vampir* of Serbia and Bulgaria, the malign and succubus-like *Baobhan sith* from the Scottish Highlands, the *Lhiannan Shee* of the Isle of Man, and the Icelandic *draugur*. From Europe to Africa to Asia to the Americas, there is a common mythology of a vampiric entity, be it corporeal or a ghostly spirit, who terrorizes, seduces, and feeds upon human victims.

But now, as I sit here and reflect, it seems Man has outgrown his fear of the vampyre. Europe has come a long way since the so-called "Great Vampyre Epidemic," a period from roughly 1725 to 1755, when cases of vampirism and fear reached their peak across the continent. Before then, our ancestors had quickly adopted the BIG RULE for survival: The dark provides cover for dangerous predators on the prowl, so it must be avoided. But as mankind developed electricity, we no longer lived with torches and candles in darkened homes, fearing the night. Modern man now rationalizes and scoffs at the ancient legends. It is so easy to deny the terrible truth that vampyres are indeed real and walk amongst us, and in the case of the Mortis, they feed on not only our blood but also our fears and dark desires. The Mortis relishes ravishing the innocent, stealing the goodness in people, and replacing it with evil and hate. And many men, willing acolytes such as Ernst Hellriegel, will gladly sell their souls for the promise of power, wealth, or eternal life. Yet, despite all this evil and chaos around us, Anna and I have found a loving refuge in each other's arms. What a stark reminder of what makes us humans who we are. Of course, humanity has its flaws, and I've spent my life chasing down our own form of human monsters. Some are clearly of criminal mind— the rapists, the serial murderers. But many walk amongst us as normal people. The current Nazi regime clearly illustrates the banality of evil—terrible and reprehensible actions carried out by outwardly respectable people. Take Rudolf Höss, for example, the commandant of Auschwitz. A rather bland, terrifyingly normal bureaucrat within the SS, a loyal functionary who carries out his murderous role with calm efficiency. Not due to any abhorrent, warped mindset, but because he has completely absorbed the principles of the Nazi regime so unquestionably—never considering their consequences from anyone's perspectives but his own—that his focus is simply to please the Führer and thus further his career with the regime and climb its ladders of power. His actions are defined not so much by thought but by the absence of thought. Someday, he'll claim he was just "following orders" and still will not understand the breadth of the evil of his crimes even as he takes the long drop at the end of a rope.

I know I'm rambling a bit in this journal entry, but I suppose what I'm trying to say is that despite its shortcomings, mankind, in general, is still capable of embracing love, characterized by care, compassion, closeness, protectiveness, attraction, affection, and trust. This is what sets us apart from the Mortis Vampyre. They know only the joys of the dead. When I am with Anna, I do not feel despair. Or hopelessness. On the contrary, her love for me invigorates me, sustains me, and makes me stronger. Because of her, I know the joys of the living.

In the evening, Stanislaw came to my flat to discuss some conclusions he had come to regarding Wojciech. As we know, Wojciech was born in Kraków in 1562. Stanislaw is becoming even more convinced that the vampyre has returned to the city of his birth for a specific reason. What that may be is still unknown. Perhaps it may be nothing more than a fit of melancholy, a sense of nostalgia for home. According to Stanislaw, vampyres often stay around the places they knew and frequented when they were alive. They feel "anchored" to familiar places. Unfortunately, this means staying around people they once knew and cared for, explaining why the vampyre often calls upon friends, relatives, and loved ones. In his book, *The Vampyre in Eastern Europe: Legend vs. Reality,* the chapter titled "The Balkans—Hotspot of Vampirism," Stanislaw cited three well-documented cases of Mortis vampyres terrorizing the inhabitants of their villages long after their deaths.

The first account was of a man named Jure Grando, a stonemason who lived in the village of Kringa within the region of Istria in what is modern-day Croatia. He was referred to as a *štrigun*, a local word for something akin to a vampyre and a warlock. Grando died in 1656, and for the next 16 years, he would rise from his grave by night and terrorize the village. He would knock on the doors around the village, and on whichever door he knocked on, someone from that house would die within the next few days. Grando would also pay visits to his widow Ivana, his rancid corpse and ghastly face, which looked like he was smiling and gasping for breath at the same time, would terrorize and rape her every night, forcing what he thought were her marital duties on her well after his death. Father Giorgio, the village priest who had buried Grando, soon put it all together. When Giorgio eventually came face to face with the vampyre, he held the monster at bay by holding out a cross and saying, "Behold Jesus Christ, you *štrigun*! Stop tormenting us!" Kringa became a village of terror, especially after county prefect Miho Radetić chased and tried to kill the vampyre by piercing his heart with a hawthorn stick but failed because the stick bounced off of his chest. It wasn't until one night in 1672 that nine brave villagers decided to end Grando's reign of terror by going to the graveyard, carrying lamps, a crucifix, and a hawthorn stick. They dug up Grando's coffin and found a perfectly preserved corpse with a smile on its face. They then tried to pierce his heart again, but the stake could not penetrate its flesh. After some exorcism prayers, one of the villagers, Stipan Milašić, took a saw and began to cut off the head off the corpse. As blackish blood began to flow, a dreadful howl was heard across the cemetery. The vampyre began thrashing and twitching as if he were still alive. At last, the men succeeded and the vampyre was dead. According to all accounts, peace finally returned to the region after Grando's decapitation.

Another well-documented case was that of Petar Blagojević, a Serbian peasant who lived in the village now known as Kisiljevo. Blagojević died in 1725, and his death was followed by a spate of other sudden deaths. Within eight days, nine of his fellow villagers perished. On their deathbeds, the victims allegedly claimed to have been throttled by Blagojević at night. It is said that he had also returned to his own home, demanding food from his son, and when the son refused, Blagojević brutally murdered him by biting and drinking his blood. After Blagojević's wife was also visited by her dead husband, she moved to another village for safety reasons. The villagers decided to disinter the body and discovered a complete lack of decomposition. The hair and beard were grown out, "new skin and nails" were noted, and blood could be seen in the mouth. The villagers staked the body through the heart, which caused a great amount of "completely fresh" blood" to flow through the ears and mouth of the corpse. Finally, the body was burned by the villagers. The Blagojević case was unique in that it was well-documented. Government officials of the Habsburg Empire examined the body, wrote case reports, and published books throughout Europe at the time.

A year later, in 1726, upon the death of another Serbian by the name of Arnold Paole, an epidemic of vampirism resulted in the deaths of at least sixteen people in his native village of Meduegna. Before moving to Meduegna, Paole had previously lived in a place called Gossowa, possibly in modern-day Kosovo, where he often mentioned that he had been plagued by a vampyre there. Paole said that he rid himself of the vampyre by finding its grave, eating soil from it, and smearing the creature's blood on himself. In 1725, Paole fell from a hay wagon, broke his neck, and died. Three weeks after his burial, four frightened villages came forward to say that Paole had visited them—plagued them. All four villagers died soon after. The villagers remembered Paole talking about how he'd been plagued by a vampyre in Gossowa and how he had rid himself of it. They decided to take a look for themselves, and so forty days after Paole's death, his grave was opened. Inside, they found Paole's corpse undercomposed—his body wasn't showing the usual signs of death. The nails on his hands and feet, the hair on his head, and his beard had all grown noticeably. Fresh blood flowed from his eyes, nose, mouth, and ears, and his shirt, shroud, and the inside of the coffin were covered in blood. A wooden stake was driven directly through his heart, which resulted in Paole shrieking, groaning, and bleeding. The villagers then cut off Paole's head, and burned his entire body. They also disinterred the four victims of Paole and gave them the same treatment to prevent them from becoming one of the undead. That spelled the end of Arnold Paole and the end of the vampyres in Meduegna. Or so the villagers thought. Five years later, in the winter of 1731, a new epidemic began, and by 12 December, 13 people had died in the course of just six weeks. Some of the villagers died in just two or three days without any previous illness, and others after a few days of languishing. By 7 January, 17 villagers had died within a period of three months, ages spanning from 10 years old to around 70. One of the girls who died, named Stanoska, became terribly ill the same night she woke up screaming that a boy, who suddenly and mysteriously died weeks before, came to her in her bed and tried to strangle her. At this point, the village reported the deaths to the Austrian military commander in charge of the administration of the area, who, fearing a possible epidemic, sent an infectious disease specialist named Glaser. He agreed to exhume some of the bodies, and what he found shocked him. Some of the recently deceased were decomposed, but others who had died earlier had not deteriorated and had blood in and around their mouths—like Paole. Unsure of what to make of this, Glaser reported back to Belgrade. A second commission was dispatched to investigate the case. Regimental Field Surgeon Johannes Flückinger, along with other military surgeons, were sent to Meduegnes. After Flückinger arrived, two more people died, and the village began to disinter the earlier victims. They found the bodies in the same state they had discovered Arnold Paole after digging him up. Some even had fresh blood in their organs and appeared younger than when they died. In his official report, Flückinger stated that the bodies were *das Vampyrenstand*, meaning "in vampiric condition." He ordered everyone recently deceased to be dug up. Forty bodies were disinterred; seventeen were in a preserved state similar to Arnold Paole. All seventeen were staked, beheaded, and burned, and the ashes were thrown in the West Morava River. The mysterious deaths of Meduegnes suddenly stopped. Flückinger wrote up his findings in an official government report titled *Visum et Repertun,* or "Seen and Discovered," dated 26 January 1732, bearing the signature of all five officers involved. The report was presented to the Austrian Emperor, becoming a best seller, with circulation all over Europe. Paole's case, similar to that of Petar Blagojević, became famous because of the direct involvement of the Austrian authorities and the documentation by Austrian physicians and military doctors, who confirmed the reality of vampyres.

As Stanislaw explained it, all three men—Grando, Blagojević, and Paole, were classic cases that documented what he called "vampiric anchoring," or the natural tendency for vampyres to remain tethered to their familiar surroundings…their family, friends, and community as they remembered it. In the case of Grando, sixteen years to continuously visit your wife and neighbors is a long time. "But Stanislaw," I had to protest, "Wojciech doesn't fit that mold at all. He didn't seem to have any compelling need to stay here in Kraków, having traveled over 300 years throughout Europe, leaving his trail of death and destruction. If anything, he was totally nomadic, not sedentary." Stanislaw agreed, but nevertheless, he felt he was on to something. "I know Otto," he had sighed, "Wojciech doesn't seem to have that anchor. But now, for some reason, he has been drawn back here. Back to his birthplace. There has to be a reason; I know it's there, but I'm just missing it." Stanislaw admitted that at first, he thought Wojciech might have returned to his old estate, which was about 23 kilometers south of Kraków. Wojciech's father had built the castle in the foothills below the Kaniowa Góra summit, with its elevation of 547 meters, and was not far from the village of Jawornick. Nearby is a large natural rock formation the locals have come to call Diabelski Kamień, or the "Devil's Stone." Stanislaw explained that the grounds fell into ruin not long after Wojciech left it, the place having been shunned by both family and locals alike. Despite this, Stanislaw had visited the site often over the years, looking for any evidence of habitation or visitation. He said there was little left except its brick foundations, now overgrown with bushes and vegetation, and a few scattered remnants of the walls. Since Wojciech's return to the city, Stanislaw has had the ruins under constant surveillance, either by himself or by Magnus familiars. Still, there have been no sightings of Wojciech, or Hellriegel for that matter. Stanislaw and I both agree that Hellriegel must be aiding and protecting the vampyre, and for that reason, we must bring all our resources to bear in finding him. Hellriegel is the key to all this, and if we can track him back to Wojciech's lair we may just be able to finally kill that monster.

5 August 1943 –

My God in heaven! My hands are shaking as I finally have time to write this entry. It is now around 5 a.m. on the morning of 6 August. I still can hardly believe it. That fucking vampyre…that evil, sick bastard! He has one of us! Elsie Best, that innocent, sweet girl. Now in the hands of that sadist. The thought sickens me. And poor Felix. The man's devasted. He blames himself for her abduction. Despite what I've said to him, his face only registers the guilt and shame he feels for not having been able to protect her. She had been staying at his flat for that very reason. She was safe there with him. Or so he thought. And as everyone else on the team had become aware, Felix's interest in Elsie went far beyond simply watching out for a colleague. "I loved her," he sobbed just an hour ago, his head in his hands, while sitting at the large table in my flat. "I loved her, and I killed her. It's my fault. I served her up to that fucking monster right on a silver platter." Felix has been inconsolable, and it took several hours to get the complete story out of him about what happened. It was so difficult seeing a seasoned homicide detective, trained to observe and report objectively, reduced to a weeping and emotionally devastated victim. Seeing my old friend in this state has been truly heartbreaking.

To start from the beginning, I received a phone call from Felix around 10:38 p.m. last night. He was nearly incoherent, rambling about "vampyres" taking Elise. I immediately contacted Manfred and instructed him to meet Anna and me at Felix's flat. Anna grabbed her medical bag and we headed out. We don't leave the flat often at night if we can help it, so we made sure we were well protected with our crucifixes and vials of holy water. We made it to Felix's flat in record time, and it was damn lucky we did, too. When we arrived, we walked into a madhouse. Our initial problem was handling Felix himself. He was nearly out of his mind with shock and anger, shouting about "the vampyres," and blaming himself because "Elise wasn't wearing her crucifix, which could have saved her." Other tenants were already filing out into the hallway, responding to all the shouting. Felix continued ranting about how he was going to "track the vampyres down" and "cut the fucker's heads off," amongst other things. He became completely oblivious to what he was saying in front of the growing crowd of onlookers. It was a miracle the Ordnungspolizei hadn't already arrived. Before they could, we flashed our badge and credentials and pushed Felix back into this flat. We knew it was imperative to keep him quiet. It would do no one any good for an SS KRIPO officer to be ranting about vampyres that snatched his girlfriend. I told Anna to give him something, anything, to get him to shut up. She ended up injecting him with a sedative, and it worked fairly quickly to get Felix calmed down.

It wasn't until nearly 2 a.m. that we got Felix rational enough to provide an official sworn statement about what happened. Well, I say "official,", but I don't intend to ever let it see the light of day. I tasked Manfred to put together a public version that would be far more believable and based mostly on the truth. After all, falsehoods are truths when based on alternative facts. As soon as the statement is typed up, we'll get Felix to sign it.

Felix told us that after he and Elsie had left Wawel Castle for the evening, they had walked straight to his flat, arriving well before sunset. They ate dinner in his flat and afterward were having fun playing records on a 78rpm phonograph Felix had bought from a German music vendor the week before. Felix's favorite record was "Lili Marleen," the famous love song recorded by German Lale Anderson in 1939, now popular throughout Europe among both Axis and Allied troops. Elise couldn't tire of listening to "Don't Sit Under the Apple Tree (With Anyone Else But Me)" recorded by the American Glenn Miller and the Andrews Sisters. It was hard to obtain, but Felix pulled out all the stops to get Elsie the American RCA Bluebird record. Felix said that Elsie liked the song so much because its lyrics are the words of two young lovers who pledge their fidelity while one of them is away serving in the war. They took turns playing the records, dancing, singing, and, well…what lovebirds do. But then, just shortly after 10 p.m. they heard a commotion coming from out in the hallway. This was soon followed by a woman's scream. Here attached is Felix's true statement as to what happened next. It's hard to read, and I pray we can find and return Elsie to Felix alive and well, but in my heart, I know that is probably a false hope.

Statement of SS-Sturmbannführer and KRIPO Senior Detective Felix Schellenberg:

It was a few minutes after I heard the clock strike 10 p.m. that Elsie Best and I first heard some noise coming from the hallway. It's not uncommon to hear voices filtering in from the hallway as these older Polish apartments tend to have thinner walls. After turning the volume down on the phonograph, we could tell the noise was not a normal conversation but seemed to be of a woman in some distress. We could hear the words "please no," "please stop," and "no, no, stop." That was enough for me to realize the woman was being assaulted in some way. As I began to get up off the sofa, I heard the woman let out a scream. The sense of terror in that scream propelled me into action, and without thinking further, I opened the door to my flat and looked down the hallway. Down near the end, near a door that leads to the stairway, I could see one of the female residents. I had met her once or twice before; she lives just five flats down the hall from my own.

Her name is Lily, and I believe she works for the Reichsbank. It looked like she was trying to gain access to her flat when she was accosted by two men. Their backs were turned to me, but I could see they were wearing Wehrmacht uniforms—uniforms of the German Army. One of them had the woman by the neck, holding her up against the wall; her face was already turning blue as her airway was cut off. The other soldier was laughing...a hideous cackle, and he had his hand under the woman's blouse squeezing her breast. I charged forward, and I may have heard Elsie's voice telling me to wait, but I'm not sure. It was as if I was on autopilot. All I knew at that moment was that I needed to stop those two soldiers from assaulting the woman further...or God forbid, raping her. When I was still a few steps back, I yelled out to the two men, "KRIPO officer! Get your damn hands off that woman!" Or something to that effect. Seeming to obey my command, the one soldier let go of Lily, and she dropped to the floor, hard. She looked to have passed out. Then, one by one, the two soldiers turned around to face me. It was only then that I realized their uniforms were not up to regulation; they were no longer clean and well-creased. There were holes, rips, and tears here and there all over their tunics, surrounded by a plethora of dirt and stains. It looked like they had just returned from battle or had been out in the wilderness for weeks. Alarm bells began going off in my head, but a second later, as my eyes moved up from their tunics to their faces, I knew these were no normal German Army soldiers. Not anymore. I recognized their faces from their Wehrmacht identity cards, which we posted in our Be on the Lookout (BOLO) bulletins. It was Feldwebel Tanz and Obergefreiter Bauer. The two missing men that Hauptmann Dietrich had last seen in the Kraków alley with his dead fiancée Johanna Liebl. Their skin was sallow and yellow, beginning to take on a greenish hue, stretched tightly over their cadaverous skulls. I took a step back, already registering what this meant. But it was too late. In my rush to help Lily, I had left the apartment with no protection against the vampyre...no crucifix, no holy water. And it was also too late to warn Elsie, as I heard her running up behind me. Why did she do that? Why did she leave the flat? Why? Feldwebel Tanz, the one who had seconds before been strangling Lily, now broke out into a malicious grin I'll never forget. It was completely devoid of any warmth or empathy but radiated pure evil and lack of humanity…the Cheshire Cat grin of a demented sadist and rapist. It was identical to the expression I saw on Helmut Brecht, the infamous "Rapist of Fasangarten," when we captured him during that big Munich case in 1938. He raped and killed six young girls, and when we interrogated him, he just sat there with the same expectant and excited expression as he told us what it was like for him to violate the young flesh of his victims. At the time, I thought Brecht's satisfied smile personified evil as it was the most vile and heinous I had ever seen. I was wrong. Tanz's grin, stretching unnaturally from ear to ear, was completely devoid of humanity. It radiated the intent of depravity and the promise of malice. That wicked grin turned my blood to ice, and I'm ashamed to admit I was frozen into place. I should have moved back faster, but the surprise and fear had paralyzed me. I started to feel Tanz's eyes drill into my own. Unlike the eyes of Helmut Brecht, Tanz's were not human; his pupils had turned to viper-like slits, and the whites of his eyes had taken on the reddish glow of a hungry, predatory beast. At last, I made a move, and just as I took a step back, my arms reaching behind in a vain attempt to grab Elsie, Obergefreiter Bauer stepped forward to join Tanz. He too was smiling, his face a hideous rictus that revealed a mouth of jagged teeth protruding from blackened gums. Two longer dagger-like incisors, glistening in the glow of the hallway lights, dripped ribbons of anticipatory saliva. I realized in horror he wasn't looking at me. He was staring over my shoulder, fixated on who was behind. And then he spoke. It sounded raspy, like dead leaves scuttling along in the wind. "Oh Günther, look. Such a beautiful fräulein. I bet her tits are as ripe and juicy as a set of Polish peaches. Let's take a closer look." Bauer's evil intent as he leered at Elsie finally empowered me to find my voice. "No!" I yelled, "Keep your filthy hands off of her!" Bauer's response was to backslap me hard, sending me reeling several feet down the hall. I was momentarily dazed, and by the time I had my senses back, they were already on Elsie. As she screamed my name, I managed to get back up and make another lunge at the men. This time, Tanz grabbed me by the throat, and in an instant, I had taken the place of the hapless Lily, pinned against the wall, my feet dangling helplessly. As I struggled to breathe, Tanz leaned into my face. His breath was foul and smelled of rot and putrescence, and I gagged despite my windpipe being squeezed nearly shut. "We're going to take your little playmate with us, SS man," Tanz hissed. "It was the plan all along…and you fell for it…stupid enough to leave the safety of your flat. The Master wants her, you see. He has a thing for beautiful girls. Like yours. So don't worry. When the Master fucks her, she'll forget all about you. She'll rut like a wild animal, and when she comes, her breasts slick with her own blood, she'll scream out the Master's name in pure animalistic ecstasy. Once tasting that pleasure, she will never come back to you. Ever." With that, he slammed me back against the wall. Hard. Two, maybe three times. Enough to knock me senseless. Satisfied, he flung me off to the side. I didn't see them leave with Elsie, but I do remember Tanz leaning over with one final warning. "Oh, and tell your boss Geissler to stop speaking with that shaman Kaminski," he growled into my ear. "The Master says he needs to stop interfering. Or his woman will be the next to join us." -------------------------------End of Statement---------------------------------

Tragically, Felix had known the Golden Rule that Stanislaw had taught all of us—that the vampyre cannot cross the threshold of one's physical abode without an invitation, be it a home or flat. It's the act of living in a place that grants the residents the power to keep out the vampyre. The threshold of the living is a line the dead may not cross. Our flats are our sanctuaries, and when we leave them, the only thing between us and the vampyre is our crucifixes and our holy water. In his haste to help that poor girl, Lily, Felix forgot that Golden Rule and crossed that threshold. The Mortis had set the trap using Lily as the bait, knowing Felix would act instinctively to save the woman. Their gamble that he would come without protection paid off, and in the end, Felix was at their mercy. Perhaps if Elsie had had a crucifix, she could have warded off the attack, but she, too, was defenseless. The vampyres took her, carrying her off into the night. It's a miracle they didn't kill Felix, but I suppose they let him live just so he could give me Wojciech's message. I hadn't heeded his warning to back off that night when he first made his appearance to me down in the plaza, and I hadn't heeded his warning to back off after he left the bloody message at the Kessler's flat. Not only have I not backed off, I found his lair at the salt mine, took his precious trophies, and formed an alliance with his nemesis, Stanislaw Kaminski, resulting in us killing three of his Mortis converts—Max Weber and the Kessler couple. Now, he's taken Elsie in reprisal. They probably should have killed Felix; it would have been more merciful for the man. As for the rest of us, with Elsie's abduction, one thing was made crystal clear: The hunters are now the hunted.

6 August 1943 –

Today was a long one. And a tough one. It was a day of grief, a day of loss, and certainly, a day for lots of explanations, none of which would be told truthfully. My only goal was damage control, to shape a story that didn't include vampyres. The first thing we had to do was determine who saw or heard what. I had the Ordnungspolizei interview all the tenants on the floor, and I felt a sense of relief to find out that only one person witnessed the altercation itself. That witness had initially heard Lily's scream and had stuck his head out into the hallway to see what was going on. Fortunately for us, his flat was on the far end of the hallway, and he only saw Tanz and Bauer from the rear, so he did not get a good look at their faces. Nor could he clearly hear any of their conversation. He witnessed the assault on Felix and, after that, stepped back into his flat and attempted to call the police. Fortunately for us, in his fear and panic, he had initially misdialed several times and then had problems getting connected, so that was why the Ordnungspolizei showed up late. By the time they arrived, we had already put the gag on Felix. That left the more significant problem of the majority of other tenants who had been drawn by Felix's rants about vampyres snatching his colleague. Manfred and I left Anna to watch over Felix, and then we proceeded to go door-to-door. I'm not big on intimidation or using my credentials as an SS officer to threaten anyone, but in this case, that is precisely what Manfred and I did. We even went one step further. As we flashed our SS identity discs, we didn't directly identify ourselves as KRIPO, but rather, we alluded that we were officers of the Gestapo. Naturally, all the German nationals in Felix's flat complex, many of them working for military or state agencies, were also members of the Nazi Party. As such, everyone knew the Gestapo was the Secret State Police responsible for political repression and arresting enemies of the state, including members of the Party who were deemed disloyal. At the mere mention of the Gestapo, it was amazing to see how cooperative and compliant everyone became. All we had to do was issue them a warning that whatever they heard, they were to forget it and never discuss it again with anyone, even their spouse or family if they "ever hoped to someday return to Germany." It was insinuated that Auschwitz was not just for the Jews. I feel terribly guilty for frightening the residents to such a degree, but at least I'm confident that any stories or rumors of a KRIPO officer gone mad, babbling about the undead, will never see the light of day.

It was around 3 a.m. when Manfred got the bogus statement typed and ready for Felix to sign. It started truthfully that the couple was listening to the phonograph in the evening, and all was peaceful and quiet (of course, we left out that Elsie had been staying in Felix's flat for days as a measure for her own protection.) Felix then heard the altercation in the hallway and went out to investigate, followed by Elsie Best. He found two Wehrmacht soldiers assaulting Lily as they tried to gain entrance to her flat. Felix tried to intervene but was assaulted by the two men. As he lay momentarily unconscious, the two men managed to overpower and abduct Elsie. Later, after they made their escape, Felix identified them as the two missing army soldiers, Feldwebel Günther Tanz and Obergefreiter Klaus Bauer. Obviously, they are not murder victims but deserters. The female victim, Lily Rascher, who suffered a crushed larynx, also identified Tanz and Bauer after being treated at the Kraków main hospital. Oh sure, this rendition of events doesn't help Felix's reputation as a kick-ass KRIPO detective, but it's better than saying he was confronting two German soldiers turned vampyres. We now have a narrative where Tanz and Bauer, AWOL and clearly deserters, attacked not just an innocent woman but a highly decorated KRIPO detective. The Wehrmacht will be under tremendous pressure to pull out all resources to find them. While that's not good for the army, it's a positive break for us. With their photos now re-distributed to every Wehrmacht soldier in Poland, even those on leave or R&R, the chances of someone spotting the pair have vastly improved. Just as with Hellriegel, if we can narrow down places they are seen, perhaps we can identify the likely location of the vampyre's lair.

By dawn, we had left Felix alone at his flat, although I assigned a pair of Ordnungspolizei to stay with him. Not because I was worried about the vampyres returning but because I was concerned about Felix's state of mind. He blames himself so much for Elsie's abduction, and I fear for my old friend's mental stability. No one on the team got any sleep after leaving Felix's flat because, by then, it was time to face the music back at Wawel Castle. My first stop was to try to call Stanislaw so I could inform him about the attack on the team and that the Mortis had taken Elsie. He didn't answer. I knew he would probably stop by my flat in the evening per schedule, but I didn't want to wait that long. I felt that the sooner he could get his eyes and ears out looking for Elsie, the better chances she could yet be saved. I knew it wasn't a realistic expectation, but I owed it to Felix to try. When I got to Wawel Castle, the first thing I had to do was brief General Governor Frank, SS chief **Krüger and** Kraków police chief Scherner on the attacks on my two colleagues. Within an hour, we had Reichsführer-SS Himmler on the telephone line from Berlin. Himmler was furious, particularly about the brazen abduction of an SS typist assigned to a high-profile murder investigation. As I had foreseen, his wrath was solely directed towards the Wehrmacht. There was certainly no love lost between the Army and the SS; the relationship between the two has always been acrimonious. The Army, seeing itself as the professional defender of the German Reich, often perceives the Waffen-SS as a less professional yet highly ideological paramilitary force whose loyalty is only to the Nazi Party. In turn, a negative attitude towards the Army by the Waffen-SS is positively encouraged. This attitude finds expression in the fact that only rarely does an SS man salute an Army officer. I'm not ashamed to say my game plan was to use this rivalry to my advantage. My priority was to deflect any unwanted attention away from Felix and Elsie, which could open the door as to why she had been staying with him in the first place, and by extension, the damage control had to ensure the term "vampyre" never came up. Protecting the integrity of the team and my investigation was paramount. Yes, I am using Tanz and Bauer as scapegoats and sullying forever their reputations as good soldiers and decent men, but what does it matter? I know they would not have behaved in that immoral way as the mortal men they once were, but it is too late for them now. Reputations do not matter. They are forever lost to their wives and families. It is easier to label them as the villains because they will never be going home, ever. I never felt a twinge of guilt as I described to Himmler the ruthlessness of Tanz and Bauer, at the same time extolling the outstanding courage of SS-Sturmbannführer Felix Schellenberg, laying it on thick that it was his bravery and chivalry that protected Lily Rascher from further assault, and quite likely saved her life. In the scenario I spun for Himmler, Felix was the role model of the perfect SS man—brave, fearless, and courageous. Honestly, I didn't have to work hard to convince Himmler of the story's propaganda value to the SS. Not only can he smear the Wehrmacht by painting Tanz and Bauer as dishonorable runaways, attacking and abducting young women, but at the same time, he can expound the honor and virtue of the SS man who tried to stop their nefarious intentions. By the time Himmler got off the phone, I even had his approval to submit Felix for an SS award for exceptional bravery!

As soon as the briefing concluded, I called Stanislaw again. This time, he answered on the second ring. "It was a fucking set-up, a well-planned trap," I summarized after giving him all the details. "Wojciech wanted to hit us. Hit the team hard and where it hurt. And if we don't lay off, he'll come for Anna next." I could hear Stanislaw curse on the other end of the line. The man had given us all the tools and information to defend ourselves, yet the Mortis had been able to snatch our youngest and most vulnerable member. And the most innocent, I thought sickly. "I had heard there was a flap of some kind last night over at the governmental apartments," he said, "but nobody seemed to have any particular info about it. You guys must have kept a pretty good lid on it." I gave a silent laugh. For once, Stan's informants weren't privy to everything. "You don't know the half of it, my friend. And I've got Himmler ready to give Felix a medal for his bravery in defending the women from the two Wehrmacht 'criminals.' I swear, I've told so many lies over the past couple of weeks I've lost count." Stanislaw chuckled. "Look, Otto, I'm sorry for what happened to Elsie. It's a dangerous business. But if it is any consolation, it proves yet again how desperate Wojciech has become to get you off his back. There has to be a reason why now, more than ever, he is feeling threatened by his pursuers. And I still think it all comes down to why he has returned to Kraków. There is something important here to get done; otherwise, he'd have moved on instead of confronting us. If I can determine the nexus, the reason he has come home, we will have what we need to find him, I'm sure of it. I'm doing some research on the city's buildings and architectural archives…using my German identification to gain access. I have a hunch, and I have to play it out. Maybe by tomorrow, I'll have something worthwhile to share with you. Something actionable we can use.

Meanwhile, I'll tell my contacts to pull out the stops looking for Tanz and Bauer…and Fräulein Best. Again, I'm very sorry, Otto. And for Felix."

At the end of the day, I received a note from Frank letting me know some heads had rolled over at the Army's Capital Defense headquarters. Three officers have been relieved of duty. One was the Feldgendarmerie Oberst who had arrested Hauptmann Dietrich for the murder of Tanz and Bauer, both of whom have now been proven to be alive. The second officer is the commanding officer of the 501st Signal Battalion. Apparently, his only crime is letting the two soldiers go on pass the night of their desertion. Lastly, the commandant of the military stockade from where Hauptmann Dietrich had "escaped" had been summarily sacked. Never mind that Dietrich had escaped from a locked cell without taking his boots; that warden was held accountable. It didn't take long for Himmler's anger to be felt by the Wehrmacht's chain of command.

Tonight, Manfred is staying with Felix. Anna and I are together of course. After all that's happened, I'm going to hold her especially tight by my side. I don't know what I would do if I lost her.

7 August 1943 –

Christ, I almost killed Felix tonight. I came within a cat's whisker of pulling the trigger of my Walther, but thank God it didn't come to that. Although I surely would have shot him if I had to. To prevent him from placing Anna's life in danger. There is nothing more important to me now. I will do anything I need to protect the woman I love. And I do so much love her.

It began after work was finished for the day at Wawel. Myself, Anna, Manfred, and Hans—had all agreed to go to Felix's flat to spend the evening with him. We hoped that in the company of friends, we could assuage his anguish, at least for a short time. It was decided we would make him some dinner, so on the way Anna and I stopped by the large open-air market at Adolf Hitler Platz to pick up some pork cutlets, potatoes, onions, and fresh ears of corn. As well as a bottle of Polish wine. The marketplace was bustling, full of people buying their meat and produce to take home for the evening meal. Even under the German occupation, there was a sense of normalcy as the centuries-old tradition of the open-air market continued to thrive. With a ration card, of course. As I looked around the crowd of people, I couldn't help but think I was living in two worlds—one, completely normal and happy, where the privileged citizens of the new "German" city of Kraków walked to and fro wearing their blinders, oblivious to the evil and genocide taking place all around them. The other is a world with people like Anna and me, whose blinders have been viciously snatched away to reveal the true reality of their existence… they share this world with creatures that will kill and feed upon them without the slightest bit of remorse. For Anna and I, having seen the brutality and savagery of the Mortis Vampyre, and recognizing their danger to mankind, how is it ever possible to return to the old world we once felt safe and comfortable in? Standing there in the market square, I realized that it wasn't. We can never go back.

We arrived at Felix's place well before sunset. As we entered the building, one of the residents saw me, and immediately turned pale. He gave me a very exuberant yet nervous "Heil Hitler!" and then retreated to his flat, almost at a run. Anna looked at me quizzically. "That guy looked downright terrified of you, Otto. What did you do to him?" I smiled as I leaned over and kissed the top of her head. "Nothing at all, darling," I replied, as innocently as I could, "He must be confusing me with someone much higher up the food chain."

We took the lift up to Felix's third floor flat. Upon reaching his door, we saw that Felix had nailed a large crucifix to the outside. It was obvious he wasn't going to be taking any more chances. I inwardly cursed, however, because I knew it would result in unwanted scrutiny and questions, and even more whispers about "vampyres." Anna squeezed my hand, as if to tell me to ignore it...at least for the time being. After knocking twice, Felix slowly unchained the door and opened it for us. I think both Anna and I made involuntary gasps of surprise when we first took a look at him. My old colleague looked several years older. Gone was his boyish grin and his ever-present humor. The dark, puffy circles under his bloodshot eyes told us that he had not slept since we had last seen him. He was completely disheveled, his blond hair remained uncombed and his face sported a dark five-o'clock shadow. He was still wearing yesterday's clothes, wrinkled and soiled. "Hello sir, hello Anna," he said. He held a glass of liquor in his hand and judging from the slur in his voice and the smell of booze on his breath; it had not been his first. "Oh, Felix," Anna cried as she gave the big man a hug. "We've got to get some food in you. Come, Otto, let's get dinner started."

Soon after, Manfred and Hans arrived. Manfred had brought some green beans, lettuce, and tomatoes he had bought at the produce market. Hans brought a loaf of Bauernbrot, or farmer's bread, and some cheese. With the rationing, we all had to chip in to buy the essentials. Manfred, as I had known, considered himself a culinarian, or gourmet chef, having learned to cook because, according to him, when he married his ex-wife Gertrude, she "couldn't boil an egg." He immediately took charge, and I let him and Anna work their wonders in the kitchen while I sat with Felix in the main room. "Felix, I'm sorry about Elsie," I told him, "but you've got to accept that it wasn't your fault. You had taken all the precautions, and you had done well protecting her. But you just couldn't have foreseen the trap that they had set." I leaned in closer to him and placed my hand on his shoulder. "I need your head back in the game," I said quietly, "Things can move quickly once Hellriegel is spotted. We're confident that wherever he is, we'll find the bastard Wojciech, and maybe the whole Mortis nest. And Stanislaw is working hard to find the real reason Wojciech came back to

Kraków in the first place. There's a nexus there, and we'll find it. Wojciech is lashing out at us because he is feeling threatened. He knows we have people looking for him, for Hellriegel. I need you back up on your feet, Sturmbannführer, and thinking clearly. I need you back in the fight. It's what Elsie would have wanted." Felix looked me in the eyes. I could still see the pain and anguish there. Pain and guilt that would probably never go away. But after what I had told him, I could see the old Felix as well. The eyes of a seasoned detective, intense with steely determination when in relentless pursuit of a murderer. At last, he smiled. "Okay, boss," he said, "You don't have to worry about me. I'm good." I squeezed his shoulder again in affirmation. His response heartened me. I believed then that the worst of it was behind him. But as events would soon prove, I was wrong. Things could get worse. A lot worse.

We had a fabulous dinner. Manfred had done a beautiful job with the breaded schnitzel, and the sauce he prepared was truly delicious. Anna had prepared the salted potatoes, beans, corn, and a wonderful crisp salad. We opened the bottle of wine, and I made the first toast—to good friends, those we have now, and those we have lost. Per our old Prussian military custom, we had left one chair and table setting empty, in remembrance of a fallen comrade...Elsie's seat. It was there to remind all of us what we were fighting for...what we facing, and who we have lost. I told everyone about my latest conversation with Stanislaw, and how he believes he is getting close to finding out why Wojciech returned to Kraków after so many years. "His attacks on us reveal his desperation," I summarized to the team, "He's up to something, and whatever it is, it is taking time, and he doesn't like us breathing down his back. Hellriegel has been bringing him supplies, such as kerosene. Probably for lanterns, so Stanislaw suspects they're in a cave, or someplace underground. Vampyres do not need light to see, so the lanterns would be for his human helpers—his familiars. Whatever Wojciech is up to, the positive thing is the longer he remains here in Kraków without moving on and disappearing in the wind, the better our chances are in tracking him down and killing him. Destroying his black heart and cutting off his head. Once and for all." It was Manfred, ever the skeptic, who spoke up first. "Yeah, but the longer Wojciech stays here in the city, and his little harem of women continues to grow, we're going to have more murders on our hands. And that's not going to go down well with Himmler. With no break in the Kraków killer case, we're all likely to end up in Dachau ourselves." We were all silent around the table for a moment. Everyone knew Manfred wasn't exaggerating. Himmler didn't take kindly to fools. He loved his SS, and held his officers to high standards. Just this year, Himmler had a camp commandant arrested and shot for embezzlement, black marketing, and overall corruption in the concentration camp system. After all, the SS had principles, and it is not tolerated for an SS officer to loot camp victims for self-gain.

It was decided we'd lighten up our moods by playing a game of Schaftkopf. We cleared off the large dining table while Felix left to scrounge up a 32-card deck of cards. Manfred suggested that to make it a bit more fun, we should have a bet of 10 Reichspfennig on each game. Soon, it became obvious why he proposed that addition to the game—the old fox seemed to have a knack for winning the trick the most consistently, and his pot of money grew exponentially. As we started to play, a thunderstorm began to roll in. It was no surprise; the day had been hot and humid and it had been brewing for a few hours. The loud rumble of thunder soon signaled the onset of the storm. Lightning flashed through the night sky, and rain began to patter against the room's window. Two hours into the card game, the storm hadn't let up; if anything, it had intensified. Through the window we could see arcs of dazzling lightning as it crisscrossed the black sky, accompanied by rolling thunder, loud and booming. The whole building seemed to reverberate with each resounding thunderclap. The rain was by then coming down in torrents, a deluge of the like that I hadn't seen since arriving in the city. I stood up and looked out Felix's window into the blackness of the night, and could see that the street down below had become a small river. After telling the group that it looked like we were going to be stuck there for the duration, we went back to the card game.

It was close to 11 p.m. when the lights in the flat first flickered. The building seemed to lose power for just a second, but then it resumed. At first, we thought nothing of it and continued to play. A couple of minutes later, the flights flickered again, but this time it continued. The overhead light and the lamps began a flashing dance of light, on, off, on, off, on, off. "Some kind of brownout," Manfred announced. "A power station must have been hit by lightning." The thing was, for the past half hour or so, the storm had been abating. The rumble of the thunder now sounded far off in the distance, and the wind had all but died down. I sat closest to the window, so I turned around to look out. I could see the rain had slacked considerably and had become just a light drizzle. "I don't know, Manfred, the storm…" My words were suddenly cut short when the lights went out completely. "Damn," exclaimed Manfred, "there she goes." Felix stood up. "I'll get some candles," he said, leaving for the kitchen. It was Anna, my sweet Anna, who already seemed to be reading my mind. "I don't like this," she said. "I've never seen a brownout like that. Otto, look out the window and see if there are any lights." I did as she asked, and after pulling back the curtain what I saw caused a shiver to go down my spine. "Everyone else has power," I told the group, "it looks like the problem is confined to this building." That got everyone's attention, and fast. "Something's definitely not right," said Hans. When Felix came back with the candles, I turned around and went back to the table. "I suppose if it's an outage confined to the building the tenants will be notified soon enough. In the meantime, we had all best stay here, together."

That was when we first heard the scratching. An unpleasant sound, akin to fingernails on a chalkboard, or a fork scraping on a plate, sending a shudder shuttling straight down the staircase of my spine. From the faces around the table, everyone had the same raw, visceral reaction. Heads began turning to try to find the source of the awful noise. "The bedroom," Hans whispered, his coroner's voice having lost its usual tone of professional self-confidence. The big man was scared. So were we all. "Everyone stay here!" I hissed, as I got up. Felix started to rise, too, so I once again ordered, "Stay here, Felix. I'll check it out." I crossed the main room, over to the door of Felix's bedroom. It was a small bachelor's flat, so there was only one. The door was open, and the candlelight from the table behind me helped to illuminate the room inside. I could see Felix's rumpled bed, and next to it was a small nightstand. Along one wall stood a kleiderschrank, or clothes closet. There was a window, curtains closed, on the far side of the room. The unholy scratching was louder, and most definitely coming from the window. Only now, it was more like a tapping. Slow, but incessant. It could be a tree branch, I told myself. Or a loose piece of the building's awning flapping in the wind. However, I knew these were hopeless and foolish thoughts. For one thing, we were on the third floor…there were no trees outside this high up. And, there was no wind. I slowly made my way around the bed. I reached the window, and through the closed curtains, I could see a shadow. A shape of something moving outside. Three stories up. And no balcony to be standing on. I took a deep breath, counted to three, and flung back the curtains.

I heard a piercing scream from behind me. I jumped in surprise and shock, momentarily averting my eyes from the horrific apparition that had been before me. I had been so focused on the window that I had not heard the group come up behind me, disobeying my order to stay in place. The scream came from Anna, who had her hand placed over her mouth, her eyes wide with terror. My heart beating wildly, I turned back to the window. A young woman was standing there on the other side of the window, her face mere inches from the glass. But no, not standing. She was floating. Floating in the air like an angel. She could have been an angel, with her sky-blue eyes and ruby-red lips set in a face with a perfect, powder-like, and unblemished porcelain complexion, all framed by long blond hair that billowed all around her like a golden halo. Only this angel didn't have angelic wings. She was hovering here, feet dangling in the air beneath her, her slim figure still attired in the dress she had been wearing two nights previously. A dress now wet with drizzle, held taut against her skin, the nipples of her young breasts jutting through the thin fabric. It was Elsie Best, coming back for her lover.

Before I had time to react, I was knocked aside as Felix pushed his way past, rushing up to the window. "Elsie! Elsie!" he cried, his voice wracked with grief, "I'm so sorry." I heard the Elsie-thing reply, her voice hers, but yet not hers, sounding deeper, raspier, like someone speaking with a mouth full of dead leaves. "It's alright, Felix," she cooed, "They didn't hurt me. I'm fine. Just a little cold. The storm was so cold. Please let me in, Felix. Let me in so I can get warm." As Felix reached for the window latch, I pulled out my Walther PPK and shouted, "Stop, Felix, you can't let her in! She's dead, can't you see? You can't let her cross your threshold!" The kind, sweet girl I once knew as Elsie turned to me, and I could see her once pretty eyes flash a predatory red in her anger. The creature's mouth widened into a shark-like slash, her red lips opening like a theater's velvety curtain to reveal her two small, almost lady-like, incisors. She hissed, snake-like, full of poison, "Fuck you, you little cocksucker. Go fuck your little whore. She's fucked about every man in Kraków, do you know that? Even women have been down there between those sweet thighs!" She laughed then, an evil cackle that sounded just like that green witch in the 1939 American movie "The Wizard of Oz." Then, within a split second, her demeanor suddenly changed, her face once again becoming angelic, her attention shifting back to Felix, as she coaxed him to open the window. "That's right, baby, just open the window," she purred. "Only you can make me warm. We can be together now. Together, forever." I still had my Walther trained between Felix's shoulder blades. I watched as he fumbled to turn the handle. I cocked the gun's hammer. I was within a slight trigger pull of sending a 7.65mm bullet straight into Felix's back. I would have done it too. If it meant protecting Anna and everyone else in the room.

Just as I felt my finger squeezing the trigger, Manfred came up from behind me and gave Felix a hard shove, forcing him to lose balance and topple over away from the window. I watched as Manfred slapped a crucifix up against the window so hard I was afraid the very act might break the glass and let the monster in. "Get the fuck away!" Manfred commanded. "Go back to Hell from whence you came!" He used no special incantation or sacred scripture, but the result was instantaneous. The vampyre took one look at the crucifix and recoiled as if it were a deadly Cobra. Eyes wide, mouth twisted in a pained grimace, the Elsie-thing shrieked a horrific, deafening scream. Then she was gone. One second, she was there, then the next, she wasn't. All that remained was the faint sound of the light rain on the window and Felix's sobs as he lay on the floor.

8 August 1943 –

Today was without a doubt the low point of our time in this accursed city: Elsie, taken and turned. Felix, reduced to an emotional wreck, a zombie of his former dynamic self. Manfred, nearly the same as he struggles to take care of his subordinate and friend. Hans, skittish and afraid, but with no choice but to return to work with the dead in the morgue. Anna, the only other woman on the team, shaken to her very core after seeing Elsie's transformation from a kindly young girl to a complete monster. Me, well, what pains me the most is the defeat I'm seeing in everyone's eyes. And there's nothing I can say to change it. Wojciech, and his vampyre minions, all growing larger and stronger by the day, now strike us at will, even where we live. Yet, we seem to be spinning our wheels in our attempts to find him. We desperately need a break, and we need it damn soon!

9 August 1943 –

Very late this evening, Anna and I were at my flat when the phone rang. It was Stanislaw. Without preamble, he said, "You're there. Good. I'll be over in ten minutes. This is it, Otto." Then he hung up without further explanation. True to his word, in ten minutes, we heard rapid knocking on the door. When I let Stanislaw in, his demeanor was animated, and his entire posture conveyed a degree of excitement that I had never seen in him before. I knew instantly that he had a revelation of great importance. "Otto, Anna, I think this is it!" he exclaimed. "This is the break we've been waiting for!" With those two sentences, he changed everything that we thought we knew. As he had mentioned the previous day, Stanislaw had been researching the records of the Kraków regional land and building archives. It took some digging, but he had discovered long-forgotten documents that revealed the existence of a second Batowski castle. Record keeping from that era was nearly non-existent, and most records that survived were too deteriorated to be of much use. Fortunately for us, the construction of castles involved a multitude of skilled workers and artisans. Stanislaw was lucky to find some correspondence between several teams of specialized craftsmen that were hired by Henryk Batowski, including masons, carpenters, blacksmiths, and laborers. The correspondence indicated that in the early 1600s, Henryk had commissioned the craftsmen to begin building a castle at a location 36 kilometers southeast of Kraków, near the Polish village of Pogorzany. It was to be located on the high ground below the peak of Ciecień, which had an elevation of 829 meters. Construction of the castle took several years to complete, but records indicate Henryk and his family were occupying it by 1610, when his older brother Wojciech was thought to have been killed at the Battle of Klushino. Additions to the castle were constructed as late as 1622, just two years before Wojciech went missing for good. Henryk's castle was much smaller and more modest than the older, original family castle that Wojciech, as the elder Batowski, had claimed for his own. It was built more for living in than for battle. Most notably, it didn't have a Keep—a castle's fortified tower built within the walls, the last resort in case of a siege or attack. Nevertheless, it was a magnificent estate, having a commanding view of the villages in the lowlands beneath it. The castle consisted of two round gothic-style towers connected by an imposing rock wall that provided fortification and security. Inside the walls was a courtyard and garden, surrounded by a granary, stables, chapel, and small servant's quarters. The main house, adorned with several turrets, had a grand hall, a large ballroom, several dining rooms, and multiple bedrooms.

Digging deeper into the history of the new Batowski castle and uncovering some period correspondence that mentioned it, Stanislaw pieced together that, overall, during the years of Henryk's residence, the castle was a happy place. Henryk and his wife raised their two children, Darek and Albina, and the sounds of their happy laughter were often heard inside the castle's walls. Henryk experienced good fortune, maintaining his family ties and service to the Polish King Sigismund III Vasa and the Polish-Lithuanian Commonwealth. The castle was the site for many receptions, dinners, and social engagements of the Kraków elite and was a welcomed refuge by many who wished to escape the busier life of the city for the peace and beauty of the Polish countryside.

However, this all changed after Henryk returned from his trip to Vienna in 1639, when he swore he saw his dead brother Wojciech, alive and well and not having aged at all. His wife said Henryk was never the same after that. The visage of his brother's horrendous, lamprey-like smile woke him up from never-ending nightmares for years after. He became moody and, just like his brother, withdrawn and reclusive. As the years progressed, Henryk's fortunes declined, alongside those of his benefactor, the royal House of Vasa. King Sigismund III's death in 1632 marked the end of the Polish Golden Age, with its era of prosperity. It was probably a blessing when Henryk died in 1652 at the age of 80. By then, John II Casimir Vasa was on the throne, and just two years later came what the Polish call "The Deluge," a series of mid-17th century military campaigns in the Polish-Lithuanian Commonwealth, comprising the Polish theaters of the Russo-Polish War of 1654-1667, and concurrently the Second Northern War with Sweden between 1655-1660. During the wars, the Commonwealth lost approximately one-third of its population—188 cities and towns, 186 villages, 136 churches, 89 palaces, and 81 castles were completely destroyed…as well as its status as a great power. The Siege of Kraków took place during the "Swedish Deluge," beginning on September 25, 1655. The Polish garrison's capitulation two and a half weeks later was inevitable; they had been just 5,000 men surrounded by a Swedish force 14,000 strong, and further resistance would have meant the destruction of Kraków and starvation of its residents. After the Polish surrender, the Swedes moved in, occupying Wawel Castle where, ironically, we Germans sit today, shining in our own supposed victory. Over the next two years, Kraków and the surrounding areas suffered greatly under military forces from Sweden and its ally Brandenburg-Prussia. Henryk's castle was initially pillaged and burned by Swedish-Brandenburgian forces looking for rumored treasures. After, it was further plundered by thieves and profiteers. Henryk's widow, ill, destitute, and with no more royal benefactors, fled to her family's home in Warsaw and died a year later. The castle's ownership fell to their son, Darek, but he didn't own it for long. In 1657, the Transylvanian-Cossack army, mutually allied with Sweden, also reached Kraków, and along the way, it burned and looted Polish towns and villages, murdering thousands. Derek was killed in a skirmish just outside of Kraków, not far from his father's castle. The fate of his sister, Albina is not known, but considering the cruel reputation of both the Transylvanians and the Cossacks, it likely wasn't a pleasant one. Looted and destroyed, Henryk's castle lay abandoned. It was a tragic end to the Batowski family line, and not long after, the end of the Vasa dynastic rule of Poland and

Lithuania, which ended with the abdication of King John II Casimir Vasa in 1668.

When Stanislaw had finished his history lesson, Anna blew out a breath. It was a lot to digest. "That's incredible," she stated in amazement, "So there is another Batowksi castle." I picked up the documents that Stanislaw had uncovered and held them out. "Okay, I see where you're going with this. We've been staking out the ruins of Wojciech's estate in case he returns there, but it turns out there is a second castle. I get that, but why would he return to his brother's castle...a place in which he never lived and has no connection?" I asked. Stanislaw held up his hand placatingly, as if saying, "Have a little patience, all will be known in due time." He smiled, apparently savoring his next big revelation. "Oh, there's more to it, Otto," Stanislaw said, his eyes wide with excitement. "I found records dating from 1627, three years after Wojciech disappeared from Kraków, where Henryk had paid for the exhumation of a set of graves that were located on the grounds of Wojciech's estate and to have them moved to a new location adjacent to Henryk's castle. He commissioned a team to disinter and move the remains, as well as the services of a stone mason, and these records survived." I stared at Stanislaw, not understanding why this was important. He could see the confusion on my face. "Look," he said, unfolding several age-darkened and brittle sheets of paper. "Wojciech's old castle was the site of three graves. Two of them were his and Henryk's parents, Stanislav and Karolina. I can understand why Henryk wanted to have them moved to his own estate. Wojciech's castle was falling into ruin, with the grounds becoming overgrown with vegetation. The walkway to the gravesite would have been increasingly hard to access. And besides, by then the castle had taken on a reputation as a "bad place," with all the local villagers avoiding the place. Not the resting place you want to leave your parents. It made sense for Henryk to move them to a new cemetery on his own land." I still wasn't sure how that was important, but I knew there was more to the story. "You said there were three graves that were moved," I said. Stanislaw grinned even wider, looking like the cat who got the canary. "Indeed," he said, unfolding another of the old paper documents. "Payment for the disinterment, movement, and re-burial of one Nataszja Batowski, dated 24 May 1627." At last, the realization hit me. "Wait. So, you're telling me that the body of Wojciech's wife is not at the remains of Wojciech's castle but is at this other place, 34 kilometers away, near Pogorzany?" I asked. "Yes! Yes!" Stanislaw replied, giddy as a young schoolboy. "I always knew the bastard had returned to Kraków for a reason. The only thing that makes sense is he wants to reunite with Nataszja, to make that connection with his old life. And this whole time, we've been staking out the wrong place. It's Henryik's castle we should be looking at. I'm sure of it. I think that's where we can find him!" I nodded. What Stanislaw found out was a game-changer. I had to agree with him. I reached out, and for the first time, I hugged the old man. "Jesus, Stanislaw, that's an amazing piece of detective work. Absolutely amazing. Hell, you can come to work for me anytime." When I let him go and took a step back, Stanislaw smirked. "Senior Detective Kaminski," he said sardonically. "It has a good ring to it. I'm sure I'd look quite dashing in the black SS uniform." I gave him a rueful smile. "Maybe after the war, my friend. When this insanity is over."

The next thing we did was to take out a large map of the Kraków area and spread it out on the table. I bent over, taking out a pencil. After a few moments of studying the topography, I drew several circles on the map, which I then connected with a line that began from here in the city. What I had suspected was now clearly evident. "There it is, Stanislaw," I said, pointing. "Ernst Hellriegel was initially spotted in the village of Dobczyce, located about 29 kilometers southeast of Kraków. Next, he's seen buying kerosene in the village of Racienchowice, a further eight kilometers southeast. From there, all one has to do is draw a line continuing further southeast, and what do you know, it runs right into the village of Pogorzany, another 12 kilometers down the road." Stanislaw nodded in agreement. "You're right, Otto. Hellriegel could have run off in any direction, but he's been spotted twice on a road that leads to Henryk's castle. That's too much to be a coincidence. He's definitely making supply runs for Wojciech. The kerosene is most likely for lamps. But maybe also for cooking stoves. We don't know how many human familiars other than Hellriegel might be encamped there, who need to eat."

With that, I agreed to make the trek with Stanislaw to the castle ruins tomorrow. Doing so will not give us much time to prepare, but we can't afford to wait even one more day. We might already be too late; Wojciech may have finished whatever he was up to and made good his escape from Kraków. We must go tomorrow, in the light of day, when Wojciech and his minions will be "resting." Stanislaw explained that the vampyre does not truly "sleep" in the day, and certainly not always in a coffin, as depicted in our German 1922 silent film, *Nosferatu*, or the 1931 Hollywood epic *Dracula* with Bela Lugosi. The sun's rays are death to the vampyre, and thus, in the daylight hours, they must seek refuge in any dark or shaded place, be that a cave, a tunnel, or the basement of an abandoned or seldom-used building. There, they will lightly sleep, akin to taking a nap, but perhaps heavier slumber if they have fed the night before. Just like any beast in the wild that has recently fed, the vampyre will shut down and rest when satiated. This is the time when they are the most vulnerable and can be overtaken by surprise if the vampyre slayer is stealthy enough. Once awakened, however, the vampyre will be able to fight back as long as it remains safe from the sunlight.

"You know I'm coming with you," Anna said after Stanislaw had left. "Anna, I don't think that's a good idea," I replied. "There are too many unknowns. We don't know how many vampyres are in Wojciech's lair. We don't know how many families are guarding him. I will not place you in that kind of danger. I couldn't live with myself if you get hurt or…" My voice trailed off, unable to contemplate the unimaginable. Anna came over and pressed her lips against mine. They tasted like honey, and I kissed her back passionately. After several moments, as I caught my breath, she stepped back. "I know you love me, Otto. And I know you want to protect me. But I've been a member of this team since the beginning. There's no way you will leave me behind. And besides, I'm a woman of science, remember? Vampyrism…it defies everything I've ever learned, all I've been taught about scientific rationality. I must, no, I need to study it further. I'm going." I wanted to argue with her, but I knew it was useless. And I couldn't deny her something she so passionately wanted. "I'm…I'm just scared for you," was all I could say. Anna gave me a strange smile and walked over to the table where I had placed my Walther PPK. She picked it up. "I may be a scientist," she said, taking out the magazine, checking it, and inserting it back into the pistol, "but I've got another skill I learned outside the lab." She racked the slide and chambered a round. "I'm a damn good shot."

Within minutes I called Manfred and filled him in. "We're going to go up there at first light," I instructed. "We need to prepare packs for each of us with our blessed crucifixes and holy water. Place a pistol in every pack, with at least 100 rounds of ammo. We're going to need several of those Daimon Wehrmacht-issue torches that can button to our tunics. Don't forget extra batteries. And a coil of, say, 15-meter rope. Also, first aid kits." When I was done, Manfred told me he'd get right on it. "Oh, and Manfred?" I caught him before he hung up. "Bring along a Schmeisser MP-40 and pack a couple of stick grenades." There was a pause on the other end. "Jesus, Otto, that's a lot of ordinance." "Indeed," I replied, "but we're probably going up against more than just the vampyres. Wojciech has at least Hellriegel protecting him, but there could be several more familiars we'll have to contend with. And crosses and water aren't going to do much against them. Especially if they are armed, too." Manfred grunted. "I see your point. And what about Felix? He's still badly shaken and has hardly spoken a word since last night. After seeing Elsie at the window. It really did a number on him." I paused for a moment to give it some thought. "Speak with him, Manfred. Tell him we're going into Wojciech's lair. He's never been one to shirk a good fight. And we really need him, if it's at all possible." Manfred acknowledged, and I hung up. But now, I have doubts about letting Felix come. What will he do if we find Elsie lying in repose, in all her beauty? Could he slide the dagger between her ribs and into her heart? Would he get in the way if one of us tries to do it? I don't have the answer. And it's too late at night to dwell on it further. Tomorrow is going to be a hell of a day, and I've got to get some sleep.

NOTE: There were no journal entries made for the next nineteen days, from 10-28 August 1943

29 August 1943 –

As I sit and write this, the August sun beams through the open window of my home in Munich; its warmth provides a gentle caress to my skin. I can hear the hustle and bustle of the citizenry in the plaza below. Their muted discussions filter up to the room, as well as the occasional laugh of a woman or the squeal of a happy child as they make their way towards the market square. The sounds of life. How I always took that so much for granted. A woman's mischievous smile, a child's inquisitive face, the eyes of a couple madly in love…we see them, but we never really appreciate them. Until it's too late. Like the man in the prime of his life being told he has cancer, it's the ultimate slap to the face, a brass-knuckled fist thrust to the gut, a bucket of ice water over the head. But once the shock is over, that man never looks at life the same way ever again. As long as he lives after that, be it only one day or the rest of his life, he will never see the world the same way again. Every morning that he awakens will be a gift, every day new and unique. People, places, and things that were once seen only in washed-out sepia are enhanced through a new prism that displays the world in sharp, vibrant colors. Sounds are enhanced—the bird's sweet song, the chirp of a cricket, the whisper of the wind…all are heard in crystal clarity.

Taste and smell are all fresh and new, just as he remembered them being as a child.

Today, I should feel like that man with cancer. I've cheated almost certain death and survived. And I'm home, back to my beloved Germany. The sounds of life down in the plaza below should sound like a sweet symphony. But it does not. The warm sun on my skin, the silky white clouds floating up in the emerald blue sky, the smell of fresh brot and smoked bratwurst wafting from the marketplace, the happy voices of the children down below…it should be like a feast to my being, a welcome reminder of how great it is to be alive. Alas, I enjoy none of it. My sepia word is even darker; the world is devoid of any color, warmth, or pleasure. I am alive, yes. But at what cost? It was a pyrrhic victory; I've lost everything dear to my heart. The world may be a bit safer now…the people in the plaza below can sleep a bit more safely tonight, but for me, the beautiful colors I once remembered are now gone, along with the love I once embraced, all dispersed in the wind like a tattered remanent of a life undone.

I've been delaying taking pen to paper and writing down the events that took place in the ruins of that accursed castle in Poland. I suppose I feel that once my account is set in writing it will become more real. It will be codified, and no longer just a nightmare of the mind. But it must be done, as painful as it may be. I owe it to the memories of those who did not make it out…to honor those who lost their lives in the battle with the Mortis Vampyre.

We left Wawel Castle a little after 0900. We took two Kübelwagens from the Capital motor pool. I left word that my team and I were headed out for a recon based on another possible sighting of SS-Haupsturmführer Hellriegel. I deliberately didn't call Hans Frank because I didn't want to get tied up with any questions. Best take the vehicles and go, and explain everything later. If I was able to. I was pleased when Manfred arrived, bringing Felix in tow. The junior man was clean shaven, and dressed for the field. "Reporting for duty, Herr Inspector," he said, as he provided a crisp salute. I looked at him. His eyes were clear and sharp, and his expression showed a steely resolve. He had the face of a man out for revenge, with no mercy in mind. I returned the salute. "Welcome back, Sturmbannführer. Grab that Schmeisser there. You're driving for me." Anna joined Felix and me as we loaded into the first vehicle. Manfred drove the second, accompanied by Hans riding shotgun. As we drove out, I took one last look at Wawel Castle. It was the scene of so many key events in Polish history— royal coronations and burials, battles and sieges, and palace intrigue during the 500 years the castle served as the royal residence for Polish kings and their families. And here we were, just five mortal men and one woman, leaving the castle's imperious gates, with no pious, zealous, or lofty intentions other than to confront the evil that had interceded into our lives. Like so many who had left this gate before us through the centuries, we were going to battle. And just like them, we were fighting for a just and holy cause that was fervently believed in. For us—Anna, Felix, Manfred, Hans, and myself, there was no more cause worth dying for than to rid the world of Wojciech Batowski and the scourge of the Mortis Vampyre.

About 13 kilometers outside of Kraków, after leaving the last of the capital's Wehrmacht checkpoints, we left the MSR and turned down a smaller, secondary road. After another five minutes, Felix steered our small convoy off onto a gravel road. We passed a solitary farmhouse, ringed by a field with a couple of grazing cattle. After another minute, we turned onto a dirt logging trail so overgrown with vegetation that branches scraped along the Kübelwagens as we made our way slowly down the path. Eventually, the trail led into a small clearing. There was a car there, waiting. A pre-war Polish sedan that looked to have seen better days. The car's doors opened, and Stanislaw and two other men got out. We had pre-arranged the meeting location, well outside of Kraków and away from questioning eyes. A bit cloak-and-dagger, but it was necessary. Stanislaw's false identification as a German citizen was solid and fully tested, and with his mastery of the language, he could pass scrutiny easily. We had taken him to our earlier crime scenes under the guise that he was a KRIPO informant. But his two friends were different; they were both living "underground" and had not yet been provided forged identification. Thus, we had agreed to the clandestine link-up there in the Polish countryside.

Without saying a word, the men grabbed several bags out of the car and walked over to our vehicles. "This is Jan," Stanislaw stated, introducing a very tall, lean man with dark curly hair who looked to be in his mid to late 20s. He had the well-muscled forearms and dark tan of a farmer. "Jan served with distinction in the Polish Army but is understandably unemployed at the present time," Stanislaw continued, his dark humor evident. "He's a Magnus familiar, so this is not his first rodeo, as the Americans like to say. He helped me kill two Mortis vampyre in Serbia two years ago. He's a crack shot with any firearm, and when it comes to killing with the knife, he's the best." I looked into Jan's eyes; they remained cold and impassionate. The eyes of a killer. But then again, with this damn war, hadn't we all become killers of sorts? It was not for me to judge. Besides, on that day, I needed the most ruthless of men if we were to accomplish what we had set out to do. As I shook Jan's hand, Stanislaw turned to the other man. "And this is Nicholas," he introduced. Unlike Jan, Nicholas was a short, stout man, but I could see right away that his heavier build was made up of almost pure muscle. His meaty arms were those of a short-reach boxer, built for pounding, and at the end of them, his huge hands looked like industrial jackhammers. He was completely bald, which helped to accentuate his almost rotund appearance. Whereas Jan was serious, all business, Nicholas greeted me with a smile. "Sounds like you fellows need help today," he said, shaking my hand, "I'm here to give you whatever help you need. Kick ass and take names, that's what I love to do." I had to smile at the round man. "Nicholas is a Magnus familiar as well," Stanislaw explained. Both he and Jan are beholden to Bethany." I remembered that name. The same woman who had recruited Stanislaw as a vampyre all those

THE FEAST OF THE VAMPYRE

years ago. The one the **Mortis** called *Rhamnousia*, the name for the Greek goddess of divine retribution. "Is she here? Now?" I asked. Stanislaw shook his head. "I wish she were," he replied, "but she is far across the continent…in pursuit of the Mortis Queen, Alexandria. Those two are locked in mortal combat, I'm afraid. Bethany is obsessed with tracking her down at the expense of everything and everyone else." I thought I could see a brief scowl flash on the face of both Jan and Nicholas…no doubt disapproving of Stanislaw's criticism of their Magnus master. "But she has released Jan and Nicholas into my care," Stanislaw continued, "And today, they are here for you. We could not have two better soldiers accompanying us on this mission. You can trust them completely." I thanked both men again, and then we finished loading their kit into the Kübelwagens. Stanislaw drove with me, and Jan and Nicholas jumped in with Manfred and Hans.

We reached the small village of Pogorzany about an hour later. It was very rural and was populated by only a few spread-out farmhouses. A few of the homes had smoke rising from the chimneys. It portrayed the most serene image; it almost looked like the war had never reached this far. We followed the road as far as it would go, leading us up to the beginning of the heavily forested terrain. At the end of the road, we parked and took out our packs. I double-checked my Walther PPK and put extra magazines into my coat pocket. As Manfred and Felix slung a Schmeisser over their shoulders, I handed another PPK to Anna. She had already demonstrated her expertise with the weapon, and there was no way I was going to let her go any further without being armed. I noticed both Jan and Nicholas had brought their own arsenal of weapons. From his kit bag, Jan took out a Sten Gun, a British submachine gun chambered in 9mm. It was a gun well known to be used as an insurgency weapon by insurgent groups within occupied Europe. If he were caught with it by the Germans, he'd be shot for sure. But at that moment, I didn't care. It was a formidable weapon; I knew it carried a 32-round box magazine and could fire 600 rounds a minute. It was similar to our German Schmeisser, but I remember a Waffen-SS officer I met once by the name of Otto Skorzeny telling me how he preferred the Sten because it required less raw material to produce and performed better under adverse combat conditions. If the Sten wasn't impressive enough, Nicholas was carrying a Soviet PPSh, a submachine gun that fired a more powerful 7.62x25mm Tokarev cartridge, at a rate of 900 to 1000 rounds per minute. He had ditched the box magazine for a drum, which he said carried 71 rounds. Both men strapped on bandoliers of extra ammo and more than one knife. They were professionals in killing, and they had the weapons for it. In a rather dark and twisted way, that realization gave me solace. Because if there were vampyre familiars up in the ruins protecting Wojciech, we'd have to kill every one of them.

We knew the castle was somewhere above us, on a high ridge line up on the mountain above. We would have to hike up to the ruins on foot. When we had our equipment ready, we began walking around the base of the tree line, but there was no clear trail that we could find to ascend upwards. The way up had long since been forgotten and overgrown. It was going to take us a lot longer to find the castle ruins than we had thought. We eventually came to an area with less of an incline and figured this was the best option to begin the trek upwards. It wasn't long before we encountered huge patches of briar, some of it consisting of vines as thick as my little finger, encrusted with rose-like thorns that tore at our clothes and exposed skin. We tried to skirt around the worst of it but often encountered patches of deadfall, tangled masses of fallen trees and branches that presented their own dangerous obstacles. We had to be very careful not to fall through it and suffer, at best, a twisted or broken ankle, at worst, impalement on the broken, jagged branches that jutted up from below. As we crossed one particular treacherous pile of fallen trees, Anna, who was walking in front of me, slipped on a branch and nearly toppled over the side. I quickly grabbed her from behind and steadied her. She turned her head and smiled, and I could see her lips mouth a silent "thank you." She looked so beautiful to me at that moment; a real trooper, hard as nails and carrying the same pack as the men, going to face God knows what, but yet so vulnerable, her eyes twinkling as she smiled. Ah, if I could just go back to that moment. To look into those loving eyes one more time and to feel the warmth of her skin, holding her hand in mine.

As we climbed higher, the forest canopy became thicker, and with it, the air grew heavy with the summer's humidity. My shirt became sweat-soaked, and this seemed to entice the mosquitos that flew around my face with buzzing arrogance. I had the sense that the forest had become almost primordial. Centuries-old trees with sprawling limbs guarded the darkness, blotting out any sunlight. Their bark was mottled and splotched as if bubbled soup had been frozen in time on its surface. Clump combs of wet moss dangled from their rotten and twisted branches. A pungent tang oozed from every sentient being in the forest. As we walked, the overhanging tree limbs, with what seemed like malady-brown leaves, hung over the path.

As we reached a point near the top of the crest, I caught the first glimpse of the castle ruins splayed out above. The exterior stone wall was shrouded in a pale mist which leaked between its cracked facade and splintered walls. With every cloud of swirling vapor, the ruins seemed to be breathing deeply, like a dragon with smoking nostrils. Clumps of rotten leaves and moss clung to the wall, and savage-looking thick vines appearing like clawed hands scraped out of the dirt and snaked around the rocks. "Looks lovely," Manfred grumbled, "the perfect place for a vampyre's lair." We continued the last of the climb, struggling to make our way past another unwelcome obstacle—this one a large outgrowth of stinging nettles, its leaves and stems covered with an abnormal amount of large hollow hairs that would act like hypodermic needles injecting histamine into any of us unfortunate enough to touch them. "Briars, nettles, deadfall, it's almost as if the damn castle has its own defensive measures," Felix mused as we finally reached the crest. And then, as I looked forward, the ruins of the castle's entrance rose up from the mist like a ghostly apparition. The wooden gate had long deteriorated into dust, and the cracked stone walls were broken up by hundreds of years of rain and moisture, their demise further ensured by the invasive, meandering tree roots.

"Keep alert," Stanislaw ordered as we walked through the gate, weapons at the ready. Jan and Nicholas fanned out, taking point, wary of an ambush by the familiars. As I crossed the threshold, I felt a peculiar mix of excitement and dread, a cocktail of emotions that one only faces when lives are at stake, particularly one's own. As we entered the courtyard, we could see that the castle grounds were also shrouded by the centuries-old overgrowth, the forest having nearly devoured it into its ageless maw. Dappled sunlight filtered weakly through the trees to reveal the weather-worn stone walls surrounded by dead clumps of decayed moss.

Many small forest creatures had made the castle ruins their home; as we walked, I caught glimpses of lizards as they moved in and out of the multitude of crevices that adorned the rock formations. Emboldened by the muted sunshine caused by the thick forest canopy, spiders spun abnormally large silken webs throughout the branches of the trees. Judging from the many silken sacs of encased prey hanging amongst the webs, they had been doing quite well. But it was the several mounds of translucent, discarded snake skins we encountered along the walk that got our attention. "The skin of the European Adder," Stanislaw stated unemotionally. "It's a snake, mostly brown in color with zigzag patterns along the back. It's not usually aggressive and bites only when provoked or stepped on." I heard Hans clear his throat behind us. "Why so many skins? Is that normal?" I looked over as Stan shook his head. "No. Probably means there is a nest of them around the rocks. Just don't stick your hand in any crevices." I heard Manfred grunt. "Great. As if vampyres and familiars weren't the only things we have to worry about. What the fuck else can be thrown our way?" I inwardly cringed. I knew from reading Stanislaw's book that vampyres sometimes have the ability to control animals, influencing creatures like bats, wolves, and rats to do their bidding. It didn't seem like a favorable scenario if snakes were added to that list. I decided it was a question better not asked. When we reached the far side of the courtyard, we found old ash scars on the stone from past fires, evidence no doubt of curiosity seekers foolish enough to have ventured out to find this accursed place. Still, I could detect no signs of a more recent occupation.

The remains of the main home were nothing but a shell consisting of decaying stone walls. However, a portion of the ceiling of what was once the grand hall was still held up by an arched, skeletal framework, which gave the eerie impression of it being supported upon human ribs. As we walked, tiles from the castle's roof crunched and cracked underfoot. What once would have been a majestic piece of architecture was now nothing but ruins and a crumbling pile of rocks. The place could now only whisper in the forest wind its tales of forgotten glory and happy times. "Here," I heard Jan say softly, and as I turned, I saw him pointing down to a corner of the stone floor, in which lay a pile of displaced slabs. Someone had unearthed what appeared to be stairs leading down to a subterranean level of the castle.

"This could be it," Stanislaw whispered. "Everyone, make sure you have your crucifixes at the ready. And keep the holy water close at hand. And stay as quiet as possible." We took out our torches, turned them on, and then, one by one, we proceeded down the pitted stairsteps into the darkness below. The stairs were at such an angle that it was necessary to crouch low when passing under the floor level to avoid hitting one's head on the way down. As we descended, the beams of our torches flashed along the sides of the crumbling wall, casting dancing shadows that followed us, seemingly mocking our every step. Down, down we went. It soon became apparent that we were going deeper than just a single level below us. The air became cool and damp, and the stone steps became slick. The walls began looking like the insides of a clogged pipe…a black mold, as thick as moss, grew everywhere, the clumps hydrated by noxious, brackish water that seeped down the wall to leave them glistening and soft. I reached over and steered Anna, who was walking perilously close to the wall, over toward the center of the steps. I suddenly feared that even a slight brush of our clothing against those sponge-like clumps of fungus would release a cloud of spores that we would not want to be breathing in.

Finally, our torches illuminated the end of the steps not too much further below. Jan and Nicholas were the first to reach the bottom. Immediately upon doing so, they fanned out left and right, no words or signals necessary between them, as they no doubt performed this surreptitious drill countless times. When the rest of us left the stairs, we found ourselves in a small stone chamber that extended out for perhaps 25 meters. On the far side, the wall opened to a narrow tunnel that looked to continue under the bowels of the castle. I wondered for what reason Henryk had built such a tunnel system. Surely it would have been a huge undertaking to have excavated this part of the mountain down to such a level. As if reading my mind, Stanislaw leaned over and whispered, "I didn't see this mentioned in any of the old documents…nor was it in the blueprints." I nodded. Whatever this place was for, we had to check it out. We reached the tunnel and shone our torches in. Our lights couldn't illuminate anything at the end except blackness, so it either went on a fair distance or took a turn left or right further in. The tunnel was even more narrow than the stairs coming down had been, so at best, we could walk through at two abreast. Every 10 to 15 meters, we'd come across an alcove or small chamber. We proceeded forward. Another room. Nothing. Then another. Nothing. Then another. They were all empty. Until, suddenly, they weren't.

I watched as Jan and Nicholas paused for a moment up ahead and then as they stepped aside to let Stanislaw peer in. "Don't shine the lights directly into their faces," he whispered as he turned his torch off and entered the chamber. In the now muted light, I moved up forward enough to where I could look inside. There, lying in each other's arms like a pair of lovers, were Johanna Liebl and Hauptmann Dietrich. Johanna was wearing a tattered, dirty dress, and her mane of brunette hair had lost its classic curls. Her hair was now a mass of tangles, full of burrs and bits of dried leaves and twigs. The skin of her face was pale white and bloodless, pulled taunt to be almost translucent to where her skull could be seen underneath. The impression of death was only broken by the ugly patchwork of blue veins under her skin that seemingly pulsed with life, flowing with blood that was no longer there. She lay at her lover's side, her head nestled in the curve of his shoulder, her arm over his chest. Dietrich, the once dashing military officer, the pride of the Führer's officer corps, now looked the part of a dirty, homeless vagrant. He was more nude than clothed, his prison uniform having long since been discarded. Just as with Johanna, Hans looked to be sleeping, his face painted with a slight smile as he held his lover. It was a touching, almost romantic scene, the illusion only shattered by the two large incisors that protruded menacingly from between Dietrich's abnormally red lips.

Without waiting further, Stanislaw nodded to both Jan and Nicholas. They understood what he wanted, and they were well-practiced. As we all took out our crucifixes, both men kneeled at the heads of the vampyres. They simultaneously took out what resembled wide leather belts or straps that had been draped around their shoulders. Stanislaw kneeled beside Dietrich, and then he looked at me. I nodded and did the same, kneeling beside Johanna. I knew what he wanted. I knew what had to be done. The thing at my side was no longer a woman…she was no longer innocent, no longer pure of heart. I looked at Anna, and she nodded. Stanislaw and I took out our silver daggers and doused them with holy water. Without further fanfare, Jan and Nicholas slapped the leather straps over the vampyre's mouths. Johanna's eyes flashed open wide in surprise, and perhaps even in terror, as she knew what was about to happen to her. Before they could even scream, Stanislaw and I thrust our silver daggers into the chests of the vampyres, directly into their black hearts. Under the leather straps, I could hear the snapping of their jaws, but they were powerless, their teeth not able to puncture the leather. It also muffled their shouts quite well. Johanna's hands tried to reach for my face, armed with fingernails as sharp as an eagle's talons. I pulled out the dagger and plunged it in again. And again. Black ichor flew everywhere as I twisted the dagger back and forth, determined to destroy the accursed heart in its entirety. At last, Johanna stopped thrashing. Jan and Nicholas removed the straps, and I could see both the monster's mouths agape in death. In their convulsions, their fangs had succeeded in biting through their own lips and cheeks, and the vile black blood had been vomited in copious amounts. Vampyres do not die cleanly. There was just one last task to perform. I watched and followed Stanislaw's lead as he again doused his blade with holy water. Together, we quietly spoke the sacred incantation, *Adjure te, spiritus nequissime, per Deum omnipotentem*, and then proceeded to saw off the vampyre's heads. In a matter of minutes, we were done with the gristly task. We knew then that we had found the vampyre's lair, because if Dietrich and Liebl were there, most likely the others were as well. Above all, I prayed that we would find the originator of all of the evil that the accused castle now welcomed between its walls—Wojciech, the King of the Mortis. Thus, we continued down the dark tunnel, even more resolute in our purpose.

It wasn't long before we found the two SS-Helferinnen, Haas and Koch. They were nude, having long lost the white shrouds their bodies were wrapped in when they walked out of the morgue the month before. They were filthy, their white skin caked with dirt and mud, the underside of their long fingernails so full of dirt they looked like blackened talons. Their hair was matted and tangled into a thick mass, full of briars and other scrub. They had been living out in the forest for weeks, I thought. They had once been young, pretty girls; now, they had been reduced to just scarecrows of their former selves. As they lay there, I almost felt sorry for them. They had been Aufseherinnen at the Auschwitz camp, yes, and would have surely faced justice for their crimes if Germany lost this war, but did anyone deserve this type of fate, to walk the night as one of the undead? I thought not. It was up to us to release their souls into the hands of God for his judgment…be in justice or mercy. We dealt with the women in short order, quietly, and efficiently. This time, Hans and Felix did the honors while Jan and Nicholas held down their thrashing heads with the leather straps. In just a few minutes, we left the room, the decapitated heads of Haas and Koch left on their chests, their eyes wide open and seemingly watching us as we continued our trek down the tunnel.

We didn't encounter any more sleeping vampyre, and after a few minutes, we began to see light further down the tunnel. As we progressed, it got brighter. "Only humans need the light," Stanislaw whispered to all of us. "The vampyre's familiars are here. Be vigilant—we need to keep the element of surprise." We all nodded and kept our weapons at the ready as we walked towards the light. Soon, the tunnel opened up into another chamber, this one much larger than the one back at the bottom of the stairs. Hanging from hooks along the stone walls were lamps…kerosene lamps. No doubt supplied by Ernst Hellriegel. The light from the lamps illuminated the entrance to yet another tunnel. It also illuminated a large slab of rock that rose in the center of the chamber like a bloated finger. Atop this pedestal was what I at first thought was a pile of grey cloth or rags. As we got closer, I could see that they were wrappings. Wrappings for a body. But not a fresh one. Not by a long shot. It was extremely old, a withered and dried-out husk. It was the mummified remains of a young woman. Her face was preserved enough for me to see she had probably once been beautiful, with high cheekbones and a Greek nose. "Nataszja Batowski," I heard Stanislaw whisper, "Wojciech's wife, dead since the year of our lord 1610." Around her body, the pedestal had been etched with various occult symbology, the largest being a pentagram framing the likeness of Baphomet, the Sabbatic Goat. Above that was some kind of cuneiform script that Stanislaw guessed to be ancient Sumerian. There was also what looked to be fresh blood smeared over the stones. The slab was some form of altar and clearly not one for the Christian faith. On the floor next to the pedestal was a scattering of books, all on the subject of black magic, spells, and incantations. I suddenly had a spine-chilling thought. "Stanislaw," I whispered, "In Hellriegel's flat, we found books on demonology and the occult...and several of them were about incantations and necromantic spells. You don't think..." My voice trailed off, unwilling to finish the thought. "That Wojciech wants to raise his once beloved wife from the dead?" Stanislaw finished for me. "What are the Mortis except consorts of Satan, themselves created by the powers of darkness? Yes, I think Wojciech is trying to use the ancient necromantic rituals, blasphemous and dangerous as they may be, to return his wife to him once again. Only by using the spells of black magic can he hope to elicit the favors of the dark demons and spirits that can grant such evil and vile requests. What he will offer the demons in return, I don't know, but it may be the sacrifice of yet another unfortunate young woman. We have to keep moving. We have to find him before the sun sets." I nodded. I took one last look at the 333-year-old corpse of Nataszja. Such a strange dichotomy of emotions, I mused. Wojciech was a sadistic and remorseless killer and defiler of women, and as such epitomizes pure evil...yet, at the same time, he was still capable of expressing the dearest of all human emotions—love. The love he had for his wife when he was still human—as a husband, nobleman, and respected military officer of the realm. Wojciech Batowski was a mass murderer, and yet the love for his dead wife had survived for over 330 years.

I put these perplexing thoughts behind me as we once again switched on our torches and began making our way through the next tunnel. I glanced down at my watch and was surprised that it was already nearly one in the afternoon. We needed to find Wojciech and the others while it was still daylight up above. Once he awakens, we would lose our advantage. An advantage...suddenly, I had an idea. I grabbed Stanislaw's arm. "I want to look at that pedestal again…confirm a suspicion. You guys keep going, I'll only be a minute." I turned to Anna, who had whispered, "I'll go with you." I shook my head. "I'll catch back up," I whispered, "You stay with the group, I'll be right back." Before anyone could object, I turned around and quickly headed back to the chamber. It only took me a couple of minutes to do what I needed to do. I was able to rejoin the group in short order. I could see Anna's relieved face as I appeared behind them out of the gloom. I gave Stanislaw a thumbs up, and he was satisfied that I had found whatever it was I was looking for. It wasn't long after that when Jan and Nicholas raised their hands in the air for everyone to stop. They had spotted more vampyres in one of the alcoves. As we filtered into the room, I could see immediately it was the two Wehrmacht soldiers, Tanz and Bauer. I looked over at Felix. He had already turned to face me. The icy look in his eyes and his ruthless expression told me everything I needed to know. Those two "men" had taken his dear Elsie, and he was going to make them pay for it. We quietly filtered into the room. Both of them were still wearing their uniforms, but they were badly ripped and torn. Buttons were missing and their tunic tops were hanging open to reveal their dirty and grimy undergarments. Both their undershirts were more brown than white; blood had saturated them and had dried to a flaky crust. They had recently fed, and fed well. Unlike the other vampyres we had encountered, Tanz and Bauer weren't lying on the floor. Instead, they sat with their backs to the wall, legs spread out, arms to their sides, and their heads down, chins touching their chests. It was an unusual position. Was this done out of instinctual habit, I wondered? Soldiers are trained to keep their backs to the wall while sleeping while facing the most likely direction of a potential threat. Stanislaw had told us that vampyres often retain many of the traits and habits they had when alive. It was eerie, and I almost expected both of them to raise their heads and smile a toothy grin as we came near. I watched as Felix drew up close to Tanz, kneeling beside him, his silver dagger at the ready. Manfred stepped forward in a show of support for his junior colleague and approached Bauer, also kneeling down at the ready. Jan and Nicholas gestured that they were going to shove the two men away from the wall so that they could get leverage to cover their mouths with the leather straps. If it was done quickly enough, we could still get it done silently and without alerting anyone else in the tunnels. Everyone nodded in understanding and we were all set. That's when the whole thing went to shit. Jan and Nicholas had taken their positions beside the vampyres, when, without warning, Hans dropped his torch. It fell to the stone floor, the metal case impacting the stone floor with a thunderous bang; the sound amplified by the close confines of the small room. Simultaneously, the bulb shattered with a loud "pop" that sounded like the crack of a silenced pistol. It was enough to wake the dead. And it did.

I once read that it takes a normal human about 250 to 300 milliseconds, or about a quarter of a second, to respond to a stimulus like a sudden noise or a visual cue. That may seem fast, but it doesn't factor in the human hesitation when faced with something incomprehensible; when the mind can't quite process what it has seen. When that torch hit the floor, it was one of those moments. Instead of reacting in that supposed quarter of a second, I wasted the remaining three-quarters staring at the broken torch in stunned disbelief. And it was a costly hesitation. On all our parts. Because before anyone had a chance to react, Obergefreiter Bauer lurched forward and bit into Manfred's neck.

All hell broke loose then. Bauer let out a snarl as he latched onto Manfred with the same tenacity of a dog clamping down on his favorite bone. Manfred screamed, his arms flailing in a feeble attempt to get loose from the vampyre's grip. Anna, in turn, shrieked as a jet of Manfred's hot blood hit her in the face. I barely had time to register all this when I saw Felix and Jan begin to wrestle with Tanz, who had been awakened from his vampiric slumber and didn't look too happy about it. Nicholas was closest to Baur, and I watched as he took his crucifix and slapped it against the

THE FEAST OF THE VAMPYRE

monster's face. Bauer let out a howl of pain as the sign of the cross burned into his cheek, leaving his skin sizzling like bacon in a frypan. It did the trick, and Manfred fell free from the vise-like grip of the vampyre's mouth. Bauer tried to turn to his side and bite Nicholas in the leg, his incisors glistening red from Manfred's blood. But because Bauer was still sitting, Nicholas just dodged out of the way and then once again slammed the crucifix to Bauer's forehead. He continued to hold it as Bauer's skin began to smoke, further immobilizing him as he writhed in pain. This gave Stanislaw the opening to plunge the sacred dagger into Bauer's chest. Bauer screeched as Stanislaw twisted the dagger back and forth. Vampiric blood erupted from Bauer's mouth and nose as the dagger found its mark and pierced his heart. I looked over to see Felix and Jan had finally pinned Tanz down on the floor. I went and stood over the men, holding out my crucifix, the gaze upon it forcing Tanz to stop struggling. Tanz had recognized Felix and had broken out into a toothy, mocking grin. "Well, well, look who we have here," he hissed in a raspy voice, "the loyal boyfriend back to look for his wayward girlfriend! How touching!" Felix bent down and held up his silver dagger. When Tanz saw it, his eyes grew wide with fear. It seemed to wipe the smug look right off his face. "You're going to die soon," Felix spat. "Really die this time. But before you do, tell me where I can find Elsie. She's here, isn't she? Tell me, you bastard!" Tanz curled up his lips into an ugly smirk. "Oh yes, she's here," he replied maliciously. "She brought back a boy just the other night. She's teaching the kid the ropes. Did you know your girlfriend likes to fuck them young, SS man? She screams in delight when he comes all over her tits! Why, she even..." Tanz's rant was cut off when Felix slid the dagger between his ribs, as smooth and effortlessly as cutting through butter. Tanz's mouth flew open, his thick tongue lolling out like a black snake. In his death machinations, his jaws clacked madly, sounding like an out-of-control typewriter. His jagged teeth severed his tongue, which plopped to the floor, resembling a link of blood sausage. Felix continued to twist the dagger even when it was no longer necessary. None of us said a word. Some things are best left to a man to sort out himself.

I heard someone's soft crying, and I turned to see Anna sitting on the floor and cradling Manfred in her arms. He had bled out, and her shirt was soaked in blood. "He's gone," Stanislaw said after feeling for a pulse. The huge gash in the side of Manfred's neck and the fact blood had all but ceased to pour from the wound already told me that. I kneeled beside my old friend. It had all happened so damn fast. A tear slid down my cheek as I picked up his hand. Why him, I wondered? He deserved to live a much longer life. Time to go boating on the Königssee in Berchtesgaden, sing "Ein Prosit" at the München Oktoberfest, or play Schaftkopf in the Englischer Garten. I felt a hand rest upon my shoulder, and I looked up. It was Felix. His tears cut lines through the grime on his face. I knew that he cared for Manfred as much as I. Manfred was his mentor, and I had the sense Felix felt closer to him than he did with his own father. "I'm going to get him, Standartenführer," he vowed. "I'm going to avenge both Elsie and Manfred. If it takes my last dying breath, I swear it, sir."

I was about to respond when another voice sobbed, "I'm sorry...I'm sorry...I'm sorry," in a continuous mantra. It was Hans, kneeling in the corner, his hands covering his face. I went over to him. The irrational part of me wanted to shout at him, curse at him for what he had done. His action had killed one of my closest colleagues. But I knew better. It had been a horrible accident. Any one of our torches could have slipped off our tunics. And who would have known the vampyre would react so quickly? Seemingly asleep one second and snapping like a rabid dog the next. We were all caught off guard. I kneeled beside the crying man. "Hans, it was an accident. And it could have happened to any one of us. And it probably won't be the last cock-up one of us makes today. What's done is done. We need you. We need you with us to finish this thing. Come on, get up, Doctor. We have work to do."

Before we left the vestibule, we had to complete the sacred rituals by beheading Tanz and Bauer. I felt as military men, they had deserved better. It wasn't their fault what had happened to them. Worse, poor Manfred had to be dealt with as well. He had been bitten, and he, too, would rise as one of the undead if left intact. Stanislaw knew we could never bring ourselves to perform the rite, so he told us to wait in the tunnel while he took care of it. I was grateful for that. Although I knew we had to keep moving, I vowed to return for Manfred if we left the place alive. He deserved a proper burial back in his homeland of Germany, not to be left in the dark bowels of the accursed castle, a feast for the subterranean rats that I'd seen scurry to and fro. A few minutes later, we were ready to continue our trek down the tunnel. I looked over at Anna. She had wiped Manfred's blood from her face, but her shirt was saturated. I knew the wetness would start to chill her in the coldness of the tunnels. I embraced her and whispered, "I can give you my shirt." She chuckled and whispered back, "Always so chivalrous. That's what I love about you." I stepped back and looked at her. "I should have left you back at Wawel. It was crazy to bring you here." She just smiled. "Silly boy, it wasn't your decision to make. I'm part of the team. And we're going to finish this as a team." She leaned up on her toes and kissed me. It was the sweetest kiss. I'll remember it until the day I die. "Just stay close," I remember telling her, "if anything happens, I want you next to me." Those words sound so hollow to me now.

Out in the tunnel, Stanislaw squeezed my arm. "I'm sorry about Manfred, Otto. Be assured he gave his life for a just and holy cause." I nodded, although I'm sure he couldn't see it in the darkness of the tunnel. I couldn't tell if it was my imagination, but the beams cast from our torches seemed to grow dimmer the further we went. The darkness was invasive, almost as if it were a living entity, swallowing up our light like a gluttonous carnivore. Even the air seemed denser, dripping with a palpable feeling of wrongness...of something malevolent and evil. As we walked, the feeling became oppressive, and judging from the small sobs I heard periodically from Hans, I knew the poor man was at a breaking point. Nevertheless, when we came to those small alcoves, we checked them all out, one by one. Although we found no more of the sleeping vampyre, we found personal detritus of those who had been there before. A woman's discarded dress and hairpin, a man's jacket and hat, some shoes, two pairs of eyeglasses, and a man's wallet. In one alcove, we found a Kennkarte, or German national identification card. The name was unfamiliar; it wasn't one on our known victim's list. We concluded it must have belonged to someone snatched recently, or his disappearance was not reported for some reason. We continued further down the tunnel. We continued to find more personal effects. It was a horrific reminder that we were traversing a killing field. It was almost a relief to all of us when we could see lantern light illuminating the end of the tunnel. The light meant familiars, and that meant danger, but as we emerged into the lit chamber, it felt good to get out of that dreadful darkness. The chamber was very similar to the last one, except there were five instead of one tunnel leading out. I watched as Jan and Nicholas fanned out to stand watch near the tunnel entrances. At the moment, it seemed that all was quiet. Our attention was brought back to the center of the chamber. Once again, there was a stone pedestal jutting up from the floor. It, too, was engraved with occult symbols and words in Latin. This time, however, it did not hold a mummified corpse. Instead, it presented an even ghastlier surprise. Above it, hanging from an iron hook embedded in the rock ceiling, was the corpse of a young woman. She was hanging upside down, trussed up like a holiday turkey. Her hands were bound behind her back with what looked like a scarf or handkerchief, and her ankles were bound with a rope that suspended her from the ceiling. She had been very pretty once, but the long gash on her neck that extended from under one ear to the other had changed that. She had died with her eyes wide open, likely having witnessed the unthinkable sight of her blood pouring down her face and into the large pan that had been placed on top of the altar. Her mouth was frozen in a now silent scream, the sound of which had probably reverberated along the entire length of the tunnels. It would have gone unheeded, however, while her captors watched in anticipation as her blood quickly filled the pan. The poor girl had been bled out like a stag killed on a hunt; the big difference is she was alive, and it would have been a slow and agonizing death. "The blood pan is empty," Felix noted. "Yes," Stanislaw noted. "The vampyres either drank it or, more likely, had used it for the rituals necessary to bring back Wojciech's bride. Many of the spells used by necromancers require the blood of virgins. This young girl is probably a local, snatched for that purpose." Felix let out a snort of disgust. "A lot of help her blood was in resurrecting that mummified piece of shit in the other chamber," he spat. "She died for nothing. Those monsters will pay for this." He pulled out a buck knife, flicked it open, and began sawing the rope that was holding the girl up. I looked over to Stanislaw, and he nodded. There was no reason to leave the poor girl dangling there, and Wojciech would know we were there soon enough, if not already. Hans and Nicholas helped to lower the girl down, and they placed her gently on the stone floor. Hans gave the sign of the cross, giving a short prayer that the girl would find peace in death.

Next, we had to decide which of the five tunnels we would go into to continue our search. Dividing the team was out of the question. There was safety in numbers, mainly strength and experience. But which tunnel led to Wojciech's lair, if any did at all? With the wrong choice, we would end up roaming under the castle for hours and on into the night. And that was not a comforting prospect to contemplate. I looked at the tunnels and mentally labeled them one through five, from left to right. I left Stanislaw and Felix to study the Latin inscriptions carved into the altar as I walked over to the entrance of tunnel five. I noted that Jan was standing guard at the entrance to the leftmost tunnel, or tunnel one, and Nicholas was standing near the mouth of tunnel three. Anna and Hans wandered over to join me. As Anna shined her light down tunnel four, I did the same at tunnel five. Hans was at my side as we looked inside. We couldn't see very far because not far in, the tunnel curved and disappeared from view. There was no telling how far it went. I turned to ask Anna what she could see when the unthinkable happened. We got caught with our pants down.

I just had time to register the sight of Anna disappearing into tunnel four. Not on her own volition; I had a glimpse of two abnormally large hands yanking her in by the hair. Initially, I thought the attacker was wearing gloves until I saw that the paw-like hands were sprouting hair. I realized that whoever was on the other end of them was a man, and he had to be monstrously huge. Anna let out a scream of pain, but this was immediately eclipsed by the unmistakable sound of a burst of fire from a machine gun, perhaps a Schmeisser. I watched in horror as Jan's head exploded into a crimson halo. He went down as quickly as a marionette whose strings had been cut. Before I had time to process what I had seen, Nicholas took multiple hits to his upper body. It spun him around in a macabre dance and he dropped to the floor. Stanislaw and Felix barely had time to take cover behind the stone altar as rounds began slamming into the slab, with exploding chips of stone flying everywhere. "Anna!" I screamed, again and again. "Anna!" It was useless; my words were lost in the cacophony of gunfire. I instinctively pushed Hans into the mouth of tunnel five and I retreated behind him. I tried to stick my head out to spot the attacker, but a hail of bullets slammed into the stone wall next to my face. I felt a sting as a shard of rock cut into my cheek. But from that quick glance, I was able to ascertain that at least one of the shooters was firing from the center tunnel; puffs of gun smoke were clearly coming from there. Even though I had to move further into my own tunnel, I could still see directly out to the altar in the center of the chamber. Stanislaw and Felix were returning fire, although I wasn't sure how accurate it was since they couldn't look up over the top of the altar, lest they get a bullet to the head. For the next minute, the room became an echo chamber as automatic gunfire came from both sides. Hundreds of rounds impacted the walls, chipping out pieces of stone and then ricocheting dangerously. Then I saw that Stan and Felix were retreating towards the rear tunnel that had brought us all to the chamber in the first place. That tunnel was behind the pedestal, and they were crawling low enough that, at least for the moment, would keep them hidden from view by the attackers to the front. But I didn't think they would be able to make it to the tunnel entrance before getting into the shooter's line of sight. I needed to do something to distract them. All I had was my Walther PPK, but it would have to be enough. I began firing measured shots at the entrance to the center tunnel. It worked. I began drawing return fire from the shooter. When he paused, I snaked my hand out from the entrance and let loose another volley. The attacker was so fixated on me that he completely missed the fact no return fire was coming from the altar anymore. Finally, I watched as the two men successfully made the last dash toward their tunnel. Too late, the shooter had noticed, and he sent a final barrage of bullets. I could only pray that Stan and Felix had both gotten deep enough into the tunnel to escape the gunfire.

A few moments later, the attacker's gunfire tapered off. "Anna!" I shouted, fear rising, gripping me like a vice. "Are you all right?! Can you answer me?! Damn it, you bastards, if you harm her I'll kill each and every one of you!" My ears were still ringing from the barrage of gunfire, but I could hear the distinctive clinking sound of metal sling swivels hitting against the side of a rifle. Someone had stepped out into the chamber. Then I heard the voice. It was different than the last time I had heard it. It was no longer polished, professional-sounding; the tone of an elitist. Words were no longer measured, but manic. There was a hint of madness to it. And definitely of malice.

"Hello Otto," greeted Ernst Hellriegel. "Don't worry about Anna. She's in good hands." His voice broke out into an insane cackle. "You know, I knew you'd find this place sooner or later. You always were the superior investigator! The pride of the Kriminalpolizei. And the favorite son of that failed chicken farmer from Bavaria!" He again chuckled maniacally, obviously pleased with the derogatory reference to his now ex-boss, Reichsführer-SS Heinrich Himmler. "You don't know how happy I am that you are here, Otto," he continued. "It saves me the risk of tracking you down. I had tried to get back into the city, but you have been very thorough ensuring my wanted poster was plastered everywhere. The Master has been displeased with my inability to get rid of you once and for all. You see, he has had enough of your meddling. And it won't do to have ordinary humans knowing the truth. About him. About the Mortis. Having that prick Kaminski on his trail for more than a decade has been bad enough. And Kaminski writing about the Master in that stupid book of his. Way too much attention. Especially now, when he's so close to being with Nataszja again." It was my turn to laugh. "You're insane, Ernst. Your 'Master' is never going to be able to re-animate that dried-out husk in the other chamber. How many innocent girls has he killed for his perverted scheme? And you've aided and abetted that monster's efforts. Why, Ernst? Why have you given up everything?" I heard the shuffling of feet over the stone floor. Hellriegel was slowly moving towards the entrance to my tunnel. He let out a chuckle, and in a condescending tone, like he was explaining what should be obvious to even the most simple-minded, he replied "Why, to be like him, of course. To be an apex predator, a superior species. Vampyres are the perfect killing machines, Otto. The SS, with all their human apparatuses of death—the euthanasia programs, the death squads, the camps, the gas chambers, the ovens—it's all so amateurish. So ineffective. The Mortis Vampyre has been killing for millennia. They are the truly efficient ones. And when you think of it, Otto, they are no different than your precious SS. The SS is killing those deemed racially and physically inferior, the weak among us. Yet, in truth, it is the Nosferatu who is superior. Superior to man. So just as the Nazis are eliminating the inferior races, the Mortis preys upon humankind. The big difference is you and I know we're losing this war, Otto. The Nazis will never complete their task. But the Mortis will continue killing and feasting upon their human prey. For all eternity.

Because they are immortal. It's exciting, isn't it? To hunt and kill whenever you want. To enjoy the taste of your victim's hot, coppery blood as you tear out their throats with your teeth. To dominate them, rape them, torture them…just the thought makes me tremble in anticipation. The Master promises I'll have it all, as long as I help him on his mission here. When his Nataszja is back at his side, he'll leave Kraków. And he'll make me immortal."

While Hellriegel was pontificating his diabolical aspirations, my mind was reeling with what to do next. I couldn't leave Anna in the hands of those monsters, but if I took just one step out of the tunnel I'd be cut down in an instant. My PPK would have been no match for a Schmeisser. And Hans and I couldn't just stand where we were, either. Hellriegel would have a clear shot at us as soon as he got in front of the entrance. We needed to retreat down the tunnel, and fast. I decided there was no choice but to continue on, and hope that it would come out to an area where maybe I could come up behind the marauding familiars, ambush them, and rescue Anna. Even as I thought it I knew it was a desperate, foolish plan. After all, the familiars knew these tunnels much better than I. It was they, not me, that probably would set an ambush. But there was no choice. "Hans, I whispered, "run down the tunnel! Quickly! Stay quiet. I'll catch up." Hans nodded in understanding, and then turned and sped away.

Moments later, Hellriegel's voice came again. Very, very close. "Listen, Otto," he said, in an almost friendly, brotherly tone, "just come on out. I promise to kill you quickly. One professional comrade to another. A headshot. It'll be painless." There was no longer any doubt of his intent. I needed to buy Hans a bit more time to get as far down the tunnel as possible. So I asked Hellriegel a question I already knew the answer to. "Ernst, if I do, will you promise not to harm Anna? Can you promise that?" After I spoke this, I started backpedaling down the tunnel, trying to keep my Walther trained on the entrance. If the son of a bitch stuck his head around the corner, he would be highlighted by the light of the chamber; a perfect silhouette. If I was lucky, I'd get my own kill shot to the head. As I receded deeper in, I heard Hellriegel's reply, and it chilled me to the bone. "Sorry, Otto, but the Master very much wants to meet her. And she is very much going to enjoy meeting him!" With an explosion of fury, I yelled back "Then your Master's as good as dead! I'll never stop until his black heart is cut out and I squeeze the life out of it!" It had been a mistake of course. With my voice echoing off the walls, Hellriegel knew I was no longer at the entrance. I had seconds to act. I took off like a shot, running down the tunnel. I heard Hellriegel curse as he let loose a burst of fire. The bullets ricocheted along the stone walls but miraculously I wasn't hit. In a moment, I came to a bend in the tunnel and mercifully got out of the line of fire. With shots still echoing behind me, I kept running. After a few minutes, I noticed the tunnel floor was at a downward incline. I hadn't noticed it at first because of the dancing light caused by my shaking torch. But I was going downwards, I was sure of it. Sometime later, I realized all had gone quiet behind me. Only my footsteps echoed on the stones as I ran. Either Hellriegel had called off the chase, or he was being very stealthy indeed. In a way, the sudden quiet was unnerving. I was totally alone…and the tunnel seemed to take on a hush that mocked me, promising death with every step I took.

I jogged on for I don't know how long, could have been fifteen minutes, maybe a half hour. I was beginning to wonder why I hadn't caught up with Hans. Eventually, I came to another chamber. Much smaller than all the rest. Enveloped in total darkness, it was foul and fetid. The decaying air and stifling atmosphere provided the perfect abode for those who worshipped the darkness rather than the light. In the dense blackness, spiders clutched their snare strings. In my torchlight, their webs shimmered like meshed steel dipped in silver. This far below ground, I had no idea what insects the spiders could feast upon, and I suspected their prey was much larger. Eyes aflame with hunger, they were akin to their vampyre hosts, hoping to dine on the bloated bodies of rats and slurp on hot blood. I left the room as quickly as I could, continuing down the tunnel. The ancient walls were stained by mold and mildew, and I could swear I could hear distant parts of the tunnel crumbling and cracking. I gave a silent prayer that it would eventually lead back to the main branch of tunnels, where I might be able to find Anna. I knew I was racing against the clock to have any chance of finding her alive. I was sick with despair and desperation. I couldn't believe our whole endeavor to find Wojciech had gone so wrong so quickly. Three of us were now dead, and maybe a fourth soon. I had to find the others—Stanislaw and Felix. And where the fuck was Hans?

Sometime later, the light from my torch began to fail. I gave a silent curse as I switched the battery out with another from my pack. I had taken only one spare. After that one, I would be in complete darkness. It was a terrifying thought. To be enshrouded in blackness, God only knew how far underground, at the mercy of the Mortis Vamypyres who would be waking up soon. That thought made me check my watch, and I came to an abrupt halt. In horror, I saw that it was already near sunset. My God, I had lost track of time wandering in the labyrinth of tunnels! Wojciech and his accursed minions would soon be walking these very tunnels. Looking for me. Looking for all of us. It was a frightening prospect. It was a disaster—we had lost our element of surprise, and we failed to get to them at their weakest time. But it was no matter. Anna was the only important thing to me at that point. It was her that kept driving me forward. If I had to die with her, then that's how it would be. At least if I could see her one more time, to look into her eyes, to hold and kiss her. I wiped the stream of tears from my face as I continued through the darkness.

Sometime later, I came to a fork in the tunnel. It diverged off in two directions. I had already hopelessly lost all sense of direction. I felt sure I was no longer under the castle, but I had no idea where I could be, or which tunnel now went where. It was a crapshoot. Since I took the rightmost tunnel earlier from the large chamber, I arbitrarily chose the left tunnel this time. In I went, hoping for the best, but expecting the worst.

Several minutes later, I noticed light coming from up ahead. I approached cautiously, my gun at the ready. Eventually, I could tell from the light's weaker, yellowish hue that it was coming from a torch, and not one of those kerosene lanterns. My heart jumped at the thought it was Hans, or perhaps Stanislaw and Felix. As I got closer, however, I noticed the light was holding steady. No shadows were dancing on the walls like there would be if one was walking or holding it by hand. Then, somewhere beyond, whisper faint, yet traveling with the exigent clarity of a minister's voice in a spacious church, came a man's voice. Not in fear, not in pain. He sounded like he was in the wild throes of ecstasy. "My God, yes, oh yes, oh yes…so good…please don't stop." The language was German, and I knew that voice. I approached the light, and I could see that it illuminated another chamber. I held my pistol at the ready as I peeked inside. The torch was lying on the floor, having been dropped by its owner. It illuminated a scene before me that was so shocking, so depraved, I was momentarily stunned. Elsie was buck naked and riding Hans, who had his hands on her slender young hips, helping to push her buttocks back and forth. Elsie's head was thrown back as she bucked, eyes closed, mouth open in a moan, her pleasure mutual. What chilled me to the bone was the blood. It was everywhere. All over the stone floor, all over Hans, and all over Elsie. The blood came from a terrible bite to Han's neck. Hans seemed oblivious to the injuries he had sustained; the poor man was bleeding out, yet was smiling as wide as a happy lover, still moaning in pleasure, his hips rocking up to meet Elsie's. Elsie had blood on her face, and smeared all over her breasts, her nipples long and erect. They almost appeared to resemble two red balloons, bouncing up and down in rhythm to her machinations. I watched in horrid fascination as she bent over, and sucked on Han's neck. As she raised her head, I could see her two, long and very sharp incisors, dripping with fresh blood. Jesus, I thought, she was taking her time with him. She would rock, then suck, and then rock some more. "Ah yes doctor," I heard her pant, "fuck me. Fuck me hard. Come into me, hot, as does your blood. Become one with me. Be with me forever." As if on cue, Han's body convulsed, his hips thrusting madly upwards, now in obvious orgasm. I watched transfixed as Elsie bent over and latched on to Han's neck, making a horrible sucking sound, her body shuddering with her own intense climax as his hot blood jetted down her greedy gullet. The horrific scene of depravity finally shocked me out of my inaction, and far too late, I recovered my wits and took a step inside the chamber. Hans was beyond saving, but I needed to kill the monster that had not long ago been my trusted secretary.

I had swung around my pack and was just reaching inside for the crucifix when, seemingly out of nowhere, I was picked up off the floor and violently thrown against the chamber wall. I saw stars as my head slammed against the unforgiving stone. I fell in a heap, momentarily stunned and breathless, onto the cold floor. When I looked up, at first I didn't know who I was looking at. It was a woman, and a very beautiful one. She had long dark hair that cascaded down over her bare shoulders and to the small of her naked back. Just like her companion, the woman no longer wore clothes. Then I recalled the family photos we had recovered from the crime scene in the flat adjacent to Jagiellonian University. The flat that had belonged to Klaus and Irma Fischer. The flat where her husband was left in his easy chair to become a fly-infested corpse. The woman leering before me, with a smile that seemed to stretch abnormally from ear to ear, was the missing Irma Fischer. There was something about her predatory stare that suddenly made me feel young, small, and weak…it was a look that seemed to say "I wonder how you taste," like an owl regarding a rabbit. "Well, well…Elsie, look what the cat brought in," she purred. Behind her, I saw that Elsie had swiveled her head, her eyes widening in seeming recognition. "Otto…" she hissed excitedly and began to slide off the corpse of the now-dead coroner. Elsie moved with the undulating grace of a predatory cat as she crossed the chamber towards me. Her lean, lithe body had a sheen of sweat, left from the litany of orgasms she had moments before. In a few moments, she had slithered up beside her naked twin. Gone was the sweet smile, the innocence of the young girl I once knew. In its place was a hungry, calculating gaze, much like a wolf eyeing its prey, and a smile that was anything but sweet.

Terror gripped me like a vice and I looked around madly for the pack which contained my crucifix, holy water, and sacred dagger. My heart skipped a beat when, to my horror, I saw that it had been thrown halfway across the chamber when I had been tossed against the wall. It was two meters away, and might as well have been a hundred. I had nothing, no protection at all, against the two vampyre seductresses who were now eyeing me with excited anticipation.

Elsie reached out with a finger to stroke my cheek. I shuddered at her touch…not because of its icy coldness, but because…I found it not entirely unpleasant. "Otto," she purred, "I am so happy to see you! You don't know how much so." She smiled wide, revealing a nightmare mouth of needle-like teeth. "You know, I have a confession to make. I was ashamed of it at the time, but now I have a new way of looking at things. I have a more, how shall I say, liberated perspective. Did you know that during all those team meetings we had at Wawel I secretly thought about us fucking? Oh, how the thought of having sex with an older man, a man of power and authority, had turned me on. I fantasized so often about you and I staying late after work, and you dropping a hint that you were interested. And with just my simple nod of acquiescence, you would shove me down on the desk, push up my skirt, and tear off my panties. I would see the need in your eyes, your wanton desire to take me. And then you'd ram your rock-hard cock into my hot cunt, pound into me, ravage me, until I climaxed again and again. And Felix never suspected. I'd be so wet from my illicit fantasies the dumb fuck thought it was because of him. When I screamed in ecstasy, it was really you I was thinking of. But you wouldn't ever look at me, Otto.

Not in that way. The way that I wanted. And that hurt me, Otto. Hurt me a lot. But now…you're here, Otto. And I'm going to fuck your brains out like there's no tomorrow." "We both are," corrected Irma, as she put her arm around Elsie's naked waist and pulled her in close. "Ever have two women at once, Otto? It's a man's wet dream." I watched as Elsie and Irma embraced, their erect nipples smashing together, and their tongues darting into each other's mouths like hungry snakes. Watching the two women engaging in their sexual delights, I crazily thought of the vampyre "sisters" in Bram Stoker's *Dracula*, who seduced the hapless Jonathan Harker during his ill-fated visit to Dracula's castle. The fact that I was facing just two of the young succubi versus three, as in the story, did not provide me much comfort.

"Hmmm," Irma moaned as she broke free from Elsie, "She tastes sooo good. Don't you want to taste her, Otto? Or better yet, taste me?" It was then I noticed that the pupils of her eyes began to take on a reddish glow. At first, like what you'd see when a camera flash reflects off the blood-rich retina in the back of the eye, but quickly becoming brighter, more intense. I wanted to look away, but something felt GOOD about looking into them. As I stared at them, the eyes began almost glowing, like there was electrical power behind them. With the pupils as the nexus, the red began to swirl in a circular motion. Slow at first, then tremendously fast. It was like watching a vortex of water cascading down an endless hole, a whirlpool sucking everything down. Kaleidoscope eyes that sucked in my thoughts, my energy, my inhibitions, my strength of will. "Yes," cooed Irma, who now had her hand down between her legs, rubbing herself. Watching her, that act, now excited me. I felt myself grow hard. I started thinking about how wet she must be, how she must taste down there. I WANTED to taste her. I knew such thoughts were not my own, but God help me, I couldn't look away from those eyes. "That's right, Otto," Elsie said, her own eyes now radiating with the prickly redness, "You can do whatever you want with us. No more inhibitions. No more moral values. Give in to your lust. Give in to your darkest fantasies, Otto." I watched as Elsie reached up and pinched her long, erect nipples. Irma reached down and began unbuttoning my trousers. I helped her by ripping off my shirt. The need for release was overpowering, more than food, water, or life itself. Irma mounted me, and her cunt grabbed me like a velvety vise. She bent forward, her breasts crushing against my chest, as her mouth eagerly found mine. Her tongue thrust to meet mine with fiery intensity. The moment our tongues intertwined, I exploded in orgasmic pleasure, a climax more intense than I ever experienced in my life, so encompassing and intense I almost blacked out. My body shuddered as wave after wave of the hot, erotic energy enveloped my senses. At the same time, my mind flashed with countless images of depraved and illicit acts like a corrupted kaleidoscope of the most sick and deranged. My head swam with unbridled ecstasy, along with perverted thoughts of depraved sexual acts—bestiality, necrophilia, bondage, and sadism. It was like a wanton power was coursing through my veins, fueling a thirst for lust and pleasure only achieved through the most dreadful, evil acts—an animalistic, hedonistic craving that knew no Christian or moral limits. I'm ashamed to write it here, but at that moment, my soul was completely lost. I had the most terrible fantasies…images…of what I would do to Anna when I next saw her. I would make her scream, and beg to die. What I was thinking was far more sadistic and horrendous than what the criminal monster Peter Kürten had ever been capable of. But yet, I relished those thoughts, and as Irma began riding my cock, I became even harder with the anticipation of a new, powerful life that lay before me.

Irma pushed down onto me, her pelvis grinding into mine, her smile widening into a shark's grin. She licked her moist, red lips, slowly, and salaciously. "Now you know true pleasure…tasting the forbidden fruit of erotic decadence…and surrendering to the complete corruption of the flesh." "Yes," I agreed, no longer having any fear, but instead reveling in the physical pleasure and the decadent thoughts continuing to flash through my head like an obscene slide show. My hips thrust up to meet Irma's rhythm; I need release ever so urgently. Elsie was beside me, and I felt her hand squeezing my balls with her talon-like fingers as she lowered her head to lick my nipples. "Yesss…" I moaned again. Every one of my nerve endings felt like they were on fire as her mouth snaked along my chest, pausing to kiss and suck hard enough to leave red rings. The pain felt like pleasure, and the pleasure felt like pain…there was no distinguishing between them anymore. Eventually, I felt her tongue licking the side of my neck, tasting, probing. Elsie whispered into my ear, "One last pleasure to endure, Otto. Better than the best orgasm. Remember this—blood is life. Blood is power. It has been that way for the Mortis since the beginning of time." There was a tone of oily glee in her panting voice, a voice that suddenly reminded me of black water, sluicing through gutters choked with decaying leaves and clumps of garbage. I looked up to find that both Elsie and Irma were smiling wickedly; revealing rows of stiletto-like teeth. As I watched, curved, viper-like incisors slid forward from a hinge-like musculature in their upper jaws. Spittal dripped downwards in anticipation of what was to come next. Nevertheless, I had no fear. I understood what Elsie had told me. I lay there in rapt excitement, waiting for the carnal ecstasy I knew would come as those beautiful fangs pierced my neck. Nothing would compare to the endless waves of pleasure that would wrack my body as the women so intimately sucked in perfect unison to my beating heart, my arterial spray spurting into their mouths as the ultimate oral copulation. As I orgasm and ejaculate my seed that initiates life, so too would I ejaculate blood…the very essence of life. I smiled, ready to be reborn into a new existence, a new state of being, never to look back.

But then, from atop me, Irma stopped her sliding upon my cock, her cunt's grip releasing my member. Wildly, the first thing I felt was disappointment; I was so close to climax that I felt anger at her for ceasing her movements, for denying me the pleasure I so desperately needed. But then I felt a different kind of release, as if a finger that had been pressing down upon my brain had suddenly let up. The suddenness was akin to a rubber band snapping within my mind. As I glanced up to see Irma's face, I could see that the hypnotic redness in her eyes had vanished, now replaced by blue eyes that were wide open in shock, surprise, pain, or a combination of all three. Without warning, black bile spewed forcibly from her mouth. It was hot and foul-smelling and hit me in the chest like projectile vomit. I watched as the noxious ichor began to ooze out from her eyes, nose, and ears, running down her chin and over her naked breasts. It was then, in the dim light, I noticed a glint of something sticking out of Irma's chest. Right where her heart would be. It was the tip of a dagger. A silver dagger. Within seconds, she was yanked off of me. What happened next, I admit, was a bit of a blur. With the vampyre's mind control now gone, I felt sluggish, like a drug addict slow to come down from a high. I shook my head in an attempt to clear it. I was aware enough, however, that Elsie had left my side. I heard her screech in anger or pain; I wasn't sure. I became all too aware that I was naked, vulnerable, lying on the stone floor, and I desperately reached for my clothes. Nearby were my pants, but I had to reach over the now prostrate body of Irma to grab my discarded shirt. It was wet, having been soaked in the black fluids that were leaking from her orifices and pooling all around us. After recovering my clothing, I once again heard a scream coming from Elsie. My eyes followed the sound, and that's when I realized who had saved me.

Stanislaw and Felix stood there, arms held out, crucifixes thrust forward. With backs straight, legs spread, eyes narrowed in steely determination, they reminded me of the Archangels Michael and Gabriel, God's fierce warriors who fight evil and protect the innocent. They had Elsie backed up in a corner, and she was spitting and hissing at them like an Indian Cobra while keeping her head turned to avoid gazing at the crucifix. She gnashed her teeth and snarled like a wild dog. She hurled a litany of evil epithets at Stanislaw. "Cocksucker! Fucking vampyre slayer!" she spat. "Your beloved Alicja is sucking cocks in hell, did you know that? And your unborn son is now getting fucked in the ass. Oh, you didn't know? It was a boy! The family you never had and never will. What are you doing now? Just wasting your life, succeeding in nothing! You poor pathetic fuck!" Stanislaw didn't even blink an eye. Instead, he took several steps forward, holding the crucifix resolutely. He began citing a passage I knew from the Bible's Book of John: "You belong to your father, the devil, and you want to carry out your father's desires. He was a murderer from the beginning, not holding to the truth, for there is no truth in him. When he lies, he speaks his native language, for he is a liar and the father of all lies." I looked over at Felix. Where Stanislaw had been unmoved, Felix's emotions were unchecked; tears were streaming down his face. It must have been like a knife to his own heart to once again see his beloved Elsie in this condition. To see the once sweet, innocent girl he knew reduced to a naked, snarling monster, a vile agent of the forces of darkness, spewing vile vulgarities like the foul demon she had become. It should have been too much for any man, but Felix stood his ground, resolute, advancing on Elsie together with Stanislaw. Elsie's head suddenly swiveled toward Felix, looking at him until the cross in his hand forced her to look away. But her voice changed, morphing from the guttural, demon-like rasp of just a moment before to that of the familiar voice we all knew. The voice of an innocent and fun-loving girl who once had her whole life ahead of her. "Felix, please!" she said, pleadingly. "Please don't hurt me. Why are you hurting me? Let me go, baby. I won't hurt anyone, I promise. You can come with me. It's not too late. We can have all of eternity with each other. Is that so bad?" She began sobbing then, and God help me, I saw a tear roll down the vampyre's cheek. Was it possible, I thought? Was there still something of Elsie inside that creature? Still a spark of humanity? To this day, I don't know how Felix maintained his resolve. I saw Stanislaw give him a sideways look, possibly also doubting if Felix could carry out what needed to be done. And I think very few men could have brought themselves to do it. But ultimately, it was his love for Elsie that compelled him to do what was necessary. He knew if he never released her, Elsie would never know eternal rest and would never enjoy the love, comfort, and protection of our God above. The demon Wojciech had stolen her, and Felix was going to put things right. I watched as Felix took two more steps forward, and then, with no hesitation, he thrust his silver dagger smoothly into Elsie's breast. Her back hit the wall hard as he drove the dagger in deep, twisting it back and forth. "I'm sorry, Elsie," Felix whispered, his voice choked with emotion. I cried along with him when I saw Elsie's face break into a smile. Strangely, not in pain, but with what, maybe a flicker of humanity? Of gratitude? I hope to think of love. Of a love shared, a love lost…and maybe, a love someday regained.

Felix took the dagger out from Elsie's chest, the sound making a sickening "plop" as he withdrew. He caught her body and gently lowered her to the floor. As she lay on her back, she shuddered, coughing up the same black ichor, and then her body lay still. By then, I had dressed myself and stepped over to the two men. I didn't know what to say; my cheeks were burning from embarrassment and shame. They had caught me performing the most lurid and decadent sex, and all the while, I had a smile on my face. I couldn't even look them in the eyes. "Stan, Felix…I, uh…" My words were cut off by Stanislaw. He turned to me and placed his hand on my shoulder. "There is no shame in succumbing to the seduction of the vampyre, Otto. Only a valuable lesson to be learned. And I know of no man lucky enough to be alive to have learned that lesson." I looked into his eyes. There was no judgment in them. I nodded. No one had to tell me how lucky I was. Thirty seconds later, I would have had my throat torn out. I owed my life to those two men. "Thank you both," I told them. You saved my life. I owe you one." For the first time in several days, Felix grinned, looking more like his old self. "Well, boss, when we get out of here, I sure would appreciate a thirty-day pass to the French Riviera. I don't think I've ever missed the sun's warmth as I do right now." Despite everything, I couldn't help but laugh. "You got it, Felix. And let's make it sixty."

My tone turned serious as I changed the subject. "Guys, we have to find Anna. When we were attacked in the large chamber, I saw someone pull her into one of the tunnels. I couldn't get to her. Hellriegel and his goons had too much firepower. I covered for you both as you made your escape, but then Hans and I had no choice but to run down our tunnel to get away from Hellriegel. For some reason, he didn't follow me. Hans and I got separated, but I found him here, too late." I pointed over to where Han's body lay. "He wasn't as fortunate as me, poor bastard. I have been praying this tunnel might circle back to where Anna is being kept. But now I've lost so much precious time. Do you have any idea which way to go?" Stanislaw nodded. "I think so. We noticed another divergence of tunnels not far from here. One of them looks to have more evidence of foot traffic than all the others. It definitely leads somewhere. We were about to go down it when we saw the light coming from down here…and heard the sounds." I once again cringed with embarrassment at Stan's last comment, but I quickly shrugged it off, heartened at the positive revelation. "All right then, let's go," I said, quickly grabbing my pack up off the floor. I took out the crucifix and stuffed the silver dagger behind my belt. Next time, I thought to myself, I wouldn't be caught flat-footed again. "Wait." I turned as Stanislaw grabbed my arm, his overly tight grip conveying that he had something serious to say. His expression had turned cold and dispassionate, his eyes narrow and devoid of his usual friendliness and warmth. I had seen that look before, back in the Kraków bierstube when we first met, when Stan spoke of losing his wife Alicja and his unborn child. The look of a man who has lost everything and had nothing to lose. A man out for revenge. "We will, of course, look for Anna. But the priority has always been finding and destroying Wojciech, that fucking spawn of Satan. He's awake now, which will make our job more difficult, but with the three of us, we can do it. This is the best chance I've had since Seville to kill the bastard, and nothing, I repeat NOTHING, will get in my way of doing so!" I looked over to Felix, who wore the same mask of cold determination. He gave me a nod, agreeing with Stanislaw. I couldn't say I was surprised. Both men had drunk from the same chalice of loss and despair, losing the women they had loved. The only thing left in their hearts was the thirst for revenge. Would I soon join them if I lost Anna? I wondered. A Trifecta of the Damned? The thought sent a bolt of panic through me. "You both have your priorities," I replied, shaking my arm loose from Stanislaw's grip. "And I'm with you one hundred percent on that. But make no mistake, if Anna is still alive, rescuing her becomes MY number one priority." Both men gave me a nod, seeming to agree with what I had said. But as I turned to leave the chamber, I couldn't help but notice Stanislaw's forefinger nervously tapping on the safety switch of his Schmeisser.

We hurried down the tunnel and soon came to the fork that Stanislaw had spoken of. He was right; the dirt on the tunnel's floor was demonstrably disturbed, and added to that was a large amount of detritus we found along the way—old lantern wicks, a couple of empty matchbooks, a 10 Reichspfennig coin, and several cigarette butts. My heart started beating faster with the expectation that we were getting to the heart of the giant underground labyrinth…and to Anna. We moved as quickly yet stealthy as we could dare in the near darkness, having covered our torches to allow only the faintest light to see by. We were caught by surprise once before, and we were determined that would not happen again. As we scuttled along, picking up our feet so as to not make any noise, navigating more by intuition than sight, I felt akin to the rats who roamed those dark depths. Just as the rats were cunning and quick, so must we be.

Then, we heard voices. In German. We quickly retreated our steps back to where we had seen a small alcove in the side of the tunnel. It was large enough that we could hide ourselves and not be seen by anyone heading our way. Felix quickly extinguished the dim light cast from the one torch we had been using, and we stood there in total darkness. The voices of two men got louder, signaling their approach. Motherfucker, I thought.

While one voice was unfamiliar, the other I knew. And the way he stiffened next to me, so did Felix. Of all the good luck. Fucking Hellriegel was coming our way. Like the fly to the spider. He had become sloppy, making the fatal mistake of talking and giving away his position.

"Jesus, Ernst, why didn't you kill Geissler when you had the chance?" I heard the unfamiliar voice say. "Now we have to comb these goddam tunnels. He could be anywhere. And the fucking slayer too. The Master told us not to come back empty-handed. He'll kill us both if we do!" "Shut up, Klaus! I don't need you telling me the fucking obvious!" shot Hellriegel's voice. Gone was the smug, pompous tone I had heard earlier. The man sounded scared. And probably for good reason, I thought. He had dropped the ball, and his "Master" was not one to suffer fools gladly. "Don't kill Hellriegel," I whispered so that both Stan and Felix could hear, "he can lead us to Anna." The two unsheathed their knives and held them at the ready. It was going to be a silent affair.

The beam from Hellriegel's torch illuminated the tunnel. I had no doubt he would be in the lead, his partner behind him. At some point, his light would give away our position, and I prayed we would get the jump on them before we were spotted. They were coming up quickly, obviously in a hurry. "The Master is too preoccupied with the pretty doctor," Hellriegel growled, "we still have time to find them, and then we'll look like heroes when we bring their heads to the Master. Just have a little…" Hellriegel's voice trailed off as he came up alongside us, his torch too late illuminating our faces. I reached out and put my knife to his neck, forcing him against the tunnel wall. "Don't say a word, or I'll gut you like a fish," I hissed. Off to my left, I heard Hellriegel's companion take a sharp intake of breath as Felix's knife found its mark, expertly sliding in between the man's ribs. For good measure, Stanislaw cut the familiar's neck from ear to ear with one quick, practiced motion of his knife, and he was left to bleed out on the ancient stones of the tunnel floor.

"Where is Anna, you sick fuck?" I hissed at Hellriegel, pushing the blade hard enough against his neck to start drawing blood. Unbelievably, he didn't flinch…the crazy bastard seemed to even relish the pain. He just smiled. What he said next chilled my blood. "Why Otto, she's with the Master," he gloated. "The Master is enjoying meeting her. And he will enjoy meeting you, too." I had had enough. I pushed the knife in even deeper. "Tell me where she is, damn you! Last chance." Stanislaw came up alongside. "Hellriegel," he spoke calmly, "if you don't take us to where she is, we'll kill you here and now. There will be no eternal life for you, no walking the world as an Übermensch. You'll be just a dead corpse on the floor like your buddy there, food for the tunnel rats. Or, you can choose to take us to the Master. Then, you might still have a fighting chance at salvation. Hell, the Master will probably even reward you well for bringing us to him. You'll have the eternal life and power over others that you so much crave." I could tell that Stan's ploy worked; he had pushed the right buttons, leaving Hellriegel with only one option. Hellriegel finally nodded but, with a sneer, said, "All right, Slayer. I'll take you. You're all dead men anyway. You'll never get out of this castle alive." I twisted Hellriegel around and shoved him face-first into the wall. "Felix, hand me that rope out of the pack. We're going to truss him up like the pig he is." I then tied Hellriegel's arms behind his back, wrapping the rope several times around his torso. If I could have, I would have tied his legs, too, but we needed him to walk. "All right, Haupsturmführer," I said sarcastically, "lead us to your Führer."

And Hellriegel did lead the way, the knife in my hand never an inch away from his neck, as I used my other hand to hold on to the rope behind his back. The torch clipped to my tunic top illuminated the way. I was followed by Stan and Felix in the rear, both holding crucifixes at the ready. The vampyres were awake and surely roaming the labyrinth of tunnels, and we walked on in a sea of anxiety, expecting one of them to jump us at any minute. We trudged on for about ten minutes, none of us speaking, until Hellriegel made the mistake of opening his mouth. "Don't expect to find your lovely Anna in one piece, Otto…the Master has a way with women, as you so very well know." I saw red and slammed his head against the tunnel wall, and reached out to cut his throat. I was going to shut his evil mouth once and for all. But then Stan grabbed my wrist. "No, Otto, not yet! We need him to get us to Wojciech. We can end it if we find him. And we don't know if Anna has been harmed yet. We can still rescue her…but we need him!" Stan was right, and I reluctantly let Hellriegel go. His eyes gleamed fiercely, unblinking, as a yellowish saliva dribbled down from a corner of his mouth to his chin. His lips stretched taut into a feral grin of bow-mouthed mockery. The man was truly insane. "Hey boss," Felix said gently, taking my knife, "I'll handle him. He won't be going anywhere." He looked over to Hellriegel. "Open your mouth again, and your teeth are the next to go." I relented, stepped back, and let Felix begin escorting Hellriegel down the tunnel. I took a deep breath and began following the others.

A minute later, we came to a fork in the tunnel. Without hesitation, Hellriegel took the fork to the left. I could see it was the route that seemed to be the most traveled, but I wondered if he was nevertheless taking us on a wild goose chase. Just screwing with us for his own sick pleasure. Or to provide his Master more time with Anna. I swore to myself that if he fucked us over, and Anna died as a result, I would kill him, but very slowly, very painfully. As we walked along, I began fantasizing about how I would do it. Maybe castration…just let him bleed out slowly as I placed his testicles in his hand. Or, cut off his fingers, then hands, then forearms, and so on, piece by piece until he lost his mind with the pain. Then again, I could pluck out his eyes, and leave him to roam the bowls of the castle entombed in his own darkness, as he hears the rats slowly close in. Yes, I imagined, let him roam blind with his ball sac dragging behind him, as the vermin latched on and slowly began munching their way towards in crotch. Suddenly I shook my head in disbelief. What was I thinking? I never had such vile thoughts before. I had chased murderous criminals my entire adult life, many of them the most diabolical and heinous of their ilk, yet I always allowed the wheels of justice to run their course. I was never one for revenge justice or vigilantism. Without an impartial judiciary to ensure that all individuals are treated equally, regardless of their background, and where decisions are made based on law and facts, free from personal biases or external pressures, we have only injustice, inequality, and instability. It was as if those accursed tunnels of death and depravity were exuding an evil that was permeating my thoughts and emotions. That's not me, I reminded myself. I resolved that no matter what happened next, Hellriegel would be kept alive to face justice for his crimes.

About a minute later, we began to see the glow from lanterns up ahead. "What's up there?" I heard Felix ask Hellriegel. "A large cavern," Hellriegel responded, "it's our meeting place. The place where the Master comes to speak with us…to give us direction." "Okay Ernst," Felix said, as he brought Hellriegel to a halt. "Honesty time. If you lie to me, I promise things won't go well for you. How many familiars can we expect? And how many Mortis?" Hellriegel replied without hesitation. "You killed Klaus, and that just leaves Tomasz. He's Polish, and just a word of warning, he doesn't understand German too well. As far as the vampyres…shit, I don't know. For the most part, I only see them when they're sleeping. At night they're out and about. Maybe ten, twelve?" That revelation made my stomach clench. By my count, we had only destroyed eight of the creatures since arriving at the castle.

Felix pushed Hellriegel forward and we walked the remainder of the tunnel towards the opening. As we cautiously entered, I could see Hellriegel had been telling the truth. Unlike the large chambers we had seen up to that point, all of them man-made from stone as parts of the tunnel system, this cavern was a natural formation, an underground cave that was indigenous to the mountain. As we stepped in further, the cavern almost didn't seem real—so fantastical was its immense structure that it seemed it had been built as an amphitheater for the gods. So large was the cavern that the lights from the kerosene lanterns that had been placed atop some of the rock formations could barely illuminate all of its vast expanses. The crystalline structures that made up the walls glittered like jewels and seemed to create images and sculptures of fantastical creatures that almost looked alive in the flickering light. The ceiling was far above us, adorned with hundreds of stalactites. Long and pointed, dripping with ancient water filtering down from the mountain above, they resembled the sharp teeth of a predator, wet with spittle. Much of the water had pooled to the floor below, creating a matching mandible in the form of stalagmites, completing the illusion of a hungry maw that only a few have escaped from. As we walked, faint echoes bounced off the cavern wall, carrying secrets from centuries past. An air of ancient magic hung heavy, whispering stories of lost civilizations. In sudden corroboration, we could see that the walls of the cavern bore witness to eons of secrets, displaying cryptic symbols of past ceremonies and rituals. This cavern had always been an important spot, I thought, even for thousands of years it served as some place of meeting and worship. But it had a feeling of wrongness; there was an inexorable hush of lurking death draped all over it. As I walked along, I noticed that there were large crevices in the cavern floor, revealing more subterranean levels beneath us. I approached one and cautiously bent over to look over the edge. The narrow vertical passage twisted like the coils of a serpent leading deeper into the abyss. My gut clenched at the thought of someone falling into those unchartered depths, and what may await them down there. Little did I know that in only moments I would get a chance to find out.

I had just turned around when I heard an impatient Stanislaw ask Hellriegel, "Where is Wojciech? We've lost enough precious time. Tell us right now or you are a dead man." I was about to walk back to join them when I heard something from above us. Very faint, but sounding like a squeak, like that of a rat, or rodent. I looked up, and for the first time noticed some movement up around the base of several of the stalactites.

Whatever it was, it was hard to see in the dim lantern light, and I immediately directed the beam of my torch, still clipped to my tunic, up above to get a better look. My jaw dropped open when I saw what it was. Or what THEY were, to be precise. A group of bats with grotesque, bulbous, hairy bodies hung from the ceiling above. But hideously large bats, the size of a man. Vampyres, in their bat form. Doused in the light, their large eyes glowed malevolently, and their wings began to flutter as haunting cries echoed off the walls. Stanislaw and Felix had also heard the sounds and had just turned to look up as the creatures let loose from their moorings and dropped straight down on both men. It was as if watching an attack by our vaunted German Junkers JU-87 Stukas, performing a pin-point dive-bombing on their target. That extra second of warning had no doubt saved both their lives because as they dived to the floor, they narrowly missed having their face and neck slashed by the talons of the monstrous bats. I saw Stanislaw roll and pull out a crucifix, and I had just started to do the same when out of the corner of my eye there was a blur of motion. It was Hellriegel, his hands still tied behind him but running towards me like one of those pissed-off, trussed-up American rodeo steers. But the most frightening thing, what scared me to my core, was his face. The maniac was smiling. Not just smiling, but laughing. The high-pitched babble of the hopelessly insane. "Let's meet the Master, Otto!" he cackled as he crashed into me, sending us both over the edge of the crevice and into the abyss below.

NOTE: There were no journal entries made for the three days, from 30 August to 1 September 1943

2 September 1943 –

It's not readily known, but I learned through my various insider police contacts and friends within the Party's inner circle that Joseph Goebbels, our esteemed Minister of Public Enlightenment and Propaganda, and

Gauleiter of Berlin, keeps a diary. A daily journal kept meticulously since 1923 when he was around 26 years of age. It's a sad truth that few of our top Nazi leaders are really literate. Fewer still could be described by any standards as intellectuals. Goebbels with his brilliant mind (but oh how distorted) probably comes closest to being the exception. As one of Hitler's closest confidants, his recollections and personal insights will be a fascinating study for future historians if his journal survives this war. He's not alone. Many well-known figures in history have kept personal journals—Leonardo da Vinci, Charles Darwin, Nikola Tesla, Thomas Edison, Lewis Carroll, and Mark Twain, just to name a few.

Not that I consider myself or my insights to be of the same importance as those great figures, but as a young boy, I recognized the value of keeping a diary, or a journal, of daily events. I had always loved history, and I liked writing, so it seemed natural to keep up a journal where I could record the meaningful things that happened in my life, keeping track of significant events, people, and places, the memory of which would otherwise dim with the passage of time. Later, as a criminal investigator, my journals became more like professional logbooks, recording cases and details for later analysis and interpretation. I suppose more than anything, maintaining my journal provided a sense of accomplishment and satisfaction. It allowed me to reflect on my daily activities and see what I had accomplished. My entries were a record of my experiences and reflections over time, which helped me see how I had grown and changed as a person.

It's often said that keeping a diary can do wonders for one's mental health and that writing about personal feelings and experiences can be therapeutic, helping to relieve stress and anxiety. Also, it can help build one's self-confidence and self-awareness. I can say now that is utter bullshit! Today, I find nothing cathartic about what I am about to write about. Picking up a pen is as heavy a burden for me as lifting a five-kilogram lead weight. But I need to finish this entry…this story of the damned. It is a tale of insanity, madness, and pure evil. And of loss. A terrible, terrible loss. An empty bottle of Schnapps lies nearby, its contents supposedly providing liquid courage, yet I find none. But no matter, I must begin. And when I am finished, I shall never write of it ever again.

Hellriegel slammed into me with a running gait, knocking the wind out of me as I was sent flying over the precipice down into the inky blackness of the dark crevice in the cavern floor. I felt a momentary sense of weightlessness as I fell, but it wasn't more than a second or two before I landed, hard. It was an outcropping of rock, a rock ledge, that saved me from a long fall to the bottom. I was extremely lucky that I didn't break my neck by landing the wrong way, instead having the good fortune of hitting the ledge on my left side. The wind was knocked out of me for the second time, and I felt a burst of pain in my shoulder as it made impact with the unforgiving rock. Before I could recover, the prick Hellriegel landed halfway on top of me, having himself fallen into the crevice, carried over by his own momentum. I heard a loud smack, like rock against rock, and I hoped the crazy bastard had hit his head against the stone wall. Before I could contemplate that thought further, I started sliding. The ledge was on a downward cant, and it was very smooth. With no resistance, I began sliding downwards, headfirst. Thank God my Daimon torch was still attached to my tunic, and in the dancing light I tried to grab onto some passing outcroppings, but I was falling more or less upside down, and I couldn't see a damn thing until it rushed past my face. I was petrified that my head was going to smash into a jutting edge of rock, splitting my skull open like an overripe watermelon. I gave up trying to grab any further outcroppings and feebly placed my hands and arms over my head in a vain attempt at some protection. Down I slid, my back and shoulders burning with the friction between my clothing and the rock formation. I was going to have some really nice friction burns, I thought wildly. As if that was the worst of my problems.

Suddenly, I was flying once again, this time as I was ejected off the end of the rock ramp. In a moment of terror, I expected to freefall further down into the bottomless depths. Instead, I landed hard on my back, with Hellriegel right on top of me. My head bounced off a stone floor and for a moment I saw stars, but mercifully did not pass out. I came to rest, and everything was eerily quiet. I pushed Hellriegel off of me and then sat up, shining my torch around to get my bearings. I saw the opening from which I had slid down. It was worn smooth— the rock formation so polished it reflected some of the light back towards me. It was a slide, I realized. Worn and polished from centuries of use, a slide used to gain access from the cavern up above. But to where? I then shone the light further around and discovered I had been delivered to another cavern. Much smaller than the one up above, but deeper, darker, and far more menacing. This one reeked of death and decay, a horrid smell that lingered in my sinuses like an unwanted guest. But on top of that was a newer, fresher stench I knew only too well, having encountered it at an untold number of murder scenes. It was the coppery, charnel house fragrance of fresh blood. With dread pumping through my veins in perfect rhythm with my jackhammering heart, I wildly cast the beam of the torch around the chamber, hoping to not find what my brain was telling me I surely would. And then there it was. In an instant, my reason for living was gone, swept into the back of my mind like shards of a broken plate, by an icy touch of terror, a finger walking its way from the pores of my scalp to the tips of my toes, threatening to smother any lingering sense of rational thought or reason in an immediate suffocation of loss and pain.

Anna was dead on the floor, her once beautiful blue eyes now lifeless and vacant. Her long hair flowered around her head matted in the blood that was still seeping from the gash in her throat. All her clothing had been torn and ripped off, and she lay nude, exposed, robbed of all her dignity. Her legs were splayed open, and it was obvious what had happened to her.

She was nearly disemboweled by the horrendous assault that had taken place, and it was clear she had not died easily.

Then, in the rocks just above her, I saw movement. The dark-colored fur had helped it to blend into the shadows. It was another of the bat creatures, but this one looked larger, and more powerful than the others. I had no doubt who it was. It lay languidly on the rocks, its membranous wings outstretched, no doubt satiated from the unspeakable acts it had just done. I could see an abnormally long, stiff, bone-like protuberance lay down and forward from the monster's pelvic area. It was massive, well over two feet long, and several inches in diameter. I realized with disgust and horror that it was a baculum, just as described by Stanislaw. The vampyre had had its way with Anna, completing its unholy ritual of pleasure and pain, sadistic sex and climactic bloodletting, domination, and destruction.

Knowing it had been seen, the bat-thing slowly sat up, taking its time, seemingly confident I was in no position to be a threat to it. Its beady, bat eyes glowed red, and I made an effort to avert my eyes so as not to look directly into them. Then gradually, the thing's body began transforming. The sounds of bones snapping and joints popping echoed loudly in the confines of the cavern, creating a ghastly cacophony. I watched as its elongated bat wings folded back into themselves, its snout-like nose flattened back against its skull, and its long, pointed ears retreated to their original size. The creature's baculum shrank and became a normal man's penis. Finally, as its course, black fur shed from its skin, the creature once again could be recognized as humanoid. For just a brief moment, I saw a man who had a face like wrinkled newspaper…grey, withered, and ancient. Probably his true form, I realize now, the visage of a man over 380 years old. But the image was fleeting, and soon standing on the rocks above was a normal-looking man. But a man I knew only too well. The same man I had seen next to the fountain outside my flat just a few weeks before. Count Wojciech Batowski, Colonel of the Polish Winged Hussars. Only this time, he was just a few meters away, and for the first time, I had a good look at him. My torch shone upon a face that, although gaunt, had patrician good looks, with the classic features of European aristocracy. His long black hair, streaked gray at the temples, hung down around his shoulders, no longer worn back in a ponytail. His bare chest and arms were muscled and toned, and he looked like a man not a day over 50 years old. Overall, women would consider him a handsome man, and I could imagine how he presented a dashing, gallant figure when he was resplendent in his Hussar's uniform so long ago.

"Why Inspector," Wojciech mused, "How thoughtful of you to, well, drop in." "My incompetent minions failed to take care of you, and then, conveniently, you come to me. I should thank you. I suppose it's a testament to your investigative prowess to have discovered my brother's castle. Or does the credit go to that shaman Kaminski?" he asked. I ignored his question. Instead, I pointed towards Anna. "You killed her," I said accusingly. "You can have me, but why did you have to kill her…to do that to her?" Wojciech looked down at Anna's desecrated corpse, and when he looked back up, his eyes were devoid of even a hint of remorse. "It was rather impromptu, I'm afraid. I can never resist the charms of a beautiful woman," he chuckled. "And when I awoke, I was so, so very thirsty." I felt myself becoming flushed with anger. The fiend was so cold, so devoid of feeling, I hated him with every fiber of my soul. "You were once a great figure in Polish history, a military officer who fought for your country…you were a man of honor and integrity. Now, you don't even have a shred of humanity in you. You've killed what? Tens of thousands, maybe millions of people since your own death so long ago? And all just for your gratification. You've destroyed families, couples, and lovers for your sadistic pleasure. You are unfeeling, as cold as you are dead." Wojciech took a step down from his perch in the rocks. His eyes took on a new hardness. "You humans," he sneered, "Saying it is a crime to kill. On the contrary, it is the nature of every being to kill. It kills to live and it kills to kill. The beast kills without ceasing, all day, every instant of his existence. Man kills, never ceasing to nourish himself. But since he needs an excuse to kill for pleasure, he has invented hunting. But that does not satisfy the irresistible need to massacre that is in all of you. It is not enough to kill simple beasts, you must kill man too. Long ago this need was satisfied by human sacrifices, but now the requirements of social life have made murder a crime. We condemn and punish the so-called murderer of men. But because you cannot live without yielding to this instinct of death, you relieve yourselves from time to time, with wars. Wars like this one. Then a whole nation slaughters another nation. And with your extermination factories, you have taken killing to a whole new level. Killing not to defend territory but to eradicate a particular people. Who is the real monster? Your war is a feast of blood, a feast that maddens armies and intoxicates civilians with stories of massacres. One might suppose that those destined to accomplish these butcheries of men would be despised. But no, they are loaded with honors. They are clad in resplendent black uniforms with death head insignia on their collars, plumes on their heads, and ornaments on their breasts. They are given crosses, awards, and titles of every kind. They are proud, respected, loved by women, and cheered by the crowds, solely because their mission is to shed human blood. For to kill is the great law set by nature and the heart of existence, Inspector. There is nothing more beautiful and honorable than killing."

"You're insane," I said. "Killing for the sake of killing is never justified. Someday, my own people will face harsh judgment for what they've done in this war. Murder is murder." Wojciech smiled. "Yes," he snickered, "for you, the unjustified murder of one is as heinous as the mass murder of a thousand. You've spent your entire life running around Europe, mad as a hatter, seeking justice for the murdered innocents. So honorable, so noble. Coming to Kraków to catch a murderer. You're such a fool! You had no idea what you were facing. But then the vampyre slayer Kaminski sought you out, and you started to believe. Started to believe in, and accept, the existence of my kind. I couldn't have that. The vampyre needs to remain a figment of fantasy, of legends, and your ridiculous cinema. I tried to warn you off, but you were too dogged in your pursuit…getting too close." Wojciech started to come down from the rocks, slowly, like a predatory snake. I watched him, carefully avoiding his eyes. "Taking my beloved trinkets from the salt mine was the last straw. You had to go. But despite my efforts, you continued to survive." I watched as Wojciech reached the cavern floor. He was now on an equal footing, just a few meters away. "But alas, your time has come, inspector. You will now join your beloved doctor. By tomorrow, you will rise with her, as one. You will be free, no longer chained to your foolish, idealistic moral values. And then, you will become the hunter, the predator, and know the true pleasure in killing."

"I know why you came to Kraków," I said quietly. "Why you returned home." Wojciech froze in his tracks. Silence. "I know why you co-opted Hellriegel, why you needed him." For the first time, Wojciech seemed unsure of himself. He stood there, mute, for several more moments. Then, "You know nothing!" he sneered. I reached into my pack which fortuitously, was still with me despite falling down the rock slide. "Are you sure?" I asked, my voice dripping sarcasm as I pulled out its content. If a vampyre could have a heart attack then Wojciech certainly looked the part. His eyes nearly popped out of his cadaverous skull, and his mouth fell open in total shock, which was probably a new emotion for him. "You…you…" he stammered, as he stared at what was dangling from my clutched hand. "That's right, you bastard," I spat, "You can thank your slayer friend…he figured it all out." Wojciech snarled, the lower half of his face suddenly grotesquely distorted by a clown's red grin, stuffed with razors. An outsized mouth, smeared on the belly of a bloated balloon. His hands became claws, and he lunged for me. I had just enough time to hold up my crucifix, which I had made sure to have at the ready. Wojciech hissed in anger, covering his eyes, as he took several steps back. "Give it to me!" he screamed. "You cocksucker. Give it to me or I'll…" "Do what?" I shouted, cutting him off.

"Kill the one person I loved in this world? Rape and torture a beautiful woman who had the heart of a saint? Defile her and leave her to die in this terrible place? Fuck you! If I can't have Anna, you will never have your precious Nataszja either!" With that, I swung the mummified head of Wojciech's beloved wife, Nataszja Batowksi, with all of my might, hurling it towards the wall of the cavern directly behind him. The dead woman's hair made a whistling sound as flew its trajectory, as straight and true as a well-placed artillery round. Wojciech let loose an unholy scream, a cacophony of guttural cries of despair, anguish, and pain. He turned and tried to catch the head as it sailed past, but it was too late. As he stepped towards the wall, the head impacted. It didn't make a wet or hollow sound like, say a pumpkin. Instead, it reminded me of the giant hornet's nests we used to find in the forests as a child. The big round ones looked like they were made out of paper-mâché, but actually built from woody tissue fibers mixed with bee saliva. I remember some of them being larger than a football. We'd take them down from the trees in the winter after the hornets had died off. I had hung some of them up in my room, admiring the intricate construction. But once, I stepped on one, to watch it implode. The sound of Natasza's head hitting the cavern wall reminded me of that. It made a dry, crackling sound, like stepping in a barrel of dried leaves, as it disintegrated in a puff of ancient dust. Wojciech stood there, with his arms outstretched, watching as the remnants of his once beautiful wife's face slowly cascaded to the floor, like wisps of snow on a winter's day. I knew I had only moments to act. My sacred dagger was already in my hand, and I simultaneously popped the cork out of a bottle of holy water as I stepped forward. I had just finished dousing the blade with the water as Wojciech began to turn around. The blade caught him in his side, just under his armpit. The air seemed to shoosh from his lungs, and his eyes went wide. "This is for Anna, you devil!" I remember whispering in his ear. For several moments, we were both standing together, in a parody of a lover's embrace, as I twisted the dagger into Wojciech's side. He coughed once, then twice, expelling black ichor that reeked of rot and decay. I knew that I hadn't hit his heart though, and that wasn't a fatal wound. I was going to have to pull the blade out and make another thrust.

Before I could do it, however, someone grabbed me around the neck and pulled me off of Wojciech. It was so sudden that I lost my grip on the dagger and it was left impaled in the monster's side. I was yanked backward as the fingers dug in deeper, threatening to choke off my air supply. I twisted to my left, and then to my right, but the attacker maintained his grip. He was panting wildly, and his breath was fetid. I spotted Wojciech, now slowly scrambling back up to the rock cliff where I had first seen him. He was bent over, obviously in distress, with the dagger still stuck in his side. He's escaping, my mind screamed. In desperation, I bit down hard on the attacker's hand. He let out a scream but didn't let go. He kept pulling me backward, and I didn't have the leverage to get out of his grip. My vision was getting blurry, but I watched as Wojciech reached the rock cliff near the top of the cavern. He turned around and glared at me. His eyes still glowed a malignant red, full of hate, but they were subdued, affected by his pain. His mouth was smeared black, like a child who got into the chocolate jar, as the ichor continued to ooze from his body. He parted his lips and bared his stiletto-like fangs like a dog would do to warn off an approaching alpha male. Wojciech made one last guttural snarl in parting, then he turned his back and disappeared up over the rocks. My feet finally found purchase, and I stomped hard on the attacker's foot, and then jammed my left elbow backward into what I hoped was the man's solar plexus. It worked, and with a painful grunt, he let me go. Gasping for breath, I wheeled around and slammed another fist into the man's chest. He dropped to the ground. It was Hellriegel. The bastard had somehow managed to cut himself loose. Judging from the ragged tears in the rope, he must have sawed them by rubbing against the sharp rocks in the cavern. I swore to myself as I turned back to where I had last seen Wojciech. He was gone.

I fell to my knees, still trying to catch my breath. Then a voice drifted into the cavern. It seemed far off, but the words echoed against the walls quite clearly. It was a familiar voice, and I burst into tears when I heard it. It was Felix, shouting my name. And the big guy was still alive. "Otto! Otto! Can you hear me? Sir, can you hear me?" I realized they never saw me go over the edge. I could be in any number of those crevices, no doubt some of them bottomless; they were calling my name, shooting in the dark. I quickly ran over to the base of the slide and yelled back up. "Felix! It's me! I'm all right! Hellriegel is down here too. You and Stan need to come down. This was Wojciech's lair. He's wounded, and we need to look for him. It's a slide, Felix. You can slide down. But come down by rope, to help us get back up!" Felix shouted his acknowledgment, and in a few minutes, both of them were at my side. Felix had a wicked-looking gash on his cheek, and Stan, too, was covered in scratches and looked like he was going to have one hell of a shiner on his right eye. We hugged each other tight, shamelessly. "Anna's dead," I said through tears, "and I thought you both were dead too," I told them. "I probably would be if I didn't have this guy with me," Stanislaw replied, nodding towards Felix. "He's a hell of a fighter. A real natural at this." I learned later that they had managed to ward off the two vampyres with splashes of holy water, then, using their crucifixes, had cornered them so they could get in close to use their daggers. Stan had come close to being bitten, with one of the vampyre's fangs only inches away from his throat, but Felix had come to his rescue. "Listen," I said quickly, "Wojciech is getting away. I've wounded him, but while fighting Hellriegel he managed to climb up there and get away." I pointed to the rock formation that led up to the cavern ceiling. "All right," said Stan excitedly, "let's go cut off that bastard's head and finish this."

But we never did. Finish it. I wish I could say that we did. I wish I could write how we caught up to Wojciech, cornered him, and then rammed that bright silver blade right into his black heart. And how his face registered shock and astonishment that his centuries-old existence had finally come to an inglorious end. But most of all, how sweet the taste was of retribution, getting justice for all the murdered victims of that fiendish monster. Justice for Stanislaw's Alicja. Justice for my Anna. Justice for Elsie, Manfred, Max and Hans. And justice for the murdered women of Kraków, be they German, Pole, or Jew. But it wasn't to be. But we tried. Oh Lord, we tried.

Stan, Felix, and I searched the tunnels under that accursed castle for the entire night. We easily found the hole in the cavern ceiling from through Wojciech had escaped after climbing up the rock pile. It led up to a tunnel that was above the cavern. Literally, an escape hatch. We found drops of the black ichor and followed this for a while. Eventually, we stumbled upon my silver dagger, discarded in the tunnel. Wojciech had managed to get it out. After that, the bleeding of ichor ceased, and we were never able to pick up his trail again. Stan theorized that the wound might have been serious enough to prevent Wojciech from transforming himself into a winged creature of the night, and if he was still humanoid, he couldn't have gone far and was probably holed up somewhere. And once dawn came, he would be trapped within the labyrinth of tunnels. So initially, we were optimistic. But as the night wore on, we found nothing. It was as if he disappeared in thin air. When dawn came, Stan refused to give up. I couldn't blame him. He had waited decades for his revenge, and we had gotten so close. So very, very close.

Eventually, I decided to leave. It wasn't easy. I felt like I was letting Stanislaw down, and I was admitting defeat. But I needed to get back to Wawel, explain the deaths of my team members, and start shaping the narrative. "Boss, I'm going to stay with Stanislaw," Felix announced as I was getting ready to make my way back to the surface. "What?" I asked, stunned. "What are you saying?" "I want to stay here, with Stan," Felix repeated. "He has spent most of his life hunting the Mortis. I want him to teach me. I want to learn everything he knows. Most of all, I want to help him. For him, this is not an ending here today. Wojciech got away, and Stan will never end his pursuit. Not just of Wojciech, but all the Mortis. One man can't do it all. Someone has to help him." I looked at my old friend, trying to come to grips with what he was asking. "You're willing to give up your police career, Felix? Your pension? Just walk away from your friends and family? I asked, dubiously. "Have you thought this through?" Felix gave a sad smile and replied "I have a feeling in another year or two Germany won't be needing any policemen, especially Kriminalpolizei officers with SS rank. As far as family, they're all gone. I suppose Manfred was more like a father to me than anyone. And none of my friends made me feel loved like Elsie. And now the bastard who killed her is still out there. I can find him, with Stan's help. And he needs me as well." I looked at my old colleague with a tinge of sadness, but also a deep admiration. He was willing to sacrifice everything to become a hunter of the Mortis…a slayer of the vampyre. Stan came up alongside and placed his arm around Felix. "He's a good man, Otto. A man of pure heart. The Magnus Clan of the Vampyre will accept him, and take care of him. He'll be given all the money and resources he needs to live a comfortable, albeit busy life. And I'm sure Bethany will take a shine to him, and help me teach him what he needs to know. I'm getting old, and won't be around forever. I welcome Felix's dedication…and companionship."

I looked at both of them and nodded my head in understanding. "Felix, you are missing but presumed dead," I announced. "Killed by SS-Haupsturmführer Ernst Hellriegel, the 'Butcher of Kraków.' Hellriegel is insane, and a sadistic killer of women. After being suspected of the recent murders in the city, he went AWOL, leaving behind a flat full of books on Satanism, necromancy, and the occult. Knowing we were on his trail, he tried to warn us off by kidnapping and murdering team member Elise Best. We finally tracked him here, and, after getting each of them alone, he managed to murder and decapitate SS-Obersturmbannführer Manfred von Albrecht, and Doctors Anna Müller and Hans Ziegler." And with that, I sealed Hellriegel's fate. The story was set. And I felt not a shred of remorse—the man was insane and dangerous. And he was damn lucky I just didn't kill him and rid the world of his evil.

Stan and Felix helped me to get the bodies of Anna, Manfred, and Hans back up to the surface. We placed them together with their decapitated heads on the floor of the main hall of the castle. I couldn't bear the thought of leaving them down below, in the dark, to be prodded and bitten by the tunnel rats, until I returned with a fresh team of investigators to retrieve them. The whole area was a crime scene after all. It was during one of those trips to the surface that a movement in the ruins of the castle's crumbling courtyard caught my eye. We went over to investigate and found a man hanging from a tree, his body swinging slightly in the wind. We surmised he was the third Mortis familiar—the Pole, Tomasz. He had taken his own life. Maybe he couldn't take it when he saw his master abandoning him, or maybe with Wojciech leaving the spell was broken. We left him hanging there, the birds already flocking around his corpse, beginning to peck at his eyes.

Our next task was to destroy the corpse of Wojciech's Nataszja. I did not take any enjoyment in doing this. She was, after all, an innocent woman, a woman once loved, and a woman that just weeks ago had been peacefully interred, her body left to the ages. I wasn't keen on having to desecrate the poor woman's body, but as petty and vindictive as it may sound, Wojciech had destroyed the women that Stan, Felix, and I had cherished and loved, and we'd be damned if we were going to leave him the body of his beloved wife. I saw the pain in Wojciech's eyes when Nataszja's head exploded into dust. If I could cause him to suffer further by destroying her body, robbing him of anything physical to cherish or memorialize, then that's what I was going to do. After finding several cans of kerosene that Hellriegel had stockpiled, we liberally doused Nataszja's corpse and lit it on fire. The mummified remains were dry, and the flames caught quickly. In a few minutes, Wojciech's beloved wife was nothing but a pile of ashes and a handful of glowing embers.

By then it was late morning, and it was time for us to part ways. Felix and Stan helped me to carry Hellriegel, tied up once again, down the mountain to the waiting vehicles. He was kicking, but I can't say he was screaming, because I had stuffed a dirty rag into his mouth. He had been rambling about his loyalty to Wojciech, and how his Master would someday come back for him to make him immortal. There was no way I going to listen to his insane ranting during the drive back to Kraków. Once Hellriegel was stowed away, I turned to my old friend. "Goodbye, Felix," I said, my voice choking with emotion. "You were a good officer and one hell of a criminal investigator." "Take care, boss," Felix said, "If we lose this war, Germany will need good men like you. Men who seek the truth and enforce justice, no matter the victim." I turned to Stanislaw and took the older man's hand. "Take care, Stan," I said. "Since meeting you, it's like a pair of blinders has been taken off, and I'll never look at the world the same way again. I don't know whether to thank you or curse you. I hope you find Wojciech someday. If you do, make sure he hears Anna's name again before he dies." Stan nodded. "I will, Otto. I'm sorry about Anna, but you can leave here proud, knowing you accomplished something no vampyre slayer has ever managed to do…you wounded Wojciech badly, and by doing that, you hurt him more than physically…you took away a piece of his pride. He was reminded he could still be killed by the likes of us. His plans here were ruined, and now he's on the lam. I think that Kraków has seen the last of him. Now…" and with this, he turned to Felix…"we will do our best to pick up his trail again." I nodded. I appreciated his praise, and perhaps what he said was true. Nevertheless, I felt it had been a pyrrhic victory…we won the battle but at a terrible, devastating cost.

I walked Ernst Hellriegel into Wawel Castle Kraków in handcuffs, and to say the place broke out into absolute pandemonium was an understatement. Heads turned and everyone stopped what they were doing as I paraded Hellriegel through the hallways and towards Han Frank's office. Doors opened, and office workers began milling out to gawk as word spread like wildfire. We must have looked quite the sight—I was disheveled, clothes torn, and covered in grime, dirt, and sweat from my 24 hours in the tunnels, hand clutching my Walther PPK, never letting it veer far from Hellriegel's back. As for him, he was still gagged, but his muffled ranting made his eyes bulge out to make him even more demented looking. By the time I got to his office, Frank was already out in the hall, standing along with SS chief Krüger. The look on their faces was priceless as I shambled up to greet them, playing the theatrics to the hilt. "Heil Hitler!" I shouted, saluting. "Governor-General, I present to you the murderer of the women of Kraków, among them your secretary, Johanna Liebl, SS Helferinnen Magdalene Haas and Irma Koch, and Reich Propaganda Cinemaphotographer Gertrude Brunner. SS-Haupsturmführer Ernst Hellriegel will also be charged with the murders of SS-Obersturm-bannführer Manfred von Albrecht, KRIPO secretary Elsie Best, Doctors Anna Müller and Hans Ziegler, Hauptmann Hans Dietrich, Feldwebel Günther Tanz, and Obergefreiter Klaus Bauer, as well as the suspected murders of SS-Sturmbannführer Felix Schellenberg and Dr. Max Weber, who are both missing." There was a clamor of gasps and expressions of shock and horror as I read off the litany of victim's names. All eyes turned on Hellriegel as they realized the breadth of crimes of the monster standing before them. Then, someone, somewhere, started clapping. It started slowly but then erupted into a loud cacophony of cheers and acclamation. Frank stepped forward and placed his hand on my shoulder. He was all smiles. "Well done, Otto, well done! Brillant detective work! The Reichsführer will be most pleased, and I am eternally grateful. You have made Kraków safe once again!" I translated that to mean he was greatly relieved his head was no longer on the chopping block. Krüger did not look as pleased. I had not kept him in the loop as I had promised, and he was getting none of the glory. I knew I'd face his wrath later, as well as criticism from my colleagues over the deaths of our fellow KRIPO officers. There would be many questions and much second-guessing in the days and weeks ahead. But at that moment, there was nothing for **Krüger** to do than to step forward and offer his congratulations for bringing such a heinous murderer to justice.

In a perfect world, that would have been the end of things…Hellriegel would be convicted of his crimes and justice would be duly served. I suppose I should have foreseen what was going to happen. I guess I am just an idealistic fool. Himmler asked me to escort Hellriegel back to Berlin immediately, but I refused. I had to go back to the castle, I said, to retrieve the bodies of my team members. And to bring them all back home to Germany for burial. That was my priority. And that is what I did. Kraków police chief Scherner ended up taking Hellriegel to Germany and that was fine with me. I guess my first clue of what was going on took place just after he left. News of Hellriegel's arrest was never printed in the *Krakauer Zeitung,* nor was it mentioned in any other state-controlled media. In the days to follow, the Kraków KRIPO began clamping down on any public discussion that the killer was a member of the SS. Some people were even arrested for speaking openly and brought in for interrogation. When I asked Frank about it, he shrugged and just said I needed to speak with Himmler about it. It was then I realized Himmler had launched a cover-up…he would never let his beloved SS be tarnished by the fact that an officer in its ranks was a cold-blooded murderer, which is quite laughable when you think about it. Someone of the likes of Rudolf Höss could kill millions of "undesirables" in the performance of their official duties, but the rapes and murders of German women would bring shame and dishonor to the SS. Well, I didn't care. I focused on what I needed to do, and by mid-August, I was back in Munich with my beloved Anna. Manfred too. I will make sure they are laid to rest properly. Young Elsie was given back to her family in Amberg. I'll let Felix know where he can find her if I ever hear from him again. As far as Hellriegel…he's a ghost. The press here in Germany never carried any mention of his arrest. His name has disappeared from the membership rolls of the SS. His wife has been sequestered, and the Gestapo has warned her to keep quiet. Himmler is probably trying to figure out what to do with him. I don't push the matter. Whether Hellriegel's fate is public or private, he is done.

I'm ending this journal entry now. I shall lock it away and I hope to never dwell on those dark days again. There lurks in each of us a haunted house inhabited by the ghosts of our worst regrets. Of what could have been. Anna's loss tears at my soul, but if that pain isn't enough, it's the never-ending realization that the monster once named Wojciech Batowski is still out there. Out there, somewhere. Some nights, I lay in bed and envision Stanislaw and Felix hot on the trail of the vampyre, and I smile. But most nights, I hear a rustling just outside my window. When that happens, the chill of fear creeps through my veins, numbing reason and leaving only raw panic. Each heartbeat echoes like a distant drum, urging me to flee, to fight, to open that damn curtain. In that icy grip, I cling to sanity, desperate for a lifeline—a glimmer of hope to pierce the darkness. But more often than not, reason slips away, shards of understanding lost in the void. Sometimes, terror is the only truth we know.

PART THREE

12 May 1990 –

Man, it's been a long week! The team and I have just about finished moving everything from the Woodland Hills condo out to our new facility in the Antelope Valley. It's about an hour and 15-minute drive to Pearblossom from the San Fernando Valley, and with multiple trips necessary to move all our files and records, it's taken several days. But I have to say, Simon and the Magnus Elders really came through for us. The contractors they used (several of them Magnus familiars) designed and built a state-of-the-art facility in the Mohave Desert that serves our needs perfectly. There are plenty of bedrooms for all the team members and more than enough space for any expansion of the team. Almost a commercial-sized kitchen, multiple fridges, and freezers to handle all our cooking needs. I think Tom, our in-house chef, took a special delight in that. A work wing of the home has a large conference room and several interview rooms. Tom is also particularly happy with the communications room, filled with his beloved police scanners and a base station for all our vehicular comms. Steve, of course, took particular interest in establishing the research rooms where we can maintain an extensive library and access all our Mortis archives and records. He's still grumbling a bit that we've set up shop in the middle of the desert so far away from his beloved beaches, but with all the amenities here, he's quickly adapting. I think, best of all,

Roxy got her wish—we have an indoor shooting range with 25-yard lanes for pistols and 100 yards for rifles. On top of that, there is plenty of outdoor acreage for long-gun and shotgun ranges and a mock town for urban tactical training. I never saw Rox so giddy as when she saw that specially designed race track she had begged Simon for…a nine-turn, 1.2-mile course to accommodate high-speed escape and evasion maneuvers, or what she so affectionately calls "crash and bang training." Kenny is likewise going nuts with the motor pool, where he can tinker to his heart's content. It's complete with an indoor garage where we can keep the operational cars parked, and a large service bay where we can do our own maintenance. Hell, even Chris Clarke, my good friend and fellow vintage car enthusiast, about blew a gasket (no pun intended) when he saw the place. I know Chris is disappointed we are moving out of the condo, but I have a feeling my offer to let him store some of his race classics out here to use on the racetrack will help him get over it. And it's not like I won't be going to the Valley ever again. I've still got my North Hollywood apartment and I'm never letting that go…it remains my only link to Bethany and her memory.

So all in all, we have a fantastic setup here, and I think everyone is happy. But truth be told, the Magnus owed it to all of us for giving them the Mortis "Liber Sanguinis Fidelis", the Book of the Faithful Blood, which provided them a complete listing of all Mortis Vampyre familiars dating back to the 14th century. Using that list, Simon and his Committee X (the euphemism for their "Mortis Eradication Program") members tracked down and eliminated hundreds of familiars here in the U.S. and worldwide. Finding them also led us straight to their Mortis masters, and while several of them got tipped off and escaped, many did not. All in all, it was a coup for the Magnus, allowing them to render the worst blow against the Mortis in centuries. And certainly, our other major victory was the discovery of the lair of the Mortis vampyre queen Tanya Lieberman, my nymphomaniac yet sadistic nemesis. When we found her nest on Kohler Street in the dilapidated warehouse district of Los Angeles, we succeeded in barbecuing nearly fifty Mortis vampyres and sending Tanya out of town with her tail between her legs. For her actions that day, Roxy wears with pride the necklace given to her by Simon and the Elders—an acorn with the ashes of the revered "Der Eisern," one of the original Magnus Elders—an "award" only given to the most heroic of the Magnus Vampyre themselves. Roxy hates it when I call it the "Grand Order of the Acorn," but really, what else would one call it?

Anyway, the news tonight was that I received a telephone call from Simon. He informed me that a Magnus familiar had come across a letter mailed last year to the Committee for the Scientific Investigation of Claims of the Paranormal, or CSICOP. My first question was what the fuck the CSICOP was because I had never heard of it. Of course, Steve, our resident paranoid skeptic and overall expert in anything occult, conspiracy, or unexplainable, knew all about it. He explained the CSICOP is a nonprofit organization that evaluates paranormal and fringe-science claims from a "scientific" viewpoint and attempts to provide the public and scholars with "scientifically reliable information" about them. Simon was excited because this letter, sent from some guy in Michigan, accompanied a journal that his father kept back during WWII. The man—his name is Geissler—was a German police homicide detective or inspector, and the journal documents a case he was working on in Nazi-occupied Poland. Specifically, it contains his detailed notes about a string of murders in the city of Kraków during the summer of 1943. Murders of women involving sexual assaults and vampiric bloodletting.

And here's the kicker. The killer described in the journal all those years ago was Wojciech, the same vampyre we've been chasing for nearly three years now. The sadistic son-of-a-bitch who's been leaving a string of butchered women across the U.S. Simon says the inspector's journal is fascinating as it provides the only known personal recollections of a man meeting and speaking with Wojciech and living to write about it. It also confirms once and for all the vampyre we knew only as Wojciech is, in fact, Wojciech Batowski, once a Polish nobleman. We suspected as much last year after learning that Ernst Hellriegel, together with his son Victor, went to Kraków, Poland in 1969, the first time the elder Hellriegel had returned there since the war. There, they had visited the city's genealogical records department and asked for records pertaining to the lineage of one of the local families of nobility, having the old surname of Batowski, and in particular an ancestor named Wojciech Batowski, a nobleman who had lived during the years of the Polish-Lithuanian Commonwealth, and who was a Colonel in the Polish Winged Hussars. We surmised our vampyre Wojciech was the one and the same, but we were never sure. Now it's confirmed. Oh, and get this! The journal indicates Wojciech was a Polish Count as well. Now why the fuck do vampyres always have to be Counts? I mean, like really? "Count Batowski," go fucking figure. And there's yet another surprise—that sadistic woman killer had once been married. The journal reveals that while at the same time he was conducting a reign of terror raping and murdering women in Kraków, Wojciech was there trying to resurrect his dead wife. Like something out of a bad horror movie. Really, one can't make the shit up. But despite all that new biographical information, the most fascinating and shocking revelation is that this Geissler detective actually wounded Wojciech with one of our silver Slayer's daggers. That must have been one hell of a confrontation. Because, as far as we know, that's the only time that bastard had been almost killed!

Simon also said the journal is invaluable because it contains much of the biographical and background information on Wojciech that was originally compiled in the 1930s by a Magnus Vampyre Slayer named Stanislaw Kaminski. Kaminski, a Pole, was recruited by the Magnus in the late 1920s, and he spent his entire life researching not only Wojciech but other vampyres in Europe. When Kaminski died, his dossier on Wojciech was thought lost. With the discovery of the journal, we now have the full dump on our elusive and enigmatic "Count." His life, his death, and how he came to be. Also, a complete compilation of his vampiric scourge through the centuries. Maybe just as important, Simon related, was that the journal fills in a lot of blanks about the mysterious Ernst Hellriegel, the father of our current nemesis, the Mortis familiar Victor Hellriegel. Last year, we uncovered Victor and his Los Angeles cult, the "Stygian Seekers of the Ethereal Light" who were recruiting familiars for both Wojciech and Tanya. One of those familiars was John Guzman, my barber and confident since my dad died years ago. Discovering that John had become a familiar in service to Tanya had been a devastating blow, a betrayal that I'm still trying to get over. In the end, John was left tied to the Cross of St. Peter, blinded and castrated in a most horrific way. Tanya had been quite unforgiving over the loss of The Book of the Faithful Blood. Simon said the journal sheds much light on Ernst Hellriegel and how he became Wojciech's familiar. That could be very helpful as we try to learn more about Victor and his motivations. As far as the Magnus records show, Ernst and Victor Hellriegel are the only father and son familiars that were ever recorded. Simon promised to drop the journal off tomorrow, and I'm very anxious to start reading it. Maybe it can provide us with useful information that can aid us in our hunt for both Wojciech and Victor Hellriegel.

13 May 1990 –

What the fuck! Simon can be a real prick sometimes but this time I'm fucking ballistic. Why didn't he tell me Bethany was mentioned in Otto's journal? My beloved Bethany. He had known she would be of course. He knew Bethany and Althea were working in Europe at that time, primarily chasing down Alexandria, the Queen of the Mortis. But to turn the journal pages and suddenly encounter the passages about Bethany…it was like a kick to the gut. All the memories of her came roaring back, and the pain of how much I still miss her. Reading Kaminski's account of meeting Bethany in Warsaw's Castle Square in 1929, how he described her as "angelic" with her "gorgeous sapphire blue eyes" and "beautiful blond hair fashioned in ringlet curls," all those descriptions of the girl I loved…I couldn't help but cry. But most of all, it was Kaminski's account of how Bethany alleviated his grief and sadness by taking his hands into hers that pained me most of all, as it reminded me all over again of her tenderness and warmth…and of what I had lost. It was like tearing off a scab and the terrible pain of losing her came rushing back. What Kaminski said about Bethany resonates so much…he described her perfectly. That's the woman of love and warmth that I knew so well. And those words, "You are a good man, Stanislaw Kaminski, of pure heart and soul." Almost the same words she told me so long ago. She found and saved both Kaminski and I. He, a vampyre slayer of his generation, and me, a vampyre slayer of today. With that realization, I cried until I could cry no longer. Good Lord, I miss her so much.

14 May 1990 –

Poor Rox. Whenever I get pissed at Simon I take it out on her. I know I shouldn't, but despite our love for each other, she is Simon's familiar and as such is beholden to him, and so sometimes it's difficult for me to see her as impartial. She often gets caught in the middle, for no reason. Worse, I've hurt her by allowing Bethany's ghost to once again come between us. I apologized to her this morning. I don't blame Simon for the Journal anymore. He had to let me read it and face my memories of Bethany head-on, allowing me to grieve in my own way. He's a damn vampyre, but the guy understands human emotions better than a lot of people I know. I guess that's why I always look up to him like an older brother; he has wisdom far beyond his years. We may look the same age, but he is, after all, hundreds of years old. That's something I have to constantly remind myself of. Anyway, it was all put to rest by the time Simon came over this evening to discuss the journal.

The first question I wanted to ask Simon was about Ernst Hellriegel. Even before the journal surfaced, there was a lot we had uncovered about the father-son familiars. We already knew from the entry in the Mortis Book of the Faithful Blood that Hellriegel was officially hailed as a vampyre's familiar on February 18, 1944. So clearly, his allegiance to the Mortis remained strong after his return to Germany from the events in Poland. We knew he went on to survive the war, and that his son, Victor, was born in Munich in April 1945, just as the American tanks rolled into the city. Ernst then went into hiding after being branded a war criminal due to his participation with the SS Einsastzgruppen. Almost two years later, Ernst was captured by the British in Flensburg, in occupied northern Germany, where he had found work as a mechanic under an assumed identity. He was subsequently tried and convicted by an Allied tribunal, and sentenced to 20 years in prison, but he was released early, in 1958. He became obsessed with the study of the occult, black magic, demonology, and vampirism, and in 1963 he formed a secret society in Munich ostensibly dedicated to occult Hermeticism and metaphysics which he called the "Primordial Brigade of the Stygian Truth." Victor joined his father's cult as a young man, and the Book of the Faithful Blood indicates he was inducted as a Mortis familiar on January 25, 1965, during the time he was attending the University of Munich and recruiting new converts for the Primordial Brigade. In the late 1960s, several adherents who later left the Brigade reported that the cult's studies became increasingly related to vampirism, and the magical qualities of human blood. In 1969, both Ernst and Victor took that trip to Kraków. In the early 1970s, when the sect was reported to have nearly a thousand members, both Hellriegels came under police scrutiny due to several strange murders in the city where bodies were found drained of blood, via some intravenous punctures on the arm. In 1975, Ernst Hellriegel died of an apparent heart attack at the age of 60. Less than a year later, for no apparent reason, Victor Hellriegel left everything he owned and immigrated from Germany to the United States. By 1981 he eventually ended up here in Los Angeles as a college professor and started his own secret society, the "Stygian Seekers of the Ethereal Light." Just like with his father's cult in Germany, one of the principal teachings of the Stygian Seekers was about the magical power of blood. Even going so far as extracting blood from human victims. The cult brainwashed its members on the mystical importance of blood…its power…and got them to drink it. At the same time, they romanticized the vampyre…making it a god-like figure. Eventually, it would prove a perfect segue to pitch a malleable member to become a familiar…with the promise of immortality and everything that goes with it. Hellriegel was using the Stygian Seekers to recruit familiars for the Mortis, and not just for his father's old master, Wojciech, but for Alexandria, the Queen of the Mortis, and later, her replacement, the teenaged vampyre Tanya.

I told Simon that I had read Otto's account of Ernst Hellriegel's arrest for the Kraków murders, but I was curious as to what happened after that. Hellriegel was never punished for those crimes. Simon felt the answer was quite simple. "Politics wins over idealistic justice, Jack," he said. Ernst Hellriegel was an embarrassment to the SS. Himmler had always taken pride that the SS served as the central institution for the broader extension of National Socialism ideology and its realization. He always insisted the members of the SS be held to the highest standards…racially, ethically, and morally. That's why he established the SS Junker leadership schools. At that time, Hellriegel wasn't the only rotten egg. Himmler also investigated and later arrested SS-Standartenführer Karl-Otto Koch, the previous commandant of the Buchenwald and Majdanek camps. Himmler had been investigating Koch for many months concerning allegations of his improper behavior at Buchenwald, which includes corruption, fraud, embezzlement of property stolen from prisoners, drunkenness, sexual offenses and even the murder of some hospital orderlies who had treated him for syphilis, an act that he feared might be uncovered. Koch and his wife Ilse were both guilty of using their positions with the SS to build their own personal wealth. After a trial, Koch was sentenced to death for disgracing both himself and the SS, and he was executed by firing squad on 5 April 1945. But the Hellriegel case was much, much bigger. It was not confined to corruption within the SS but involved the murder of German civilians. Himmler was even afraid the resulting scandal could jeopardize his position as Reichsführer-SS. So he had to keep it quiet. Since the arrest took place in Poland, it was easier for him to put the wraps on it. He used the full power of the SS and Gestapo to make sure no one who knew the "truth" talked. The easiest option would have been to have Hellriegel quietly executed, but because he was an SS officer, that would have only raised more questions. So, Himmler sequestered Hellriegel with a "desk job," and with his demented state it was easy to say he had been traumatized over the death of his team members in Poland. By 1944, events moved on, there was the invasion of Normandy in the West, the Russian advance in the East, and the 20 July bomb plot and attempted assassination of Hiter. By early 1945, Himmler was only concerned with negotiating with the Allies behind Hitler's back, trying to save his own ass upon Germany's surrender. Hellriegel was forgotten and survived the war. He was one lucky son-of-a-bitch. Otto Geisler should have killed him when he had the chance. Before the evil bastard had a chance to set in motion the chain of events that would create a cult of vampyre worshipers. Before he had a son named Victor who would carry on his evil legacy for almost another fifty years.

As far as Otto Geisler, he got the short end of the straw. He knew Himmler sandbagged him and that Hellriegel would never face justice. I can't help but wonder if he ever followed Hellriegel's activities after the war. And if he knew Hellriegel had never let go of his obsession with Wojciech. But I doubt it. By locking up his journal, Otto was locking up those memories for good. When he lost his beloved Anna, he lost a piece of his heart. I know his pain; I felt the same with Bethany's loss. I suppose Otto and I are very similar in that regard. But where Otto bottled up his pain and locked it in a box, abandoning his country and career to begin a new life abroad, I chose to stay and embrace the pain. I couldn't run away from the Mortis, I was going to make them pay for what they did. I guess that makes me more like Felix Schellenberg. We both took the path of vengeance and became Slayers. But I can't condemn Otto for taking a different path. I truly hope that after the terrible events of that bloody summer in Kraków in 1943, he had finally found some inner peace.

And what of Wojciech? Yes, indeed, what of Wojciech? We know he survived Otto's attack and got away, of course. He either escaped out into the night or, in his weakened state, continued to hide in the tunnels, somehow evading the searches by Kaminski and Schellenberg. From everything we know, Wojciech left Kraków, never to return again. A lot then changed, and quickly. The Nazi's days in Kraków were numbered, and less than seventeen months later, on 18 January 1945, the city was liberated by the advancing Russians. The citizens of Kraków were then condemned to live under Communism for the next 44 years. From one totalitarian master to another. The Magnus records on Wojciech are sketchy for the first two decades after the Second World War, but for the most part, he went dormant, with little to no killings attributed to him. Perhaps Otto's attack had changed Wojciech somehow. Maybe Kaminski was right; the wounding hurt him more than physically. As with anyone who has a near-death experience, it may have reset his priorities or his way of looking at the world. Less audacious and more careful. At the very least, it took him down a few pegs and reminded him that he might be immortal, but he is not God (or, more appropriately, the Devil). It didn't last, though. Although there were just a handful of killings in Europe attributed to Wojciech in the 1970s, things suddenly changed in the 80s. After centuries, Wojciech left his homeland of Europe and showed up in the United States. In late '87, we began seeing vampiric killings in different states that involved horrific attacks on young women. The Magnus Elders became very concerned, and in May of '88, we tracked him to Brewsterville, West Virginia, where he had bought an estate as a hideaway while feasting on the local women. We narrowly missed him but ended up adding his erstwhile employee, Kenny Grimes, to our team of Slayers. Why did Wojciech come to America? New victim pool? New opportunities? After five centuries of Europe, looking for a change of venue? Is it because he's a fan of American football? Who knows. That's the question that has been plaguing us…Kenny, in particular. One thing is for damn sure…his long period of benign dormancy is over. Not only has the number of his attacks been growing, but his sexual sadism is increasing, and the staging of bodies is becoming more sexually prolific and vile. And so, too, his taunts, personal ones, directed at Kenny. Wojciech never got over Kenny's betrayal, and with each killing, he places a guilt trip on Kenny for being powerless to stop him. The last time we encountered his handiwork was last fall in a small town called Marshall, Missouri. There, Wojciech left a note for Kenny in the mouth of a teenage victim. Sick bastard.

And what about the people mentioned in Otto's journal? I was curious what happened to them all. Of course, the fates of the more well-known historical figures are already documented. We know that Josef Goebbels, Adolf Hitler's Minister of Public Enlightenment and Propaganda, followed the Führer's example and committed suicide in the Berlin Bunker, together with his wife. Just before, Goebbels killed his six children by giving them cyanide. His partially cremated corpse was found and autopsied by the Soviet Army and then buried once, exhumed, and then reburied in 1946 on the territory of a Soviet military compound in Magdeburg, East Germany. Twenty-four years later, in 1970, upon orders from Moscow to finally destroy the remains, the Soviet KGB dug the Goebbels family up. The corpses, along with those of Hitler and his wife, Eva Braun, were burnt on a bonfire outside of the town of Schönebeck, 11 kilometers away from Magdeburg, then ground into ashes, collected, and thrown into the nearby Ehle River.

Reichsführer-SS Heinrich Himmler, the failed chicken farmer turned architect of mass murderer, said during an October 1943 speech, "This is a glorious page in our history (the liquidation of the Jews) that has never been written and shall never be written." He was wrong. The crimes of the SS were quickly realized at the end of the war, and it was declared a criminal organization by the International Military Tribunal in 1946. Unfortunately, it was Otto Geissler who was right—his beloved KRIPO under the Nazis was forever tarnished; at an institutional and individual level, the KRIPO was deeply complicit in the crimes of the Third Reich, including the Holocaust. The entire SS and police apparatus was responsible for the total murder of six million Jews, 1.8 million non-Jewish (ethnic) Poles, 3.3 million Soviet prisoners of war, up to 500,000 Romani, 300,000 persons with disabilities, and tens of thousands of German political opponents and "undesirables." As for Himmler, he was captured by the British and committed suicide by cyanide poisoning while in their custody on May 23, 1945. His corpse was unceremoniously bundled up in an army blanket and camouflage netting, bound with telephone wire, and buried in an unmarked grave in the woods near Lüneburg, Germany, the exact location remaining unknown to this day.

SS- Obersturmbannführer Rudolf Höss, the longest-serving commandant of the Auschwitz extermination camp from 4 May 1940 to November 1943, and again from 8 May 1944 to 18 January 1945, was sentenced to death following a trial before the Polish Supreme National Tribunal. It is believed that around 1.1 million people perished in Auschwitz during the less than five years of its existence; the majority, around 1 million, were Jews, 70 thousand were Poles, 21 thousand were Roma and Sinti, 15 thousand Soviet prisoners of war, and some 12 thousand prisoners of other ethnic backgrounds. Quite fittingly, Höss was hanged next to Crematoria I in his former camp on 16 April 1947. His cremated ashes are believed to have been scattered in the nearby Auschwitz forest.

Likewise, SS-Hauptsturmführer (he was promoted April 1944) Amon Göth, the "Butcher of Płaszów" was tried by the Polish people and sentenced to death. He was hanged on 13 September 1946 at the Montelupich Prison in Kraków, not far from the site of the Płaszów camp. His remains were cremated, and the ashes were thrown in the Vistula River.

SS-Obergruppenführer Friedrich-Wilhelm Krüger, who strangely is not as infamous or well-known as Himmler, Höss, and Göth, was in many ways even a worse monster, as he was personally involved in the progressive annihilation of the Polish nation, its culture, its heritage, and its wealth. With blood on his hands from the extermination of six million Poles, three million of them Jews, and massive destruction, degradation, and impoverishment of the Polish state, he didn't wait for the hangman. Krüger committed suicide on 10 May 1945 in Eggelsberg, Allied-occupied Austria. As with Himmler, he was buried without fanfare or ceremony, and the site of his grave is forgotten.

Similar to Karl-Otto Koch, SS-Oberführer Julian Scherner, the police chief of Kraków, had a proclivity for enriching himself with the confiscated goods of the Jews he killed, and in late 1944, he appeared before the dreaded Hauptamt SS-Gericht, or SS Court Main Office. As a result, he was demoted to Hauptsturmführer and assigned to the infamous Dirlewanger Brigade, a Waffen-SS penal unit made up of convicted criminals and the most cruel and barbaric men. Scherner's death was as murky and obscure as his career. He was found dead shortly before the war ended in a wooded area between Heidese and Markisch Buchotz in Brandenburg, Germany, around 70 kilometers west of the Polish border. How he died is a mystery; he may have committed suicide, been killed by the Soviets, or even by his own men when trying to stop them from retreating.

And what became of the ill-fated members of Otto's investigatory team? And the vampyre slayer Kaminski? I asked Simon to research the Magnus archives to see what he could find. He also asked the Magnus familiars in Germany to do local research on death records. When put all together, this is what we know:

The enigmatic Stanislaw Kaminski, AKA Josef Fischer, had indeed been a Magnus Slayer, after having been recruited by Bethany in 1929. To avenge the murder of his pregnant wife, pursuing Wojciech Batowski became a lifelong obsession. Kaminski is thought to have killed over 540 Mortis during his quarter century of service, making him one of the most prolific and successful vampyre slayers. He died in 1954 at the age of 69, remarkably from natural causes, unfortunately having never gotten his man. The Magnus Vampyre clan gave Kaminski a hero's funeral. He is buried in Powązki Cemetery, the oldest and most famous cemetery in Warsaw, Poland. His grave is often visited by taphophiles and the curious, drawn to the lavish yet gaudy tombstone depicting an angelic-winged man (looking remarkably similar to a young Stanislaw) who, as with the Goddess *Nemesis,* is holding a majestic sword in one hand, and a severed head in the other.

SS-Sturmbannführer Felix Schellenberg "officially" disappeared without a trace on the night of 10 August 1943 while investigating a murder case in Kraków, Poland. His fate was listed by the SS as most likely killed by an "unknown assailant." However, in the months to follow, up until the end of the war, a rumor persisted that Schellenberg had not been killed, but may have gone AWOL—Absent Without Leave. This was due to several unconfirmed sightings by one family member and various friends residing in Germany. In truth, as we know from the journal, Schellenberg chose to leave the Batowski castle with Stanislaw Kaminski. He became Kaminski's apprentice, learning everything he could from the older man. Ultimately fulfilling his wish to become a vampyre slayer, he worked together with Kaminski hunting down the Mortis until Kaminski's death. For the next two decades, he was the main Magnus slayer of the Mortis vampyre throughout Europe, racking up a record of kills that rivaled that of his mentor. On 12 January 1976, Felix Schellenberg went missing for a second and final time. Magnus records indicate he was on the trail of a Mortis who was only known as "Marco," who attacked several women in small villages around Gothenburg, Sweden, before moving on to the area around Bergen, Norway. Schellenberg eventually tracked Marco to the Icelandic port city of Reykjavik. Schellenberg had checked in to his hotel on 10 January and was seen driving his rental car out of town the following day. Hotel employees saw him return later that night, but the following day, the maid service noted that his bed had not been slept in. Two days later, when there was no evidence that the room was being occupied, the authorities were called in. They found all of Schellenberg's personal belongings, including his passport and wallet with traveler's checks, still there. The only missing items were what he likely had on his person at the time—his wallet and keys to the rental car…which had been left parked in the hotel garage. The only disturbance noted in the room was an open suitcase lying upside down on the floor. Scattered under it were numerous crucifixes, rosaries, bottles of what was later tested and determined to be ordinary tap water, and an odd, antique-looking silver knife with a Latin inscription. These were all taken into evidence, but strangely, twenty-four hours later, it was discovered the knife had disappeared from the police evidence locker room. Schellenberg's disappearance remains one of Iceland's most mysterious missing person cases.

Elsie Best was brought back to Germany and buried in the Katharinenfriedhof in her hometown of Amberg, Germany. Her marker simply reads "Died as a hero in the service of the Reich, Kraków, Poland, August 1943." Her parents and younger sister Elke were devastated by Elsie's death, but all three survived the war. During the post-war years of economic ruin and personal hardship, a mysterious benefactor began sending the Best family aid packages of food rations, clothing, medicine, cigarettes, alcohol, and other contraband items. Soon after, cash began arriving that the family used to move to adequate housing. Even years later, sufficient money was sent so that the Best family could afford to send Elkie to attend university. Their generous benefactor was never identified, but the family surmised he had to be a lover of music; in one of the boxes left at their doorstep was a collection of wartime 78rpm records, one of them Elsie's favorite—Glenn Miller's "Don't Sit Under the Apple Tree (With Anyone Else But Me)."

SS-Obersturmbannführer Manfred von Albrecht, Dr. Hans Ziegler, and Dr. Dr. Anna Müller are all three buried side by side in the Munich Waldfriedhof, one of the largest and most famous burial sites in the city, known for its beautiful, park-like design. They are buried in good company, with many of their fellow war heroes—1,789 of the First World War and 1,459 of the Second World War. One of the tales that gets passed along between those who operate and maintain the cemetery, for only they would take note of such things, is about the plot they have come to call "the grave of never-ending love." This is because beginning sometime around 1946, and for the next 43 years without fail, someone had made arrangements to have a single red rose placed on the headstone of Dr. Anna Müller…on the tenth of August—the anniversary of her death.

20 May 1990 –

Big break today! We just got a solid lead on Victor Hellriegel. We lost the professor's trail last fall after he fled to Mexico City, abandoning his cult's temple and leaving behind his vile library consisting of some of the most evil tomes ever written on the occult, black magic, and Satanism. I still shudder when recalling standing before Hellriegel's copy of *The Grand Grimoire*, considered one of the most dangerous books in the world. A black magic spell book, it contains instructions on how to make magic talismans and amulets, how to summon demons to do one's bidding, and even how to summon Lucifer for the purpose of forming a deal with the Devil. Having such a book says all that needs to be said about Victor Hellriegel—he is truly an evil man. But now, Magnus sources south of the border believe

KEN JOHNSON

they have spotted him and his mysterious travel companion, Emma Schultz, in a small desert town in the Mexican state of Durango. Better yet, they were seen by the source in a cantina meeting with a girl, described as maybe 16 or 17, very petite with blue eyes, a spattering of freckles, and chestnut brown hair. She had on low-riders, flared at the bottom to show a pair of scuffed cowboy boots. The jeans hung low around her hips, and above that was an olive-drab halter top, exposing her flat, teenage belly. The source said that even from a distance, the girl exuded so much raw sexuality that he could almost "taste" it. There's no doubt about it...it's Tanya! The Queen of the Mortis. And there's only one reason for her and Hellriegel's cultish familiars to be back together...Tanya is looking to build a new enclave, a new nest, and Victor is there to help her. There is no indication that Wojciech is part of it, and as far as we know, he's still holed up somewhere in the Midwest...not far from Marshall. Wojciech prefers to be a loner, and his circle of minions is always small. Tanya, on the other hand, just like a typical teenager, craves attention, status, and social acceptance. That's always been her undoing. And now she's tipped her hand. With any luck, we can catch both Tanya and Hellriegel by surprise and finally kill them both. I'm going to notify the team. We're heading for Mexico!

ABOUT THE AUTHOR

Ken Johnson retired from the United States Army with the rank of Colonel in 2013 after serving 30 years supporting sensitive Defense Department intelligence operations around the globe. His assignments include two combat tours in Iraq, a peacekeeping mission in Bosnia-Herzegovina, service along the Korean Demilitarized Zone (DMZ), and diplomatic duty as the Assistant U.S. Army Attaché in the American Embassy, London.

Just as with his fictional character, Steve, Ken considers himself a student of history and a conspiratologist. With a lifelong interest in the unanswered questions surrounding the assassination of President John F. Kennedy, he maintains a library with one of the most extensive collections of books, literature, and historical artifacts on the subject.

Ken is a fan of horror in both literature and film, but it had always been the legends of the Nosferatu, Wurdulac, and the Vampyre that captivated him the most. Beginning as a young boy in the 1960s, when he would rush home from school to watch the ABC daytime gothic soap opera *Dark Shadows* and follow the exploits of the campy vampyre Barnabas Collins, Ken has continued a lifelong love of vampiric horror. Now retired and with the time to dedicate to writing, he plans to be a continuous contributor to the vampyre genre. With the *On the Trail of the Vampyre* series, he strives to harken back to Bram Stoker's literary roots of portraying the vampyre as a sexual being, exemplifying the link between horror and eroticism. As with Stoker's *Dracula*, the dominant theme in Ken's stories is sexual menace and the dreadful perception of sexual perversity. Ken's Mortis Vampyre do not "sparkle" in the sun and turn into romantic saps; they are predatory creatures, violent, amoral, and hedonistic.

Ken has a son and daughter, both U.S. Army officers, and he lives in Northern Virginia with his wife of 38 years. He is currently working on future installments of the On the Trail of the Vampyre series. Ken's books are available on Amazon, and his author's page with the latest news and updates can be found at www.facebook.com/Skiller189X.

OTHER BOOKS BY THE AUTHOR

On The Trail of the Vampyre Series

OTTOTV Diary Entry #1: "Past is Prologue"

OTTOTV Diary Entry #2: "Manifest Destiny"

OTTOTV Diary Entry #3: "Revenge is a Dish Best Served Cold"

OTTOTV Diary Entry #4: "In Hot Pursuit"

OTTOTV Diary Entry #5: "The Trouble with Familiars"

On The Trail of the Vampyre Universe

The Vampyre Tapes (Prequel to OTTOTV Diary Entry #1)

How I Became a Reluctant Vampyre Slayer (Prequel to OTTOTV Diary Entry #4)

The Feast of the Vampyre (Prequel to How I Became a Reluctant Vampyre Slayer & OTTOTV Series)